PASSING STORMS

A Novel
By
Kathleen Haun

Published by Aventine Press
55 East Emerson St.
Chula Vista CA 91911
www.aventinepress.com

ISBN: 978-1-59330-973-2

Printed in the United States of America
ALL RIGHTS RESERVED

Cover photo by: author
Design and layout: Brad Allen Fine Art
www.bradallenfineart.com

Dedicated to

the pioneers of Inyo and Mono Counties,

past and present

PROLOG

The West of the 1800's has been referred to as wild for a good reason. When thousands of people determined to trek across the United States in search of gold, their only transport was that of wooden wagon or horse, and the journey became a human evolution that chose for survival only those strong enough to endure. These survivors tended to expect, if not demand, a great reward for their sacrifice, and consequently allowed nothing to get in the way of their achieving it.

Some of these people came to the Owens Valley of California in the early 1860's. Towns were quickly knocked together out of wood or adobe, and homesteaders and miners put down deep roots.

In 2003, I had purchased an old trunk filled with letters written from the Eastern Sierra in the late 1800's. Once I saw them published, I thought that was the end of my involvement with the people who wrote and received those letters. However, one day when I had the letters out of the trunk in which I still kept them, I realized that the dark floor of the trunk was not as smooth as I had previously thought.

Carefully prodding around the edges, I pulled back the heavy cloth bottom and found sheets of paper covered in typing produced on an old manual typewriter. It was a manuscript written by Whitney Eastman, the daughter of the woman who had written the letters, covering the events in Whitney's life during the first eight years of the twentieth century. (See the historical fiction novel, *Dear Carrie, Letters from the Eastern Sierra 1878-1899*)

The heart of Whitney's memoir, and that of her mother's letters, is Lone Pine, California in the Owens Valley. It is the deepest valley in the United States, bordered on the west by the Sierra and blocked from Death Valley to the east by the Inyo Mountains. When Whitney was growing up, the dark blue waters of the Owens River visited on its journey south a number of small green towns laying like jade pearls in the naked cleavage of a grand lady: Bishop, Sunland, Big Pine, Aberdeen, Taboose, Independence, George's Creek, and finally Lone Pine. Those towns still on the map give new meaning to the phrase "slow growth".

Dry, sable brown hills and huge piles of granite boulders called the Alabama Hills separate Lone Pine from the high peaks of the Sierra. The tallest of the ancient mountain spires, and the defining presence of the area, is Mt. Whitney at 14,496 feet, as it was thought to be in 1900.

The Sierra is made for snow. In its white winter dress it rises above the Valley as the regal overlord, no longer bare and stark but soft and glimmering. Before the aqueduct syphoned much of the valley water, spring's warmth released this frozen reserve into hundreds of creeks, lakes and underground springs. Much of this drained into the generous flow of the Owens River. By the early 1900's Valley ranchers had dug almost 300 miles of irrigation ditches from the river to their fields of wheat, alfalfa, barley, corn, potatoes, and grape vines crossing carefully tended sections of land like lines on old dusty sheet music.

For thousands of years prior to the presence of these settlements, the Owens Valley Paiute had gently cultivated the land and hunted its abundant wild game. When reports of gold and silver lured homesteaders to the Valley in the early 1860's, settlements were built and ranchers brought in large herds of cattle and flocks of sheep. This disrupted the fragile agricultural life of the local tribes. Not surprisingly, after a few stray killings of both Paiute and settler, events escalated to the point where the homesteaders requested help from the Cavalry. Over 157 soldiers arrived at Oak Creek east of the pioneer town of Putnam's (now Independence) on July 4, 1862. The soldiers raised their flag to the top of a fifty-foot flagstaff, gave "three times three cheers" while firing salutes, and attached the name of Fort Independence to their rude cabins and caves dug into a ravine. Deeply impressed by the physical suffering and struggle they had endured to reach the area even before coaxing from the land or a mine enough productivity to support a family, the settlers proclaimed, "We worked hard for this land, so now it's ours."

In the following years many settler and Indian lives were lost when a series of treaties were broken, sometimes by Indians unwilling to compromise and sometimes by irrational ranchers. Although a strained peace was eventually achieved, so unspeakable were some of the atrocities experienced by the Paiutes during the "Indian troubles" that over a century later their descendents will seldom speak of those events passed down to them by their elders, even between themselves.

Soon after these events, the largest silver mine in California history was discovered on the eastern shore of Owens Lake just south of Lone

Pine on the 9,184 foot crest of the Inyo Mountains. Eventually 5,290 tons of bullion worth over $2,000,000 was shipped to Los Angeles and the ports. The freight wagons returned to Cerro Gordo filled with Southern California produce and other goods, prompting Los Angeles newspapers to claim that the city was set to become a great city. It was the beginning of a long and fragile relationship between Los Angeles and the Valley.

At the turn of the century, the main road between the towns was a ribbon of rutted dirt referred to as the road north or the road south, there being only the one. Although the paving of it was not completed until the 1930's, it was named El Camino Sierra in 1910, and eventually changed to the less romantic designation of Highway 395. For every stretch of paving completed, the citizens celebrated with picnics, toasts and speeches, so important was it to their prosperity.

Where now a four hour drive is sufficient, in 1900 families traveling south to Los Angeles or San Bernardino Counties would load up a stout wagon pulled by as many horses or mules as their circumstances allowed. With only a few small towns available for supplies, and the concept of motels years into the future, they camped on the open desert each night for several weeks. After all, it took the fastest of the stages from Bishop three days to reach Mojave, the main town 175 miles south. Travel north to the Lake District (now Mammoth Lakes) or the Mono Basin, was an even more difficult ordeal because of the sandy roads and steep grades. But at least the narrow gauge railroad headed north.

These are the details that rushed through my mind as I gathered together the pages of Whitney's memoir. So many questions had formed in my mind when reading her mother's letters. Whitney's manuscript gave me those answers, although I must admit they are not the ones I expected.

CHAPTER ONE

The ropes cut into the flesh of my wrists that were tied behind my back while curious children stared intently at me from the floor where they sat at my feet. Unwilling to accept my silence, they hurled questions at me until I sobbed over and over, "I can't tell you." Thankfully, that was when I awoke, but I was haunted for days by the memory of the dream-children's accusing eyes. Even after the real children represented in my dream became adults, they continued to press me to reveal secrets they knew I'd hidden from them their whole lives.

Having experienced the terrors of the Great War, the bumptious 1920's, the upheavals of the 1930's, and *now* the beginning of the 1940's that bode not well, I never hesitate to speak out about these decades. Born in 1880, I also enjoy talking about my first twenty years lived in what is often referred to as *the Wild West*. However, the events in my life during the first eight years of the twentieth century I always avoid.

When I recently told a friend that I still don't think I can talk to the my children about those events, she said, "Then, Whitney, maybe you should write about them. It may release old ghosts." After thinking it over, I have agreed to do just that. Besides, more than my family and future generations realize, they have a right to know what happened during those years. And only now do I realize how much the world in which I lived, and the influence of the people in my youth, affected my adult choices. It is important, therefore, to understand what composed the substance of my life during my formative early years.

The Owens Valley along the Eastern Sierra in California was my back yard. Mt. Whitney, the tallest peak in the continental United States and within view of our house, was the inspiration for my name. It shows to what lengths Father would go to please my mother, since he was who named me. Mother had developed an odd rapport with that mountain peak when she first saw it in 1878. The Paiutes call it "the Old One". Mother called it "my old friend". Thankfully she only used that phrase with family.

When I achieved my twentieth year in 1900, lady's jackets rode on the hips just above the protrusion of the bustle, an affectation that gently rounded the body's posterior portion. The corset wasn't as strictly worshipped as it was in the East, and Western women were breathing more deeply than they had for decades. But women still spent twenty minutes donning layers of white, smoothly ironed underclothes--muslin drawers, dress shields, sleeveless vest or chemise, corset (laced up the back with assistance or front hooking), hip pads and bustle form, petticoat (cotton in summer and flannel in winter), and cotton or lisle hosiery. Blouses were called a waist and gripped the throat in near strangling modesty, but were always covered by a form-fitting jacket when the woman was in town. Button or lace-up shoes ended just above a woman's ankles, and society dictated they not lift their long skirts above the tops even when stepping over a puddle in the dirt roads.

Women in Lone Pine when cleaning house or working outdoors moderated much of this, and a cotton or wool dress was more common. Bonnets were smaller and less ornate than in earlier years, but few women would be caught in town without one, and even the young or poor would wear a bit of ribbon in their hair. Many women were beginning to rebel against wearing animal parts on their hats as decoration, and if any woman was bold enough to do so in Mother's presence, they would receive a lecture on the decimation of species for the selfish pleasure of "we women" (as though the generalizing of the criticism would take the sting out of her words).

Men's shoes were lower on the ankle than those of women, but in ranch country where I lived men wore tall boots. Although Father had simple work boots purchased from the Montgomery Ward catalog for $1.75, he also had many more with square toes and heels and decorative stitching up the stovepipe uppers to stiffen the supple leather.

The townsmen, especially during hours of trade, wore carefully brushed and usually out of date suits over stiff white shirts. If they didn't wear a tie or bandana, at least their collar button would be tightly fastened. The ranchers, cowboys and transient laborers were commonly arrayed in denim pants with plaid or striped shirts that showed several days wear less obviously, and were carefully tucked into a tight waistband.

Men who spent only a small portion of their pay in a saloon might cover their shirts with leather vests, the more prosperous of them adding sheepskin lining in winter. But all men wore one-piece lightweight underwear that covered their bodies from neck to wrist to ankle. And all men wore a hat, whether of felt, canvas or straw, depending more on their nationality than the type of work they did.

Even now, my parents loom largest in my thoughts, because they seemed to me brighter versions of all those among whom they moved. The only ones as bright were Vince and Charlotte Perry, the dear ones I called Aunt and Uncle but who were really only family friends. Their close bond with my parents began when they lived near one another in the infamous mining town of Bodie, California, during the mining boom of 1878 through 1881.

My mother, Emily Eastman, was twenty-three when I was born, a handsome fine-featured woman who carried herself tall. My "Aunt" Charlotte offered to the world a soft expression that belied the astuteness of her mind. When the two friends walked down the street together it was like watching two proud and sleek mares contentedly in double harness showing themselves off to those less splendid.

As they advanced in years, they were less matched in appearance, as my mother was a bit taller with a graceful yet slightly voluptuous build. Her dark brown hair was lightly streaked with gray and held back on the side with combs, forming short tight curls at the base of her neck. Charlotte was more petite in her shape, with her dark golden hair almost a memory among the darker gray strands, but always worn swept up into soft curls with little tendrils framing the sides of her intelligent and watchful eyes. When together, they laughed easily and often exchanged knowing glances that I couldn't interpret, and which shut me out of shared secrets they never explained.

However, being with Father and Uncle Vince always brought me a deep sense of comfort and belonging. When I was allowed to trail along with them, it was like being with two long-time members of a men's club, and all comers were welcome. Men greeted Frank and Vince with smiles and handshakes, women offered warm smiles, and young girls quickly averted their eyes so as not to be seen staring at these handsome older men in their mid-forties.

Father was a little taller than the average, lean and strong, with thick black hair and dark eyes set in a face tanned by long hours in the sun. Quick to smile and having a deep gentle voice, he could if provoked shed his open good humor and present a hard, unreadable mask that was as good as a closed door. At such times, only Mother would be let in.

Uncle Vince was even taller, thick through the chest but with narrow hips and long legs. He had enviable dark lashes fringing eyes always warm and full of humor, which was appropriate for a man so slow to anger and quick to laugh. His light sandy hair lacked the gray of Charlotte's, and it had more natural curl. Uncle Vince walked with a slight limp and sometimes would flinch if he turned too sharply to the left, the lingering effects of having been trapped beneath a stack of barrels that fell on him back in the days when he owned a warehouse in Bodie. Mother had just returned to Lone Pine and was waiting for Father to join her hopefully in time for my birth, so Aunt Charlotte nursed her husband alone, unsure if he would survive.

Uncle Vince once said, "I owe my life to my sweet wife."

Aunt Charlotte waved away such sentiment, telling him, "I owe you for the substance of my life, so it was a good trade." She would never say more about those long anxious days by her husband's side.

When my parents met in Lone Pine, Father had been working as an engineer for local mines and spending much of his time around a poker table or racing his handsome quarter horse Royal with bets on the side. But nothing prepared Frank and Emily for the strength of their immediate attraction. For both, that first meeting was a homecoming after a long journey, and they wanted no more travel unless it was together. Whatever the difficult challenge encountered over the years, they were one another's mainstay and champion. As I grew up, I looked forward to the day when I too would have such a marriage.

My most treasured possession is an 1879 photograph of my parents taken on the occasion of their first wedding anniversary, after living many months in the unremitting filth and violence of Bodie. It shows two handsome young people staring seriously into the camera. Unlike so many photographs of that era, my parents stand beside one another rather than him sitting hat in hand and her standing behind. Father wears a dark suit, white shirt boiled stiff, and hair unusually shiny. Mother stands proudly erect in a black walking suit with a tight bodice over a small corseted waist, the long skirt gathered into a modest bustle. A high collar squeezes her neck, allowing only a small foam of white lace to fall forward under her chin, while a ribbon holds long dark ringlets from her face.

Mr. Kemp, the photographer, told them, "Frank, you must remove your arm from around Emily's waist. Showing such familiarity in a photograph just isn't done." The only response he received was a glare from Frank, and Emily moving a bit closer to her husband. That's when Mr. Kemp snapped the picture.

Father worked with cross-breed cattle for awhile until he realized no one wanted his "fancy cows". He then grew crops, only to be disappointed when the train passed far to the east of town and shipping charges cut deep into profits. Finally, he settled on building a large herd of Hereford cattle and growing alfalfa. Although he had made profitable investments during his mining days, Mother said his success locally mattered greatly nevertheless. Only when I was older and had more knowledge of men did I understand.

Mother and Charlotte seldom focused beyond the town, both tireless supporters of all its needs and causes. Not least of Mother's activities was keeping alive the idea of women's suffrage. Maybe that's why several times I heard her criticized as "having views about things", something a woman was not encouraged to have unless they mirrored that of her husband.

Father seldom attempted to curb Mother's ardor, more than to simply offer a word of advice, which she seldom followed. It didn't seem to bother him, and if her frustrations turned to tears over the intractable attitudes of those with less vision and harder natures, he lent to her his shoulder and his arms.

But the topics Father and Uncle Vince discussed while sharing a beer at the end of a long day interested me most. While scrubbing vegetables for dinner, I would listen to them discuss their growing cattle business, fields of crops, and Uncle Vince's uncertain venture into raising hogs. Sitting in the middle of the kitchen at the big wooden table, their talk would inevitably turn to Valley politics or the local economy. One such exchange in 1893 stands out in my mind.

"I wish we could increase the prices we're asking for our beef," Father said, "or at least the alfalfa. I thought we'd be able to do that by now."

Uncle Vince answered with his usual refrain. "The boom will come. It's only a matter of time."

"If we could find an easier way to get crops and beef to the rails, it'd help."

"Yeah, well," Vince sighed, "if only we could lower our other costs, then the transport time and the railroad's rates wouldn't matter so much."

"Notice how often we use that phrase?" Father chuckled.

Vince looked up and thought a moment before smiling. "You mean 'if only'?"

"Yeah."

And they fell into a pensive silence.

This attitude of expectant optimism was common, people often wondering what grand enterprise would eventually bring the Valley into prosperity. For those maintaining themselves just above subsistence, this faith was all that kept them going. No one knew when or how, but all were sure something would put our Valley on the map. As it turned out, when it happened, it was far from the way any of us would have chosen.

The big yellow house surrounded by sycamores at the south end of town, on the east side of Main Street and facing west, was the core of my world. One of the few large houses in Lone Pine, it was originally a popular boardinghouse when my mother first lived there in 1878. Mrs. Kennedy owned it then, a welcoming woman who quickly took on the role of surrogate mother to twenty-one year old Emily. When Mrs. Kennedy died, I was only nine days old, and her will left the house to Mother as "sole trader", with Father's full approval of course.

Mother's first letter to her childhood friend Carrie, dated April of 1878, described it in enthusiastic detail.

"I was invited into a long narrow entry, the dark wood floor laid over with a burgundy braided rug. At the far end of the entry a steep stairway angles to the left, leading to the bedrooms upstairs. To the left is the parlor, and across from that a large kitchen filled with warmth and good smells. The walnut paneled dining room is behind the kitchen, so it can be entered from there or the entry hall.

"The parlor is the heart of the establishment, its walls covered in flocked rose red paper. The windows overlooking the street are accented with dark red drapes puddling lavishly on the floor, and allow for good light and views of the Sierra. A blue velvet Eastlake sofa with a curved mahogany frame sits in front of the window, along with a well-used Reed rocker with full roll arms to its left.

"A large stone fireplace covers the center of the far wall, its walnut mantle holding two small tin-types of an older couple, two daguerreotypes in silver frames of Mrs. Kennedy and her husband, and a walnut pipe rack. On either side of the fireplace tall windows cast muted light onto green velvet-covered game tables. Two brown leather arm chairs sit across the room from the sofa, conveniently arranged next to small tables where I could faintly smell the oil lamps on them. Above the chairs two large portraits covered by a blister of glass look down upon the room, hanging from burgundy cords attached near the ceiling. One is of a younger Mrs. Kennedy and the other is of a distinguished gentleman which she informed me is a good likeness of her late husband."

Remarkably little of this room had been changed over the years. Card tables and spittoons had been moved into the large room behind the parlor next to the stairs, originally Mrs. Kennedy's bedroom. This created a room where men could relax and, as Uncle Vince once declared, "There's no damn doilies!" For us, Mother placed two large comfortable chairs on either side of the fireplace, and from the time I was five this was my favorite place to curl up with a book.

Most evenings anyone passing the house would see Emily and Frank Eastman on the front porch swing watching the last glow of sunlight fade behind the Sierra crest. In summer, the open windows of my bedroom that fronted the street allowed the soft indistinct murmur of their voices to reach my room, lulling me into contented sleep.

Our small front yard was edged by a low white fence along which ran flower beds filled with daisies, black-eyed Susan, lilacs, lavender, rosemary and wild roses. Out back on the northeast corner of the house was Mother's vegetable garden. We grew more than one family could possibly consume, so we either shared the excess with neighbors or traded it at the stores for things we couldn't grow or make.

But I always knew we had more than most of my friends. Many families in town had little more than what they raised in a patch of garden, along with a few chickens and a cow. They obtained flour, sugar, and coffee in trade for a sack of potatoes or a basket of eggs. We had our own water and a pump in the kitchen, but well into the twentieth century many families still hauled their water from the creeks or town wells.

In back of the house was a tool shed next to a big red barn that housed the milk cow and two horses used with the buggy. Our chickens were back of the barn next to the hog pens and near two small pastures that allowed Father's riding horses Royal and his son Noble to graze near one another.

On the south side of the house, facing the road leading east to the cemetery, was a small bath house where black iron kettles on a small iron stove heated hot water. Being close to the clothes lines, once a week a big iron pot was set up to heat water for the Paiute woman who did our laundry. When I was eight, her two lively little girls the same age as myself started coming with her. But although I always asked to play with them, it was not allowed. Their mother made that clear to me whenever I tried.

Spreading east were the acres of fertile pasture where Father grew alfalfa and grazed his cattle, the property abutting that of Mr. Siliah. Beyond that, interrupted by the narrow gauge railroad tracks running between Owenyo northeast of town and Keeler southeast of town, the land swept gradually up into the Inyos--tall mountains brushed with streaks of lavender, red and pink.

But no matter what memory I recall, I am assured of finding within it Steven Perry. No single person was more pivotal to my world. Ten months after my birth, Charlotte and Vince had brought forth a handsome and intelligent son, and from that time on our parents raised us as though we had fledged from the same nest. Taller than me by the time he was ten, with dark hazel eyes flecked with brown, he saw the world with a wisdom and calm beyond his years. A grade behind me in school, he nevertheless sat next to me in the one-room schoolhouse on Locust Street, and often served as the tutor that helped me pass a test.

I sometimes think Mother and Charlotte forgot that we were not brother and sister, for regardless of which parent was present to witness our mischief, we were disciplined with equal impartiality. But our reactions were quite different. I would snuffle or pout for hours while Steven showed no reaction beyond twisting his face into a grimace of stoic resolve.

He also never gave in to a challenge, even if in pain or with blood running down his cheek after a fight with a bully. He wouldn't even admit that it hurt. When I was eleven, I walked to the Perry house and heard shouts of pained protest coming from the barn. Peeking around the corner, I discovered Steven standing up from a prone position across the knees of Uncle Vince. There was a tear running down the father's cheek, but not that of the son. Steven never did admit to me that he had hollered.

Some of our best times were when Steven and I climbed in the back of Father's wagon and he took us south to the small lake on the old Diaz Ranch property. A small pond had been there for years, surrounded by a marsh where mules and horses were turned out to graze while ducks and geese splashed in the surrounding puddles. After the great earthquake of 1872, which shifted and broke apart the floor of the Valley, the pond gradually became a lake. Steven and I would sit very still by the edge of the water, listening for the chortling call and fluttering rush of gleaming red-winged blackbirds. Soon a flock of the birds would rise like a single huge creature from the reeds, then quickly settle back down only a few yards farther along the shore.

Although Lone Pine was small (4,377 in 1900, compared to Los Angeles at 102,479) and of course oriented to the basic needs of ranchers, homesteaders, miners and employees of the soda ash plant on Owens Lake, we never lacked for something to do. A favorite place for our play was in the grove of trees on the north end of town just the other side of the plaza from the Robinsons Livery Stable andwith its stage stop. It was a small forest of pine, black locust, birch, cottonwood and willow shading Lone Pine Creek. If the gritty winds weren't blowing, it was a wonderful place to wade in the creek, play hide and seek, or race among the trees. We also played board games, marbles, jacks, jumped rope for hours, and ran foot races through sand and mud.

Sometimes kids helped each other with chores so we could get back outside to play. Oh yes, all children had chores to do, even pampered little me. You did them because you were part of a family, and receiving an allowance was an unknown concept.

If hunger struck while out seeking adventure, we simply raided orchards or back gardens, whether our own or that of a neighbor. Rule one, however, was never touch the watermelons. They were counted carefully as they matured and it was the quickest way to get into trouble. As Steven and I wandered the dusty roads talking of the great things we would accomplish in our lives, our favorite treat was to find a farmer's unguarded bee hive and continue on our way chewing sweet honeycomb as it crumbled into the crevices of our teeth.

If at dinner that night we claimed a lack of appetite, we were still made to clean our plates. Complaining of a stomach ache would only earn us a large spoonful of a thick bitter goo from a brown bottle. Yet we never changed our ways. Until, that is, we passed adolescence. Then such rambunctious days were sacrificed to the self-conscious fear of not acting one's age, a criticism that can make a young person question their place in the order of the universe.

But whether we were infants surrounded by toys, children at the mercantile with a handful of candy, kids doing school work in the tiny library off Main, or young adults racing horses around the granite boulders of the Alabama Hills, people would see Steven Perry and Whitney Eastman together. If I was hurt or bullied by another child, Steven was there to protect, comfort, and wipe away my tears before seeing that I got home safely. And he never once made fun of me or betrayed my trust. I blush to admit that my behavior toward him was not always so reliable.

CHAPTER TWO

In the summer of 1896 I was sixteen and eager for new experiences beyond the familiar abundance of the Owens Valley. So I was very excited when Father announced that he was going to Bridgeport, the County Seat of Mono County. Although 150 miles from Lone Pine, I talked him into taking Mother and me with him.

As we rode north out of town early in the morning, Mother commented on how nicely the trees along Main were shading the storefronts. Although I thought them less than what a shade tree should be, when Mother had arrived in Lone Pine eighteen years earlier, they had been little more than saplings. She took that opportunity to lecture me about gratitude.

Two men were hammering a nail into a wood plank in the sidewalk outside Mr. Carrasco's Saloon, while the man himself leaned against a post watching them work. When Mr. Carrasco looked up, we waved in greeting, but his only response was to glare at Mother. I quickly hid a smile. If the narrow wooden sidewalks were not kept in good repair, it was not unusual for the business owner to receive an angry earful from any woman whose child had tripped on a loose plank, or whose dress had caught on a nail. I assumed Mother to have put herself into the latter category.

Because of all the stops along the way, it took almost a month for us to complete the trip. But I loved every minute while riding my new quarter horse gelding next to Father. How grown-up I felt. But although I was allowed to ride astride while on the road, Mother insisted I wear a long, split skirt instead of denim pants. Then, before entering a town, she made me dress in a regular long skirt and ride on the seat beside her in the wagon. She inevitably had to remind me to stop fidgeting.

Along the way we stayed with friends my parents had made over the years, in every town greeted warmly by people who sang the praises of Frank and Emily Eastman. Some of them Mother had nursed through illness, while others had turned to Father when in jeopardy of losing their homestead or business, or needing someone to bail them out of jail. Others were simply old friends like the Shepherd family at George's Creek; the Skinners in Independence who were old friends of Mother's; and at

Taboose Ranch the man who would be the old stage station's last keeper. How proud I was to present myself as their daughter!

The two days we spent in the Lake District were my favorite of the whole trip. We stayed with a family who I remember laughed a lot, and where the woman baked the best pies I had ever eaten. Early the morning of our first day there, we rode up into the mountains, through an area called Mineral Park, and on to the ruins of the Mammoth Mine. Mother was deeply affected by this area of abandoned and deteriorating buildings. She had been there in 1878 when the Mammoth Mine was first being developed and so many people were looking forward to great wealth. Unfortunately, it was not to be.

After riding higher into the mountains, at tranquil and beautiful Lake George, Mother walked away from us and stood near the edge of the shore. Smiling wistfully, she stared for a long time at a large outcropping of granite on the far side of the small tree-lined lake beneath Crystal Crag, a huge thumb of granite rising above the mountain's crest. Sensing her thoughts to be private, I didn't ask her to explain. But several years later when I discovered Mother's letters to her friend Carrie, I remembered our time at Lake George and understood.

A stop near Mono Lake, with wide views of its dark blue water, was a relaxed idle filled with hours observing birds the likes of which I had never seen before. It also gave me the time to write a long letter to Steven describing the trip thus far.

We finally arrived in Bridgeport on the 25th day. I have not commented on the dusty roads, hot days, cold nights, stinging insects, chafing wind, dirt crusted on skin and hair, saddle sores, difficulties feeding and watering the horses, and the tedium of hours waiting in misery for the next resting place. It was simply to be expected on a wagon trip of that length.

Approaching Bridgeport, we passed through an Indian camp with its ramshackle shelters and grazing horses munching the long grasses near the river banks. Our wagon rumbled over a wooden bridge crossing the swiftly flowing river near a large marsh that covered much of the area to our left, passed the lovely Towle house with its three chimneys and inviting shade trees, and finally stopped in front of the stately white stone courthouse. Its tall arched windows across the second floor gleamed in the light. Ruts of wagons cut deep into the mud surrounding the building, and several cows nibbled at the sparse grass growing by the road. Evidently at least one wagon had cut too sharply over to School Street, the main route heading north out of town, as scrapes showed on the left front corner of the building. In an effort to abate further damage from such impacts, a cedar post had been shoved into the ground at the corner. But it too had taken the brunt of at least a few collisions.

Father went into the building to set his appointment for the next day, which gave me time to cast an appraising eye over the town. It sprawled in the heart of a large grassy meadow by the narrow flow of the East Walker River. In the near distance the granite barrier of the Sweetwater Range rose up as if to embrace the town, mountains of a reassuring character but certainly not the looming giants seen from Lone Pine. However, unlike Lone Pine, there were many large trees throughout the town.

I was impressed by the careful maintenance of the buildings, and the wide main road gave evidence of communal caring, even as the considerable wagon traffic on the streets produced the typical raucous noises of a busy supply depot. Rigs passed us filled with hay, lumber, and miscellaneous supplies in wooden barrels and crates. Even larger bull rigs of two or more wagons linked together rolled slowly forward under the burden of their heavy loads while the drivers whistled and yelled. Only the cracking of their long black whips over the heads of their mules and horses was louder than their bellowed swearing. Smaller freight wagons left town with supplies for the ranchers, miners and businesses that for many surrounding miles counted on Bridgeport for their provisions.

To house and feed the large number of people traveling through town, and the grateful citizens serving them, several two-story hotels and restaurants had been built, with shops and markets stuck in between. Large brick warehouses, saloons with fancy signs out front, livery stables, and the post office, completed the street. The noise and strange pungent smells generated by all this activity made my heart race with excited anticipation.

The following day, Mother and I rested on the porch of the Leavitt House, waiting impatiently for Father to complete his business. Although Mother refused to allow me the freedom to roam the busy town alone, I could see much of it from in front of the hotel.

A stage arrived and pulled up in front of the post office with chains rattling, horses snorting, and dust filling the air around it. On its way to Bridgeport, the stage had come in by way of Bodie, possibly explaining why the driver looked so exhausted and was covered in layers of grime. But this trip had been a relatively easy one for the stage, unlike those during winter when even with special snowshoes on the animals' feet, the snows would eventually become so deep that horses and mules could no longer navigate the Bodie/Bridgeport road. Then men on snowshoes and skis carried the mail, one from Bodie and one from Bridgeport. They met in the middle, then turned around to struggle as best they could back to their rigs waiting at the nearest freighter's station.

The Leavitt House barn was two doors down on our side of the street, just the other side of Sinclair Street. Its big wooden doors were wide open, and we could hear the striking of hammers on iron while horseshoes and wagon parts glowed red in the large hot forge. I wanted to walk down and watch the smith do his work, but there were so many wagons, horses and mules around the opening that Mother thought it too dangerous.

Even more interesting was watching the local Paiutes walk down the street, the women in their calico dresses and head scarves tied tightly under their chins with only the long fringe of their bangs showing. Although I knew they wore the scarves this way so the frequent gusty winds wouldn't blow them off, I thought about joking to Mother that it looked as though they were afraid their ears would fall off. But I didn't dare, as she was very disapproving of anything that showed the least hint of disrespect toward the native tribes.

So instead I sat silently watching two old Mono Paiute men walking together down the sidewalk, dressed in faded jeans and red cotton shirts under vests of tanned hide and rabbit fur. Old straw hats pulled down low on their foreheads cast deep shadows on their dark-skinned faces, making it easier for them to avoid meeting the eyes of the men they passed, and especially those of the white women.

Wondering why they projected such an attitude of apology, I watched them approach a white man in a suit who continued in a straight line, forcing the Paiute men to walk in the road to get around him. Mother told me that they must do whatever was necessary to avoid a confrontation or they could end up in jail, or worse. I didn't ask what that meant, having heard stories about Indians being burned out of their homes or dragged behind a horse into the foothills until just this side of dead.

Mother explained that at sunset all the Paiute women and children, and all but the most reckless of the Paiute men, would disappear from the streets. Five years previous a law had been passed to make it a misdemeanor for an Indian to be on the streets after sunset. They were allowed back in town only after the sun rose in the morning. Before I could jump to the conclusion that no one trusted what they might do under cover of darkness, Mother explained that it had more to do with keeping them away from the saloon crowds where prejudices escalated under the influence of drink. Although the whites, Mexicans, Irish, Chinese and Paiutes tolerated one another during the day while tending to business and the making of money, there was little desire on the part of most of them to mix together while socializing in the evening.

Watching the two Paiute men continue past, I was struck by the thought that only four decades earlier the meadows had been home to tribes living off the natural abundance of the land in peace, without interference or threat. Pondering how reduced life had become for these proud people, I suddenly felt uncomfortable, and more than a little sad. Glancing sideways at Mother, I found her watching me with a gentle smile, understanding glistening in her eyes.

But all of this sensitive social introspection abruptly ceased when we saw Father ride down the street toward us, Noble tossing his head when forced to stop at the hitching rail. Although I was allowed to ride his gentle sire Royal, I was strictly forbidden from riding the three year old son still trying to figure out if there was some mischief he could attempt without being disciplined.

As Father approached, his eyes only briefly swept over me before settling on Mother. As I watched her react to him, the nurturing caretaker of hearth and home disappeared and was replaced by Emily Eastman, proud wife of the man she loved. A hint of eager passion showed on her face as she rose to meet him, and the present moment then existed only for them. As their eyes conveyed unspoken thoughts to one another, he leaned down to kiss her cheek. They smiled at the same time. Often their exchanges held a look so intimate that it made observers uncomfortable. Or maybe it was envious. But I don't think it ever occurred to either of them that anyone noticed. Watching then, I once again found myself looking forward to the day when I too would gaze into a man's eyes and find there whatever it was that Mother always reacted to with blushes and smiles.

After lunch we explored the town, purchasing supplies from the Hays Brothers store on Main next to the granary, then the new, large brick building that served as the Leavitt warehouse. Opposite the Leavitt House, Ella Brady Hayes distributed the mail from the old Crowell Building, a small structure of vertical slats in need of paint and fronted by a narrow door next to a window through which the mail was handed out. Dave Hays, an early Bridgeport pioneer, had been the postmaster from 1887 to

1891, but now Mrs. Hayes was the postmistress (no relation to Dave), and her efficiency and warmth had gained her much respect.

We quickly passed by the noisy Stanton Saloon, one of the first buildings constructed in the town during the Aurora boom of the 1860's. Mother took my arm to hurry me along, and I wondered if she was trying to keep me from seeing the men inside or the men inside from seeing me. The only thing she accomplished was to increase my curiosity. Father distracted me from straining to look over the swinging doors by commenting that Bill Stanton, original owner of the saloon, had died six years earlier of consumption. He didn't say whether or not he had known Mr. Stanton, but the subdued tone of his voice indicated that probability.

We also passed too quickly the busy and crowded Hughes' Blacksmith. The jarring clang and woosh of the forges, the shrill whinny of nervous horses, the shouts of impatient and sweaty men, the pungent smells of animals and hot iron—it all stirred in me an arousal of curiosity like nothing I had experienced before. I longed to spend more time there, captivated by the young blacksmith's sweat-soaked shirt and his smile when glancing in my direction. But I said nothing about lingering for fear of being misunderstood. Or maybe Mother understanding only too well.

At the Bryant Store, Mother and I enjoyed the abundance of its sundries. The Bryants, another early pioneer family, had built the store in 1866. The front porch was now covered by an upstairs balcony held up by four substantial white pillars and several men leaning on them while loudly arguing local politics. We didn't notice Father fidgeting by the door until the loudness of his bored sighs permeated our chatter. Quickly paying for our purchases, we joined him on the sidewalk where Mother slipped her arm through his while laughing. He didn't join in her laughter, but he did offer the hint of a resigned smile.

We stopped by the newspaper office, turning off Main onto School Street. At the rear of the courthouse we passed a large open area where the remnants of twenty cords of wood were scattered, then walked toward a narrow white wood building with a sharply peaked roof. It looked more like a small schoolhouse than a business, fronted as it was by a single door to the left of two tall windows. A large sign across the front proclaimed 'Chronicle-Union'. Pressing to the rear of the building was a small house and a graying wood barn belonging to the Folgers, who ran the paper.

While we waited for Father, Mother said that during their time in Bodie the paper had been the *Bodie Chronicle*, a copy of which was framed under glass on the wall. I read it studiously in an effort to connect to my parents' past, their stories of living in Bodie having taken on the proportion of legend in my young mind. Leafing through more recent papers, I read the following comment from the February 10, 1896 edition:

"Dull is no name for the times in this town and county at this time. There is absolutely nothing going on out of which a fellow can manufacture an item. The dogs won't even fight, and our horses are too well bred to run away and injure a body, or mash a buggy; and our community is too moral and religious to get up any fights or domestic unpleasantness that would be public property—and so items are as scarce as hen's teeth. The town is quiet as a cemetery, the practicing of the band now and then being all the noise one hears excepting when school lets out."

Showing the article to Mother, I said, "What a nice place to live. Maybe someday we'll be able to spend more time here." Someone should have told me to be careful about the forming of wishes.

We continued to the end of Main where the Kirkwood home faced down the street toward us. Needing to turn left or right, we chose left and crossed the street to a white L-shaped house near the corner. It was surrounded by a whitewashed picket fence and had a large red barn anchoring the back of the property. As we passed by on our way back to the hotel, I noticed a dignified older man standing on the small, covered porch, and he was looking our way. Mother suddenly stopped and turned back just as the elderly man left the porch and hurried down a gravel path toward us. Father mumbled, "Well, I'll be damned!"

Meanwhile, Mother had rushed forward, impulsively throwing her arms around the stranger's neck with a cry, "Harvey!"

He hugged her back, laughing with obvious joy. "Frank!" He hurried to Father and shook his hand hard enough to prime a pump.

"Whitney, come here," Mother beckoned. "I want you to meet Mr. Boone. Harvey, this is our daughter, Whitney."

Beaming down at me was a clean-shaven man a good dozen years older than my parents, and now his gentle eyes a bit wetter than I think was normal for him. Instead of feeling shy as I often did in the presence of adults I didn't know well, Mr. Boone's friendly smile warmed me to him immediately. He invited us into the cool interior of his home and made us comfortable in the parlor with glasses of tea and the remains of a small cake.

As I sipped my drink, Mother proudly explained that Mr. Boone was a direct descendant of Daniel Boone, and had demonstrated his own pioneer spirit there in the West. It was while running his general mercantile store in Bodie that he had met my parents. Mr. Boone told us that since the 1880's he had spent most of his time on his ranch in the Bridgeport Valley, having married Ada Murphy five years before.

Mother leaned forward. "Is she the daughter of the man who ran the station on the road from Bridgeport to Bodie?"

"That's right. It was also known as the Clearwater Station." He grinned. "We've been very happy here."

"If I remember correctly," Father said, "you've owned this place for a long time."

"I've had roots in this area even while I had the store, the stable, and the freighting business in Bodie. In fact, they've named a local creek after me." He laughed heartily at that.

The rest of our visit was composed of reminiscences of their shared experiences in Bodie, and filling in the details of lives that had not intersected for many years. The thing that impressed me most was Mother's obvious fondness for this old man. When we parted from him, I could tell it was with great reluctance on her part, and even Father shook Mr. Boone's hand a bit longer than he did that of most men.

As we entered the hotel, Father put his arm around Mother's shoulders and squeezed gently. "We'll see him again."

Mother's only response was to cast him a doleful glance full of doubt before sighing deeply. "I suppose I should be grateful for having this unexpected opportunity to catch up and tell him how special he was in my life. One visit is better than none."

As they walked away after leaving me at the door of my room, I heard Father say, "He was more understanding of your feelings back then than I was, wasn't he?"

Mother responded graciously. "He could afford to be. It wasn't his wife taking the risks I did."

"When you were writing Carrie all those letters back when we were in Bodie, did you tell her about that business with Kitty?"

"Yes."

"Then she'll love hearing about today's visit."

On our way to Bridgeport, I had asked if we could visit Green Creek about seven miles south of Bridgeport to see the Dynamo Plant there, but

Father said it was too difficult to reach with our wagon. As we walked through town that evening, I asked him if we could go there if we rode our horses.

"No dear," Mother replied for him, "we've planned to go in a different direction tomorrow and it'll take all day."

Dad chuckled softly as we sat down in the parlor of the hotel. "I sure would've loved seeing the lights come on in Bodie when electricity first arrived on those transmission wires from Green Creek."

"That was two years ago," I piped up, "but it wasn't the first place to be wired for electricity. San Francisco had it by 1892."

Eager to show how well informed a daughter he had, I waited for a sign of his approval. Instead, his thoughts still on Bodie, he said, "But it was the first time electricity was relayed over such a long distance. Thirteen miles and the wire laid in a straight line directly to the Standard-Consolidated Mine. They were afraid the current might jump off the transmission wire if it was bent around a curve." He chuckled with the mirth of one better informed before adding, "They say if the experiment hadn't worked, after closing the mine down for a month during its installation and the miners getting no pay, they would've hanged Levitt. It was his idea and he was in charge of the work."

I gasped. "They wouldn't actually have done that surely?"

Mother smiled at my youthful wide-eyed incredulity. "Don't ever under-estimate what might happen during mob rule. We saw violence there you can't imagine, and which I certainly hope you never see."

Early the next day we hired a horse for Mother and the three of us rode down the long, winding road that cut through the open range of Big Meadows. Our canteens were full and our saddlebags packed with a blanket, sandwiches and fat slices of cake. Although we passed several large ranches, mostly there was around us only acres of green pasture with countless narrow ribbons of water trickling through the long grass. Enjoying all this lush bounty were more cattle than I'd ever seen. After two hours of riding we reached the rocky outcroppings at the start up into the mountains. Following a steep but good trail, we finally arrived at two lakes linked by a wide land bridge. The narrow, rocky trail continued upward along the edge of the water while weaving between tall Jeffrey pines.

The two lakes were the color of blue gemstones and were surrounded by a thick forest of giant trees, many along the very edge of the water, and scenting the air with the spice of their peculiarly enticing perfume.

The still water glistened and reflected the tree's green shadows onto the water along the edge. While dappled sunlight glinted through overhead branches, bright blue and black jays hopped and squawked among the tree tops as though cheering the occasional large fish that jumped up from the water before disappearing in the center of a neat ring of rippling water.

Having happily anticipated our being there alone, I was disappointed by the intrusive presence of several men fishing from the shore. Father, however, enjoyed talking with them while Mother and I availed ourselves of a recently constructed privy among the trees.

Mother insisted we eat the packed lunch before venturing further along the lake's edge, but I was too distracted to eat much. Something about the smell of the pines triggered in me a restlessness that merged with an odd primal impulse barely controllable. I longed to run and skip by the shore like a child, inhaling the sharp sweet air while laughing with squeals of delight. But I was a proper young lady and constrained to walk sedately ahead of my parents, who I felt were dawdling something awful as they walked close together while talking in low voices. Occasionally, one of them would laugh, making them hard to ignore. I wanted to be alone in this splendor of raw wilderness, imagining it to be my private world where I could ponder strange longings just beginning to fill my daydreams.

Eventually my parents decided to rest on a small boulder. They were immediately transformed into Frank and Emily, wrapped in each other and their quiet conversation. When they gave me permission to continue down the path a short distance, I hurried to get as far removed from them as possible before they thought to call me back. Basking in the beauty of the mountains, I looked up at the tall peaks and the wispy fluff of clouds forming above them. That's probably why I slipped. The searing scrape of rocks and branches cut into my legs as I slithered down the side of a steep bank toward the cold water and partially submerged rocks. Catching up against a fallen log like a bit of debris, I clung to its rough sides only a foot from the water's edge.

My cry as I fell must have alerted my parents, because suddenly Father was there lifting me into his arms. He carried me up the steep incline so quickly that I still can't figure out how he had the strength. Watching from the trail was my poor mother, hands clasped beneath her white face as though in prayer. When Father set me down, I saw that he too was pale, and his hands trembled as he wiped the dirt from my face.

My guilt was overwhelming and my contrition immediate. Over and over I apologized as they brushed me off and kept asking if I was injured.

That was the first time I realized how important I was to them. Having only considered how they fitted into *my* life, it was a shock to realize that I was the core of theirs. Crying more from guilt than pain, I clung to Father while promising never to upset them again, too young to realize that such promises cannot always be kept.

The next day Father said he was going to visit with some men he knew there in town, but I think he actually went to play poker with them. After Mother and I had lunch, we waited for his return while reading and relaxing with a cup of tea in the hotel's parlor. Noting my restlessness and disinterest in the book on my lap, Mother surprised me by suggesting I explore the town by myself for a short time. As I hurried down the hotel's steps, I wondered if the drama of the day before had somehow influenced her willingness to grant me small freedoms.

Setting out on a walking tour of the town, I decided to explore Sinclair Street on the west side of the hotel. It ended at a road parallel to Main called Kingsley that was lined with small wooden houses. Most had tiny front porches facing the road, with the rest of their property continuing back toward the meadows.

A girl about my age was throwing a stick for a little brown dog in front of the nearest house, a small neglected dwelling surrounded by a low fence badly in need of paint and the replacement of broken slats. Although what little yard there was showed nothing but dying plants and flourishing weeds, some distance behind the house was a large red barn that glowed with new paint. Irene Baxter introduced herself to me and we fell into conversation, both happy to be talking with someone our own age.

Tall and thin, with pale hair and even paler skin off-set by dark smoky eyes, she seldom looked directly at me the entire time we spoke. Instead, her eyes darted so constantly around us that I began to expect something dangerous to pop out from behind a bush.

We had been talking for several minutes when her father stepped out onto the porch and hollered at her in a low, gravelly voice. "You're not to go away from home!" His long brown beard blew sideways in a sudden gust of wind, and his scowl as he looked at Irene dropped shaggy brows near the bridge of his nose. "You're still in mourning, you know. Try acting like it!" Turning on his heel without acknowledging my presence, he disappeared inside. The front door slammed loudly behind him.

I asked her gently, "Did someone in your family pass away?"

"No." She hesitated only a moment before adding, "The man I was promised to had an accident and was killed."

"Oh, how horrible for you!"

But she merely shrugged as she said, "My father wanted us to marry, but I didn't. The man was ten years older than me and had a big spread in Carson that impressed my parents. But I'm only seventeen and I didn't love him."

"I'm certainly not ready for such a big thing." Truth be told, however, I was a little titillated by the thought of being that intimate with a man.

"My father doesn't care if I'm ready." She looked into the distance and a frown wrinkled her forehead. "He wants me to marry a man with money. He thinks he'll be able to get some of it for himself." She picked up the little dog that had sprawled at her feet and scratched his ears.

"What's your dog's name?"

"Oh, this isn't mine." She gave it a quick squeeze before putting it down. "Father would never let me have a pet. He won't even let me put flowers in the garden. He says they both take up room and expense without producing something we can eat or sell."

"What about your mother? Doesn't she understand how you feel?"

Glancing at the house, then quickly away again, she added, "She always takes his side."

"Will he push you to marry someone else soon?"

She seemed startled by my question and her delicate brows drew together. "I suppose he might. I'll just have to convince him I'm still mourning too much to bear the attentions of another man."

"That's a clever idea. But how sad that you have to manipulate things like that."

She shrugged and asked, "What else can I do when no one cares about what I feel or want?" When she looked me full in the face for the first time and continued to stare at me, I realized she seriously wanted an answer.

"I...I don't know."

She nodded as though expecting nothing else from me. "I'll figure out something. Of course, when I'm of age, I'll just leave home."

"Are you still in school?" I asked.

"No. Father took me out. He said I read enough at home and he wanted me available to help him around the place. Mother's too frail for ranch work. Are you in school?"

"No. We don't have a high school, and my parents didn't want to send me to Los Angeles to boarding school. So I read lots of books and they ask me questions about them."

"Do you have a boyfriend?"

"No." Then I added, "But I do have a friend that's a boy. We were raised together."

"Oh my! I've never even talked to a boy, more than to say hello when introduced."

"And yet you were supposed to marry a man so much older than yourself?" It seemed indecent, and I shuddered.

She smiled a little and shyly looked sideways at me. "At least now I have a new friend. Can I write you sometimes?"

"I wish you would." I gave her my address, and we departed from one another with a backward glance and a wave. She didn't seem eager to enter her house.

Overwhelmed by a sense of appreciation for my kind and loving parents, when I returned to the hotel, Mother was surprised at the enthusiasm of my hug. But for some reason I couldn't explain, I told no one about my conversation with Irene.

CHAPTER 3

My parents did all they could to give me a balanced and joyous childhood, and they were mostly successful. But there were random events in the Valley that were anything but joyous. My first experience of this was when I learned the Paiute's history. When miners and settlers arrived in the Valley, their presence and their cattle immediately usurped the Indians' ability to prosper from the land as they had for thousands of years. For the whole of my young life, Paiute workers on the ranches were an every day event. Although most kept to themselves, some were more open and even willing to share their talents.

It was the Paiute cowboys that taught Steven to rope when he was only eight. They were men Uncle Vince admired and respected, but they spent time with Steven only when Uncle Vince wasn't around. Steven in turn taught me. His Indian teachers observed him doing this and smiled with benign tolerance, unlike Mother and Charlotte's friends who condemned me for a lack of feminine comportment even though I was only nine.

Over the years, I learned much from the skills of the Paiute cowboys and ranch workers, the stoic loyalty and good humor of the Paiute women who did our laundry on the iron stove in the side yard, and the serenity of those who talked to me about working in harmony with nature as they planted and helped in the garden. When I was six and had a fever, an old Paiute woman taught Mother how to make a tea by steeping dried leaves from a desert plant. Father wanted to pay them all more than the low common wage, but he couldn't break with the other ranchers. Instead, he began giving bonuses for work well done, and consequently never lacked for extra hands when he needed them.

By the middle of the 1870's, the Indians were allowed to file for homesteads, but only with the proviso that they renounce any tribal affiliations. Most would never consider doing that. The few who did try to file found an almost insurmountable number of hurdles raised in their way during the processing of what was called the *necessary proofs*, including paperwork unaccountably lost. When Uncle Vince found out this was still happening in the late 1880's, he helped several families wade through the tedium of the process and get their deeds. The next time he went in for a beer, some of the men at the bar turned their backs on him. But he continued in his efforts, and his kindness was not forgotten by the tribes.

On several occasions our alert youthful ears overheard the adults talking about a Paiute man that had been sold liquor, which was against the law. Surprisingly, when damage resulted as suppressed resentment found release under the influence of alcohol, the blame went to the seller of the liquor as much as the Indian. It was always a fearful episode for the town, but especially for us kids who didn't understand either side of the issue.

Another confusing mix of communal denial and shame regarding this co-existence occurred for me when I overheard the parents of a friend say they were relieved that men from the town could no longer rape a Paiute woman with impunity. Discovering that such an ugly thing had taken place within my own community, and little done about it, was a revelation that cracked the basic foundation of my youthful innocence. For a long time after that, when gathered together with others in church or a town hall meeting, I would study the neighbors or shopkeepers around me and wonder if it might have been one of them. It may have been none of them, but for a long time I went out of my way to never be alone with any man other than Father or Uncle Vince.

By the turn of the century, the Indians had for many years worn the clothes typical of all people in the West, including leather boots instead of moccasins of rabbit skin or reeds. I asked Steven once if he thought the Paiutes' native ways would eventually disappear as they blended into our society. He smiled knowingly and said there was much the Indians held back from the non-native population, their tribal traditions and ancient stories carefully preserved by their wisest elders.

"Did you ever consider," he asked me, "that by agreeing to work for those who took over their land, they're still staying on that very land? And getting paid to do it."

On the land they certainly were, but the native people I knew as a child would not be accorded U.S. citizenship until 1923. I don't think most of them cared, since to their way of thinking they were simply *the people*. Sensing layers of meaning in such a simple yet self-assured identity, I have often wondered if anyone but a Paiute can truly grasp the significance of such a claim.

By the time Steven and I were in our late teens, we had developed many friends of our own. More often than not, however, we arrived together at a party or public event, and even if we might separate to spend time with someone else, it would always be Steven that would see me home.

Not long after I turned seventeen, Steven jubilantly teased me as we left the town hall following a dance. "Well, another helpless idiot has fallen under your spell."

"What about that poor besotted girl I saw you dancing with?" I teased him back. "You know, don't you, that she's now waiting to receive an invitation from you?"

What these boys and girls, temporary amusements and dancing partners, felt when unceremoniously left behind, I have no idea. And only now do I realize how cavalier we were with their feelings. We simply wrapped around ourselves the smug satisfaction of invulnerable youth reinforced by the complacent acceptance of our life-long bond.

Progressing through our teens, we matured along with the Valley. But while the ranches struggled through lean times brought on by closing mines, dwindling markets for cattle and sheep, drought and failing crops, Steven and I flourished. Raised in households full of love and encouragement, and enough money to feed and clothe our ripening bodies, we progressed effortlessly from children into young adults, never considering that the future would be anything less assured.

Then one morning in the summer of 1899, I looked into the mirror over my dressing table much as I did every day. But that morning something was different. Looking back at me was an unfamiliar young woman with long auburn tresses cascading in natural curls over wide shoulders. Soft brows arched over green eyes that looked back in surprise, high cheek bones accentuated clear rosy skin, and full sensual lips slowly smiled. I stood up and dropped my robe, revealing a narrow waist above rounded hips, and full breasts straining the fabric of my chemise. When, I wondered, had the freckles and thin angular planes disappeared? Realizing with dismay that I was now a woman, I knew instinctively that from then on life was going to be very different.

With my newly awakened perception at the fore, I looked more carefully at those around me. My parents, half way through their forties, still appeared to me quite young. Gray strands in their hair, skin no longer smooth, and lines around their eyes were barely noticed when caught up in their exuberance. Charlotte and Vince were closer to fifty, with more gray and fine lines, but with no less a zest for life.

While I easily kept a realistic perspective of these people so dear to me, for a reason I couldn't understand it was more difficult for me to be objective when thinking of Steven. Still perturbed by this new self-awareness, I approached the Perry barn later that morning. Steven was mucking out the end stall nearest the open double doors and I stopped to watch him. The low sun slanted through the opening and poured brightness into the dim interior, glistening off the sweat beading on the bare skin of his broad shoulders. An old felt hat shaded his eyes and I could see his lips pucker as he softly whistled a tune I couldn't hear but knew was "My Old Kentucky Home".

As I continued to watch him, I was again struck with the wonder of change. Where was the skinny boy, all arms and legs, with a smile too big for his face? Hearing my steps crunching on the gravel, Steven hastily put on his blue work shirt, the muscles of his arms bulging the fabric of a garment recently outgrown. Leaning the hay fork against the old wood of the barn, he stretched slowly, wiping calloused hands on hard muscled thighs encased in tight denim. The jeans were obviously in need of replacing with a larger size, but I hoped it wouldn't be too soon. Gasping with surprise, I chastised myself, "What a thing to think about Steven!"

Then he turned toward me, the slow smile that greeted me formed by a sensuous mouth now fitting well into a strong jaw. When he removed his hat to wipe an arm across his damp brow, there at least was the same long wild hair, now matted by sweat and the tight band of his hat. He ran long fingers through the tangled curls, allowing the breeze to dry them into soft waves. When his hazel eyes twinkled at me with delighted surprise, I noticed that he too had lost the freckles once scattered across the bridge of his nose.

So it was true. We were a man and a woman. But I didn't know what to do with this knowledge, and even less did I know how to deal with the rush of heat that filled me to bursting. I turned to run away from this stranger who was at the same time my most intimate friend.

"Hey!" he yelled.

I stopped and turned back at his call. Drawn to him with a feeling of helpless surrender, I waited for him to reach me with my head down like a sheep waiting for the shearing to begin.

"Why did you come here just to turn and walk away?" he asked.

Avoiding his eyes, I stammered, "I...I just remembered something I was supposed to get from the store for Mother."

"What?"

My cheeks flamed. "Um...coffee beans."

"She was grinding some yesterday. There were plenty of beans left."

"Oh. She must have forgotten."

"Then come sit in the shade with me while I cool off. You look hot, too."

As I arranged my skirts next to him on the wooden bench under the old walnut tree, he mopped his face with the kerchief he'd removed from around his neck. "I hope I don't offend you." Startled, I looked at him without saying anything. "Because I've been working in the stalls," he clarified. When I shook my head, he frowned and asked, "Is everything okay?"

"No. I mean yes. Everything's fine. I'm just, well, looking at things differently today, I guess you could say. What are you doing?"

He looked up from the jumble of items he'd pulled from his pockets. "I have a splinter in my finger. But I guess I left my pocket knife on the post of the stall where I was working."

"I'll get it." Before he could object, I walked quickly to the barn feeling his eyes on me. Glad of the cool dim interior, I took a few seconds to gather my wits. Sitting next to him so close had been unnerving, causing my pulse to race and a bead of sweat to slide down my cleavage.

Walking back to him, rather than bothering to step around a small mud puddle, I lifted my skirts almost to my knees and jumped over it. Looking up, the startled expression on Steven's face was unlike any I had ever seen before. He was staring at my legs, and his cheeks glowed red. Lowering my skirts, I stopped to look up at a hawk passing overhead in order to give him a moment to collect himself. But I knew then that our awareness and development was on the same time-table.

When I returned his knife to him, he looked at me with a sense of wonder so intense I started babbling about petty events among our friends. It was such mindless chatter that I couldn't now recall it even if my life depended on it. Indeed, at the time it felt like it did.

Mother's best friend from the east, Carrie Nurrey, moved with her family to Bishop in January of 1900. Mother was ecstatic and soon after the Nurreys arrived, she brought me with her to Bishop to meet my "Aunt" Carrie. She was a big bosomed woman with gray hair smoothed back from her face and captured into a round bun at the nape of her neck, and I was immediately warmed by her bright smile. She embraced me with an enthusiasm that left no room for shyness on my part and then released me almost reluctantly. Mother and Carrie stayed up late every night visiting, but they were always up early to begin the unpacking of crates and the decorating of the ranch house.

While Carrie's daughter Wanda and her son Evan, and their spouses, unpacked in the main house and worked on the ranch, Carrie's sixteen year old daughter Mary and I were assigned various odd jobs. It was while completing one of these tasks that I discovered an old trunk in the storage room off the service porch. It was filled with letters my mother had written to Carrie beginning in 1878. The last one was dated only two months previously on December 31, 1899.

For the rest of the month that we were there, whenever I could get away from the others, I read the letters and was amazed at the many surprising things I learned about my parents and their life together. It made a big difference in my attitude toward them, and what I in turn expected from marriage.

But I was mostly surprised by what was not included in her letters to Aunt Carrie, especially about Lone Pine. There was no mention of the violence in the numerous saloons, or the Chinese section and the atrocities regularly perpetrated there with little fear of punishment. But the same could be said about incidents between the whites and the local tribes, although since the Indians were so much a part of the work force, the law usually stepped in to mediate any conflicts. There was also little mention of the large Mexican population present in the town, and who were families of miners who had been part of the town from its beginning.

Nor did she make more than casual mention of the arson fires set as warnings and retribution by arguing factions--enraged Indian farm workers, ranchers in disagreement over property lines, and miners angry at mine owners. She commented only in passing on any type of crime in the area, and what was mentioned was mostly anecdotal. And although she acknowledged the prostitutes in Bodie (even forming a friendship with one unfortunate girl), nowhere in her letters does she mention the prostitutes that made their home in Lone Pine or Bishop.

This apparent lack of a social conscience surprised me, because Emily Eastman was known to be a woman of endless resolve and compassion, as well as a supporter of greater rights for women and the local tribes. But she also had rigid opinions that once set were difficult to influence, and sometimes she was shortsighted when her emotions were highly charged.

Mother often acted as though she had little awareness of what society thought appropriate for a woman in her circumstances. When animals were mistreated and Mother spoke out in protest, she was amazed that others didn't back her up or thought her an interfering busybody. When a woman moved to town with a baby and the rumors began that she had not really been married to its father, Mother went out of her way to help the woman and introduce her to those most willing to give her the benefit of doubt. But it took her weeks to forgive those who had shunned the young woman.

One day I took time away from my chores at Aunt Carrie's ranch and the reading of Mother's letters and went into town. I was in the hope that I might see someone I'd met the previous fall when Mary and I had attended a dance at the town hall. Having just that summer become aware of my blossoming femininity, I was gratified to experience for the first time men a little older than myself responding to me with interest. But only one of them generated my interest.

His name was Alexander Roberts and he was visiting from Bridgeport where he and his father had a large cattle ranch. We were so taken with each other that we seldom danced with anyone else, and even when we did, it was difficult for me not to stare over the shoulder of my neglected partner at this handsome, dark-haired man with eyes as blue as a Sierra sky. He had worn a closely tailored buckskin jacket and dark brown pants that broke on top of a boot that had met the iron of many a stirrup.

Through the early winter of 1899 Alex and I had exchanged a few letters, and I could tell Mother was anticipating a wedding at the start of the new century. But when I visited Mary that February of 1900, I admitted to her that I hadn't received an answer to my last letter at Christmas. Of course, mail between Bridgeport and Lone Pine in the middle of winter was always a dubious proposition. But after we returned home from Bishop and spring arrived, I still hadn't heard from Alex, so I relegated our meeting the previous fall to that of just a pleasant one-time event, that nevertheless continued to haunt my memory.

At the end of May, Steven went to Bishop to attend a large horse auction. While there, he made a new friend and after several days together at the auction and in the saloons, Steven brought him to Lone Pine so he could consider purchasing a horse that Vince had for sale.

When they arrived at the Perry ranch at the south end of Washington Street, I was standing with Father and Vince by the barn. As the young men dismounted and led their horses toward us, I recognized the man with Steven as Alexander Roberts. When his eyes shifted in my direction and his prepared smile broadened into pleased recognition, my chest tightened and I felt my face flush. To keep anyone from noticing, I turned away and patted Steven's horse on the cheek.

Steven proudly announced, "Everyone, I'd like you to meet Alex Roberts from Bridgeport."

Shaking hands with Father and Vince, he murmured to each a polite, "Nice to meet you, sir."

This seemed to please them, but when he took the hand I boldly offered, both Father and Steven frowned.

"How do you do, Mr. Roberts?" I murmured, looking boldly into his eyes and smiling.

Few of the young men I knew in town handled this well, and I had enjoyed their discomfiture as they strove to be respectful and hopeful at the same time. But Alex merely met my gaze and allowed the tiny suggestion of a smirk. This subtle message of understanding and challenge tickled me so much that I laughed outright, and so did he. When the others frowned at us, including Vince this time, I told them that Alex and I had met the previous fall.

While watching Alex out of the corner of my eye, I said, "We even exchanged a few letters, although Alex must not have found mine very interesting. I haven't heard from him for several months."

"I can only plead for forgiveness." He did look contrite. "After the deep snow melted enough to allow it, business took me away from the ranch. I was intending to mail you a letter from Bishop while I was at the auction."

And indeed, he took an envelope from his pocket and handed it to me. Looking down at it, I told him, "I must forgive you then." And againm we looked into one another's eyes and smiled.

Steven removed his dusty hat and beat it against his leg, suddenly the picture of chagrin and disappointment. He crammed the hat back on his head and poked his fingers into the pockets of his leather vest.

"Are you looking for your watch, son?" Vince asked Steven.

"Yes." He swung around toward the barn while commenting over his shoulder to Alex, "I'll get the horse out so you can look at it. Then you can get on your way home."

"I signed on two more men today," Uncle Vince commented. "Let them get it out."

Stopped in his tracks, Steven only said, "Fine."

Never having seen Steven so uncomfortable and at a loss for words, I was even more puzzled by the look of resigned defeat that settled on his face. But Alex's presence quickly distracted me from everyone else.

Father turned to Alex. "If you don't have to leave town right away, why don't you stay with us tonight? The Whitney Hotel is probably full. Our home used to be a boardinghouse, so we have plenty of room." Wreathed in a pride that lighted his lean face, Father ad ded, "My wife is a great cook, too."

Alex's eyes flicked toward me and back again to Father as he answered quickly, "That's very kind of you. I don't have to be back any time in particular. I'll look at the horse and then Steven can take me to your home."

Around the dining room table that night, we got to know more about Alex while Mother and Charlotte served a wonderful dinner. They insisted I stay seated with the men.

"How big a spread do you have in Big Meadows?" Father asked.

"About a thousand acres. Most of it's pasture, but we also have a large pond we keep stocked with trout." He smiled broadly. "Our land is between town and the mountains, so in spring it's practically a marsh."

"When I was sixteen," I interjected, "we took a trip through the meadows while staying in town. In fact, we must have passed by your ranch on the way to the lakes." Abruptly changing the subject, I asked, "By the way, do you know a girl about my age named Irene Baxter? We met when I took a walk onto Kingsley. I've written her several times, but received only one reply shortly after my first letter."

"Yes, I know her." He looked down at his plate and after a slight hesitation, said, "Her parents were killed a few years ago."

"Oh, no!" I couldn't imagine anything worse happening in my life.

"How did it happen?" Mother asked.

"They died in a fire. Irene came home from errands in town and found the barn on fire. It looked like the Baxters had been working inside in the hayloft and were overcome by the smoke. I was in town at the time, on my way to see Simmons in his barn near their property. We heard Irene screaming for help, but by the time a bunch of us got there with buckets, it was too late."

"Poor Irene," Mother murmured.

Father quickly changed the subject away from fires, probably to spare Mother from focusing on the loss of her own parents in the great Chicago fire years before. For some time after that, the men discussed cattle prices and Alex mentioned that they sold beef to the citizens of Bodie.

Knowing this would open the floodgates to stories from my parents and the Perrys, I fell into a long-suffering silence. Up to then I had avoided looking at Steven, but now allowed my eyes to steal in his direction. It wasn't me he was watching with great intensity, however, but rather Alex. In fact, his expression was just this side of extreme dislike with maybe a touch of fear. I quickly looked away.

But Aunt Charlotte had been watching all of us. When our eyes met, she looked down at her plate with a puzzled frown followed swiftly by surprise and alarm as an unexpected idea occurred to her. Only good breeding and a wish to avoid an awkward situation kept me from pulling her into the kitchen to ask what she was thinking.

Forcing my attention back to Uncle Vince's current story, I noted that Alex was genuinely engaged in what he was saying. From August of 1878 until the end of 1880, the years of Bodie's greatest boom, Frank and Emily Eastman had lived at the south end of the town. While Father worked as a mining engineer, Mother struggled to maintain a home in the midst of harsh zephyr winds, muddy streets, explosions, mines caving in, and crime of such violence and frequency that some today believe the stories are merely part of Western myth. But it was indeed all real, and took place during long winters below zero with snow piled to the eaves and short summers with days hovering at 100 degrees. A close friendship with Vince and Charlotte Perry helped my parents maintain their sanity, especially Mother.

"This is wonderful fried chicken," Alex mumbled as he accepted another piece.

"Thank you," Mother and Aunt Charlotte responded at the same time.

When the laughter died down, Alex asked Father and Vince, "I noticed quite a number of ducks on the edge of Owens Lake the last time I was in the area. Do you hunt them for the table?"

Everyone shook their heads as Vince answered. "They've been past eating for years. The lake water is so low, and the soda content so high, that the ducks taste awful."

Father related what Beveridge Spear, a longtime resident of the area, had once told him. "He said back in the 1860's they hunted ducks on Owens Lake when there were millions there. He said the roar of their wings was so loud that the sound could be heard at Cerro Gordo, ten miles up the Inyos. Some were so fat from eating the rich brine fly along the lake edges, that when the hunters shot them, the birds burst apart in a spray of yellow fat."

After that vivid image was dealt with, the men discussed the ditch companies and the practice of the ranchers bringing the river water to their fields before the drainage could reach the lake. There was little critical debate about it, since it was a practice that had been going on for over two decades. But they had to acknowledge that the small quantity of river water that reached the lake was not sufficient to offset the rate of evaporation.

With a sudden change of subject, Alex turned to me and asked, "What did you think of the Bridgeport Valley?"

"I liked it very much," I answered with enthusiasm. "It's a very beautiful area."

"Have you lived there long?" Aunt Charlotte asked. It was the first time she had questioned him. Steven still hadn't spoken, stoically observing all that was going on around him with a frown that never softened.

"We've lived in Bridgeport my whole life," Alex explained. "My father, J.B. everyone calls him, grew up in Long Valley. But he decided to settle in Bridgeport after winning a big poker hand in Virginia City back in the 1870's. He bought our land and some cattle from a man selling up and leaving the area, and then slowly built that into the large spread we now have."

"That must have required a lot of work," Mother remarked.

Alex glowed as he talked about his father. "Yeah, but he had several loyal hands that helped, and most of them are still with him. He earns respect easily. They built the barns and sheds and fenced in the pastures. He built the house after he met my mother." He chuckled. "Until it was finished, they lived in one of the sheds, so he worked fast. The house has been added onto a couple of times, the last being a bigger kitchen and back hallway with a room for Sing, our Chinese house help. There's also a large room there for Mrs. Lewis, our housekeeper, a caring older lady that practically raised me."

"Is the house so large then?" Charlotte asked.

"Well, besides those rooms, downstairs between the kitchen and the great room is a good sized dining room. Then upstairs is a guest room, two connecting bedrooms, my study and J.B.'s room. The bedrooms face an open corridor that looks down on the great room below where the end wall is covered in river rock around the fireplace. It's so big that we can get the trunks of small trees in it."

"Oh, how lovely," Mother exclaimed.

"Must put out a lot of heat," Uncle Vince mused.

"Yes, but our winters are colder than yours here. We can have deep snow for months, so we need it. In fact, back in November of 1890 we had temperatures 40 degrees below zero." We were all appropriately impressed. "There's also a smaller fireplace with a raised hearth on the other end of the great room that's open to the dining room as well. But it's the big one that impresses people as soon as they walk through the front door."

"So Bodie has gotten beef from you for a long time?" Father asked, less interested in the house than the ranch's operation.

"Yes. Of course, Bodie isn't what it used to be when you lived there, but it counts almost a thousand people. Since I've been running things for J.B., I've introduced hog production and we've found buyers for them in Bodie as well as towns north, the Mono Basin and Lundy Lake."

"Oh, Lundy," Mother exclaimed. "What's it like now? I was there at its start and it had such great potential."

"It's almost deserted now."

"But it's so beautiful," she protested, "what with the lake and the narrow canyon covered in trees!"

"There was a resurgence of interest in '89 when a ten-stamp mill was built in Lake Canyon. Then the new cyanide process helped the reclaiming of gold from the old tailings. But even that hasn't been able to get the town up and running again. The Lake House Hotel is a popular spot in summer though. And, of course, the lake is terrific for fishing."

"But the May-Lundy mine isn't producing?"

"I guess there's still something there because the Crystal Lake Gold Mining Company recently bought it and added twenty stamps. They're digging a new tunnel to intersect the main vein."

Mother sat forward. "How exciting! That'll surely revitalize the town."

"We'll see," Father commented. "I don't think anyone will ever be able to get out the gold in that mountain. I think its in there so deep that it'll always cost too much to get it out."

"But engineering techniques continue to develop," Mother argued.

Uncle Vince laughed. "By the time someone figures out how to get it out, the world probably won't want it."

"Well," Mother mused, "maybe that's a good thing. The area's natural beauty is so great, I'd hate to see it spoiled by man's greed like so many other places." She looked out the window at the Sierra. "Somewhere in this world there should be wild places treasured for their pristine beauty and value to Nature alone."

As though none of her comments had touched him, Uncle Vince picked up the subject of his own efforts with swine, receiving some valuable information from Alex that would help him in the future. Father then carried the coffee into the parlor for Mother. Suffused with the soft glow of the kerosene lamps, we gathered there for dessert.

I talked little, rather choosing to memorize Alex's face--his strong jaw beginning to show the shadowed evidence of a shave many hours past, and the sparkle in eyes nestled like bright blue jewels under even brows a little lighter than the dark hair he occasionally brushed from his forehead. His right eye would sometimes partially close in a squinted reaction to strong emotion, showing he wasn't as relaxed as he appeared. Steven, however, I studiously ignored as he slumped in his chair at the end of the room, dividing his glare between Alex and myself.

During the last of the evening's conversation, Alex mentioned, "This September we'll be driving cattle to pastures in Nevada and some down around Bishop. The snows are too deep for them in our area, so we have to move them out before any chance of snow."

"It's only three months until September," I needlessly observed.

Later Charlotte informed me that my tone had nearly crossed the line into unseemly over-eagerness, and sharply encouraged me to maintain more decorum now that I was no longer a young girl. My cheeks flamed as I listened to her. Although my stance was one of submission, my mind roiled with unspoken tart responses.

But that night in the parlor Alex matched my eagerness. "When I do get down here with the herd, might I call upon you?" He quickly included everyone in the sweep of his glance, but it was clearly an afterthought. My parents graciously gave him permission to call, while Steven stood up and walked from the room and into the kitchen.

After a little more discussion of general topics, Steven came back into the room to remind Alex that he was planning to be on the road early in the morning. Alex thanked Mother for a wonderful dinner and took my hand in his a little longer than might have been considered proper. He then retired to the room Mother had assigned him for the night.

As I always did, I walked with Steven to the front gate, where he blurted out, "Bishop is a long way for Alex to come unless he has important business."

"He'll only be a few hours ride from here."

"Like I say, it's a long way." He stuffed his hands in the pockets of his jacket and looked up at the sky peppered with so many stars they almost formed a solid canopy of light.

I suddenly lost patience with his strange petulance. "You don't act like you want to see him again."

He shrugged. "He's just a casual acquaintance." A long pause followed where neither of us spoke. Then Steven said, "He talks a lot about his father, doesn't he?"

"What's wrong with being proud of your father? Aren't we proud of ours?"

"Of course." He glared at me. "But I've never gone on and on about mine like he did his. It just seemed a bit excessive, is all."

Probably because I agreed and didn't want him to know it, I told him, "Well, I think you were rude. It's not like you."

"What did I do that was rude? I barely talked to him."

"That's the point." Then, before he could respond, I said, "I don't want to continue this conversation." Turning away, I walked quickly toward the house.

"Whitney, I'm sorry," he relented.

But I kept going, unable to cogently explain why I felt so confused, but the intensity of it frightened me. It was easier to escape inside to my room, just down the hall from one source of that confusion. Sleep resisted until late, and I was still wrapped in fitful dreams when Alex crept out of the house just before dawn.

As soon as he got home, however, he wrote me a polite letter expressing his delight in having met me again, and his happy anticipation of seeing me again in a matter of months. He enclosed a newspaper published in the town of Bridgeport.

When I told Aunt Charlotte that I thought this sweet, she merely pressed her lips together and grunted, "Uh-huh." She then scrubbed more fiercely at the skillet in the sink. After that I didn't share anything related to Alex. Being in a romantic frame of mind, I wanted no prying questions or anything of the practical to shake me from it.

Good to his word, Alex didn't think it too far to travel, and just under three months later he was back in Lone Pine. He stayed two weeks, and I always recall that time as a blur of activity: dinners at the cafe, a church dance, visiting with friends, a town hall meeting, watching a traveling troupe of actors, fishing the streams around the town, a picnic in the grove by the square, and rides among the jumble of huge boulders in the Alabama Hills.

The late September evening air was perfect as we sat on the front porch swing, wrapped only in light jackets and the excited flush of awakening passion as yet not acted upon. Our conversations covered a wide range of subjects, and served mainly to bring us closer together by acknowledging similar experiences and attitudes. We laughed at small humorous things, and touched our shoulders together, something considered daring by the older citizens going by.

As we rode away from the house one afternoon, I glanced back at my parents watching us from the porch. Father put his arm around Mother and she looked up at him with a pride that lit her face. I glanced at Alex, who after seeing their exchange, smiled at me and held out his hand. I took hold of it briefly before encouraging my horse forward, but for the first time I knew something of what Mother felt so often. I knew what it felt like to be a woman in love.

My parents continued to welcome Alex into our home and there were many meals shared where I could see Father growing increasingly fond of him, even one time calling him *son*. Mother was always eager to hear the stories about his father and their life on the *Double R*.

On one such occasion after dinner, in the parlor with our coffee, Mother asked Alex, "Where did you say your father was raised?"

"In Long Valley." He hesitated a moment, then said, "I really don't know too much about his youth. It doesn't seem to be something he wants to talk about. I get the impression it wasn't all that pleasant. However, I do know that my grandfather was a farmer and sold his excess produce to the miners in Bodie and Aurora back in the 1860's and early '70's. My father speaks of his parents with fondness, but also a hint of sadness."

"Why do you think that is?" I asked.

"Whitney!" Father chastised with his usual mildness. I almost laughed as my ever-curious mother frowned at him.

"Well, he brought it up," I defended.

Alex only laughed, a wonderful light sound of delight that broke free in a spontaneous burst. "She's right. Besides, I'm so comfortable with you all that I don't feel any question an intrusion."

I shot a look of victory at Father, who turned his attention from me to wink at Mother. I asked Alex, "So why do you think he has a sense of sadness regarding his parents?"

"Well, about my grandmother it's easy because she died young, like my own did. But although my grandfather has been portrayed to me as strict in his expectation of hard work and discipline, I don't think he was overly harsh. But I've gotten the impression there was some kind of falling out between them. I do remember him saying that when he was twenty-one, my grandfather moved to Nevada and never returned."

"Why was that? What did he do in Nevada?"

His cheeks colored pink and he traced the lip of his cup with his index finger, round and round several times as was his habit when nervous or disconcerted. "I don't have the answer to either question."

Mother asked him, not unreasonably, "Haven't you asked him?"

Alex looked at her with a sadness I have seldom seen in a young man's eyes. "No. He has a way of turning off the flow of conversation that makes it clear there'll be no more of it on that subject."

"Does it bother you not knowing?" Mother asked kindly.

Alex flashed his beautiful smile. "Not really. Everyone should be allowed the privacy of their memories."

He reached out and poured himself another cup of coffee, and therefore missed Mother's look of disappointment. But I felt the subject closed between us, and knew that Mr. Roberts was not the only one with the skill of ending a conversation with finality.

While Alex was with us, I wasn't prepared for the surprised looks from those to whom I introduced him at gatherings. They would almost always look past us, as though searching for something they were surprised not to find.

Finally, someone was bold enough to ask, "Where's Steven?"

These good people, who had always been part of my life, evidently assumed that one day Steven and I would be together as a couple. I laughed out loud at the thought. We had been raised, after all, like brother and sister.

From that time, Alexander Roberts merged into my life like a soft breeze on a summer night. His knowledge of ranching and his respectful manner impressed Father and Uncle Vince, while his humor and prosperity impressed Mother. Charlotte was the only one to hold back from him, although she was always polite. I often caught a look of sadness in her eyes when she looked at Steven, and I assumed she was wondering when he too might develop an attraction to someone.

Arriving earlier than expected one morning at the Perry home, I stood on the back porch preparing to enter unannounced as always. But then I heard Charlotte say to Steven, "My dear, don't fret about Whitney. I doubt she'll be anything more than a brief infatuation for a man like Alex.".

Steven mumbled something I couldn't hear, but his tone was sharp and unkind. Baffled and hurt by the direction of their conversation, I silently withdrew from the porch. Walking blindly, I stopped beneath the shade of a large locust tree not far from home.

Pondering what I perceived as their lack of enthusiasm for my happiness, I eventually decided to conclude that their actions were motivated by love. After all, if I became involved with someone who lived so far away, they might lose me from their lives. I ignored the fact that my own parents hadn't shown such a concern.

But I soon had little time to think about what anyone else thought. The spring of 1901 brought an end to a long winter of letters between Alex and myself, carried by trains, intrepid mail carriers on snow shoes and skis, and more than a few stagecoaches and wagons. Then, as soon as the passes were clear of snow, Alex returned to Lone Pine. He wasted no time before asking me to marry him, and I wasted no time in thinking it over before I said yes.

CHAPTER 4

On April 1, 1901, Alex and I entered the small church at the end of Locust Street in Lone Pine. It was filled with my family and closest friends, which meant a gathering of about thirty people from the town. Standing beside Alex was Steven, a reluctant and surly groomsman. Uncle Vince several times made gestures at him to smile, but Steven ignored him, not so much from defiance as from the inability to comply. Finally, Charlotte told Vince to shut up and leave Steven alone. She used a tone I had never heard from her before, as I doubt Uncle Vince had either. It was immediately effective.

I looked over at Mrs. Bowman and Mrs. Faber, the last of mother's friends from the original 1870's quilting circle. Both women had been part of the great pioneer migration to the West in the 1850's and '60's. My long dress of fine ivory cotton and lace had been made by these dear, elderly ladies. As they watched me walk to the altar, they had their hankies at the ready, unashamedly prepared to enjoy with gusto the wedding of their dear Emily's daughter. But they were comfortably seated on Alex's side of the church to lend balance, as were several of the young people that had been told to sit there by their mothers.

Alex's highly lauded father was conspicuously absent. Mr. Robert's telegram merely said that due to pressing ranch business he couldn't leave soon enough to reach Lone Pine for the wedding. Alex made no comment, and in fact, seemed to accept his father's absence at face value. I, on the other hand, felt he could have made the wedding if he had really wanted to put forth the effort. Of course, I said nothing.

Immediately after the brief but reverential ceremony, we returned to the house. Surrounded by close friends and my family, we cut into a large sheet cake in the center of the dining room table sparkling with Mother's best china and silver.

However, Father's toast to our happiness was interrupted by the entrance of young Elmer from the telegraph office announcing a message for Alex. Opening it with a smile, expecting his father's congratulations, Alex's face fell as he instead found the curt instruction to return home as quickly as possible. Almost all of the ranch hands had left, heading for a mining resurgence in Bodie and Dunderberg. The Double R had been left short-handed and new hands needed to be hired.

Not wanting him to see how disappointed I was, and eager to give at least the appearance of an understanding wife, I generously suggested he hurry on home by train and horseback. The Carson and Colorado Railroad had just the month before been purchased by the Southern Pacific and the trains were running a regular schedule north. I promised to follow within days by taking the train to Benton and then a stage from there to Bridgeport.

Our parting that afternoon was a hurried packing of saddlebags, kisses of incredible passion, tantalizing whispers that made me blush, and much shaking of Alex's hand by the men. Standing in front of the house by the gate, I watched my husband of only hours ride away from me until the white clouds of road dust enveloped him. Turning back toward the house, thinking myself alone, I was startled to see Steven standing under the large sycamore tree next to the path leading to the house. I was also surprised at the intensity of my pleasure.

"Steven!" I hurried to his side. "I'm so glad you're still here." As we had done so often over the years, we sat on the old bench in the shade of the tree.

Steven twirled his hat in his hands while the breeze ruffled his sandy hair, as always in need of a trim. I watched him look down at the shiny gold band on my left hand, his long dark lashes laying on his cheeks like startled butterflies. He stopped playing with his hat and lifted his eyes to mine. The look of plaintive sadness in them stabbed at my heart and I thought to myself, "How can I ever leave him, this friend so close and so dear most people think of us as brother and sister?"

He began talking about a new saddle he had just purchased, and that was followed by a sharing of information about some of our friends. But I sensed his interest was forced, as well as his cheerful tone of voice. He suddenly stood up and moved toward the gate.

Grabbing his hand, I pulled myself up beside him. "Steven, what's wrong? I know I'll be far away, but we can write. I'll always be your best friend."

He looked me in the eyes and slowly shook his head. "I know that. But it won't be the same."

"No, it won't," I admitted. "But please be happy for me. This is such a huge step in my life."

After a long hesitation, he blurted out, "I just don't think he's the right one for you."

A slap on my cheek wouldn't have startled me more. "Steven! He's your friend!"

"No!" Lowering his voice to a harsh whisper, he said, "He's your husband." Before I could ask what one thing had to do with the other, he walked away as suddenly as his words had pierced my happiness.

Entering the house, I looked around my life-long sanctuary from all in the world that had lacked grace and benevolence, and suddenly realized that this was no longer my home. My disturbing conversation with Steven fled from my thoughts as I was forced to face the fact that my home was now far to the north in Mono County. But I didn't know what it looked like.

Filled with a vague sense of loss and doubt, I longed for something intangible that I struggled to name. Tears hovered at the back of my eyes, but I wouldn't allow them release since no one would have understood. Neither of my parents had suffered even one moment of doubt after committing to one another, looking to the future with assurance and certainty because they would be facing it together. I found it deeply disturbing that I couldn't claim the same thing.

Finishing my packing for the journey to Bridgeport late in the afternoon, I heard a breathless Aunt Charlotte downstairs calling my name.

"Whitney? Where are you?"

"Here," I answered, running down the stairs into the entry hall. "Is something wrong?"

"No, no. Quite the opposite." She smiled at me with obvious satisfaction. "I'm sure you're concerned about not being able to take all your personal things and wedding gifts with you immediately."

"That's true. I'll have to wait for them to be shipped on the train and then carted in by wagon."

"No, you won't," she declared with a big smile. "Stan and Helen Moore and their son Andy are leaving tomorrow morning for the Mono Valley just north of the lake. They're going to spend the summer with their daughter. Andy said he'd drive a second wagon with your things if Alex can send someone down to meet you there."

"But that's a longer trip than going most of the way by train," I reasoned.

"Yes, but you'll see more of the country, and you'll have all your things with you when you get there." She finally noticed my confusion and looked at me with contrition. "Oh, my dear, I thought it would be what you'd enjoy."

"No, no. You're right. It'll be wonderful fun. But Alex may want me there sooner."

She blushed. "I telegraphed his father and received an affirmative response. So you can leave here tomorrow as planned."

"And Alex and his father know where I'll be staying?"

"I got directions and included it in the telegram. Please stop worrying. Your mother took a side trip on her way to join Frank after they were married, and he didn't mind."

If this was to become a family tradition, it certainly was an odd one. But I didn't say anything.

Charlotte took my hand and held it tight, pleading her case. "Alex will be very busy when he gets home, helping his father. This way once you get there, you'll be able to have your things to add to the house."

Why did it sound like so much justification? Was she trying to make amends for her earlier reluctance over my marriage? Whatever her reasons, I accepted the plan and rearranged my thoughts so I could look forward to the unexpected adventure.

Early the next morning I found dressing to be a protracted chore. After putting on layers of cotton under things, I stepped into a dark skirt a few inches shorter than most to facilitate climbing in and out of the wagon, hooked the long row of buttons on a light gray waist and tossed a loose leather traveling jacket onto the bed. I then sat down and began lacing up new kid leather shoes until each was wrapped tightly a couple of inches above the ankle.

Meanwhile, Father, Vince and Steven loaded the wagon with my traveling valise and the crates holding my clothes, our few wedding gifts, the fine linens I had embroidered since a young girl, a favorite picture from my room, a new set of Rogers Brothers' silver plated flatware, a soup tureen of Mother's that I'd always loved, and a small crate of books selected from my shelves with great care and anguish for those that had to be left behind. In my trunk were the few pieces of jewelry received from Father over the years, each piece protected in a velvet pouch.

At the last moment I slipped over my neck a long gold chain from which was suspended a pink shell cameo. The white figures carved upon its surface were those of a baby boy and a baby girl sitting with their feet touching. The boy holds out a daisy to the girl, a tiny diamond chip nestled in the center of the flower, while a swath of flowing scarves binds them together in a moment of sweet innocence. Steven had given it to me on my sixteenth birthday.

Tucking the personal treasure beneath my waist into the warmth of my cleavage, it was secreted away along with the dawning awareness of how dear to me was Steven. The pain I felt when contemplating our parting was physical in its intensity. With difficulty, I pushed down a growing sense of panic.

"What have you done?" a small voice at the back of my mind whispered. Placing my hand over the hidden cameo, I looked at my reflection in the mirror and whispered aloud, "What have I done?" The hard pounding of my heart beat out the answering refrain, "too late, too late, too late". A wave of dizziness swept over me.

"Whitney!" Mother's steadying hands took me by the shoulders and led me to the edge of the bed where I perched carefully. "You really should have eaten more this morning."

"It's not that."

"You're not wearing your corset too tight, are you?"

I looked up into the concerned and loving face that was so happy about my successful marriage, and smiled. Receiving from me a promise that I'd eat something before leaving, she rushed off to put a few things together from the kitchen.

With a shake of my head, I stood up and walked downstairs, refusing to look back at the shelter of my room. After a quick few bites of egg and toast in the kitchen, I joined my parents on the front porch. As I hugged them a final time, I tried to ignore a small tear gathered at the corner of Father's right eye and the quiver beginning in the center of Mother's delicate chin. As I turned away quickly and hurried down the walk toward the wagon, I noticed Steven standing in the deepest shade of the old tree by the path. But I allowed him to think I was unaware of his presence, not trusting my emotions at that moment.

As soon as I settled myself in the seat next to the tall lanky form of Andy Moore, a young man I had known since early school days, he gave a shout and the horses moved forward. Turning in the seat, I fixed a smile on my face and raised my hand to wave good-bye to Steven, wanting him to know that after all I was aware of his presence. Of all those dear to me, I wanted Steven's face to be my last reminder of home. But only empty shadows filled the space beneath the tree. I quickly returned my raised hand to my lap. I felt tears forming, but managed to keep them from falling.

Andy tried to commiserate. "Leaving home must be really hard for a girl like you. Wish I could say something to help."

Sniffing and dabbing at my eyes, I mumbled, "Thanks, Andy. There's nothing that can be done now."

This being only too true, I took a deep breath and eased the tightness in my throat. Passing the Meysan's old store, Aunt Charlotte stood on the porch watching us pass by, a forlorn expression on her face as she peered from beneath the wide brim of her new bonnet. Raising her hand, she wiggled her fingers slowly in farewell.

"Bye Aunt Charlotte," I called out. "I love you." Her mouth formed the same words and I quickly faced forward. Leaving all the familiar people of Lone Pine, the town that had been witness to the years of my maturing, my heart ached for one last embrace with them all.

"Lovely lady that Mrs. Perry," Andy broke into my thoughts. "She's been like a second mother to you, hasn't she? And Steven like a brother."

I longed to shout at him, "But they're not. She's a dear friend and Steven is so much more than a brother!" But I only nodded.

"Alex is a nice guy. I bet he's real eager to see you. You'll certainly be settling in a nice area. My dad says your father must be very happy you've made such a good match."

As Andy fell silent at last, so did the temptation to jump off the wagon and run back to Lone Pine. Yes, Alex was waiting for me, probably with exciting plans and an eagerness only a newly married man denied his honeymoon could know. After focusing my thoughts on the adventure of married life, I too began to feel the eagerness a bride should feel.

Slowly, and with many stops to water the horses and ourselves, we progressed through the Valley. We passed the small settlement of George's Creek, many small ranches set well back from the road surrounded by growing fields of alfalfa, crossed bridges over the wider streams and rolled through the smaller ones where the horses had a quick drink, and finally entered Independence. There we spent the night with mutual friends. The next day we left at sun-up and traveled through miles of desert blooming yellow, purple and white, with the mountain peaks still packed with snow. After a brief stop at Aberdeen, we arrived late in the day at the small agricultural hamlet of Big Pine. There we spent the night, camping with some other travelers at the edge of a pasture on the northwest edge of town beneath the cover of cottonwoods.

A few years later I remembered how the men hotly debated the presidency of Theodore Roosevelt and what he'd accomplished since he took over. Some commented on his reputation for fairness. If I'd known the role he was to play in the future of the Owens Valley, I might have listened more closely.

The next day we passed through Bishop. Thankfully, it was only 16 miles from Big Pine, so we had time for a meal and a nice visit with Aunt Carrie and her family before we had to get to bed. As we left the following morning, Carrie hugged me to her ample bosom with the strength of loving sentiment, and the biceps of a ranch woman who found it difficult to allow others to do all the work.

The road began to climb more steeply, especially over the Sherwin Grade where the wheels turned with difficulty through miles of deep sand. We gave assistance by walking and even occasionally lending our shoulders to the rear of the wagons. Not far from the road to Convict Lake, our wagon rolled over a large rock and landed with a hard jolt. Upon inspecting the wheel, it was found to be cracked.

"Damn," Andy commented with feeling as he climbed in beside me after discussing the situation with his father. "We'll have to head up Monte Diablo Canyon toward the creek. Dad knows a guy that has a cabin there and he can help us make repairs."

To lighten our load, we transferred some of the things from our wagon to the other one, and slowly made our way toward the upper canyon. Although we held our breath as we thumped over every rough spot and hole, the wagon held together, and after two hours of this slow progress we finally reached the small cabin situated near a grove of willows. Nearby was a swiftly flowing creek filled with tumbled rocks and over-hung with willows, aspens and pines. While the men worked on the wagon and Mrs. Moore gave thought to dinner, I brought her water from the creek before walking to the lake.

The hot sun intensified the dusky spice of pine and cedar as I stepped around lingering areas of slippery ice covered with pine straw. Melting patches of snow watered dozens of knee-high saplings hovering near the shelter of their parent's rooted feet, mature versions promising what they would someday become.

I had heard about this dark blue lake many times, a lake of such extreme clarity that I could see the bottom covered in small tumbled rocks. But its setting was what made it so special. With desert scrub to my back, I faced a triptych of granite walls towering over the far side of the lake. Whorls of pink, blue, and lavender washed across the lower reaches of these scarred and barren slopes, just below the upper half still frosted with thick coats of snow. This bizarrely shaped rock was created millions of years in the past by the slowly moving mass of a glacier. After pushing its massive, grinding boulders to the near shore, the frozen mass then melted and created this cold blue lake to hold its ancient remains.

From very early times the area had been known by the Paiutes as Wit-sa-nap, and then by the miners around the time of the Civil War as Monte Diablo. But in the 1870's people began referring to it as Convict Lake after escaped convicts from the Carson Prison in Nevada shot it out with a posse near the lake.

I looked up into the trees around me, some just showing the bright lime green of new spring growth. With the sun lending shine to their feathers, birds called from the branches as a cool breeze rocked them gently in their green aerie. Feeling the gentle sway of my skirts mimic this action, I realized that I had not felt this relaxed for weeks.

At the end of the fifth day we reached Windy Flats, although some called it Mammoth Meadows because of the mine established there for a short time in 1878. We stayed for three days with friends of the Moores, the kind but quiet Hernandez family that included six well-behaved children. Although impatient to reach Alex and my new home, I was still happy to see this area again.

We were snug in a cabin only a stone's throw from Mammoth Creek where it flowed through a thick stand of quaking aspens still standing in snow along the edge of the fast flowing water. The roof of the house was partly caved in, the result of too many heavy snowfalls, and the siding was badly in need of paint. But the curtains at the windows, made from flour sacks imprinted with tiny blue flowers, were so welcoming that one couldn't object to the few cracks in the glass.

The next morning we rode up the steep road from the wide meadow toward the defunct Mammoth Mine, the scent of pine growing stronger as we gained altitude. Rounding a curve in the narrow road, off to our left in the shelter of the forest, we saw a grave surrounded by a battered picket fence. This was the last resting place of a woman who made the mistake of wanting to stay in the mining camp with her husband through a Sierra winter two decades earlier. She had wanted a home with a white picket fence, and after her death from exposure to the harsh winter, her husband saw that she got one. Instead of a sentimental reaction as the men expected of me, I felt a surge of pique. The husband's creation of this quaint shrine may have satisfied his sense of guilt, but to me it felt like a hollow gesture. Riding on, we found mounds of snow blocking the trail and so were forced to return to the meadow without seeing the site of the old mining camp.

We left the comfort of the Hernandez home on the eighth day of our journey, refreshed and eager to be on our way. We soon found ourselves traveling through miles of Jeffrey Pine forest. The coolness and heavy scent uplifted our spirits as the closeness of the trees hugged us in welcome. Then we entered the Mono Basin.

Here was a very different view--a land of barren white stretches of desert dotted with blue-green sagebrush surrounding an inland sea of immense dimensions. This glare of blue water was Mono Lake, its two volcanic islands floating in its midst like dumplings in a pot of salty soup.

No one from the Double R was waiting for me at the home of the Moore's daughter and her husband, Melinda and Chris Fowler. Their ranch was situated near other small ranches on the northwest corner of the lake, and sat in the midst of a large garden of vegetables just starting into life. It was no doubt liberally fertilized by the cattle grazing in the surrounding scrub. Numerous dogs danced around our feet while two young girls stood on the porch with large, resigned cats held dangling from their embrace. Two boys in outgrown overalls were cleaning leather tack at the other end of the porch.

The problem of where I would sleep came immediately to light, although they offered me the hay in their barn. Andy barked laughter at that, and although about to accept the offer, I realized that it would hardly set the proper tone for Alex's ranch hand to find me in such circumstances. Mr. Fowler said I could no doubt find reasonably comfortable lodging at the Hector Station, a stage and toll stop near the Bridgeport Canyon Road. As I stood exhausted in the press and chaos of barking dogs and squealing children, I figured the stage station couldn't be any noisier.

While it was still early enough for me to reach the station before dark, we said our good-byes and they promised to direct Alex's man to me. As I climbed into the wagon and took the reins in my hands, the horses turned their heads to stare at me. Neither one looked happy to be traveling again so soon.

An hour later I pulled up in front of the small wood and stone building fronted by a raised porch with no railing. There was a long hitching post in front of the building hosting several dozing horses still saddled, with more horses standing in a number of corrals waiting to change places with the exhausted stage teams soon to arrive. I left the wagon to be picked up later by Andy and was shown to my room. It was not much larger than a closet, and was to be shared with another lady traveler. But it was better than a pile of straw, and the dinner in the saloon's small dining area was palatable.

The next day was Sunday, and when I stepped outside in the morning to enjoy a view of the lake, I had to walk around a congregation of Paiute women with their hair tightly wrapped in colorful bandannas or bowl-shaped woven reed hats, and their calico dresses topped with colorful shawls. They were accompanied by dark-skinned men dressed in jeans and cotton shirts, all sitting on the edge of the porch playing "hand game", a wagering game similar to dice but played with sticks and what they called bones.

Just as I finished breakfast, my transportation arrived. A small, lean man with a dirty face, but surprisingly clean clothes, stood next to a buckboard loaded with barrels and burlap bags full of supplies. Failing to remove his hat as he addressed me, which anyway looked permanently affixed to his head by a band of grime, the man moved forward and asked, "You Mrs. Roberts?"

When I assured him that I was, he announced that he was Parson, there to take me to the Double R. Without waiting upon further conversation, he picked up my bags and loaded them onto the back of the wagon along with my things from the Moore's wagon. He neither helped me up onto the wooden platform that served as a seat or said anything more after himself climbing up next to me. Here I would perch the rest of the way to Bridgeport, clinging to the seat's low iron rail until my shoulder ached. The woman with whom I'd shared a room at the station watched us move forward with a jerk, obviously none too certain whether or not she should let me go.

I will not detail the long ride, except to say that we had only one stop of any length, and where I was able to rest for half an hour while Parson changed the horses back to those that had been hitched to the wagon when it had left the Double R. We had only two other short stops to water the horses in streams, and where I was able to find shelter behind some brush to accomplish that which all must do. The road was steep most of the way, only occasionally leveling off before once more forcing us to strain upwards. When the road was deep in sand, I got out and walked to help lighten the wagon. When the trail was thick with rocks, roughly jostling the wagon as we rolled over them, I held my breath. When the trail was narrow and near the edge of a precipice, I thought of Steven behind and Alex ahead, and commenced to pray.

Arriving in Bridgeport, we passed through the Paiute village on the outskirts, and with the town's long main street stretching into the distance before us, crossed slowly over a bridge spanning a narrow tributary of the Walker River. It was a sturdy wood and iron bridge, the banks of the East Walker River flowing beneath cribbed with quarried stone, and the edges of the bridge blocked by large triangular beams. The river banks on either side of the bridge showed a wide trough of mud created by livestock crossing the river when herded in and out of town. Parson called it "the new bridge", as it had been completed only three years before.

As we rolled onto the main street and merged with the other wagons, the nerves of my stomach began to clench. After a final longing glance back at the bridge, the portal from the south and my beloved Owens Valley, I faced forward. We continued down the wide street bordered with warehouses, shops, saloons, residences, the inviting Leavitt House sporting new paint, and the white regal gleam of the Mono County Courthouse. It was all as I'd remembered it, and I felt comforted by a sense of familiarity.

While Parson picked up a barrel at a warehouse, I stayed with the wagon and gazed around at the busy supply town. The street was lined with horses tied to hitching rails in front of saloons and businesses, most animals shedding out the long hair that had kept them warm during the winter, and all looking extremely bored.

Freight wagons passed us slowly, groaning under heavy loads of hay, lumber and livestock on their way to the Mono Basin and nearby towns of Bodie, Lakeview (later called Lee Vining), and Lundy. Other smaller wagons belonged to ranchers I supposed could be my future neighbors, hauling home supplies. A few were headed to homesteads miles from town, bringing with them enough supplies to last through the summer, and not returning until fall for the supplies that would have to last them through the winter.

The few women I saw there in town were making their way slowly along the wooden sidewalks with baskets over their arms. Now that winter was past, with an early spring emerging and the roads clear of snow, they were eager for their regular trips to town. Not one of them passed another woman without stopping to visit. Men always complained that it took their women a long time to complete simple shopping, but after a long winter of fighting "the lonelies" far out in the surrounding countryside, such social contact with other women was part of their survival.

Men flowed in and out of the Stanton Saloon to our right.

"That looks like a popular place," I commented after Parson returned to the wagon and moved us slowly forward.

"Yup," he responded. "Bill Stanton took it over in '73."

"Nice man?" I asked, matching his clipped tone.

"Yup."

"Do Alex and J.B. visit Mr. Stanton there?"

"Nope."

"Why not?"

"'Cause they visit him at the cemetery. Dead since '90. Tuberculosis."

"Oh."

I think it was the most complex of the conversations we'd shared since leaving Mono Lake behind us.

Parson reined in the wagon with a suddenness that startled me. A group of four rowdy cowboys on lathered horses cut across the road in front of us, pulling up at the Hughes' Livery Stable with shouts into the interior. Not far from them, several sweating men wrestled with a wagon beneath a large gallows frame, while a group of cowboys next door on the porch of the Stanton Saloon shouted suggestions. This prompted the blacksmith and his helpers to shout a few choice curses at them, along with, "Why don't you lazy sons of bitches come help?" The harassers quickly retreated into the saloon.

Having made our way to the end of the street near the Kirkwood home, we turned left past a number of clustered wagons and left behind the noise, dust and chaos.

"Is it always this busy here?" I asked Parson.

"Naw. Sometimes it's busier."

We quickly passed beyond the view of buildings and entered a world of spreading green where hundreds of small, meandering streams (which Parson referred to as stringers) sparkled through young grass just gaining height. After years living in a valley of broad gray desert broken only by green-edged creeks and fields of alfalfa, to be in the midst of such a lush green expanse was an experience so intense it felt like a different planet.

Our wagon bounced down the long, rutted road curving through acres of pastures surrounded by barbed wire strung between posts that had not long before been large branches. Only occasionally did a sprawling wind-twisted tree rise above the rich grass, adding visual interest to the flat countryside that ended near the rolling hills at the feet of mountains still partly covered in snow. The chortling call of red-winged blackbirds gave us music through the rising wind as dozens of their black bodies fluttered upward out of the grass. Fighting the temptation to picture Steven at Diaz Lake, I focused instead on the road ahead.

Beyond the fences a scattering of dark cattle stood staring without interest into the distance, their massive jaws moving from side to side. One stood with its forelegs in a stream, lowered head sucking up gallons of water. Only a few bothered to look in our direction. Soon the pastures would be full when the rest of the herd was brought home from the warmer climes of Smith Valley in Nevada, Adobe Meadows southeast of Mono Lake, or the rich grasses near Bishop.

Most surprising to me was the amount of water swamping the area. Parson unhinged his jaw long enough to explain that there was so much run-off from snow melt that the ranchers had dug ditches to Green, Summers, and Dogtown Creeks to the south, and Buckeye, Swauger and Robinson Creeks to the north. These creeks intersected north of the town in a wide depression of land.

A little more than two miles from town we approached a large ranch on our left. Set well back from the road not far from where it curved sharply to the right, I could see a scattering of buildings, barns, pens, corrals, and a pond.

Parson said, "There it is."

Surprised at the size of what lay before me, all my attention and curiosity became riveted on the prospect of my new home, especially the house. Highlighting the landscape was a large, two-story log structure on a high river rock foundation topped by a steeply pitched roof. Adding grace and visual balance, three chimneys rose above the roof, the tallest at the near end. Steep split-log steps led down from the railed porch accenting the front of the house and affording a view to the north toward town and the Sweetwater Mountains beyond. A small grove of willows clustered invitingly at the far end of the house, just showing the hint of new slender leaves.

While I stared in surprise at the beauty and size of the property before me, we swung off the main road and passed beneath a square arch of rough-cut logs. Looking up, I saw an iron medallion encircling the Double R brand, a symbol of the two Roberts. Only now there was a third.

Recalling Alex's stories of the adventures and hard work he and his father had shared over the years, I glanced back at all the cattle carrying the Double R brand and felt each brand to be an accusation of my intrusion.

Had Mr. Roberts thought of this too? Would he receive me as someone only to be tolerated in this bastion of male enterprise?

Both sides of the quarter mile road to the house were lined with tall, long-needled pines and old lilac bushes dripping with lavender blooms that perfumed the warming air. The shadows of the trees washing over us was so pleasant, and my anxiety so intense, that I almost asked Parson to stop while I collected myself. However, by the time we pulled up at the foot of the wide steps, I had steeled myself to the inevitable while also eagerly looking for Alex on the porch.

But only a tall, thin woman stood there near the front edge. Hands clasped in front, back straight and shoulders squared, she looked down at me with cool gray eyes. My steeled resolve almost faltered as I took in her high cheekbones, small sharp nose, and tight thin lips now pressed together with disapproval ill-concealed. But she was beautifully gowned in the latest of Eastern fashion, the bell-shaped skirt of her black moiré dress smooth over a small bustle and wasplike cinched waist. Only a hint of gray showed at the temples of her black hair slicked back into a tangle of short, tight curls.

Parson threw a furtive and uneasy look at the woman, but made no introduction. He did, however, move a little faster to unload my things. The woman told him shortly, "Take the crates around to the back door and carry them in from there." I didn't hear what he mumbled under his breath, but it didn't sound amicable.

A small Oriental man with a long S-shaped braid of hair down his back came forward to get the luggage. To this man Parson did introduced me, calling him by the singular name of Sing. Observing his diminutive stature and aware of how heavy were some of my cases, I worried he might hurt himself. But he picked them up as though they were empty, passed me with a nod of his head, and gave me a warm smile.

"Good afternoon, Mrs. Roberts." The woman's voice was almost as deep as a man's, but softened by a husky quality that caught one's attention like a whisper in a noisy room. "Welcome to the Double R. I'm Mrs. Lewis, the housekeeper."

She appraised my person from toe to hair as I climbed the steps and prepared to take a proffered hand that didn't after all appear. When she concluded her observation of me with the saucy comment of a cocked eyebrow, I resisted the impulse to curtsey.

"Hello, Mrs. Lewis. It's nice to finally meet you."

Hoping I was successful in hiding my unease, I wondered how Alex had managed to give the impression of a housekeeper of maternal and nurturing character. Instead, I was to share a house with this angular package that had made up her mind to resent me even before we had met.

Mrs. Lewis turned and walked into the house while I followed like a servant expected to obey. It was a feeling most unpleasant, and I told myself that only the fatigue of the long journey kept me compliant and silent. I would not admit to intimidation.

We entered straight into the large great room where I stopped, surprised at the scattered arrangement of heavy, over-stuffed furniture covered in animal fur or blanket throws. To my far right was the gaping maw of a huge stone fireplace where the remains of a small tree smoldered amid glowing red coals. Although a number of rag rugs covered the shining planked floors, in front of the fireplace the hide of a large black bear reclined at the feet of four sofas haphazardly shoved together. Resting against the rock, and near the ceiling, was a large iron Double R medallion matching the one over the front entrance to the property. No one visiting this ranch was left in doubt to whom all this belonged.

To my left was a smaller fireplace with a raised hearth confronted by a cluster of chairs and a low table covered with a scattering of books and ashtrays. Looking down from the wall above a wide mantle were the heads of a deer with a large rack and an elk with an even larger one.

In the center of the room between these fireplaces and their seating arrangements was a large roll-topped desk with heavy chairs on either side, and supporting a large copper oil lamp with a clear glass chimney. Completing the furniture in the great room was a round game table with six chairs. It sat in front of large windows affording a view of the approaching drive and the far Sweetwater Mountains.

The tall ceiling above was crossed with dark rough-cut square beams hewed from the trunks of pines. A large crystal chandelier holding ten candles was unexpectedly suspended from one of the beams. Stairs at the far left of the room ascended to an open hallway in front of five dark, paneled doors. Between the doors the walls displayed two paintings of horses, three of mountain scenery and a prized fish mounted on a board. The whole within view reminded me of an elegant hunting lodge temporarily empty of men and seldom visited by women. I couldn't wait to see our bedroom.

"Your room is ready," Mrs. Lewis informed me with little enthusiasm.

Following her up the stairs, I looked down over the railing into the great room and felt a surge of excitement as I realized I was now the mistress of such a grand place.

"Mrs. Roberts?"

Turning toward the throaty voice now tinged with impatience, I found Mrs. Lewis standing back from an open door. When I brushed past her unyielding form, it was to enter a large room where I was faced with a four-poster bed covered in a pink and black crazy quilt.

Against the wall to my left and next to a dressing table of dark wood, a tall armoire stood with its doors open ready to receive my clothes. Modestly positioned in the near corner and partially hidden by a tri-fold wooden dressing screen was a marble-topped wash stand of dark glossy wood. A stack of white towels sat next to it on a small table with a new bar of Ivory soap on top of them. A lidded porcelain chamber pot painted with pink roses was beneath the wash stand on a shelf. To my right a small iron stove against the wall was cleaned and laid ready to light. I laid my shawl across the back of a small chair next to it, just beyond a small walnut table. The pink glass kerosene lamp in its center gave off a dull glow and the familiar musty smell.

"This is lovely," I exclaimed happily. "But I'm a little surprised."

"Why is that?" One brow rose a little above the other.

"It's so light and airy. So feminine. I'm surprised Alex would have a room like this."

"He doesn't."

Turning to her in surprise, I said, "I beg your pardon?"

"This was the large guest room. It's been done over for you."

"For me?"

"Yes. Alex has a room connecting with this. There's a dressing room between."

"Oh, yes. Quite proper." Although a common arrangement among the upper classes in the East, I was nevertheless surprised that it was what Alex preferred, considering the lack of marital intimacy such an arrangement suggested.

"Where's Alex now?" I asked eagerly. "Has someone gone to tell him I've arrived?"

The corners of her mouth slowly turned up, but it was difficult to interpret the emotion back of the action. "Shortly after Alex returned from Lone Pine, he was called to Carson City by J.B."

Stunned at her words, I almost gasped in surprise. But not wanting Mrs. Lewis to know the degree of my consternation, I quickly tried to recover my poise. I knew I wasn't successful when her smile broadened. "When will he be returning?" My voice sounded small and plaintive, and I hated it.

"One never knows. Especially if he's with J.B."

I said nothing, having no words and not wanting to express my disappointment to this woman, who I felt would only enjoy seeing it.

"I'm sure you don't want a heavy dinner," she informed me without inquiring if it was true, "so tea will be served downstairs in fifteen minutes. Sing will bring you hot water. If there's anything else I can get you, please let me know."

Giving lie to the sincerity of her offer, she turned away without waiting for a response. When she reached the door, she briefly turned to look back at me and met my eyes with an undisguised hostility. The crisp rustle of her skirt was the only sound in the room as she turned away before closing the door behind her, a little more firmly than was necessary.

CHAPTER 5

Before I could collect myself following Mrs. Lewis's abrupt withdrawal, a sharp knock at the door announced the arrival of my hot water. Sing bustled in with a big smile and a large enamelware kettle with steam rising from the spout. After filling the white porcelain bowl centered on the wash stand, he poured the remainder into the matching pitcher next to it. When he turned back toward me with a slight bow, his smile glowed in the room as he hesitated, awaiting further instruction or a request.

"Sing, I can't tell you how nice it is to see someone smiling." Relief flooded through me. "Parson hardly ever talked, much less smiled. And Mrs. Lewis seems to find my very presence difficult to bear."

He chuckled. "Oh, yes. You not mind them. Parson has toothache and Mrs. Lewis always that way, 'cept 'round Mr. Alex or J.B."

I leaned against one of the tall posts of the bed. "Does everyone address Mr. Roberts as J.B.?"

"Oh, yes. Always. He want it that way. Very ... ah, relaxed fella."

"This isn't a formal household?"

"Oh, no. Well, when guests here, yes. But not rest of time."

"Have you been here long?"

"Oh, yes. Started day after J.B. and wife move into big house. Not want to cook for miners. I promise to make good grub and he hire me." His smile grew wider.

"Do you know where Alex and J.B. are right now?"

"Telegram for Mr. Alex come from Carson City, but they be anywhere now."

"When might we expect them home?" I continued to press.

"Expect? Not good idea." He shook his head firmly. "But you be comfortable here. I make sure." He flashed his radiant smile again, shifted the enamelware kettle to the other hand and quickly left the room.

Fifteen minutes later I obediently reported to the dining room where Mrs. Lewis served me tea. To her credit, or possibly that of Sing, a hearty meat sandwich was set before me along with a generous portion of apple cobbler with heavy cream, and a pot of excellent coffee. With an appetite that surprised me, I consumed it all. But I did so alone, in a house so quiet I felt the sound of my chewing to be an intrusion.

After complimenting Sing on his delicious food, I decided to familiarize myself with the layout of my new home. One of my favorite finds was in the hallway extending from the foot of the stairs, past the rooms of Mrs. Lewis and Sing on the right, past the kitchen door on the left, and ending at the back door. Floor to ceiling shelves lined the hallway walls and were filled with hundreds of books covering a wide range of subjects.

Passing through the back door, I stood on the wide covered porch and took inventory. The grove of willows to my left, that I'd seen in the distance when approaching the house, looked peaceful and inviting. A newly planted vegetable garden was close to the house and surrounded by currant bushes just beginning to leaf out. I looked forward to helping with the harvest.

A gravel path cut through the garden and continued until it passed the bath house, a smoke house, two chicken coops and several hog pens. Walking along the porch to my right, it turned the corner of the house and I stood at the back of it where I could see in the distance two large barns and several sheds partially covered in the tendriling vines of hops. Beyond those was a maze of wooden corrals, the odor of their occupants well away from the house.

Returning to the hall, I was drawn to the warmth emanating from the kitchen. Good smells wafted from the stove, a modern iron monster with a fire box roaring next to a steaming hot water well lined with white porcelain. Above was a warming closet positioned between iron resting plates to keep food hot until all the cooking could be completed. Ornate nickel-plated oven doors gleamed in the light pouring through the window above the sink that overlooked the garden. I had only seen a stove like this once before, and that was in a Sears, Roebuck and Co. catalog. Mother had yearned for it, but had baulked at the $30 price tag.

Curiously surveying the rest of the room, I was happy to see an iron pump rising from the side of the wide, deep sink. It assured me of easy access to water from a well rather than carrying buckets from a creek. At the center of the large rectangular room was a chopping block work table held up by thick, elaborately carved legs. To my left, just beyond a small kitchen table, a door opened into the dining room. I passed through it into the great room, and ended my tour near the foot of the stairs where I had begun. Recalling what Alex had said about the deep snows that frequented the area for weeks or months, I envisioned myself walking this circuit in winter as a means of exercise. But really, I questioned, does the deep snow last for months?

As I returned to the dining room, I was puzzled by the predominant rustic influence mixed with an odd assortment of more delicate items. If Alex's mother had not died so long ago, I would have assumed they had belonged to her, but they looked to be of a more recent style. Outstanding was a large collection of fine crystal and china in a tall delicate cabinet behind what I learned later was J.B.'s place at the head of a rough-hewn dining table.

Both rooms had large, fancy crystal chandeliers hanging from the heavy beams, and some of the hand painted glass two-globe lamps on the scattering of heavy tables were excessively delicate. Fancy gilt frames on the walls displayed paintings of flowers and overflowing bowls of fruit, while rough wood frames highlighted mountain and hunting scenes.

Attributing the eclectic mix to the fact of two single men living together for too long without the softening influence of a woman, other than the dour Mrs. Lewis, I still wondered how they had come to own so many furnishings.

With an elaborate mental shrug, I put my curiosity aside and headed outside. However, I got no further than the porch when hit with the piercing chill of evening, forcing me back inside. After another solitary but satisfying meal, I read by the fire for awhile and then retired early to bed.

My routine varied little over the next week as I waited for my new husband to return from his business. I spent as much time outside as possible, basking in the lush green landscape so different from Lone Pine. From my bedroom window at the back of the house I could see in the distance the jagged crest of the Sierra, a reassuring granite connection to home. The peaks within my view quickly became new friends from an old familiar family.

The first time I went out to the big red barn that sloughed a bit to the north, the result of strong winds and heavy snows, I could hear the sounds of horses snuffling and the low conversation of deep-voiced men. As two cowboys in dusty jeans, striped shirts and dark hats walked past me toward the corrals, a tall muscular man wearing a long leather apron approached me. A dirty gray hat almost hid his watchful eyes, but it was the large wad of tobacco bulging in his leathery cheek bristling with gray stubble that held my attention. Walking slowly, just before reaching me he briefly turned his head and spat dark juice onto the ground where it landed with a splat that raised a small puff of dust.

Rearranging the cheek bulge, he asked, "Can I help you?"

"I'm Alex's wife, Whitney."

His alertness level elevated. "Oh, Mrs. Roberts. How do, ma'am. I'm Mort, the hostler and blacksmith. Welcome to the Double R."

"Thank you." Looking into the barn, I asked, "Do you think it's possible for me to ride for awhile? I'd like to get some exercise and also see the ranch."

"Of course. We have a nice older mare just right for a lady."

Choosing not to respond to this assumption of maidenly fragility, I followed him into the barn. While he headed to the stall of a horse showing considerable gray around the nostrils, I continued down the row of occupied stalls, running an appraising eye over each horse as I passed.

"I'd rather have this one," I called out to him, standing in front of a low door between myself and a sleek, dark gelding with soft but alert eyes.

"Uh, that's one of Alex's horses." He nervously shifted the cheek wad. "He's never let anyone ride Comet before."

I smiled sweetly. "He's never had a wife before either."

Mort frowned, started to say something, stopped to eject another brown glob onto the ground, then said, "Comet has a lot of spirit and he hasn't been out for awhile. He'll be frisky."

I opened the stall and walked in, talking softly to the horse as it watched me with ears twitching. As I slowly ran my hand up and down his neck, he stood still and allowed the familiarity. Taking a twist of sugar from my pocket, I poured it into the palm of my hand, letting his lips and tongue deftly scoop it into his mouth. That and a piece of carrot soon won him over.

Taking the bridle out of Mort's hand, I slipped the headstall onto Comet's head while getting him to take the bit in his mouth, all with minimum effort.

"Could I ask you to saddle him for me?" He seemed happy to accommodate me, even though it was not a side-saddle that I had chosen.

It felt grand being astride a good horse again, and Comet seemed unconcerned that it wasn't Alex on his back. The split skirt of my conservative riding outfit hid my legs from view while allowing me the ability to center my weight in a way familiar to Comet. From the look on Mort's face, I could tell the new lady of the ranch would be a topic of conversation over that evening's meal shared with the other ranch hands. Hopefully, the meal would be seasoned with at least the beginning of respect.

"Would you like me to go with you this first time?" he asked.

"No, thank you." I smiled at him. "I don't want to take you away from your work and I'll stay within sight of the buildings."

"Okay then." As he made a gesture that hinted at the raising of his hat, I applied gentle pressure to Comet's sides. He moved forward eagerly.

The cool breeze stirred the grasses through which we walked, Comet's long legs stepping over the many narrow streams slicing through the meadows. He tossed his head at the slowness of our pace, but it gave me the opportunity to survey the property. I looked back at the barns, one for the horses and mules and the other for the buggy, wagons, plows and other equipment. Next to the horse barn was a small building used as a tack room, and other sheds beyond that held tools, grain and various other things needed on a ranch of such size.

I could now see not only the out-buildings I had viewed from the back door of the house, but also a turkey run near a small swiftly flowing creek over which a cold house had been built for the storage of vegetables and dairy. A large holding pond beyond the corrals caught the run-off from the snow melt and rains, as well as a controlled diversion from a small tributary of the East Walker River running across a corner of the property. Two tall windmills near the edge of the pond turned slowly in the wind, pumping a supply of water to the wash house and the troughs at the corrals.

The reeds and sedges along the edge of the pond attracted frogs and birds, although I could hear more of them than I could see. Overcoming the urge to use Comet's height as a vantage point to observe the birds' antics, I instead returned to the barn. Comet was greeted by a solicitous Mort ready to wipe him down and make sure he was comfortable. I wished my husband was waiting in my bedroom to do the same for me.

Over the next few days, I worked hard to learn the names of the ranch hands that worked for the Double R on a permanent basis, eager to assume the role of ranch owner's wife. As I watched how hard the cowboys worked, I also gained considerable respect for them. They were men of many nationalities, although mostly Mexican, and lived a frugal existence while sharing a bunk house and cooking on a sheet iron stove. Most of the workers were transient, traveling from one ranch to another as they adapted themselves to whatever work was available. It could be branding, haying, harvesting, digging canals, riding the fence lines looking for needed repairs or building new ones, felling timber, or a host of assigned chores. If they wanted to take care of their families, living near or far, they learned to do it all.

Alex often hired three Negro cowboys, brothers who traveled the ranches helping with branding in the season. They were big, strong, fearless and always a step ahead of the any steer, cow or calf thinking itself clever. The youngest workers were often sons of ranchers who needed the practice so they could learn the necessary skills needed to run their own spreads. They were seldom of much help, but Alex or J.B. either owed their fathers for a past favor, or hoped to get one from them in the future.

The one constant on the Double R, other than Mort and Sing, was the foreman Hank, somewhere close to sixty. No one seemed to know or care about his last name, being variously referred to as Hank, Mr. Hank, Senor Hank or Sir, depending on the nationality and degree of respect or supplication involved. Tall and lean, with skin dark as strong coffee, his black hair was topped by an old brown Stetson hat of a remarkable cleanliness. When he spoke, he immediately gave away the fact of a good education.

At first, although always polite, he didn't seem disposed to be anything more than formal and distant. But as I asked more questions, hoping they ranged in the direction of intelligent, he became more inclined to full sentences and eventually formed close to half a dozen of them together.

Our first long conversation took place when he showed me his work room located in one of the rough-timbered sheds. Hanging along the wall or laying on work benches were tools for any task needed on the ranch. I recognized many of them, naming them aloud while pointing to them, such as the felling-axe for cutting down trees and a broadax for hewing; an auger for boring; several hatchets; a long two-handled cross-cut saw; a sledge-hammer; a maul for striking; hitting-beetle-and-wedge for splitting logs; hitting mallet and cornering chisel for squaring holes; reaping hooks for harvesting; and a hollowing-gouge for making holes in wood. But there was so much more I didn't recognize. When I asked Hank to describe the use of several items, he happily did so. I think he felt that more the correct order of the universe.

By the end of the week, I had forged tentative friendships with Mort and Hank, their greetings when I approached genuinely pleasant. And since I evidently hadn't overly irritated Parson on the trip to the ranch, several of the men he worked with began to greet me with a tip of their hats. Walking around the ranch became the most pleasant part of each day.

One afternoon, taking advantage of Hank's fulsome mood, I gleaned two new facts. The first was that Hank had no knowledge of J.B. before he came to the Big Meadows area. Either that or he was doing a good job feigning ignorance, which I had an uncomfortable feeling might be the case. The second bit of information was that after Alex's mother died, J.B. never brought another woman to the ranch. I wasn't sure what that meant, but sensed it was significant.

One day when Mrs. Lewis was in town, I was able to visit with the young Indian woman who did our laundry. She implied at one point that her mother had known J.B. well. She said this with a wink, adding that no doubt several of the white women in town could make the same claim, and not just the saloon floozies. I was increasingly eager to meet the elusive J.B.

But it soon became obvious to me that the men considered that Alex was "the boss man" instead of his father. When I commented on this fact to Hank, he admitted that it was true, but didn't know what J.B. felt about it. Of course, he assured me that whenever J.B. was present, he was accorded the utmost respect. Hank claimed to be puzzled by the increasingly long absences of J.B. from the ranch, and said that it was from one of these trips that Alex and J.B. were expected "soon".

When Alex finally arrived home, he was alone. I was sitting with a book near the small fireplace late in the afternoon when the front door burst open and there he was--unshaven, rumpled, dusty, and gloriously handsome. We came together in the middle of the room where I wrapped my arms around his neck and eagerly met his lips. For a long moment his arms tightly encircled my waist, but then he pulled back so suddenly that it threw me off balance and left us several feet apart.

Looking over my head toward the stairs, he said, "Hello, Mrs. Lewis."

She stood with hands clasped in front of her skirts, her face set like stone and lips tightly pressed together. Turning back to Alex, I murmured, "Don't worry. It's not the first time I've seen that expression."

He looked down at me in surprise, then slowly smiled. Taking my arm, he tucked it under his and turned toward Sing who had entered from the dining room.

"There you are, Sing." Alex smiled with great affection as he accepted the glass on the silver tray Sing held out to him. Bringing to his lips the crystal goblet half full of whiskey, Alex downed a good size swallow. "Ah, you take such good care of me, Sing."

"Oh yes! Now I put hot water in bedroom. You wash and get nice for Mrs. Whitney." Flashing his smile, he hurried to the kitchen for the big water kettle that he carried up the stairs and into Alex's room.

"I'd better do as he says." He kissed my cheek. "I'll be back down in a few minutes."

Mrs. Lewis had disappeared, something she was very good at doing, and I tried to settle by the warming fire, although returning to my book was out of the question. In fact, I was so excited at Alex's sudden return that I wasn't even sure I could eat supper.

The candlelight in the diningroom that evening was soft and calming. Alex sat in his chair to my left with his back to the great room, while I sat at the head of the table with the kitchen door to my right. Trying to ignore J.B.'s empty place at the other end of the table, I picked at the food on my plate. Alex ate with gusto as he detailed minor events from his trip: the weather, Carson City gossip, and the details of a stage holdup near Bodie. He even repeated a couple of slightly risqué jokes making the rounds in the towns north. But there was no mention of J.B. having been with him, or the reason for their trip. He did ask about my journey to the ranch from Lone Pine, but even though I glossed over it quickly, I could tell he was bored thirty seconds into my recitation. During the rather long and awkward lull that followed, I asked him who had chosen the beautiful white china and crystal glassware that filled the dining room cabinet.

He laughed shortly. "Neither of us, that's for sure. J.B. won it in a poker game years ago."

"An odd bet for someone, wasn't it?"

"One of the men at the table was out of money. The game was at his house and he thought he had an unbeatable hand. At J.B.'s suggestion the man put up the contents of his wife's china cabinet." Alex grinned. "As you can see, the man lost."

My sympathy for the poor woman upon being told the fate of her beautiful things soured the taste of the wine I drank from one of her glasses. I certainly wasn't thrilled with Alex for finding the event humorous. But I said nothing, not wanting to bring dissention into his homecoming.

"That's how we got a lot of the stuff in the house," he added.

Veering from that uncomfortable topic, I commented, "Sing mentioned that there's a new community church in town. Might we attend this Sunday?"

"I guess so. Up until a couple of months ago the building it's in was the old Wedertz store."

"Really?"

Responding to the interest in my tone, he continued. "The store was near the bridge by the Towle house. Then in January last year Washington Brandon's team of twenty mules, hitched together four across and five deep, pulled it all the way to Emigrant Street where it is now. They moved it along on skids across the snow. It was quite a sight."

"I assume everyone in town turned out to watch."

He laughed. "You can bet on that!"

After a quick coffee on the front porch in a temperature barely warm enough to allow for our presence, Alex suggested we retire each to our own room. Hoping he didn't mean for us to be apart the whole night, when I reached my room I dressed in a white muslin nightgown that had been planned for our wedding night.

Weeks after the wedding it might be, but Alex was as eager as I was, and it wasn't long before he made his way to my room through the connecting dressing room. To his credit, he was patient, gentle and sweet, and we spent that night enjoying one of the great pleasures of being married.

Awakening the next morning, I realized that Alex had left my bed some time after I had fallen asleep. Passing through the dressing room and entering his room, I found his rumpled bedding thrown back and the room empty. When I realized that he had spent even less of the night with me than I had first thought, I was surprised at the odd sense of betrayal that stabbed at me. But over the next few weeks, I resigned myself to this pattern as each morning I awoke alone with Alex already somewhere on the ranch or heading for town.

My routine varied little. After dressing in a simple skirt and waist, I would review the day's menus planned by Mrs. Lewis and receive the twitch of a smile from Sing as I handed them to him; do a bit of light cleaning to assert that it was my house, too; write letters to friends and family; change into riding clothes and head out across the meadows or along the roads; change into an afternoon frock and allow Sing to serve me tea; and finally greet Alex in late afternoon. If on the rare occasion people from town or another ranch were to join us for dinner, I changed yet again into a dinner frock. If alone, after dinner we would read, play checkers or cribbage, then linger on the front porch with a brandy prior to retiring to our rooms.

I routinely avoided as much contact with Mrs. Lewis as was possible. It wasn't difficult, since I think she was guided by the same purpose. But I hated the fact that she would pass me on her way to complete a task or run an errand for the household, while I would be on my way to do busy work not really necessary.

When the 1901 calendar in the kitchen was turned over to June, the days were still comfortably warm. At the end of supper, I folded my napkin and slid it back into the ornate silver ring with my initial on it. The napkin would be used again the next morning, after which time it would be ready for the laundry.

Leaning back in my chair and looking up at Alex as he read a letter from someone, I interrupted him gently. "I thought J.B. would be back by now."

He answered without bothering to look up. "He's visiting with friends."

"Where?" I persevered.

After a moment, he folded the letter and looked steadily at me. "Carson or Virginia City or Bodie. Maybe Lundy Lake if the snow is melted in the canyon."

Taking his coffee cup with him, he walked into the other room and lowered himself into his chair by the large fire. I curled up at the end of the sofa across from him, and tucked my feet beneath me.

"Don't you know for sure?"

"No." His eyes focused behind me as he said, "That was a wonderful dinner, Mrs. Lewis. Your table arrangement was very nice, too."

"I'll give Sing your compliments," she smiled. "I'm glad you're happy with the wild flowers. They're starting to bloom in the meadows. The cutting garden needs more time yet."

Glancing over my shoulder and seeing the smile she focused on Alex, I was surprised at how much real warmth there was in it. For a brief moment she looked approachable and even friendly as she asked him, "Can I get you a brandy?"

"Thank you. That'd be nice."

Alex seemed not to notice that she hadn't offered to get me anything, and he didn't request it for me. As Mrs. Lewis entered the room with his drink, I asked Alex, "Does J.B. go away often?"

"Yes."

I started to ask more, but Mrs. Lewis gave me a look of such severity that I changed my mind.

The next day I found Mrs. Lewis at the kitchen table making out a list of things needed from town. Summoning my courage, I pulled out a chair and sat next to her, nervously straightening the lace cuffs on the sleeves of my dress.

"Mrs. Lewis, I'm new to this house and this family. I can occasionally use a little guidance and would appreciate being able to turn to you for that."

"Is there something you want to know, Mrs. Roberts?"

"You can start by calling me Whitney."

"I'd rather not." She looked at me without expression. "Is there something else you'd like to ask me?"

Refraining from a tart response, I took a deep breath and asked, "Why do I get the impression that questions about J.B. are not open to inquiry?"

"Are his actions really anyone's business but his?"

Realizing her answer was an oblique way of telling me to mind my own business, I took the hint and retired to my room.

A week later, J.B. was still off on his extended absence. Alex was in town on business and Mrs. Lewis was laying down with what she called a sick headache. Sing was in the kitchen experimenting with a new recipe, and I was even more bored than usual.

Wandering around the house with a feather duster, I stopped before the door to Alex's study in the upstairs corridor. As a gesture of defiance, I turned the knob of the door expecting it to be securely locked. But it wasn't, and the door swung open on silent hinges. I had never seen Alex enter without first unlocking the door with a key carried in his pocket, so for a moment I was startled into stillness. Then, gathering my skirts and my wits, I quickly passed through and closed the door.

I began dusting, but was careful to move nothing from its normal place. Until, that is, I spotted a small ledger wedged between two large dictionaries on the shelf behind the desk. Carefully flipping through its pages, I saw it was a record of various sums of money entered by date. It started three years before and ended with an entry the day before J.B. had left the ranch prior to my arrival. All of the entries were in Alex's handwriting. The spacing of these distributions, ranging from $100 to $300, was about every two to three months depending on the season. During the last winter there was an entry in early November and none again until well into March, the period when the area would have been deepest in snow and the passes closed. And just before he left on his current foray.

Replacing the ledger exactly as found, I returned to the corridor, softly closing the door behind me. When Alex came home and went up to his study, I arranged to be nearby. When he reached the door to his private sanctum and discovered the door unlocked, there was an interesting series of expressions that passed over his face--surprise, confusion, a search through memory, and a final effort to establish a look of unconcern while it was obvious that he felt the opposite.

When he cast a furtive glance in my direction, I asked him as nonchalantly as possible, "Would you like Sing to bring you some coffee, dear?"

"No, thank you."

With that, he disappeared into his study. As I hesitated on the landing of the quiet house, the sound of the key turning in the lock seemed to echo for seconds. My feelings were thrown into a confusion of hurt and curiosity, and I instantly wished that I had not heard.

Walking slowly downstairs, I recalled a conversation with Mother and Charlotte the previous year while sitting on the back porch on a hot summer day. We drank sweet cold lemonade in heavy glasses that dripped beads of water onto our dresses. After I had wiped off the glass with my bare hand, I transferred the cold water to the back of my neck just as Father had passed us on his way out of the house. He then turned to Mother and asked, "Isn't that a new dress, Emily?"

Mother had run a hand across the white gauze of her dress and smiled. "No dear. I wore it home from last year's trip to see Carrie."

"Did you? Well, you look cool and delightful. As do you all," he had quickly added, glancing at Charlotte and me. With a gentle squeeze to my shoulder as he passed, he had continued down the road toward town.

"When did you actually buy the dress, Mother?" I asked.

"Last month."

"Why didn't you tell him that?"

"Because he'd feel bad that he didn't remember something so recent. If he thinks it was a year ago, he won't be embarrassed that he didn't remember."

"So it's okay to lie to one's husband if it's to save his feelings?"

"Well..." Mother had blushed and groped for words.

Charlotte had rescued her. "It's a fine line that a wife walks in this regard, Whitney. Sometimes leaving one's husband uninformed of your actions is simpler than triggering a reaction you're both better off not having to deal with."

"Or dealing with their ideas of how a woman should behave," Mother had added. The two old friends had then exchanged one of those looks that always left me feeling left out of the joke. When I told them how this bothered me, Mother had been effusive in her apologies.

But Aunt Charlotte had just laughed. "There are simply some things a woman can more easily share with a close friend than she can with her husband and children."

"And husbands sometimes forbid us to do things through a misguided sense of protectiveness." The scorn in Mother's voice had been clear. Then she caught one of *those* looks from Charlotte and they both started laughing again.

"Such as?" I had prompted.

They then told me of their adventure of going down into a mine while living in Bodie. Father and Vince had not actually forbid them doing so, but both women knew the men would have refused if asked for permission. So while the men were away, the foreman of one of the mines escorted them underground into the dangerous tunnels beneath Bodie Bluff. It had almost been the worst mistake of their lives, as I discovered when I later read of this adventure in one of Mother's letters to Aunt Carrie.

Recalling that conversation as I sat in the great room of the Double R looking up at Alex's closed study door, I felt better justified in what I had done. However, I carefully ignored the difference between their adventurous lark, and my having invaded my husband's privacy.

J.B. returned two days before the town's raucous July 4th celebrations. When he walked in, I was writing letters at the desk in the center of the great room. I stood up and faced him, no doubt in my mind who he was.

"You must be the lovely Whitney."

"And you must be the elusive J.B.," I returned.

His expression remained serious as he took my hand in his. He was in no hurry to let it go and gazed boldly into my eyes as though trying to glimpse my soul. But even though I was uncomfortable with his scrutiny, I didn't pull back. Then he smiled, and in that moment, I thought him the most personable and charismatic older man I had ever met.

Not much past fifty, he stood only a few inches above me. His build was wiry and his arms strong, as any man's would be who was used to an outdoor life. But his hands showed no calluses and it was easy to imagine the long fingers deftly handling cards. Although his face was thin, it was not gaunt by any means, with silky dark brown hair falling sideways just above even brows and large brown eyes flecked with gray. His nose might have seemed a little large if it hadn't been for a wide mouth that smiled easily with mirth, irony or chagrin.

That night, right after Alex and I had climbed into my bed, I turned to him and made a casual comment. "For some reason, I expected J.B. to be much taller."

"What the hell does that mean?" he snapped, sitting up and looking over at me.

Quick to defend myself, I said, "Nothing special. It's just that after listening to your descriptions of his accomplishments, and then seeing what he created here, I pictured him as a towering presence. But he's just a nice man."

"Just?" His brows furrowed together. "You don't think he accomplished all that much? Isn't the ranch big enough for you?"

"Alex!" Putting more distance between us as I sat up, I told him, "That's unfair and I've done nothing to warrant such anger from you."

He shrugged reluctantly. "It just felt like a veiled criticism." The twitch of his right eye attracted my attention, not having seen that nervous reaction since we were courting.

Laying a hand on his arm, I softened my voice. "Alex, I like J.B. immensely. I'm looking forward to spending more time with him. Beyond that happy anticipation, I don't feel anything. Why are you being so defensive?"

"I'm not being defensive." He threw back the covers and climbed out of the bed, wrapping a robe around his naked body. "I'm not sleepy. I'm going to get a brandy and do some work in my study. Good night, Whitney."

So there I was, alone with my knowledge that he may not have been ready for sleep, but he had certainly come to my bed ready for me. Trying to figure out what I had said that was so wrong kept me awake for several hours.

J.B. awoke late the morning following a full day in town celebrating Independence Day with Alex, Hank and Mort. Informed by Alex the night before the big day that it was a boisterous occasion suitable only for men, I had been left behind at home. Although not happy about being excluded, I chose to assume that the men wanted to be free to enjoy the more rowdy, masculine activities available. Mrs. Lewis, however, must not have thought it beneath her dignity, because she had followed them into town in the buggy.

After finishing a substantial breakfast, J.B. suggested we ride together for awhile. Alex had already left the house, and since I had nothing useful to do, I readily agreed. It was a relaxed and pleasant few hours, although J.B. spoke little about himself. He did, however, ask me many questions about the Owens Valley and my years growing up there.

After that, at least several times a week we would ride across the pastures, into the foothills, or up to the twin lakes above the meadows. Little by little he brought me up-to-date with Valley politics and the history of the area.

Since the early 1860's the town had been a freighting stop between the rail lines to the north and the mines to the south and east. When Bridgeport formally became the county seat of Mono County in 1864, it was also the place where mining claims were filed and legal disputes settled in a court of law. This was especially necessary when the 1877 mining boom hit Bodie. The first courthouse was in a small, rickety two-story hotel, but in 1881 the current shining white structure was constructed out of large blocks of cut granite. From then on, the town continued to grow steadily, if slowly.

When I told J.B. that I had a friend living in town, Irene Baxter, he gave me a look even more restrained than the one I had received from Alex when he first learned of my acquaintance with her. "Her parents died in a fire in their barn several years ago," he told me.

"Yes, I know. It must have been devastating for her. When I came to this area with my parents back in '94, we became fast friends."

"Have you seen her since you've moved here?"

"No. But she did send me a letter inviting me to her house. Do you know her?"

"I knew her parents pretty well. Irene was always hovering in the background. After they died, no one saw much of her for months."

"Why do I feel something unspoken?"

He looked at me, his face unreadable. "You should make your own judgments."

And that was the end of the conversation. But I wasn't surprised that J.B. and Alex were uncomfortable about Irene. She lived a reclusive existence, alone and self-sufficient, and apparently happy without a man in her life. In that era, to live that way by choice was considered unusual, if not abnormal.

J.B. was home for a month before leaving again. He said nothing at dinner the warm August night before he left, but he was gone before first light. No one commented on it at breakfast. It felt like we were all keeping the same odd secret, and everyone was determined not to be the first to speak of it.

Alex never again forgot to check the door to his study when leaving it, prompting me to wonder what it was that he was so carefully protecting, and from whom. After seeing J.B. use his own key to the study, entering at will, my curiosity grew even stronger. So did my feeling of exclusion.

CHAPTER 6

Throughout the remaining summer months, I worked hard at making the ranch feel like my home. It wasn't easy. Sing did the cooking, changed the bed linens, and washed the windows. Mrs. Lewis did the light housekeeping, overseeing a Paiute daily girl who came in early each morning to do laundry and ironing, wash the floors, and beat the rugs. That left nothing for me to do in the maintenance of the house other than occasionally wander around with a feather duster while flicking at non-existent dust.

When the cooler temperatures of fall settled in, I had a burst of energy that I channeled into the rearranging of the great room. Enlisting Sing's help, I moved the furniture so that instead of the usual disorganized scattering of sofas and chairs, all the mismatched pieces were arranged into two distinct yet unified seating areas. The grouping with the greatest amount of seating was near the large fireplace, while a cozy arrangement of a sofa and two chairs faced the small fireplace. Since this area was so near the hallway with the book cases, I positioned the largest of the reading lamps there. Sing and I were very proud of our design, as it allowed easier passage through the room and a better representation of the way we used the space.

Returning from a long ride later that day, I found the room arranged in its original configuration. Sing took one look at my angry surprise and Mrs. Lewis coming down the stairs, and scuttled into the kitchen. Focusing on the high collar of her black dress, I pictured my hands there in its place.

"Did you do this?" I asked, barely in control of my rage.

"Of course." She stood erect, her hands clasped at her waste like a stern school teacher addressing a young child. "You should have asked before changing what the men prefer."

I took a deep breath. "Possibly. But you also should have asked me before changing what I had done. I am, after all, the mistress of the house."

Sing said later that he heard her sniff of indignation all the way into the kitchen, not to mention the slam of her bedroom door. It took some persuasion on my part, but Sing helped me once more arrange the furniture the way we had positioned it earlier. Just as we finished, Sing ran to the kitchen to greet Alex and J.B. coming in the back door after a day spent breaking horses. I could tell from their non-reaction when they joined me in the great room that Sing had quickly described to them the situation.

"Very nice, dear," Alex nodded after kissing my cheek, careful not to transfer dirt from his clothes to my white waist.

After noting the studied blandness of his expression, I felt a shock of realization. "Oh, my God! She was right, wasn't she? You like it better the other way!"

"No, no," Alex assured me. "This is just different, that's all."

"It's a change from what we're used to," J.B. said as he walked through the room. "But, uh,..."

"Yes, J.B.?"

"Well, this arrangement may be useful for those of us living here, but when we have large groups of people over, the other way really is better."

My chin up, I took a deep breath and simply remarked, "I see. Since I've not seen any such gathering in the months I've been here, I wasn't aware of their importance in our life." Moving toward the stairs, and hoping to shame them into keeping the room as I had it, I tossed my next words at them over my shoulder. "Do as you like with the room. Far be it from me to contribute anything to the household."

Passing Mrs. Lewis as I climbed the stairs, I knew she had been listening. There was no mistaking that smirk. She will never know how close I came to angrily shoving her out of my way, but she wisely chose to step aside.

My pride wasn't salved the next morning when I found that the room had again been returned to its original arrangement. The subject from that moment on was ignored by us all.

Early in November, upon receiving a note from Irene, I made it clear to Alex that I was accompanying him the next time he went into town. Although reluctant, he did deliver me to Irene's little white cottage between the meadows and Main Street.

Irene greeted me at the door in a dress of silver gray with white lace at the neck and wrists. She was a vision of calm repose, as thin and pale as I'd remembered, but now exuding the refined maturity and poise of a cultured lady. A glow suffused her cheeks, and I'd never seen a woman who radiated such complete self-possession.

We quickly established the ease felt at our first meeting, and I found it wonderful talking to a woman with whom I felt I could be myself. She voiced the same feeling to me.

After a delightful tour by the home's proud owner, I exclaimed, "Oh, Irene, you've done wonderful things to this house. Alex said it was very dark, but this is anything but that."

"It *was* dark," she smiled, tossing her long ringlets back from her shoulders. "It had ancient rough brown fabric on the sofa and chairs, and dark maroon drapes. The tables were dark mahogany and the pine floor was covered in a sea of tattered rugs."

The house I'd toured was the complete opposite, especially the bedroom with its rough walls now painted white, and white lace curtains draping the sides of the windows. But the bed was its central focus. It was covered in white sheeting laid over with a large square of dark gray, open lacework that might have once been a table cloth. Pillows with their cases covered in colorful embroidery, some with tatted edges, were piled at the head of the bed. Stacked in the corner on a white wooden chair were four quilts neatly folded. Next to the bed, a small multi-hued rag rug was positioned to cushion her feet on a cold morning's rising. Within reach on a small pine table sat a fine crystal drinking glass, a clump of yellow flowers in a white ceramic vase, and a pink china kerosene lamp with a clean chimney.

Returning to the parlor, I noted a tall bookcase of rough pine in the corner. It was filled with books, some covered in leather with tooled titles, while others were red, green or blue cloth with gold impressed lettering, these being of newer publication. One book lay on a table between two overstuffed chairs covered in colorful old quilts with the worn spots carefully mended.

"Odd title," I commented.

"Odd book, too. A peddler passing through town had it on his wagon. It was published a year ago."

I picked it up and read out loud, "*Wizard of Oz*. You'll have to let me borrow it when you're finished. Heaven knows I have plenty of time to read."

She brought in a tray covered in a white cloth starched and ironed smooth. Set with thin white China plates, she offered me tiny sandwiches without crusts and small hand-decorated cookies. Such delicate food, along with the room's tattered elegance, produced in me an uneasy sense I couldn't define. Irene had obviously put forth an inordinate amount of effort to create this environment, but it lacked a feeling of substance. There was, however, enough feminine dazzle to draw one's attention away from that fact.

"Everything in the house is so light," I complimented. "You've even painted the old tables white. I love the flowered chintz fabric on the ottoman." In fact, the flowers from her garden were on almost every table. Bunches of lavender also hung from the beams in the kitchen, along with yarrow and several herbs I didn't recognize.

"My parents had a heavy and solemn sense of life," she suddenly commented.

"Was it driven by religious convictions?"

"No. We didn't go to church." She laughed bitterly. "We didn't go anywhere."

"You went to school," I pointed out.

"Yes," she agreed. Her eyes strayed in the direction of town beyond the room's freshly washed windows. Turning back to me, she said, "I went to school and I came home from school. But I was forbidden to linger or visit with other girls. The most freedom I had was to occasionally stop on the way home at a shop for something they needed." A brief shadow of sadness passed over her face before she brightened. "But I suppose they meant well. No one should go the way they did."

I merely smiled and said, "Well, you certainly have freedom and light in your life now."

"I know." A gentle smile played around her mouth and she sighed with an obvious contentment. "I've become quite a home body. There isn't anywhere else I'd rather be."

We discussed an article in a magazine that described the eastern pastime of people gathering together to view moving pictures. Irene commented, "The article says they're becoming quite popular, but that people are becoming a little bored by the same panoramas of nature and men clowning around doing silly things."

"Nevertheless, I'd love to see pictures that move." I then ventured to ask, "I know it's impertinent on my part, but how do you support yourself?"

"My dear Whitney, you could never be impertinent." She took a moment to pour out more tea. "I do several things to supplement the money my parents left. I deposited most of that in a Wells Fargo account. In the beginning, while mourning and adjusting to my situation, I lived off the sale of the heavy ranch equipment and wagons. I also sold the stock, except the chickens and the cow that I breed to a neighbor's bull. That gives me meat, eggs and dairy. With the bounty of the vegetable garden and apple trees, I eat quite well. During winter, I have what I've canned and dried."

"I must say I admire your self-sufficiency. Not to mention your beautiful flowers."

"Now that my gardens are established, I sell my flowers in the summer to the hotels, and sometimes to the freighters passing through on their way to Bodie. They can get a good price for them there."

"No wonder you're doing so well."

But she wasn't done with her recital, flushing at the unusual opportunity to describe her accomplishments. "I also substitute at the school, and do a little sewing for the wealthier citizens."

"Well, aren't you the innovative lady!" I laughed.

"Yes, I am," she responded seriously, passing me the plate of cookies. "It keeps me from the necessity of having to consider a proposal of marriage."

"Have you had many?" I tried not to sound surprised.

"Several. But I'll never accept any of them." Although said casually, the finality of her tone left no doubt that she meant what she said.

"Were you not in love with any of the gentlemen?"

"With one I was."

"Was there something distressful that you knew about him that caused you to decline his offer?"

"No." She met my gaze directly and said, "If I marry, I'll have to move to his place. Or worse yet, I'd have to share this house and change it to include him."

Speechless, my mind locked up and I couldn't think of a thing to say. Such a concept was past my comprehension.

Looking at my face, Irene chuckled and said, "I know, by the way, how odd that sounds." She shrugged. "But it's nevertheless the truth. I love living by myself and the patterns of my days are pleasing to me. But mainly, I just don't want to share this house with anyone else."

"But you said you loved one of the men who proposed."

Cocking her head to one side, she mused, "I guess it wasn't enough."

"No, I guess not." I sipped my tea and nibbled a cookie. For something to say, I commented, "These are the best cookies I've ever eaten."

"I also sell my baking to the hotels." Her face beamed with pride and I couldn't help but laugh.

When we finished eating. she showed me her home Graphophone talking and music machine, complete with large curved horn rising above the box. Cranking the handle to start it playing, the room was filled with the sound of a woman singing "A Bird in a Gilded Cage". I almost choked on my last sip of tea, the irony so poignant and to me obvious. But Irene seemed oblivious of that aspect of the song.

"The machine was horribly expensive at $5.00, but I'm enjoying it so much."

"Irene, if you're happy, that's all that matters."

"You might be surprised to know that most people feel that way now. The local ladies have learned to tolerate me as a likable eccentric, and I've learned to not care that they see me that way." She smiled mischievously. "It saves me from boring social obligations, since I'm asked to attend very few."

However, when Christmas arrived, she agreed to spend the holiday with us at the Double R. The men found her straight-forward manner and practicality surprisingly refreshing, and I think Alex enjoyed watching me interact with a woman so obviously settled in the town. J.B. even seemed to have overcome his odd ideas about her, whatever they may have been. And we all enjoyed the cakes and cookies she brought with her.

The long, snow-packed winter passed uneventfully, full of mundane routines intrinsic to life on a ranch. I never traveled further than the edge of the icy porches, but my gaze often roamed to the far, white mountain peaks with an ache of longing. For what, I wasn't sure, but I would have settled for almost anything if it would have gotten me away from the limited boundaries of the Double R.

Alex and J.B. were always busy with various chores and repairs on the ranch between storms. They also spent hours in Alex's study, or in the barn with Mort and Hank. I sometimes suspected they were playing cards in the hayloft, but that might only have been my resentment of what appeared to be their purposeful lives. By late March, even Alex took in each morning's weak light casting blue shadows on melting snow and sighed. J.B. often gazed out the windows with obvious longing, causing my curiosity to grow about where he might be planning to go when the snow melted. Consequently, we all greeted the spring of 1902 with joy. Part of *my* increased good spirits was due to the anticipation of our first wedding anniversary on April first.

Alex asked Sing to prepare a special dinner for us and gave me a beautiful ink pen, teasing me that I must have worn out several by then. I hadn't realized he was so aware of my many letters home. My present to him was a gold watch chain that I'd asked Irene to purchase for me so the clerk couldn't spoil the surprise when next he saw Alex.

That night we went to bed early for the final celebration, although shortly after I fell asleep, I was awakened by Alex leaving my bed to return to his room. The celebration, and the intimacy, had ended. More often than not after that, Alex retired later than I did, and he joined me in my room no more than once every couple of weeks. I had no idea what had triggered this change in his desire for me, but I missed it less than I would have expected.

Late in May Alex set out with two dozen men to bring the cattle home from their winter ranges. I watched them ride off, part of them heading to Adobe Meadows and others to the Bishop area, and chafed under the restriction of staying behind.

But other than frequent trips to town, J.B. stayed on the ranch. This afforded us the opportunity to spend considerable time together. We talked about local events, plans for expanding the ranch, and he even shared a few stories of his time in Virginia City, Aurora, and Bodie, giving me more insight into his early years in the Valley. But it occurred to me after a week passed that very little of our talk had revealed anything substantive about the man himself.

One evening as we sat on the front porch after dinner, I poured our coffee into white china cups and passed him one. After taking a sip, he smacked his lips in exaggerated pleasure and grinned at me.

"Ah! You do make good coffee, Whitney. Did your mother teach you?"

"No. Actually, it was a friend of my mother, an elderly lady named Mrs. Carrington. She taught my mother the art of cooking soon after Mother arrived from the east where 'cook' had done all the work. When I was in my early teens, I determined to learn from the master, too. She and her husband were killed a short time later in a buggy accident near Little Lake."

He nodded his head and looked off across the green meadows. "It'll be good to see the pastures full again. It always gives me great satisfaction when I see what we have all in one place."

Looking down at his hand resting on the arm of his chair I reached out and gently touched a gold ring on his pinkie finger.

"That's an interesting ring. I've admired it before. The snakehead raised in relief must have been done by a master jeweler."

His eyes followed mine. "I guess so. I won it in a poker game."

Deciding to jump into deep waters, I asked, "Were you raised on a large ranch like this one?"

The tanned skin of his face immediately changed to a pale mottled redness. "No. It was very small."

"I'm sorry. I didn't mean to speak out of turn." In truth, I didn't feel the least contrite.

Quickly recovering himself, he rushed to reassure me. "No, not at all." He laughed lightly, but with little conviction. "It was just a change of subject in a direction I wasn't thinking about, that's all. I was raised on a very small leasehold in Long Valley. We didn't have much, but enough livestock and garden to keep us fed."

"What did your father do?"

"He did some mining in the Homer District for awhile, a little hauling, and worked at the Mono Mills for a few years."

"So your roots go deep in Mono County."

"Yes." He looked across the view to the north, gave a slight uncontrolled shudder and said, "Do you need anything from town? I'll be going in first thing in the morning."

"Can I go with you?"

"I have some business to attend to. I don't know when I'll be home. If you have a list, I'll get whatever you need."

"I'll have it ready for you before you go."

"Fine." He stood up and stretched his lithe body. "Well, I think I'll do some paper work before going to bed early."

But he didn't. I heard the floor boards in his room creaking until just before midnight as he moved restlessly around his room. I felt inexplicably guilty, afraid I had awakened unpleasant ghosts for him.

He left early the next morning and stayed until late afternoon, arriving back barely in time for supper. I asked nothing about what he had done all day or why he had left too early to get from me a list of things from town, and he didn't volunteer any information. After that our evenings passed pleasantly enough, but our conversations were carefully bland in their topics.

Then late one morning clouds of dust and the whistles of men filled the air. I ran to the front porch to watch hundreds of cattle tightly pressed together bouncing along the narrow road and funneling into pastures through wide breaks in the barbed wire. The calm and quiet we had known for months was gone, replaced by the bustling energy of shouting cowboys overlaid with the bawling of calves looking for mothers answering them in even louder bellows. By the time Alex walked up the path and onto the porch, the noise had only slightly settled down.

Throwing my arms around his neck, I met his lips with eagerness before he pulled back from me. "I've probably gotten your dress dirty."

"I don't care." Again pressing myself against him, we shared another hungry kiss.

His hands slipped to my hips and he said, "I hadn't realized that having been married so short a time, it would make being away from you so difficult."

"Well, you're home now. Come in and get cleaned up and have something to eat."

The next morning, as he stood by my bed, he said, "It sure is nicer waking up here with you in a soft bed."

Instead of pointing out that he could do it all the time if he wished, I asked, "Nicer than what?"

"Than sleeping in a bedroll on the hard ground while men all around you snore loud enough to scare away the coyotes. Then waking up to Cooky yelling at us, 'Get your sorry dirty carcasses up to greet the new day given us by the Lord Almighty.' Every day the same disrespect wrapped in the praise of God."

"Is his coffee as good as mine?"

"Considering that he boils it near to the state of lye, yes, it is."

I looked at him and laughed. "That's not the answer I expected."

Hearing Sing knock on his door and enter to deliver his hot water, Alex walked to his room while I slipped into a wrapper and followed. After pouring hot water from the pitcher into the matching porcelain bowl on his shaving stand, Alex stropped his razor and asked me, "Did I forget to lie in order to save your feelings?"

"No. I just forgot how honest you are."

He stirred lather in the heavy porcelain mug, then brushed it onto his face in thick swirls. "You make honesty sound like a fault. If we can't be honest with each other, then what kind of real trust is there between us?"

"I agree. In fact, it's one of the things I most admire about you, that honesty is so important to you."

"Well, I just think some men offer women small lies that soften the truth, instead of giving plenty of compliments that are sincere. It may seem easier in the short term, but it's really only laziness and lack of courage."

Catching my reaction of surprise in the mirror, he raised his brows as a question, the razor hesitating at his throat.

I answered his look. "I'm just surprised to hear such a thing from a man. Mother might say something like that, but its harsher judgment on your fellow men than I would expect from you."

"Well, don't think I'd say that to the men I know!"

"So much for your honesty!"

He turned to me for a moment, stricken by the implied criticism until he saw that I was smiling. "I'm going to have to watch you," he chuckled. "You're more clever than I thought."

Watching him wipe smudges of shaving cream from his temples, I thought his comment interesting, but I only said, "Back to the subject of my coffee. Your father likes it very much."

"The two of you spent time together, did you?"

"Yes."

"You sound unsure. You either did or you didn't."

"For the first week we did. Then I asked him about his childhood. After that, I think he avoided being alone with me."

Alex turned to me with puckered brows. "I thought I'd warned you about that back when I first met you."

"About what?"

"J.B. doesn't like talking about his childhood. I told you that." His tone had sharpened and the nerve near his eye jumped.

"Does he avoid the subject even with you?"

"He's said a little here and there. But..." He lowered his voice and looked pensively at his reflection in the small mirror over the wash basin.

"What is it? What bothers you?"

He moved to his chest of drawers and took out a clean shirt, standing with it in his hands. "It's just that several times I realized my memory of what he had previously told me was better than his."

"We all forget details sometimes."

"I mean he contradicts himself almost every time he talks about his teen years. Especially names of people and places."

"Are you saying you think he made up some of what he told you?"

"The thought has occurred to me."

His frown deepened and for a moment the thought of Steven flashed into my mind. Quickly pushing away that unexpected and even more uncomfortable thought, I walked back to my room and began dressing, first in the required layers of under garments, then a fitted waste with a high standing collar, a yoke of delicate lace inset in a front of tiny pleats, and snug sleeves ending with lace at the cuffs. Lastly, I stepped into a long black skirt that flared gently. The result reminded me of a schoolmarm with a generous budget, but it was stylish and conservative, and that was the effect I wanted.

Just as I finished dressing, I realized that Alex was taking a long time doing the same. Walking back into his room, I found him sitting on the side of the bed only partially dressed and staring out the window. The morose look on his face startled me. Suddenly realizing that I had seen this look more than once, I wondered if he didn't have a tendency for this direction of mind.

"Finish getting dressed, my dear," I cajoled cheerfully. "You have a hungry wife to contend with, and Sing is probably laying out a big spread for the returned king."

He pulled me to him between his legs and I cupped his face in my hands as he looked up at me. "I'm only the prince. J.B. will always be king."

"You fool," I murmured gently as I mussed his silken hair. "Don't you know that's not the way the ranch hands think about it? You deposed him long ago simply by working with them more than J.B., and treating them fairly. They respect you greatly."

The look of satisfaction and pleasure in his eyes was radiant. "Really?"

"Yes. Now let's eat!"

I kissed his slightly damp hairline and left the room so he could finish dressing in peace. Reaching the stairs, I thought to myself, "I just hope he never notices how the men always stand a little taller or work a little harder when J.B. is around."

After breakfast I walked out to the porch with Alex. It was so nice having him home and once again feeling his arm around my waist.

He kissed my cheek and said, "Walk with me to the corrals." I smiled in response and stepped off the porch, clutching his hand.

As we approached the horses being tended in the corrals, the smell of the stock became more pungent, and I felt a harder beating of my heart. How I yearned to ride out into the pastures with the men! They would soon be bringing into the near pens those calves that needed branding, as well as adding the Double R brand to the steers and cows newly acquired.

The men that had ridden in with him were now busy stretching ropes as their patient horses waited, tied to the row of hitching rails along the

side of the big red horse barn. These ropes were the most important tool
the cowboys would be using over the next few days, and the men were
rightfully proud of their ability with them.

You seldom saw a saddled horse without a neat coil of rope hanging
from a loop of leather near the cowboy's hand. Out on the trail he might
use it to pull a clumsy steer out of a bog or ravine, to tie it down for
doctoring, or use one end as a whip on a balky horse or steer. Some of the
older cowboys even used it as a crude form of adding machine, looping
a coil of rope over their hand for some specified number of cattle being
counted.

Some of the ropes I saw that day were made of braided rawhide, which
was the choice of the vaqueros. Others were twisted grass ropes, cheaper
and a little tougher, making them strong enough to hold a wrestling 1,200
pound steer that wasn't in the mood to have a hot piece of iron pressed to
its rump. Whatever its construction, it had to be a perfect combination of
firm and supple so that when a broad loop was sent flying over the head of
a steer, the loop stayed flat and open until it settled over the target.

As I watched the cowboys, I remembered how I could never master the
throw as a young girl, but that Steven had excelled at it even when very
young. Watching Alex practice, I mused to myself, "He's not nearly as
proficient as Steven." Gasping in surprise at this thought, I shook my head
and chased it away. It wasn't the first time I'd done this comparing, and as
before, it left me disconcerted and uneasy.

Standing by the string of horses, my hand resting on Comet's neck, I
nodded good morning to those men who were regular hands, noting the
cuts and bruises they'd sustained on the drive back to the ranch. But after
the grueling work of the next few days, this would be nothing compared to
what would follow for some of them.

"Charlie Bean! What happened to your thumb?" I spoke to an old
Paiute whose skin was the color of dark tea. He had started his career as
a ranch hand with J.B. twenty years ago, and had been given his English
nickname because of his love of the baked legume when sweetened with
molasses.

"Morning, Mrs. I got my thumb caught. It's only a rope burn. Mr.
Alex and Cooky fixed me up."

"You might want the doctor in town to look at it to be sure."

He stared at me with reproach, as though I'd been disloyal by suggesting
those two great men would not do right by him. I quickly made an effort

to correct my gaffe. "On the other hand, I can't imagine the doctor doing any better than Alex or Cooky. Good luck during the branding."

He beamed upon me the benevolence of his gentle personality, and I moved on, having learned a valuable lesson. It wouldn't do for me to shame my husband in the eyes of the hands.

The next morning Alex joined me for breakfast in the kitchen while Sing happily conveyed more pancakes to the table. I then tentatively shared with Alex what was on my mind.

Speaking so rapidly that most of my words blended together, I asked, "Can I help round up the cows and calves from the pastures?"

"I've hired extra men, so I've plenty of help." He continued to read the newspaper folded neatly on the table next to his plate.

I laid my hand over his, gaining his attention. "I'm not talking about necessity. I'd really enjoy doing it."

His reply was long in coming, and I realized he was having difficulty choosing his words. It took a great deal of effort not to show my impatience.

"I know you're an excellent horsewoman," he complimented carefully. "But you're my wife."

"So?" But the answer occurred to me before he could respond and I fought the urge to drum my fingers on the table's surface. "Are you saying it wouldn't be seemly for the queen to be seen working with the serfs?"

"This isn't the first time I've seen your facility for sarcasm." He didn't smile and his voice was sharp. "It's not pretty."

The coldness of his tone was surprising, not to mention the hard look he focused on me. I was tempted to respond in kind, but it wouldn't have gotten me what I wanted, so I wisely took a deep breath.

"I'm sorry. But the principle is the same, isn't it? You're worried about your image."

"Not worried. Just careful. I need the men to respect me."

"I understand that. But I don't see how my cutting out a few calves would destroy their regard for your authority."

A muscle on his cheek bulged as he clenched his jaw. "Whitney, this conversation is over. What we'll be doing is men's work. You will not be riding with us."

Rising abruptly, I started to leave the kitchen, knowing better than to reply right then.

He called after me, "You do understand, don't you?"

Stopping at the door to the hall, I could feel my anger rising like bile, but I spoke carefully. I was sure he would like my anger even less than my sarcasm. "During the branding, may I at least stand somewhere off to the side if I promise to minimize the obviousness of my presence?"

He chose to ignore the hint of vinegar in my tone. "Of course. You can join J.B. I've convinced him to sit in the grandstand above the round pen where we'll be working. His foot has been sore lately and he won't be on the round-up."

His reference to the grandstand usually made me smile, being only a small tier of six wooden boards, but on that day, it seemed a place of exile.

"Oh, good," I answered, returning to my now infamous sarcasm, "women and the lame together. How fitting."

At that moment I looked across the kitchen and saw J.B. enter from the dining room. Realizing he must have heard me, I was immediately embarrassed, but he only grinned.

"It's all right, my dear. You're quite right." He winked at me before adding, "Together we'll represent those who have used up their usefulness and those who never get an opportunity to prove they have any."

"You're both over-reacting to this." Alex didn't try to hide his exasperation.

J.B. turned to him. "We might feel better if we were at least allowed to sit on our horses while watching."

"Oh, for heavens sake," Alex snapped, "do so by all means. And in the meantime, vilify me for my concern about my father's comfort and my wife's dignity." He raised the paper so it hid his face from us.

Not bothering to thank Alex for his permission, I went upstairs to my room. Sitting in the window seat while hugging an embroidered pillow, I gained scant comfort from its softness. Outside, beyond the stable yard, the sun glinted off miles of streams meandering through the pastures toward town. Low green hills rolled up to the granite mountains in the distance, jagged peaks stretching upward toward the billow of white clouds offsetting the bright blue sky. A hawk soared into view, its shadow washing over the horses in the corrals. But I was in no mood to appreciate the scene's beauty.

It was hard to accept the idea that my love of working with the cattle, which I had done my whole life, was now to be relegated to something indecent and unbecoming to my husband's status. Remembering how accepting of my riding astride Steven always had been, I suddenly missed him with an intensity that brought the sting of tears to my eyes.

How wonderful it would have been to talk to him, to tell him of my frustrations, my homesickness, my loneliness, and my longing to be more productive in my own home. But I couldn't fool myself into believing that a conversation with Steven would be anything other than constrained. Our lives were too different now, and we had both left too much unsaid between us when we should have been more forthcoming.

Changing into my riding clothes two days later, I went to the barn, walking around the cowboys now gathered together awaiting instructions from Alex. While I mounted my horse in the barn, I heard Alex hollering to get the men's attention. From where he stood on the mounting block, usually used for ladies who needed assistance arranging themselves on their side-saddled horses, he spoke briefly to the men.

"You all know what to do. For those of you working with us for the first time, I want you to understand one thing. This isn't a rodeo. There's no need to do any hard busting. If I see anyone try it, they'll be fired immediately. Is that clear?" They all nodded, some more willingly than others.

He was referring to the practice of a lone cowboy catching the horns of a running steer with his rope, then running out slack and flipping it around the steer's rump. When the rider then quickly turns his horse at a forty-five degree angle and leaps forward, the rope twists the steer's head around and back at the same time. The rope under the hind quarters knocks the animal off its feet and flips it over so hard it reverses the direction in which it had been running. The point of this exercise is that when released, the animal is headed in the direction you want, and it should be happy to go there. Of course, that isn't possible if its neck is broken.

After a few more instructions, most of the men mounted their horses and set about separating the cattle in the pastures and driving them into the corrals. In the big round pen next to these, two men piled up wood to keep the branding fires going. Another prepared the tools that would snip off any sharp horns, eliminating the chance of scarring the hides of steers that might come in contact with them. Scarred hides brought a lower price after slaughter. One cowboy carefully sharpened the knives used to separate the calves from that which would make them a bull, since steers provide better meat and are easier to handle. This wrangler, while waiting the few seconds it would take the cowboys to bring in the next calf, would hold the knife in his teeth to keep it out of the dirt and sanitary.

As agreed, I rode my horse to a place where I could watch unobtrusively, looking for J.B. but not seeing him. It occurred to me that he might feel uncomfortable being present without participating, and I was beginning to understand. Several of the men looked in my direction, and more broad-minded than Alex about the role of a western wife, were obviously puzzled as to why I was sitting on my horse just watching them. I decided to put the horse away and sit in the grandstand after all.

It was interesting to watch the coordinated efforts of these men, each doing his assigned task with an efficiency and grace that was not unlike the choreography of a dance. Once a cow and calf were herded into the large pen, one cowboy held back the roped cow while a second one tossed his loop and caught the calf's front legs. With another man's rope around the calf's back feet, when the two riders slowly backed up their horses, the calf was stretched out and fell on its side, remaining very still.

That was the point when men swarmed over the prostrated calf--one to the rear with the branding iron, another with knives to castrate it, and if necessary another to its head to snip off any horns beginning to show. With one loud bawling roar of surprise and pain, it was all over in seconds. The rope was removed from the calf's front legs and the back rider dragged the calf a few feet into a holding pen. The mother, no longer tethered, followed without prodding. Going directly to her calf, she comforted her off-spring as it stood up and dripped out its cut area until it dried up naturally.

A man by the gate made marks in a tablet so that at the end of each day a tally could be made. A back-up check would be the bucket where the "mountain oysters" had been tossed at the time of castrating. After counting, they would be fried in corn meal and flour, and served at that night's dinner for the men.

Amid the noise of yipping and whistling cowboys catching and moving the cattle, I watched the first of the calves undergo their ordeal. The smell of singed fur, burned flesh and fresh blood mingled with the hot dust soon wafted in my direction. When the bellow of the calf's pain was added to this, I felt a cringe of repulsion followed by a vague protective maternal rush. But after dozens of calves had passed in and out of the pen, it became merely a mechanical function of numbers counted and human stamina sustained.

One old cow in the pen with her shaken calf looked in my direction and produced an especially loud bellow. Laughing to myself, I felt like reminding her, "If you'd given birth to a milk producer you wouldn't be in this predicament." As though reading my thoughts, she glared at me a moment before turning to her calf and licking his wounds. It was only a brief light moment in the long morning, but it adjusted my perspective and snapped me out of my resentful mood.

When the men stopped for dinner at noon, I went into the house and immediately to the kitchen. "Is Alex's dinner ready?" I asked Sing.

He looked up from the chunks of meat he was stirring into an aromatic gravy and smiled. "He eat with men. Very wise."

Realizing he was probably correct, I sat down at the kitchen table where Sing had laid a lovely place setting and a white china bowl. When he placed a small tureen on the table, I lifted the lid and inhaled the steam of a delicious stew. After watching the morning's endeavors, I wasn't sure I was in the mood for beef, but one taste triggered my appetite and I enjoyed it fully. So much for human sensitivity for the creatures of the earth.

"What will the men be eating?"

"Whatever Cooky decide they eat. Oh, yes. Cooky sure can cook!"

"What's his real name? I haven't heard him called anything else."

"He work for J.B. from time he settle here. I think only J.B. remember real name."

I later learned that the men were sated with baked beans thick with big chunks of pork and extra molasses, warm bread and fresh butter. For dessert they had apple cobbler with a thick crust and heavy cream.

The activity of the afternoon was a repeat of the morning, and after the first hour, I chose to return to the house. The dust, the heat, and the strong odors finally overcame my enthusiasm, and even my stubbornness.

That night Alex ate a light supper, crawled into his bed, and was sound asleep before the moon was fully at rest in the sky. This was our routine for most of the week, the branding averaging about 300 animals a day. When it was over early on Friday afternoon, the men took a nap and then played cards for a couple of hours.

At sundown that night, they gathered together in a celebration that included a large meal followed by lots of beer, girls visiting from the town, and big cigars provided by J.B. Only after that did they get their pay packets. That prompted a few more games of chance, and a dance with the girls to the tune of one man's fiddle and another man's harmonica. However, only the winners from the card and dice games left with a fair damsel on his arm.

All this I watched from my bedroom window, since even I realized that it was no place for Alex's wife. Alex wasn't going to be there either, instead spending the time in his study. This was revelry for the men only and not the bosses.

Later in the week, as J.B. and I sat on the front porch waiting for Alex to return from town, I looked closely at his face. It was a study in casual disinterest.

"J.B., about what you said the other day in the kitchen." I laid a hand gently on his arm and looked into his eyes. "No one in their right mind would ever call you useless."

"Do you have any idea how many people aren't in their right minds?" He chuckled when he saw my surprise.

I laughed then, and he grinned in response as he reached out and squeezed my shoulder. Looking up, I saw Alex riding toward us. He was watching us closely with an odd look on his face as he observed this moment of obvious rapport between his father and his wife. Unsure if it had been a look of resentment or simply surprise, it nevertheless haunted me for a long time.

CHAPTER 7

With the continued warmth of bright summer days encouraging a sequence of wildflowers into bloom in the meadows, I was eager to be outside every morning. But when the winds were strong enough to rattle windows and scatter sprays of sharp sand, the eagerness disappeared. On one such morning, resigned to staying in for the day, I found it difficult to settle myself to anything. Tossing aside my book for the second time, I wondered what I could do to fill the hours.

Alex had joined the men for some unnamed project that was supposed to take all morning and possibly the afternoon. As usual, I wished I could put on my riding clothes and join them. Even more, I wished that doing so would meet with the approval of my husband.

Surprisingly, Mrs. Lewis came to my rescue by asking me if I would help her sort through old clothes. The quilting circle in town was making crazy quilts for those less fortunate and needed fabric pieces cut in various shapes. Piled on the kitchen table was contributed shirts, pants, dresses, skirts and waists. We cut around worn or stained spots and created a mound of usable pieces on the floor between our chairs.

There was little conversation at first, but I was still hoping that we could develop a more cordial communication. After all, it was the first time in the year I'd lived there that she had invited me to join her in any activity.

Following a long silence, I finally spoke. "Mrs. Lewis, I'd like to ask you something."

"Yes?" She didn't look up from her cutting.

"I've heard very little detail about Mrs. Roberts. I must admit to being curious, but I hesitate to ask Alex or J.B."

"That's understandable. But I'm not sure it's my place to talk about her."

"Why not? Alex said he'd add to the little he told me when we were courting, but as yet the subject hasn't come up."

I leaned forward to drag a skirt off the table onto my lap as she said, "In that case, I suppose it's all right." After thinking a moment, she continued,

"I was very fond of Alex's first wife, although some thought her not very kind."

The tea kettle began to boil and she excused herself to attend to the making of our tea. The screaming kettle expressed perfectly the turmoil roiling through my thoughts at that moment. Alex's first wife? I had been referring to Alex's mother, but my curiosity in that direction was, to say the least, abruptly diverted.

Why had Alex never told me that he'd been married before? Why had he allowed everyone in Lone Pine to assume ours was his first marriage? Or had he? He'd never actually said he hadn't been married before, but he had to know that we would make that assumption. Or had there been something said by him purposely so we would think ours was his first marriage? A sharp pain shot through my right temple.

Mrs. Lewis set a tray with a tea pot, two white cups in their saucers and a small pile of cookies on the table. Thankfully, she poured out the tea. I couldn't have done it. My hands were clenched so tight in my lap that I felt the muscles in my arms begin to spasm.

As she handed out the tea, she smiled with a warmth I had never seen in her before. "Lavinia was a truly beautiful woman, tall and slender and almost regal. She'd never be seen without her corsets laced as tight as I could get them when helping her dress. When out in the sun, her long blonde hair would shine like spun gold, setting off her cornflower blue eyes. They'd actually sparkle whenever something struck her as funny." She chuckled. "I loved walking behind her when we were in town so I could watch men turn their heads to watch her walk past. Of course, she never gave them a glance. It was just the thrill of having so much power over others that made it fun for us."

Ignoring that Mrs. Lewis spoke of Lavinia more like a proud mother than a housekeeper, I asked, "Was she a good rider?"

She tossed her head. "She disdained such activity. Oh, she could ride of course, but only side saddle. After all, she was a lady." I didn't miss the insult, but let it pass as she continued. "She preferred the buggy, claiming horses were part of the men's realm. She rightfully felt it inappropriate for a woman to insinuate herself into men's activities."

Considering how much riding I did astride, and my requests to accompany the men during branding, the scorn beneath her words was clear.

I couldn't help but wonder what had happened to Lavinia. Was she going to reappear in our lives someday? Surely not or Alex would have told me about her. So I made the assumption that she was dead. If wrong, I would expose to Mrs. Lewis my true ignorance of the situation. "How did she die?" I ventured. "I especially was loath to ask Alex that."

"She took the buggy out early one morning, telling Sing that she'd heard of some strange wildflowers closer to the mountains. He tried to talk her into waiting until Alex could go with her, but she said she didn't want to wait for him to find the time. He'd been very busy for weeks, and she was feeling neglected.

"When she didn't return by dinner, Alex and some of the hands went out to find her, supposing the buggy to have lost a wheel or something. They found the buggy just at the beginning of the road up to the lakes, the rig wedged between two large boulders with the horse still hitched to it. They figured the horse must have bolted through the opening, but it wasn't wide enough for the buggy to get through." She took a sip of her tea and I noticed that her hands shook.

"And Lavinia?" She pursed her lips, I think at my familiar use of the first name, so I rephrased my question. "Was Mrs. Roberts injured?"

She sighed deeply and shook her head. "Mrs. Roberts was nowhere to be found."

"What?"

"They found a shoe and one glove several yards away. There was also what looked like drag marks and big cat tracks. But the area was rocky and they couldn't be sure."

"Then what happened?"

"Nothing." Her eyes were moist, but she was in rigid control. I couldn't help but feel compassion for her evident lingering grief as she continued. "Days of searching became weeks of revisiting the area by Alex, J.B. and even some of the ranch hands. But nothing was ever found of her. That was five years ago."

I had wondered why a man like Alex had waited until he was in his late twenties to marry. Now I knew he had wed for the first time in his early twenties.

"It must have been agonizing for you, being so close to her and all."

"Yes. At first I only liked the way she pleased Alex. How happy she made him!" She actually smiled at the memory. "But then I saw her cleverness and spirit, and I liked her even more. She could always get her way without upsetting anyone. Well, really without them even realizing it wasn't their idea in the first place."

"Was she happy here?"

"Oh, yes. Of course, being from San Francisco, she sometimes missed all that a big city offered. But don't we all?"

I smiled at that. She started to say something more, but fell into silence instead. As she retreated into her memories, I tried to understand why Alex had not told me of Lavinia. Resisting the temptation to think of it as a betrayal, I knew it was at least a sin of omission. But I didn't know whether or not I should confront him with my new knowledge.

In the end I decided to see if he would eventually bring it up himself. Of course, I now realize this decision was a sign of how little real trust had developed between us. Certain that Mrs. Lewis would not broach the subject of the sacred Lavinia, I joined the ranks of those who kept the secret of Alex's wife; a secret that was after all common knowledge. But secrets seldom stay hidden forever, and I would come to learn that they can reveal themselves in the most surprising ways.

Alex came home from town one day in early July, smiling broadly. He mentioned that he had run into a man he'd known for years.

"Oh?"

"You know about the Sierra Club trips into Yosemite?"

"Yes." I screwed up my face in irritation. "Women aren't allowed on the trips."

"Well, now the Club is encouraging women to go along." His tone broadly casual, he said, "There's a trip being organized now. This guy belongs to the Club and he's invited us to go."

I jumped up, then quickly sat down again. "What did you tell him?"

"I told him I'd have to check with you, but from the look of excitement on your face, I guess you're up for it. Actually, I already told him we'd go." A smile split his face as he finished speaking.

Unable to restrain my enthusiasm, I sat on his lap and wrapped my arms around his neck. "You know your wife better than I thought!" We then shared a kiss filled with more passion than I think either of us had felt in a long time. However, before it could lead to anything beyond that, I went to the sideboard in the corner by the fireplace and poured him a small whiskey.

"When do we leave?" I asked.

"This Friday."

"Oh, my goodness. So soon. What should I wear? Will my riding outfits be appropriate?"

"They suggest you wear a split skirt for riding, astride I might add, because of the poor trails. But also bring a woolen dress to change into at camp. Maybe an additional waist. Also, a hat with a brim since the sun may be harsh during the day. But it'll be cold at night, so pack a heavy jacket or shawl."

"And it all has to fit in my saddlebags?"

"That and a small valise tied on the pack mules. Make sure whatever boots you wear will be comfortable enough for both riding and climbing over rocks."

Those few women who had made this trip at the end of the last century had sometimes worn bloomers under short skirts that fell several inches above the ankle, thick boots and large floppy hats, and most had used a side saddle. They couldn't have been comfortable, nor for that matter safe in their seats. But in 1902, I chose to wear a wool split skirt, white waist with a man's bolero tie, a leather vest, a western felt hat with a "stampede string" under my chin, and strong leather boots tall over the calf. Tied behind my saddle would be a heavy jacket as well as a slicker in case of rain, and in my valise a long flared skirt, the only attire acceptable for a woman around the evening's campfire where we would be required to "dress for dinner". Except for the rare occasions when we would stay in a hotel, tents would be set up for us, two for the women and two for the men. At night we women would take off our corsets, tied much looser than usual while mounted, and slip on a flannel night dress over our underthings. While sleeping, the men would wear their long underwear or even their pants, and thus would be able to dress quickly if an emergency arose, such as a bear venturing into camp.

After a week of planning and excited anticipation, we arrived by horseback at Vining Creek near the small village of Lakeview, and not far from the blue expanse of Mono Lake. We were soon joined by three other couples and a man who introduced himself as David Moore, our guide. After introductions, the men and women seemed to naturally separate into two groups. We were all in our mid-twenties to early thirties, and other than our guide, none of us had undertaken this trip before.

Early the next morning we began our journey up the Great Sierra Wagon Road, parts of it climbing to elevations over 10,000 feet. It sliced through

Lee Vining Canyon from the east and headed up into the Sierra toward the cut-off at Big Oak Flat. Blasted and excavated by Chinese labor in 1883 on behalf of the Consolidated Silver Mining Company, the road had been created so that people and freight could reach the mines near Bennettville in the Tioga Mining District. Originally it conformed to the old trade routes used for centuries by Indians crossing the range, the Paiutes trading their obsidian for the acorns of the Yo-semite Indians. The road up from Lee Vining had several times been improved by various mining companies thinking to start up the mines, but each time fate had intervened to stop their success. By 1915 it would be called the Tioga Road.

Although I couldn't see up the road very far, I felt a tingle of anxiety forming in the pit of my stomach. As I realized how rugged would be our journey, especially for us women, I realized that this trip was going to be an extreme test of hardiness and courage. Into my mind crept the tales of the courageous women who had come to the West over the Oregon Trail in the middle of the last century, described to me by those in Mother's quilting circle. So I squared my shoulders with resolve and decided not to complain.

Most of the men, I was sure, would take the rigors of the trip in their stride, regularly spending so much more time in the saddle than any woman. Then I noticed that some of the men who owned shops in Bridgeport and Bodie were wearing wool suits and jackets, as though this was to be a simple day's outing. Thankfully, Alex was in jeans and a buckskin coat over his shirt and tie.

We made our way up the canyon above Vining's Rancho, planning to stay at Bennettville, a tiny hamlet of mining shacks near the summit of the road. Although $350,000 had been spent in developing the area, no gold or silver had ever been removed and it was early abandoned.

Much of our upward route had fallen into ruin and was strewn with downed branches and boulders dislodged during periods of heavy snow. Consequently, some narrow sections were almost blocked and it slowed our progress considerably while the men cleared away the obstacles. Much of the trail was little more than a narrow shelf where we were forced to hug the mountain wall to avoid being pitched into a rocky, tree-lined gorge. By the end of the second day, our horses' heads were drooping in exhaustion and I pitied them greatly, when I wasn't preoccupied with my own self-pity.

Several times we crested a rise in the road, and I wondered how our tired steeds could clamor down such a steep trail without sliding on their haunches. Sometimes we walked while leading our horses, not just to spare them our weight but to ease the strain to our knees after bracing in the saddle so long during the descent of a steep grade.

We rested at Tamarack Flat, the highest point on the trail. Being on flat open ground, I was finally able to look beyond the instability of my feet to see a large meadow blanketed with tiny white flowers next to more vibrant patches of yellow. We walked across this huge open expanse on a spongy carpet of thick, green moss toward a wide but shallow stream where we found along its edge several boulders sporting interesting lichens.

Sitting on a low rock by the stream, I dipped my fingers in the clear and very cold water while watching orange butterflies and tiny bees busily visiting the blossoms around me. One of our guides talked to us, as he did at every rest stop, about the surrounding geology, indigenous plants, trees, and animals, and the need to preserve it all for future generations. He went from scientific facts and numbers to rapturous prose when describing the beauty and inspiration an individual could enjoy when in places such as we were currently inhabiting. As much as I agreed with him, I eventually became saturated with his proselytizing and my attention wandered. For although I enjoyed learning the facts he presented, I preferred to experience the impact to my senses that such grandeur generated, without over-analyzing the elements that created the moment's rapture.

As we advanced into the Yosemite Valley, we passed down a rough, narrow stairway carved out from the rock and earth. Our horses had to step cautiously and very slowly, the hollow clop and clank and occasional ping on rock of their hooves the only sound. No one dared speak for fear of startling a horse, and I prayed that an animal wouldn't flush from the brush along the trail. To make this tension even harder to bear, we suffered sharp pain as the horse's weight shifted from side to side, wrenching our torso first left and then right as they stepped down the rough stair steps. Stones loosened by the horses following behind me rolled past under my horse, clattering over the side into a deep crevasse that I dared not look into for fear my nerve would break. Although we all knew that a slip of a horse would mean certain death, each of us tried not to acknowledge it. We simply leaned toward the side of the mountain, kept our feet loose in the stirrups in case we had to jump off quickly (a futile effort with nowhere to land), and looked forward to our next rest stop on flat land.

At one point we walked more than half the way down a 500 foot section of the trail while I cursed the builders of the road, thinking they could have done a much better job of it. Our guide told us to keep our horses in front of us as we walked, holding onto the halter by a long thin rope, although he chose to walk ahead of his trusted horse. But there was no room on the trail to walk next to the horse's head.

Even now, after the passing of so many years, I remember vividly the moment we crested a gentle slope and stood next to a beautiful clear spring. We were in the midst of a grassy plateau surrounded by a grove of aspens and our guide said, "We're here. That's the Yosemite Valley below us."

My mind still retains memories of stirring views from Glacier Point at just over 7,000 feet, and where we could see the whole lush valley and the majestic mountain peaks beyond. The awesome green view seemed to stretch endlessly, merging finally with the blue horizon. Engineered by John Conway, master trail builder in the Valley, the winding road climbed four miles up the 3,254 foot cliff to the summit. Other than the difficulty of our exertions at such a high elevation, it was not a difficult climb.

We finally reached our first hotel. The two-story Mountain House had views looking over the vast panorama of a long green valley cradled by granite peaks rising on either side. The hotel was a welcome place to settle our weary bodies after several nights in the primitive shelter of a tent.

After refreshing ourselves in the comfort of our rooms, we gathered at the front of the hotel. There we inched our way to the flimsy railing at the precipitous edge of the hotel property, looking straight down into a deep gorge. Every one of us gasped at the magnificence of such huge trees and soaring granite cliff faces with foaming white ribbons of water pouring off their edges. Above us glowed an endless canopy of dark blue sky scattered with puffs of white slowly altering into new shapes by a breeze that was just beginning to rattle the pines around us.

Early the next morning, we were instructed to stand as a group by the same railing. A man came from the hotel with a chicken in his arms, walked to the edge and calmly threw the fowl over the railing. Why? Simply so we could watch it get smaller and smaller the further it fell away from us down the mountain. Of course, a number of us expressed great displeasure, but he told us not to worry about it. And indeed, on the way down the mountain we passed the chicken walking back up the trail with an unconcerned swagger and not a feather out of place.

While I lingered outside the hotel after Alex and some of his new friends had retreated to the hotel's saloon, one of the older men in our group joined me at the railing. After the required comments using many superlatives to describe our trip so far, he told me about some of his previous adventures in the Yosemite Valley. But the exchange between us that I remember most vividly was when he pointed across the valley to a tall peak and commented casually, "I've decided not to go to the top of that one."

Surprised at the finality of his tone, I asked, "Why?"

"Because then I'd know what's there."

"Isn't that good?"

"It's neither good or bad." He shrugged and offered the suggestion of a smile. "I just don't need to know what I'd see there."

"But you'd have a beautiful view from there."

"I already have a beautiful view from there. I have it here." He tapped his temple and smiled. "And I wish not to lose it."

"But it's not real."

"It is to me." And his smile broadened.

Later that week we stayed a night at the luxurious Cosmopolitan Hotel where we were amazed at the comfort and extent of the accommodations. Besides a large saloon and barber shop, there was a billiard room for the men, a private sitting room for the ladies, and a reading room with long tables provided with stationery. Private bathing rooms with shining clean tubs, large Turkish towels and imported soaps was a luxury I will never forget.

Our sleeping room had a fully stocked bar, an arrangement of delicate colognes for me and bay rum for Alex, a pin cushion with pins, needles, buttons and threads all under a glass dome sitting beside a small ornate scissors, and a full-length mirror on one wall. I had quite a time trying to picture all this delivered over the road we traveled, then found out there were other routes leading into the Valley.

One night I sat in the lady's sitting room and wrote in a journal brought with me to record my impressions of such a unique adventure. Journal writing was a popular activity for travelers, both men and women. One evening I wrote, "*On our way here we passed a series of crystal blue lakes set in a surround of green pines, some with cinnamon colored bark and taller than any building yet constructed in the West. We stood in awe of far views more endless than hope itself; between the far horizons and ourselves a gulf of deep green chasms that to us would always remain a mystery unsolved. To be among such giant trees as we see every day is also to hear the soft susurration of the Sierra breeze in the top boughs, nature murmuring conversations that we mere humans cannot imagine and to which we will never be privy.*

"Amid the far views thick with trees and bare cliff faces we caught glimpses of plummeting water falls hundreds of feet in height, but perceived by us so far away to be a trickle against the giant rock walls over which they were cascading, but creating a roar so loud we could hear their echoes miles away. When we approached closer to some of the falls, the wind blew the water sideways in lacy sparkling mists that usually evaporated before reaching us, but twice dampened our clothes. Sometimes the roar of the water was so intense that we could not talk above it.

"Today we walked along the rocky edge of creeks rushing over water-smoothed boulders where a small black bird dove beneath the water for food before preening its feathers at the edge. As we viewed all this incomparable beauty, the sharp tang of pine and fresh air filled our lungs, making me think that I have never really breathed before. All this and more we experienced of that which Nature has so perfectly situated within the view of one hardy enough to approach it. Whether looking up from the bottom of a valley or gazing down from an ancient crag of rock perilously climbed, I am enraptured. My favorite views are those where the far peaks are so distant that they appear only as a blue suggestion dotted with vague forms assumed to be trees."

Another entry in my journal reads: *"Tonight we have set up camp in a clearing beneath a thicket of pines and near a creek so clear we could be looking through window glass at the pebbles that line its bottom. The men shot fat grouse for our dinner and we feasted well. For entertainment we have a thick blanket of stars above, broken once briefly by the path of one star too impatient to remain in place. After dinner, while the men cleaned their guns in anticipation of breakfast, we women cleaned the cooking utensils and talked quietly among ourselves. Shouting would be as unseemly here as belching in a cathedral. Finally, by the last glow of the fire, Alex and I sat on a low boulder, speaking little but all the while holding hands. Right now he is checking the horses, and then we will retire for the night, unfortunately to separate tents."*

Throughout the trip, underlying my enjoyment of Yosemite's glorious beauty, was the warm pleasure of sharing it with a relaxed Alex in a good mood. Often I caught him looking at me when he thought I was too focused on a view to notice. But I saw; oh yes, I saw. The admiration in his eyes was not disguised, and the love showed plainly. I thought of the many times I'd seen such a look exchanged between my parents, and I felt outrageously satisfied.

We stayed only one night at the Hutchings Inn, later called The Sentinel Hotel, mainly so we could meet the well-known champion of the Sierra,

John Muir. I had read of Mr. Muir's glaciation theory, which presented the idea that much of the Sierra had been carved by ancient glaciers grinding their way down from the crest. He claimed this activity had created the scarred slopes and deep canyons visible today across the Sierra. But I also knew that most of the leading geologists and scientific minds disagreed with him. I was eager to let him know that his theory made perfect sense to me, being my whole life familiar with the mountain range. Of course, I doubted he'd care about a mere woman's opinion.

Mr. Muir often led tours through the Valley for James Mason at the hotel, but the day we were there they had just returned. After the rest of our party retired for the night, including Alex, I hesitantly approached the great man whose long legs were stretched out before the hotel lobby fire. His welcoming smile told me I wasn't intruding, so we settled down with the last of the tea in the pot and talked quietly.

Everything about him was subdued, except for the light that flared in his clear blue eyes when the Yosemite area was the topic of discussion. His soft Scottish burr was soothing, issuing from lips set in a long, scraggly beard that seemed to fit him as a neater one would not. His auburn hair was lighter than mine, but frankly softer. More than anything, I was surprised at his dry sense of humor and quick wit, showing a willingness to laugh that I was not expecting from one so serious in his goals.

When I told him that I supported his glaciation theory, he smiled gently and simply asked, "Why?"

"Well, anyone that has really looked at the mountains, such as around Convict Lake, has to realize the accuracy of the idea."

"But many don't."

"Then they're inflexible and not really seeing, although they claim to have looked." When he said nothing, I added, "And maybe they're afraid for their jobs, afraid of what others will think of their lack of vision, not having thought of it themselves."

He chuckled at that, and proceeded to talk about shadows in the Valley along the south wall and how quarried it was there, eroded far more than the sunny northern cliffs. He felt that the shadows on the Valley floor could be interpreted to coincide with forest growth on moraines and that there was an important relationship between these shadows and the way the meadows grew, and even the way the rivers bent and flowed.

I understood little of what he was saying, only knowing at the time that while he spoke, I was glimpsing ideas that fascinated and challenged my thought, and created an intense desire for more such mental stimulation. I felt an overwhelming awe that a mind could actually interpret nature, rather than simply admire it like most of us. His unique ability went beyond reading the land to know best where to reap its bounty of wildlife, minerals or timber, and spoke to the why of the earth itself. This meant that he didn't just attempt to answer common questions, but instead offered questions no one had previously thought to pose.

At one point I dared to ask him, "When the big earthquake in March of 1872 occurred, did you really run outside calling out, 'A noble earthquake'?"

"Do you think that an odd way of classifying such an event?" he asked.

"Actually , I think it quite apt. But few people would call it that while the ground still shook beneath their feet."

"Possibly. But I felt no fear, only a deep gratitude at the rare opportunity to experience something that is after all quite natural to the planet."

"Then you must have wished it to last longer than a few moments," I smiled.

"Oh, but it did," he gently corrected me, his face suffused with excitement. "The earth shook noticeably and often for days, and to a lesser degree for weeks. I kept a bucket of water on the table in my cabin so I could observe the way the water would slosh, depending on the severity of the jolts."

We spoke of Lone Pine and how I grew up in the Owens Valley, which he referred to as a uniquely spiritual place. The flash of longing for home that hit me in that moment almost overwhelmed my aplomb. Mr. Muir's keen perception didn't miss my angst and asked, "How long has it been since you've been in Lone Pine?"

"A couple of years."

"That's a long time," he commented, but with no hint of judgment.

"Yes." I swallowed carefully. "I never thought I'd be gone this long."

"There's a train out of Benton that would take you quite near, isn't there?"

"Yes. I...I don't know why I haven't put forth more effort to go home. But I don't think my husband really wants me to go."

He was too polite to pry, and I was too shocked by the realization of what I'd said about Alex to discuss it further.

He looked into the fire and said, "We usually know the why of our actions. We just need enough quiet in which to contemplate ourselves, and enough courage to confront what we find there."

After a moment I raised the subject of avalanches, since it had been discussed at dinner. He described to me the ones he had seen on his wanderings through the mountains during those winters of exceptionally heavy snow fall, something I could barely imagine doing. I then told him about the avalanche I saw as a young girl when riding with my parents near the old Kearsarge Mine location north of Independence. He listened as though he himself had never witnessed its power, making me feel terribly complimented, and therefore emboldened to describe my thoughts at the time.

"The trees stood braced for the onslaught, as though the snow would part around them only if they were very still. I felt an urge to reassure them that when the snow melted, they'd still be there, tall sentinels keeping watch on the mountain." And then I blushed at having admitted such absurd fancies. But although Alex would have scoffed, Mr. Muir did not. He merely gave me a penetrating look and smiled.

The last of our conversation was related to the state's desire to flood the Hetch Hetchy Valley north of Yosemite Valley, creating a reservoir for water needed by the growing California population. In his view, it was a place at least as beautiful as the Valley in which we sat, and would be an incomparable loss to the spiritual enrichment of future generations, not to mention only a temporary solution of the water problem. As President of the Sierra Club, and a fighter for the rights of nature to endure undisturbed, he couldn't suppress his concern.

"To keep it from happening," he sighed, "will necessitate quite a battle."

"How long a battle?"

"A very long one, I fear. I only hope I live long enough to see it protected."

Unfortunately, a dozen years after our conversation, the Hetch Hetchy Valley would disappear beneath the waters created by the O'Shaughnessy Dam across the Tuolumne River.

We arrived home from the Yosemite trip in early August when summer had established itself. Because the afternoons were very warm, we accomplished the heaviest tasks during the morning and evening hours, and often rested during the hottest part of the day. Baking was also completed early in the morning, with the pungent yeasty smells of it lingering well into the day. Sometimes Sing would slice off the end piece from a crusty loaf and hand it to me while it was still hot. Rich butter would glisten on my fingers while tart raspberry jam tingled on the back of my tongue, the flavors a perfect blend of sweet and tart. The last bite was swallowed with regret, and it was impossible not to sigh.

At the end of one such afternoon, Alex and I sat in the deepest part of the shade on the front porch, he reading the newspaper and I a book. When I refilled his glass with cold lemonade from the heavy crockery pitcher, he grunted his thanks. Bored with my book, I leaned back in my wicker chair and studied Alex as he read while sitting stiffly upright in his chair. His only concession to relaxation was the crossing of his legs.

I set my drink on the small table between us and announced, "I received a letter from Father today."

"Anything interesting?" he asked from behind the paper.

"Not really. He bragged about the local agriculture being sold to the gold mines still active in Nevada."

"Oh?"

"Tonopah especially."

"That's good."

We'd had more sparkling conversation certainly, but it was after all a warm day and he was trying to relax. Not a woman to let that stop me, I added, "He also said that engineers from the new Reclamation Service have been investigating the area."

This brought down the paper to reveal a glint of interest. "Toward what purpose?"

"They're thinking of building a reservoir, possibly in the Long Valley area north of Bishop. It's part of an effort of the government to reclaim arid lands to see if they can be irrigated. Crops raised would be shipped north and south to help the growth of the state, and even those cities beyond the state's borders."

"That ought to make the ranchers happy."

"Father said the man in charge seemed nice enough."

"No doubt Frank enjoyed talking to another engineer. What's the guy's name?"

"Let's see. It's a rather odd name." I pulled the letter from a pocket of my dress. "Here it is. Joseph Lippincott, Chief of the Reclamation Service. Father describes him as tall and very detailed in his questions about the area."

"Well, I'll hold my judgment in abeyance," Alex smirked. "Things move slowly on our side of the mountain."

I didn't for a moment question to what mountain he referred. Most of us spoke of the Sierra as though it was the defining element in our world, ignoring that the White/Inyo Range across the Owens Valley from the Sierra had peaks almost as tall. But I had begun to also appreciate the lovely Sweetwater Mountains to the north of the Bridgeport valley.

"Has Frank or Vince been to Los Angeles recently?" he asked. In the back of my mind flitted the question of why he hadn't included Steven in his inquiry.

I referred to the letter. "Um...yes. Uncle Vince and Steven went."

"Any mention of the drought there?"

"Yes. Vince said the people in Los Angeles are very concerned. He doesn't understand why the city continues to promote its virtues to the country when it can barely support the water needs of the citizens currently living there."

"I suppose that's why they set up a Department of Water last year, so they could manage such things. They'll sort it out."

"How?"

He stood up and stretched. Kissing me on the cheek, he mumbled, "That's what they're getting paid to figure out. I'm going to work in the tack room."

"See you for supper then."

I listened to his steps slowly crunch across the gravel toward the barns. He tripped once and although he caught himself before falling, I could hear him snap out his favorite swear word. He was very tired, worried about ranch business he declined to discuss with me, and maybe the frequency of J.B.'s absences from the ranch. I certainly thought it was odd for him to be gone so often.

On the other hand, if I'd been given the opportunity to return home for awhile, my bags would have been packed and in the wagon before the cock crowed. Visions loomed in my mind of Lone Pine and the big yellow house on south Main with Mother working happily in her garden. Before the picture took on more detail, however, I quickly stood up and went inside where I joined Sing in the kitchen to assist with supper. He had given up protesting when I did this, I think finally realizing that it filled my need to be busy with something productive and was not a suggestion that he needed my help.

After we ate, when Alex said he was retiring early to bed, I told him I wanted to read for awhile and would see him in the morning. But the air in the house felt close, so I retired to the porch and my favorite wicker chair. Relaxing as I breathed in the fresh cooling air, I didn't even care that it was laced with bovine scents.

Resting my eyes upon the soft curves of the dusk-darkened silhouette of far mountains, I listened to the gentle rustling of the leaves in the trees and the crickets' slow chirruping. The rising breezes ruffled my hair as the tree frogs began their night songs, and my senses were at rest even if my mind was not.

Once again visions of Lone Pine rose in my mind, and I ached to hear again the reassuring murmurs of my parents' voices coming from the front porch as I drifted off to sleep. I especially wanted to sit beneath the shade of a cottonwood on Lone Pine Creek and listen to Steven talk about... anything. When the strength of the longing gathered as a tight knot in my throat, I remembered too late to distract myself with conversation or activity. Tears pooled at the edges of my eyes and soon were trickling slowly down my cheeks. The tightness in my chest heralded waves of black desolation that led me dangerously close to panic.

Fighting for breath, I raced to the foot of the steps, gulping in the night air. The sensation of being chased by something I couldn't escape followed my steps past the back of the house into the small knot of aspens near the back garden. The branches embraced me while blocking the shine of the lighted windows, and I finally felt sheltered and safe. Slumping down on the hard ground at the base of a spindly tree, I buried my face in my hands and unleashed sobs that could no longer be suppressed, grateful for the wind carrying my anguish away from the house.

Coyotes not far away began their regular evening routine of howling as they celebrated their family bonds, a plaintive accompaniment to my distress, but giving me something familiar and comforting to focus upon, and soon the last of the desperate feeling passed. Soon I was able to return to the house where I gave Sing the cursory instruction that I wanted no dinner and was retiring early.

Leaving my clothes on the floor where I shed them, I slid under the covers and fell almost immediately into an exhausted slumber. But it was only to spend a restless night full of odd dreams where Mother and Father talked in yips, and Steven sat atop Lone Pine Peak howling my name over and over. I was more than happy to greet the dawn.

CHAPTER 8

Once again I watched the lush green grasses of early summer slowly fade through the months into golden brown thatch. As the evenings cooled in October, yellow and orange leaves from the trees around the house fell and were carried away on the wind, leaving only the stiff architecture of bare branches. It wasn't long before all color disappeared beneath a carpet of white powder laying deep beneath pine branches heavy with the evidence of a winter set to stay well into the spring of 1903. The flakes fell wet, its accumulation making everyday existence indoors relatively cozy but limited, and outdoor chores laborious and often dangerous. Avalanches scarred the mountain sides and chased miners and loggers down to the valley floor for the remainder of winter.

Alex and J.B. worked with the ranch hands, repairing equipment and preparing for the eagerly awaited spring thaw. During the worst of winter, I sat by the front window sewing, reading or creating menus for future gatherings. Alex's scowl when I ventured outside was more than I chose to trigger unless I truly needed to leave the house. So I finished a quilt partially constructed that I found in a cupboard, and made so many rag rugs from a store of old cloth that I found in the closet under the stairs that my hands began to ache. When I needed physical activity, I cleaned floors that already sparkled and dusted furniture that had no dust. After reorganizing the pantry, I calmly suffered the rebuke of Sing when next he tried to find something in it. At no time in my life was I ever so bored for so many collective days.

Alex only saw my eagerness and high spirits whenever he returned to the house. He received my hugs and savored the attention I then lavished upon him, never guessing that it was all mainly for something to do. J.B. saw and understood, yet he said nothing to Alex. The holidays relieved much of the boredom, but they passed too quickly, and we had only a few visitors. J.B. seemed to always have many reasons for us not to have more.

At supper one evening J.B. brought up the news of two brothers having built a flying machine they had recently launched in a place called Kitty Hawk in North Carolina.

"It seems these Wright boys think it's just the beginning," J.B. told us, "and that someday people will be using such machines for transportation."

Alex made a funny noise and said, "Flying people. That's absurd. What's wrong with horses and trains?"

Although I knew his question was rhetorical, I nevertheless commented, "I'm sure someone said the same thing when trains started rolling across the country." That got me a smirk from J.B., but a scowl from Alex.

In early summer the cattle were once again herded home from winter pastures and the routine of branding again took place. And we continued to act the roles we had accepted, carefully staying in character so as not to disrupt the harmony of the play, or its repetitious performances. There were bright spots, of course. I spent considerably more time visiting with Irene than Alex approved my doing, enjoyed a few dinners with neighbors, assisted at several charity events in town, watched a group of townsmen participate in a fishing contest in our trout pond, and found the holidays pleasant. But overall the year dragged interminably from month to month, including another long winter.

Spring of 1904 brought forth another delightful display of bright green new growth popping out on branches and fresh blades of grass furring the meadows. As the joyous display of wild flowers peaked in the early summer, Mother sent me a new novel she said I'd love. Indeed, I spent a glorious few days immersed in "*The Hound of the Baskervilles*" by Arthur Conan Doyle. When done, I hoped there would be available at least one more book from this author, and wrote Mother to tell her so. Alex was reading "*The Virginian*" by Owen Wister, and I eagerly waited for him to finish. Anything out of the ordinary was something I could look forward to as a special treat.

At the end of July, hoping to distract myself from the intense heat, I took myself off to Irene's house where she greeted me with ice cold lemonade. She couldn't wait to show me the paper announcing that Gustave Marsh of Lone Pine was starting construction of a pack trail out of Lone Pine to the top of Mt. Whitney. Together we excitedly reviewed the article. How thrilled I was to think that someday I might be able to stand on the top of that grand mountain.

As she fed me thin, cold soup and small sandwiches, I told her, "I just love your house. How fortunate that the fire didn't spread to it."

"Yes. It wasn't that difficult to rebuild a smaller barn and other out buildings. But the house is a real treasure." She looked around the room and a slightly pensive mood settled upon her.

"I'm sorry. Maybe I shouldn't have brought up what must still be a very difficult subject for you."

She smiled at me. "Actually, it's a relief to be able to talk with someone who genuinely cares about my feelings, and isn't just morbidly curious."

"After all this time, you still encounter that?"

"Only a little. I've mastered the blank stare that immediately puts people off."

We laughed heartily at that. She then opened the newspaper to another page and pointed to the advertising of local real estate. 'The beautiful Owens Valley' was advertised in several places on the page. 'Irrigated farms in small and large tracts', it stated, 'for as little as $625 and as much as $65,000.'

"Evidently they've decided to promote fishing and the area's natural beauty," Irene pointed out. "Do you think this will attract people to this side of the mountain?"

"Probably. I can't imagine anyone not loving Inyo or Mono County once they see it." I looked out the window and felt a stab of longing so intense that it could have been a physical blow to my mid section.

Irene laid a hand gently on my arm. "Whitney, how long has it been since you've seen your family?"

"Three years." Swallowing with difficulty, I pressed my lips together and tried unsuccessfully to control the quiver in my chin. "I wanted to go home for Thanksgiving last year. But just as Alex had done when I brought it up the year before, he said he'd invited a lot of people to dinner and I needed to be there as hostess."

Her surprise was obvious. "But it was only me and the Bryants."

"I know." I fought the clutch of betrayal in my stomach, much as I had when I realized that Alex had made up the excuse of a large gathering simply so I wouldn't go home.

Unwilling to leave the subject alone, Irene commented, "You must be very homesick by now."

"You have no idea."

After a moment, she asked, "Is there someone there you don't want to confront?" There was an eagerness in her tone I couldn't understand.

"Well, yes. But that isn't why I've not gone home."

"Is it your father?"

"Oh, no," I quickly assured her. "He very much approved of my marriage." After a moment's hesitation, I added, "It's Steven."

"Oh." An odd note of disappointment had tinged that single word. It made me uncomfortable without knowing why and created a momentary awkwardness between us, although she seemed oblivious of it.

I forced myself to ask, "Why did you think it was my father that I wanted to avoid?"

"Oh, well, girls and their fathers, you know." She smiled with an effort. "I thought maybe he hadn't wanted you to marry and move away."

"Oh. He wasn't happy about my moving away, but it sometimes happens. Of course, I wouldn't have left Lone Pine if I'd married locally. I daresay a lot of people thought that would happen."

"Is that the reason you don't want to see Steven? Did everyone expect you to marry him? How did he feel about your marrying Alex?"

"Oh my, such a lot of questions." I got up from the table and walked to the window overlooking Irene's carefully tended garden of blooms and vegetables. "For a long time, I thought of Steven as just a friend, or even a brother. But then I realized that wasn't true." Smiling at the memory, I said, "I certainly didn't feel like his sister. When I was with him, my heart raced and I yearned to touch him. And, dear God, how I wanted him to touch me."

Not at all embarrassed by my bold admission, Irene calmly asked, "Then why were you attracted to Alex?"

I turned to face her. "Because Alex was magnetic in his smiles and looks. It made me feel desirable, and mature. He made it obvious that he was attracted to me, while Steven said nothing about his feelings. There was an air of mystery about Alex, and I was feeling the awakening of strange stirrings in my body. The trouble is, I didn't realize who was awakening them until after I was promised to Alex."

"Lord, Whitney," Irene sighed. "Are you afraid that if you go home, you'll return to those feelings for Steven? Especially now that Alex has become so often distant?"

"Maybe." I sat down and finished my tea in two gulps, not correcting her use of the phrase "return to". I had never lost those feelings for Steven.

The next day I brought up to Alex the idea of my going home. He said he'd rather I wait for late summer when the crush of activity at the ranch wound down. I fought the urge to ask what that had to do with me, but I set aside the subject.

Early August continued July's heat, and promised to get even warmer as the month progressed. Since my visit with Irene, my ache for the Valley and my family had become a familiar presence so natural that I no longer avoided it, accepting the pain as part of life. When I broached the subject of a possible visit home for a second time, Alex appeased me with the promise that *soon* we would both go there for a visit. I could tell it irritated him that I'd once again brought up the subject.

On an unusually cool morning, I found myself alone in the house while Sing and Mrs. Lewis went into town. Taking advantage of their absence, I spent the morning baking, and thus enjoyed a rare opportunity to contribute to that night's dinner. Looking up from trimming the crust on a raspberry pie, I found J.B. watching me from the door to the dining room.

"Lost in private thoughts?" he asked in his typical low, soft voice.

I smiled. "Just thinking of...Lone Pine and wondering how the bee hives are producing."

"You started to say you were thinking of home, didn't you?"

"Well, yes." My cheeks felt warm with embarrassment.

He picked up a raspberry that had escaped from beneath the crust and chewed slowly on the juicy fruit. "I hope some day you'll think of this ranch as your home."

"I do in many ways." Placing the pie in the oven, I began to clean up. "You and Alex and Sing have always been very welcoming. You've gone out of your way to make me feel comfortable here."

"I notice you didn't include Mrs. Lewis," he chuckled.

"No." Then I added quickly, "But we've established a coexistence that works for us, mainly by staying out of each other's way. I think of her as a nettlesome specter, and she tolerates my presence like an irritating insect one doesn't squash because of the mess it would create." When he laughed, I quickly added, "Don't mind me. I'm just feeling a bit blue."

"It's the heat. But it's even hotter up canyon in Bodie. I got a letter from a friend who lives there. Last winter's twenty feet of snow is just a bad memory for them now."

"Yeah, well, it could return any time." We shared a companionable laugh. "I've heard enough stories from my parents to know about the harsh extremes there."

J.B. nodded. "Back in the late 1870's when your parents lived there, they had some of the worst winters that area has ever seen. Did Alex tell you about the few days in October of 1890 that we here had temperatures forty degrees below zero?"

"Yes." Not ready to leave the subject of Bodie, I said, "I've never been to Bodie. I'd love to see it though."

He pulled out a chair from the small table, twirled it around to face him and threw a leg over, sitting with his arms crossed over the back. "Would you indeed?" His eyes twinkled.

I carefully wiped the butcher block island clean. "I asked Alex to take me with him the last time he went there, but he said it was too rough a trip."

He laughed when I rolled my eyes and made a face. "Well, maybe early this fall you and I'll go. You can satisfy your curiosity with a protector in tow. You'll find it considerably reduced from the time your parents lived there, and the infamous bad man from Bodie is a rare occurrence. Several fires and the extreme weather have eaten away at the structures, but it's still wild enough for the need to be careful."

"Speaking of my parents, Mother wrote to say that Gustav Marsh completed his pack trail to the top of Mt. Whitney in the middle of July."

"Really? That had to be quite an undertaking."

"I guess the Smithsonian Institution has been forming expeditions to the top for scientific study. So he decided it was a necessary project." I stopped wiping a dish and looked over J.B.'s head as I pictured what Mother had described. "Mr. Marsh had with him three pack trains loaded with wood, so the night he finished, he built a huge bonfire on the top of Mt. Whitney. Mother said everyone in town stood outside and watched the glow, applauding and cheering when Mr. Marsh set off fireworks."

After several minutes of silently watching me move around the kitchen, J.B.'s voice came to me shadowed with caution. "Would you still like to redecorate part of the house? You can place an order for what you want now and it'll be here in the spring. We've got a Sears and also a Montgomery Ward catalog."

"That's very kind of you, but I remember how against it you were when I first came here."

"There's other rooms you could change."

After a moment, I said, "I could do a few changes to my bedroom and our dressing area. Do you think I could change the chandelier in the back hall? And move the bearskin in front of the large fireplace to Alex's study and replace it with a big braided rug?"

"So this isn't something new to your thought?"

Blushing, I responded, "No, I can't say it is."

"I can understand why a lady might prefer looking at something more refined than a chandelier of antlers spattered with years of candle wax." He stood up and replaced the chair by the table as he said, "You go ahead and play house all you want. I trust your judgment. Let's make this a home by all means. It's been a ranch house long enough."

When I told Alex what J.B. had suggested I do, he gave his approval, albeit grudgingly. He didn't relish change.

The following week was for me a delight of catalogs, lists and sketches. Alex spent much of this time working in the tack room or away on business. After heading north to collect a debt from a man in Fales Hot Springs, Alex planned to continue on to Coleville, then a homestead near Alkali Lake (changed to Topaz Lake in the 1920's). He would then go on to Gardnerville and Genoa to visit friends. This allowed me the continuity of days immersed in lists and dog-eared catalog pages. Over the next few years, I would look back on the pure joy of that time with bittersweet delight.

By the time Alex returned, it was early September and I was again full of enthusiasm for life. Filled with an energy fueled by days of creative thought and the satisfaction of finally contributing to the household, I ran down the porch steps with my long skirts billowing in the breeze and a smile on my face, unable to wait patiently for Alex on the porch. There were too many new ideas spinning through my mind, and I was too eager to share them with my husband.

As he always did when eager to be home, Alex rode his horse right up to the hitching rail near the steps rather than going directly to the barn. He dismounted practically into my arms. But the look on his face when he turned toward me was not one of welcome, but rather the fragile restraint of strong emotion.

"Alex, is something wrong?"

"Everything. I'll talk to you later." He roughly shoved me aside and ran up the steps two at a time. The front door banged behind him, leaving me outside to cope with my disappointment, which was quickly replaced by the dread of hearing what had so badly upset him. But as fear and hurt feelings tend to do, they by-passed reason and ignited suddenly into anger. Wrenching open the front door, I entered the house and prepared to do battle.

"Alex! I don't know what's upset you, but I don't appreciate being treated like a stranger who's in your way!"

He stopped half way up the stairs and turned slowly in my direction. "I'm sorry." His voice was tightly controlled. "I know you were expecting a happy homecoming. But right now I can't be concerned about the tender feelings of a pampered girl." With that he turned his back and continued up the stairs.

"I'm a *woman* and your wife, and deserve to be accorded a basic semblance of courtesy."

His only response was the slamming of the door to his study. Turning around, I found Sing standing in the kitchen doorway, his eyes stretched wide with surprise at the exchange he had just overheard.

"Sing, what's going on?"

"Don't know. Never see Mr. Alex like this. Most courteous always. Must be very bad what happened."

My sigh was deep and resigned. "Okay. Would you mind putting some food on a tray and taking it to him? I don't think he wants to see me right now."

As Sing passed me with the tray, I stopped him. Removing a few daisies from a near arrangement, I placed them next to the bottle of beer, knowing Alex would realize it was from me and that things were okay between us. If he even cared.

Although I retreated to my room, after half an hour of waiting for Alex to appear, I went back to the kitchen. Setting about the packing of a lunch, I told Sing I was taking the buggy into town. Of course, he offered to prepare the lunch and even drive me there, but I told him, "No, I'll do it myself. It's your day off and you're planning to visit your friend. You go ahead. Whatever's going on, neither of us can do anything about it."

He reluctantly left for one of the near ranches, riding the small mare he often favored with carrots and apples when he thought no one was looking. On my way out a few minutes later, I passed J.B. coming in the back door. He took one look at my face and his brows rose in surprise.

"Is everything okay?" he asked with concern.

"I don't know, but I refuse to stay here. I may stay the night with Irene."

"What's happened?" Alarm suffused his face.

"Alex came home in a foul mood. He's in his study and refuses to speak to me. I need to be away from this house."

Suiting action to intent, I slammed the back door as I passed through. Angry mumbled words poured from me all the way to the barn. Then

I stopped and looked at the mountains wreathed in gray and white thunderheads and realized I had no jacket or rain slicker with me. Before reaching the barn, I stopped and forced myself to admit that maybe even my hot temper might not be enough to keep me warm if it started to rain. Besides, I knew better than to think I could run away from whatever was wrong. That was what Alex tried to do whenever he holed up in his study, and it was what J.B. did when he disappeared from the ranch to gamble.

I determined right then that running away wasn't going to be what I did when confronted by a problem. Returning to the house, I stepped quietly into the long hallway with the intention of reaching my room unseen.

"I demand an explanation!" Alex's angry shout greeted me from the great room, stopping me dead in my tracks in the hall. "And you'll give it to me now!"

Who on earth was he talking to in such enraged tones, I wondered. I walked quietly to the end of the hall and looked around the corner into the great room.

"There's nothing to explain," J.B. told him, his voice casual but unusually tight. Just short of exposing my presence, I changed my mind and took a step back into the shadows of the hallway.

"The hell there isn't!" Alex countered. "You've been lying to me my whole life!"

"I haven't lied!" J.B. shot back quickly. "I just haven't told you all the details of my past."

"Justification? That's all you're going to give me?"

Silence from J.B. was the only answer.

Alex tried again. "My whole life I've set you up as a perfect example of all a man should be."

"Don't exaggerate," J.B. reproached him. "I told you enough of my mistakes and wild behavior that you shouldn't have any delusions about me."

"I wouldn't have thought of this." It was a statement of defeat and sadness.

Asserting his dignity, J.B. countered. "I don't owe anyone an explanation."

"You sure as hell do!" Alex yelled. "I carry your name and share your life, a heritage that someday I'm supposed to pass on to my children. But now I don't know what that heritage is. If I don't know who *you* are, how do I know who *I* am?"

"You're your own man, Alex." Irritation underlined his words. "Your successes or failures aren't tied to who I am. That would be too easy an out for you, and a damn sight too much responsibility for me!"

I heard the creak of the floor boards as Alex crossed the room to where J.B. stood before the smoldering fire in the large fireplace.

"The people I was visiting at Fales were talking about the old Monte Diablo area. They knew the names of the prisoners," Alex spat out, "the ones that escaped from the Carson Prison back in '71. One was a nineteen year old kid named J. Bedford Roberts. You were born in 1852, making you nineteen at that time." His voice rose in a shout. "Are you going to tell me there was another nineteen year old with the same name in this area back then?"

After a long silence, J.B. relented. "Okay, I'll tell you everything. You won't like it, but after hearing what happened, maybe you'll understand why I never told you the details."

Standing in the hallway by the bookcases, I knew J.B. wouldn't hesitate to speak up, since he thought I was gone for the day along with Sing and Mrs. Lewis. I don't think Alex thought of anyone but the two of them. So instead of showing myself, I kept out of their line of vision and shamelessly listened to their conversation.

Alex reminded him, "You said you broke horses in Nevada and did a little gambling in Virginia City until you met Mother here in Big Meadows and started buying up land."

"Not exactly."

"What the hell do you mean?" I heard the air whoosh out of the big leather chair by the fireplace as Alex sat down heavily.

"I mean, son, that I've never told anyone the truth of how I ended up here in 1874, or what went on before I did."

The silence lasted so long that I began to wonder if Alex was still in the room. Finally, he said, "What is the truth then?"

Alex's tone was so hard that I felt a stab of pity for J.B., who took a deep shaky breath and let it out slowly.

"The truth isn't something I want to think about at this point in my life. Believe me, I've done a good job of pushing it to the back of my mind." He snorted with bitterness. "Well, most of the time. The fear of discovery never really goes away. It just slowly eats at your guts."

"Tell me!" Alex demanded impatiently.

"Okay. You do deserve an explanation."

"Oh, let's not kid ourselves this is about what I deserve," Alex snarled. "You wouldn't be telling me now if I hadn't confronted you."

"And just when do you suggest I should have told you? Your sixteenth birthday? Or maybe when you turned twenty-one?"

"I get it. Just tell me now."

Hidden in the hallway, I sat down on the floor and made myself comfortable. However, if I leaned forward a little, I could see the side of Alex's face beyond the arm of his chair. J.B. was facing his accusing and angry son, striving to find a way to explain himself. But to be sure I wouldn't be discovered before I too learned the truth, I leaned back against the wall.

"I was a far wilder kid than I've ever told you," J.B. began. "My father was a stern man and a strong disciplinarian. No more than many other fathers, I suppose, but I resented every rule he set for me and everything he told me to do. I never knew my mother. She died when I was a baby. So there was little softening influence in our home. That's why I hired Mrs. Lewis for you after your mother died. She wasn't even out of her teens, but she was capable and had family not far away."

"Keep this about you, damn it!"

"Fine. Anyway, after years of rebellion and petty crime, I fell in with a group of guys who were planning a stage robbery they said couldn't fail."

Alex sniffed with derision and J. B. nodded ruefully. "Yeah, never believe that one! But they treated me like an equal, like an adult when I was just a dumb, snot-nosed kid. We took in a big haul and got away with it, so we tried again. One of the stage drivers was shot and we were all captured soon after.

"The trial was a sham, with so-called witnesses who hadn't been anywhere near the holdup. The guy we hired to defend us was hung over and barely coherent. Before I knew it, I was headed for the Nevada State Penitentiary in Carson City with an eleven year sentence hanging over me. At that age, I didn't know I'd probably be paroled long before that. I only knew that it seemed like forever.

"As you know, Carson City is on the north end of the Carson Valley, between the Sierra and the Pine Nut Mountains. It's been Nevada's capital since 1864, so by 1871 there was commerce in big buildings in the main section of town, large fancy houses and small homesteads, churches, schools, and a courthouse. And a long stone prison next to the Warm Springs Hotel. The hotel had served as the territorial prison in the 1860's, but in 1871 when I was there, it was billed as a resort. Now there's irony for you! Its owner, Abe Curry, had even been the first warden.

"Carson is only ten miles from Gold Canyon and Virginia City, so it became a main freighting hub, especially when the railroad came to the area."

"Quit stalling," Alex snapped. "What happened?"

"I'm coming to it!" The tightness in J.B.'s throat made his voice higher than usual and he took another deep breath. I could hear him pacing as he talked. "The prison was a little more than a mile east of the town. I've never forgotten the feeling of doom that settled over me when we approached that big stone two-story hell, dwarfing the much-ballyhooed hotel next door. The stone had been quarried on site by the first prisoners. The windows were covered in a honeycomb of iron bars, and there was a hexagonal guard tower protruding from the second floor like a hot blister on a long gray reptile. The wagon stopped in front of a pair of large arched wood doors braced closed by several sliding iron bars. The big doors could be opened for wagons if necessary, but we were herded through a small sheet iron door set within one of these larger doors. Our shackles clanged on the stone floor as we shuffled along. Soon I was sitting in a tiny cell on the back side of the second floor.

"It had been a hot summer and the cramped cells alternated between stifling heat during the day and damp cold at night. Part of the prison had burned the year before and was being rebuilt by prisoners. Still, we endured long boring hours in our cells after our assigned jobs were done, which was usually breaking rock in the quarry. We were probably allowed too much time together.

"But they must have thought the prison was secure, because the warden, his wife and his six year old daughter shared apartments beneath us off the stairwell landing, with their bedrooms on our floor at the opposite end from the cells. The warden was the respected, and by some, feared Lieutenant Governor John Franklin Denver. Denver, Colorado was named after his brother. Deputy Warden Zimmerman also slept on the second floor, next to the ammunition room."

"I don't need the domestic arrangements of the staff."

"Yes, you do! Let me tell this my way."

"Fine!" Alex sat back and folded his arms across his chest.

"The only other member of the household you need know about was Bob Dedman, a lifer that worked for the Denvers as a servant. He slept on the ground floor. We could sometimes hear the warden and his family moving around, a taunting reminder that we couldn't. I was young, miserable, and terrified of the other men. They talked about the people they'd killed like most people talk about the pesky flies they swat at. I was eighteen, for God's sake, and the worse thing I'd done was tag along on a stage holdup. These men were older and bigger than me. Well, I guess Leander Morton was close to my build, but he was so tough and wiry I always felt smaller."

"What were they in there for?"

"Robbery, petty-thieving, attacks on women, and murder."

"Nice." Alex's voice was rough with constrained emotion. "Did they bully you?"

"Only in the beginning. For a reason I was to learn later, after they found out I was from Long Valley they treated me like a younger brother. Even toasted me with their coffee when I turned nineteen."

"Do you remember them?"

"God, yes. I see them in my nightmares. The ones you need to know about included Charlie Jones, early twenties and muscular, probably from years as a teamster. But he was paler than you'd expect, with cautious hooded eyes and very small ears. He was in for stabbing a man during a fight, and I never trusted anything he said. He seemed to dislike me more than the others did.

"Then there was John Burke. He was in his early twenties, average build, with striking blue eyes. He was in for manslaughter and having broken out of some other jail. I liked him more than the others, although he was on the jittery side.

"Burke seemed to be pals with Tilton Cockerill, who talked a lot about his days as a miner. In his late thirties, he had a long shaggy black beard, and already showed a receding hairline. Cockerill had a bit of a reputation as one of the leaders of the Verdi train robbery near Reno. He was in for 23 years.

"Close to his age was Moses Black, large and heavy with lots of dark hair and beard. His dark eyes always seemed afire with some malevolent force fed by an anger he never explained. I was terrified of him. I don't know what his mother had in mind when she named him Moses, but he was about as far from anything holy as Satan himself. He'd gotten seven years for grand larceny with violence, and had only arrived six days before the events that I'm going to tell you about.

"Black immediately gravitated toward Leander Morton, who was looking ahead to thirty years hard labor for mail robbery. Leander was a small, twenty-seven year old thug with a perpetual sneer.

"Then there was me. I was a clean-shaven kid still wet behind the ears in a group of hard men numbed by the hard knocks they'd experienced. And God help me, it made me feel like a man.

"They spent a lot of time together, usually talking in low voices. I could only catch a few words here and there because they sat apart from me while I watched for the guards. I wasn't sure it was a wise thing to do, but refusing would have been fatal.

"Frank Clifford was always central to whatever was happening. He was a surly horse thief that seldom spoke to me. Then I noticed Clifford was talking to certain prisoners, and their discussions always ended in a handshake. From the terrified look on the faces of the prisoners while their hand was grasped, it looked like there was also a threat involved.

"The hot August days of 1871 passed into a cooler September. Eventually the guards, needing to be somewhat perceptive in order to survive in their jobs, became suspicious of all the low talking, and I think they reported some of this activity to Warden Denver. He must not have given it any credence, because nothing about our routine changed.

"Finally, the men came to me and laid out a plan for an escape. I was terrified. When I thought about balking, Jones, one of the meanest of them, gave me a look that brooked no disagreement. Besides, I knew that now they'd told me of their intentions, I was dead if I refused to go along. But I also knew that if we were caught, the rest of my sentence would be served in worse conditions than up to then."

"So you were forced to go along?" The lilt of hope in Alex's voice was pathetic.

J.B. hesitated a bit too long, and I peeked around the corner as Alex's jaw clenched.

"In one way I guess I was. But I have to admit that I was miserable and just wanted out. So I agreed.

"They showed me an arsenal of cached weapons. It included sharp pieces of metal sewn into the cuffs of their loose-fitting prison pants, sling shots, butter knives sharpened to points on the stones under their cots, and rocks chipped into rough knives. But the crux of the plan was based on the fact that above the second floor ran a long unbroken attic space.

"On Sunday, September 17, while a strong easterly wind blew dust as thick as smoke over the valley, we finished our six o'clock supper in the large room across from our cells. When the only guard on duty, Volney Rollins, came in to lead us back to our cells, one of the prisoners jumped him from behind and struck him on the head. A couple of prisoners who disliked all guards on principle started beating on him. But he was really a decent sort, and Pat Hurley, one of the prisoners who didn't want to go along with the scheme, grabbed hold of Rollins and dragged him into an empty cell and locked the door. There was only time for a few shouted oaths by those thwarted of their blood lust before we were given a signal by Black and about thirty of us moved into position.

"The escape was triggered at that time not only because the wind was blowing dust, but because it was Sunday. On Sundays we were locked in our cells and the guards that were usually on top of the outer walls were given time off. We anticipated a few guards in the common yard, but we thought they could be easily over-whelmed by our numbers."

"I don't suppose anyone discussed how to do that without killing them?" Alex's voice was bitter with disappointment.

"No. I deluded myself into thinking we could get out without anyone being badly hurt or killed."

"So, how did you get out?"

"At first it was pretty easy. We climbed on top of our cells and cut a hole through the thin plaster ceiling into the attic. We crept along to the area above Zimmerman's room, and thinking he would be downstairs with the Warden's family, chopped a hole through, crashing down into the room. And there was Zimmerman in his bed. For a moment we were all stunned."

"Was he killed where he lay?" Alex asked bitterly.

J.B. gave him a dirty look. "No. He fled downstairs while we broke into the storage room next door, grabbing rifles and ammo. As we came down the stairwell that ended on a wide landing by the warden's apartments, I was back far enough to have several men in front of me. Frank Clifford, the ring leader of the plan, was in the lead.

"Suddenly the warden came out of his room with a small derringer in his hand and the lifer servant Bob Dedman behind him. Warden Denver immediately shot Clifford in the stomach and then ducked back into his room. But Clifford wasn't down, and when Denver came back out with a six-shooter, several men rushed him. One of the prisoners hit him on the back of the head with the butt of a gun and another prisoner above on the stairs hit Denver on the forehead with a projectile from his slingshot.

Denver wasn't all the way down on the floor before Morton grabbed his gun and shot him."

Caught up in the tale regardless of his other feelings, Alex asked, "What was Dedman doing all this time?"

"'All this time'. God, it happened so fast that it takes longer to tell than it did to live it. Dedman had no weapon. The warden was so cocksure of his superiority that he thought he could handle it all by himself. Dedman just picked up a chair and swung it at us as we rushed down onto the landing."

"Not very effective!"

"Huh! He knocked several prisoners off their feet. Of course, Dedman was out-numbered and someone knocked him out."

"Was Clifford dead?"

"No, he was still giving orders even while blood oozed between his fingers pressed to his abdomen. We had three Henry rifles and four double-barreled shotguns, a number of hand guns and several thousand rounds of ammo. We felt pretty invincible right then."

"Is that all you were feeling?"

"No. Hopeful as well." His tone was belligerent. "My heart was beating hard and there was a pulsing in my temples that made me feel like I'd just downed a quart of whiskey. I moved along with the rest, caught up in the urgency and a longing to get beyond those rock walls. I suppose part of what I felt was fear, but it was mixed with an excitement like none I'd ever felt before. I was almost euphoric with a sense of power."

"God!" I could see the side of Alex's face and it lacked all color.

J.B. looked at his son with tenderness and despair. "There isn't any way I can justify it or get you to understand. But you have to have the whole picture, or you won't understand why I kept my past a secret from you."

"Go on then." Alex's sigh was ragged with tension.

"There were a couple of guards in the open area of the front yard who greeted us with six-shooters drawn. I recognized old Isaacs and John Newhouse, two pretty decent men as far as guards went. Of course, they began firing at us. Isaacs was hit in the leg, but even as he fell, he kept shooting. He must've taken another hit, because he stopped firing when he was all the way down. But several of the prisoners lay bloodied from Newhouse's rapid firing. Then, thinking we were in the clear after those two guards had been eliminated, we headed for the wall.

"But another guard had earlier run into the hotel next door and now came out with guns blazing. He got three of us before being hit in the groin and falling against the prison door we'd just escaped through.

"The young guy in charge of the hotel, Max Pixley, foolishly fired through a prison window into the guard room at the prisoners that hadn't gotten outside yet. I watched him go down with a bloody hole under his left eye. That's when I pressed against the wall of the prison and thought maybe I should go back in and try to pretend I hadn't been one of them. I wanted desperately to be away from the blood and noise, but I also wanted to be in the mountains again.

"Just as I started to rush forward, the warden's six year old daughter, Jennie, ran past me into the yard crying and confused. Ed Goyette, one of the prisoners, picked her up and ran from the yard to the hotel, handing her over to Burgie the bartender. After that I didn't see Ed Goyette again.

"Our plan was to be well away before word reached Sheriff Swift in town. Twenty-two of us started walking and running, two abreast like an army on the march. Most of us headed east over the hills and then south. Five broke off and headed northeast toward the mills outside of town. Two others left us too, but I didn't see them leave. We couldn't travel very fast because we'd left no wounded behind, only the dead. There were about a dozen bleeding from various parts of their bodies and they were soon having a hard time keeping up."

"Weren't you afraid to move so slow? You had to know a posse would be on your tail."

"We were sure of it. I learned later that by seven that night, Governor Bradley's Private Secretary telegraphed General Batterman at Virginia City. Three hours later 27 specially trained National Guardsmen were joined by 15 men from the Emmet Guard, and they all headed out to find us. Just after midnight they were joined by the county's Deputy Sheriff Tom Harkin and his eleven men."

"What did you plan to do next?"

"Oddly enough, no one seemed to have thought that far."

"What?"

"I know. During the general planning, it was left pretty vague as to what we'd do at that point, at least the part I was in on. Anyway, three miles from the prison we crossed the river and then split up. Some went up the river and some down, but myself and twelve others headed south toward the Pine Nut Valley."

"What happened to the wounded?"

"We didn't have any of them with us by then." Leaning forward, I caught the look of deep thought on J.B.'s face, as though it was the first time he had ever considered the question. I found the callousness of that particularly unsettling.

"Well, go on," Alex pressed him.

"Near the Pine Nut Valley, we divided again and I was left with those I previously described to you." He walked to the liquor cabinet in the corner. After downing a small shot of straight whiskey, he looked out the window, keeping his back to Alex and therefore myself.

"We passed quickly through the sand hills along the rock ridges of the Pine Nuts toward Sunset Pass. As we carefully made our way through the Valley, we saw smoke from a cabin chimney, and we knew our first forage for supplies was at hand. I was afraid the old man we surprised inside would be killed by the others, so I quickly overpowered him and whispered to him not to fight me or the others would kill him.

"He let me tie him up without a struggle and kept so quiet the others paid him little attention. But after taking all the food we could find, some of the others tore up his out buildings looking for anything they might use. The most valuable find was his four horses. After that, I rode two-up with Morton since we were the lightest. Jones and Burke rode together on another, leaving the large train robber Cockerill and the burly Moses Black each with a horse of their own."

"How cozy." Alex sat with his arms clasped across his chest, his face pale and tight. J.B. ignored his son's sarcasm and went on with the story.

"Our plan now was to head south through Smith Valley to Aurora for supplies, then on to Benton where Jones knew a man who might be willing to help us escape into Nevada. If we had to go further south, they were counting on my familiarity with Long Valley, the Owens River Gorge and the Sierra west of there. Burke and Jones talked about nearby springs where we could find water, so I knew they were at least familiar with the layout between the prison and Long Valley. I was confident in our combined knowledge of the area, and was sure we'd be able to outwit those on our tail, if we hadn't already lost them over the mountains and rough rocky trails.

"But unknown to us at the time was the fact that Sheriff Swift had with him a couple of Indian guides. One was Mono Jim, an incredible tracker who could lead them over the mountains even at night. They camped at the same spring where we'd stopped on the crest of the mountain, easily picking up our trail the next morning. They were only six hours behind us.

"By late Monday night we were in Smith Valley and just past midnight on Tuesday we reached Hot Springs on the East Walker River, just ten miles northeast of Wellington. We took time to rest ourselves and the horses.

"But instead of going down to Wellington, and there joining the main freight and wagon road to Aurora, we skirted around east of an old mining camp and hit the main road closer to Sweetwater at Sulphur Springs. There was a stagecoach station there and we hoped to get fresh horses."

When J.B. stopped and drained his glass, I knew nothing good was going to follow. Alex too stiffened, well aware that this was no youthful escapade being retold.

J.B. sat down heavily on the sofa across from Alex and ran his fingers up and down the sides of his head. He avoided looking directly at his son as he continued.

"It was mid-afternoon on Tuesday. We were almost to Sulphur Springs when Burke remembered that there was a milk ranch up ahead. I was a growing lad and very hungry, so was glad to hear this. Morton told me to go see if a single man or a family lived on the milk ranch. When I asked why, he said, 'If it's a single man, we'll kill him so he can't tell the posse we've been here. I'm not eager to kill a man with a family though, or the family if it comes to that.'

"Just as I was about to take off, a rider was heard coming our way and we all hid in the bushes. It was the old man whose horses we'd stolen! After waylaying him, much to my surprise the men laughed and tied him up by a boulder. I didn't have much hope he'd remain alive long, but we left him there. As we rode off, Morton told the others, 'Kill anyone else we come across. We can't waste this much time. We've got to protect ourselves.'

"Jones agreed and said he'd do any killing with Morton. At that point I left them to go to the milk ranch, hoping to hell there was a big family there, although I was beginning to doubt now that would save anyone."

"Couldn't you have just kept on going at that point? You had a horse."

"Not with me. I was on foot, and wouldn't have gotten very far. And to tell the truth, I wondered if maybe sending me off alone like that was a test of my loyalty, and that they were watching me."

"Was there a family there?"

"A man and his wife, but I planned to tell the guys it was a family. They also had a large potato patch, so I filled my pockets for our dinner that night, thinking maybe it would earn me a little gratitude from the others.

"Before I dug up very many, though, I heard a rider approaching. I threw myself on the ground and lay flat along the vines, watching a young kid with mail sacks on his horse pass by at a fairly good clip. I stuffed a few more spuds in my pockets and started to run back to the others. It was then I considered the idea of getting away from them while their attention was distracted by the rider. But I didn't know where to go, so I started forward slowly. It must have been about ten minutes since I'd seen the rider, and when two shots rang out, I wasn't sure if it was from him or at him. I ran into camp and found the kid on the ground with half his face blown away.

"'Why did you kill him?' I screamed as I ran forward, trying not to throw up as I saw the spatter of his blood over the dirt. I looked from Morton to Jones for an answer, then noticed that they were dressing in civilian clothes. Looking down at the kid, I saw he was wearing a prison uniform.

"Black said, 'We stopped him to ask about Captain Dingman. We heard he'd be coming this way. He's the guard that killed some prisoners during an attempted escape awhile back. The kid said he was coming down on tomorrow's stage.'

"Morton gave Jones a dirty look and said, 'You son of a bitch. If you hadn't let the cat out of the bag by telling him you wanted to cook Dingman's goose when you saw him, we could have tied him up or even let him go.'

"Jones laughed, but then so did Morton. It was clear to me then that no one was about to be let go from that point on.

"Cockerill pulled me aside and told me not to ask any more questions, that Morton and Jones had smelled blood and were now dangerous to even us. After seeing the look in their eyes as they stood over the boy, he didn't need to caution me again.

"That evening as we ate the potatoes I'd stolen, I heard Morton laughing with Jones.

"'He begged real nice,' Morton said.

"Jones answered him, 'We didn't give him much time to do it though, did we?'"

J.B. closed his eyes briefly. "I learned from listening to them that they'd both shot the kid in the head. His identification said his name was Billy Poor. They each had a ring they'd removed from the kid's fingers. Jones joked that he'd probably wear his into hell. He didn't sound as though he cared much.

"Not long after that, about eight o'clock, I dozed off. Their voices woke me, and I lay still to hear what they were talking about. It had something to do with the kid's body, but I couldn't make it out. Then Jones kicked me in the side and told me to get the horses ready. I said nothing and just ran to do what I was told, exhausted from fear as much as from lack of sleep."

Leaning against the bookcases, I thought to myself that none of *us* was probably going to get much sleep that night either. Not so much because of what J.B. had presented so far, but rather because of what I feared was coming next.

CHAPTER 9

J.B. got up and refilled his glass again, and I marveled at the fact that he moved and talked like a man who hadn't been drinking steadily for over an hour. He swallowed half the glass while his back was turned to Alex, then tossed another log on the fire. But he didn't turn back after he stood up, and told the next part while looking out the front window. I had to strain to hear his words.

"When I walked back into camp leading the horses, the glow of the rebuilt fire filled the clearing.

"'I thought we were leaving,' I said.

"'We are shortly,' Morton told me. 'First we need to fool the posse into thinking some poor convict son of a bitch got killed.'

"He and Jones dragged the body to the fire and placed the kid's head in the flames. The smell of burning flesh and hair blew in my direction, and I turned and stumbled into the bushes to retch.

"Strong hands gripped my shoulders and Burke's soft voice was in my ear. 'Steady boy. Don't show them you're weak. They could think you're not to be trusted.'

"Knowing he was right, I fought to pull myself together. We mounted up and rode toward Sulphur Springs and the milk ranch. As we passed it, Jones talked about wanting to kill the rancher and hide his body in the cellar, taking his clothes for Burke. But Burke didn't want them, saying, 'I don't go for such cold-blooded murders as that. We'll have the whole country down on us.'

"After a few minutes of arguing with Jones, Burke said, 'To hell with this. I'm leaving this crowd. I'll take my rifle and horse and go.'

"I was about to ask if I could go with him, when Morton flushed red and told Burke, 'Oh no, you won't!' His hand moved toward his gun and Burke shouted back, 'If any of you bother me, I'll shoot out your guts!'

"Cockerill spoke up, bringing reason into the mix. 'There's no use in this. We need each other too much to be fighting among ourselves.' Everyone agreed and we moved on.

"By two o'clock in the morning on Wednesday we passed the stage stop at the Elbow Ranch on the Walker River, about seventeen miles north of

Aurora. I was so hungry I thought of nothing else, unless maybe sleeping in a soft bed for a week. But none of the others showed the least sign of flagging, and I knew I had to act the same.

"We now had five horses, so only Morton and I had to double up. The kid's horse was a strong one, trained as it was to carry the mail long distances.

"When we got close to Aurora, we stopped to water the horses at a spring and the others gathered together without inviting me to join them. At that point I didn't care. I felt like a spare part anyway, something held in reserve until they needed my ability in territory unfamiliar to them.

"When they were through talking, they informed me we were going to slip around Aurora, since the sheriff there had probably received telegraphed notice about us. I was crushed with disappointment and tried to silence the rumbling in my stomach, even while knowing they were right. So early Wednesday morning we rode east of Aurora toward Benton, passing some men in a wagon. We kept riding and they only nodded as we passed them, showing no curiosity about us at all.

"But Jones looked back and his hand hesitated near the belly gun hidden under his coat. I was riding next to him on the back end of the horse I was sharing with Morton, so it was easy for me to reach the toe of my boot to his horse's flank. By the time Jones settled his horse and finished swearing, the wagon had disappeared over a small rise.

"Not far from Adobe Meadows we got to the McLaughlin Ranch. A woman there was good to us, cooking us a meal and giving us some provisions."

"Why?"

"Burke gave her some song and dance about our being miners whose diggings had played out and our supplies stolen. After we left though, her husband came home and must have figured out who we were because he went to Benton to tell the posse.

"Late Wednesday, we reached the Hightower Sawmill near Benton, passing through Taylor Canyon fourteen miles west of Benton. Jones went into the mill while the rest of us waited in the trees. He wore Billy Poor's boots and coat to disguise himself, but I knew that if he didn't get what he wanted, he'd be willing to kill for it. Soon he came back with salt and flour and a little corn meal.

"'What did you tell him?' Morton asked.

"'I told him I was with some miners waiting in the woods. He looked out the window and saw Burke sitting on a big rock with his boots off, and then seemed right friendly. Why were you doing that?' he asked Burke.

"'I had a rock in my boot.'

"A simple thing, but it would have shown us as non-threatening to anyone looking out their window. And other than myself, Burke with his fair skin, blue eyes and cleft chin was probably the least hardened in appearance.

"I looked again at Black. He didn't talk much, but when he did his dark eyes seemed to shine with a malevolence that even Morton and Jones respected. I felt the most at ease around Burke and Cockerill, but I knew better than to rile even them. Burke had been in prison for manslaughter, so I knew he was capable of killing and Cockerill was almost famous for the Verdi train robbery."

"My God, it sounds like you admire them even now."

"No, not *admire*, but I was in awe of them. Look, you said you wanted honesty. Well, here it is. Now deal with it."

"Okay, okay. What happened next?" Impatience borne of anger and disappointment was now present in everything Alex said.

"That night we made camp in Adobe Meadows. We didn't know it at the time, but right behind us was the posse. I think by then we were developing some kind of strange itch when danger was close, because we were all eager to break camp and move on several hours before sun-up.

"It was at this point that the posse changed. Sheriff Palmer from Aurora turned the chase over to Deputy Sheriff Hightower, who owned the mill we'd stopped at for supplies. Mono Jim was still with them, and a Wells Fargo agent from Benton called Robert Morrison had joined up with them. By this time, posters with a reward of $500 had been circulated, so the men in the posse were well motivated.

"We'd passed along the Aurora Road towards the Owens River, around the east side of Mono Lake at a trudging walk through the deep sand, through Adobe Valley with sagebrush raking our legs and yellow rabbitbrush making some of us sneeze, around Bald Mountain, up Taylor Canyon's rocky narrow paths, and across McLaughlin Creek. We were a tired, desperate and frightened bunch that couldn't have been more dirty, torn and ragged if we'd been laying on a garbage heap for a week.

"Finally, as we rode across a beautiful meadow at the head of McLaughlin Creek, we were in Long Valley and could see the Sierra spread out before us. We hoped it would offer a refuge that the rough, open scrub had denied us. Even our horses seemed to have more energy as they sniffed the new air. When the men turned to me for advice, I'd be a liar if I said it didn't feel sweet. But I wasn't fool enough to play it up too much.

"We followed the old wagon road next to the creek through tall bushes of red berries, and wild rose hips. Finally, we crossed the Owens River at a shallow spot, glad it wasn't during the spring melt, and trudged on to the Hot Creek area where we found a cow and calf near a homestead. We grabbed the calf and continued south until we were about three miles north of Monte Diablo Lake. That night we feasted on young beef and our energy surged. We then made our way east to the mouth of the canyon that leads to the lake.

"Black asked me, "'What makes this area so good for us?'

"I told him, 'At the far end of the lake is a creek coming down through a cut in the mountains. We can pass over this rock, through the thick cover of the willows there and up the mountains and over the ridge. There's a number of other routes we could take from there, but before they figure out which one we've taken, we'll be over the ridge.'"

J.B. poured more whiskey into his glass and Alex said, "If you're hesitating again, this must be the point you didn't want me to know about. How much worse can it get after what you all did to Billy Poor?"

"I didn't do it," J.B. responded quickly.

"You were part of it!" Alex sat forward and buried his face in his hands. "Just get on with it," he mumbled between his fingers.

"My plan of escape over the mountains beyond the lake at Monte Diablo seemed to please them." J.B.'s face hardened. "It's because of us that they now call it Convict Lake."

"Oh, hell, that's right." Alex lay back in his chair and closed his eyes. "I've heard several versions over the years. What really happened there?"

"We followed my plan and made camp on the creek a short way from the east end of the lake, planning to start around it after we'd eaten. Burke suggested that we collect some of the berries on the bushes along the creek, so Jones and Cockerill started off with him, following the creek toward the lake.

"About an hour later as I was describing to Morton and Black how we'd make our way around to the far shore, we heard the rattle of rocks being walked on along the creek. Again, I'm surprised at how much happened in the space of the few minutes that followed.

"The three of us jumped up and ran, trying to find a place to hide. I was confused with terror and shock that we'd been discovered so close to success. Evidently the posse realized it'd be impossible to ride unheard to where they rightly assumed we'd be camping by the creek, so they left their horses back down the creek with the Indian, Mono Jim. While the clear-headed Black and Morton ran into the trees, I ran in the opposite direction and ended up in the open. Before I could correct my mistake, I felt a bullet graze my shoulder, followed immediately by a searing pain on the side of my foot. As soon as I felt the ground slam into me, I started crawling until I was huddled behind the other two. There was only a large pine tree between ourselves and the posse, who was now disappearing into a stand of willows.

"Morton told me, 'Get into the willows behind us. If they surround us here, we'll get it.'

"I did as I was told, peering out from between the yellow leaves, too full of fear and excitement to notice too much the pain in my foot and shoulder. I was barely bleeding anyway, and it soon stopped altogether.

"Almost at the same time we all spotted Robert Morrison, the Benton shop keeper and Wells Fargo agent. He was sneaking up on us from up canyon. I was surprised to hear Black mumble, 'There's a brave one. Wish I didn't have to kill him.'

"Morton grunted and said, 'That's the best kind we can kill now. Then we won't have as much trouble with the rest that aren't as brave.'

"Black then crawled into the brush toward Morrison. I was higher in the willows, and could see that Black had actually passed him a bit. Because of that, Morrison saw him and took aim. I mentally cashed out Black from our group. But after the explosion of his gun, Morrison stood there with a surprised look on his face. His gun hadn't actually discharged the bullet. Before he could switch to another gun, Black had spun around and gotten off a shot at Morrison. He didn't miss and Morrison grabbed his side as he fell to the ground.

"Morrison was losing blood faster than tomato sauce from a broken jar, but even so he still tried to raise up to get a shot at Black. A wave of admiration swept over me. If Black felt any such emotion, it didn't show on his face as he towered over Morrison, calmly putting his gun barrel to the back of the prone man's head and pulling the trigger. The bullet passed out just above his right eye in a splatter of tissue.

"The rest of the posse had evidently watched this performance too, because just as Morton had foreseen, they fled from the canyon.

"After they helped me onto a horse left behind by the posse, we saw the Indian Mono Jim coming towards us from a small aspen grove. He was holding the reins of several horses belonging to the posse. We figured he was retrieving them after they'd spooked during the gunfire and broken free from him. I think he recognized the horse I was on and for a moment must have thought we were part of the posse, since he called out to us. But as soon as we turned to face him, he realized his mistake. Dropping the reins, he began running, all the while screaming a high whining series of words in his native tongue, probably begging not to be killed. No hope there. Black shot him in the back without hesitation.

"But the Indian had a gun we hadn't seen. As he lay on the ground, he got off two shots, hitting the horses of Black and Morton. As he jumped off his falling horse, Morton drew bead on Mono Jim and shot him right through the eye. He then calmly walked over to the Indian's horse and jumped on. Black took one of the others that the Indian had been holding and we were set to ride out of the canyon."

Alex asked, "What about the three that had gone down to the lake?"

"Either they were hiding or they'd already gotten out of the area. When I asked if we should wait for them, Morton said, 'They're not our problem.' I sure would have preferred being with them, wherever they were.

"We took off down the canyon at a gallop, crossing near McGee Creek toward the Owens River with me doing my best to keep up while my foot throbbed with pain. Then we saw old McGee and some guy he called Inman coming our way. We got in the bushes and prepared to pepper 'em, but they suddenly stopped and rode back the way they'd come. After that we detoured around the McGee cabin and crossed the creek about half a mile above it. We got through Round Valley to a point between Rock Creek and the river canyon, then south towards Pine Creek in the Round Valley foothills where I told them we could get over the mountains.

"The last time I'd seen the canyon was years before and I'd forgotten how steep the trail was. I'd also forgotten how long it was to the trail end. The pain in my shoulder and foot was intense and I started to feel an underlying hysteria welling near the surface. I wasn't sure if the greater threat was in the posse behind us or the two men next to me.

"On Sunday morning, September 24, after much effort that strained my wounds and set them to bleeding again, we decided to abandon one of our horses that had gone lame. We put most of our meager supplies on the Indian's horse and led the other. Only a few minutes later, on a narrow shale-covered portion of the trail, the Indian's horse slipped. I don't think I'll ever forget its screams as it went over the cliff and slid down the steep canyon.

"Morton looked over the edge with disgust and offered a short eulogy. 'Stupid beast! A mule wouldn't have done that.'

"I think Black had an idea of how close to striking Morton I was right then, ready to explode from the pain and fear and pressure of a situation I'd never bargained for. Black laid a hand on my good shoulder and squeezed. The look in his eyes would have been enough.

"We'd lost one of the Henry rifles with the horse and all our food. I was so wrung out from loss of blood and hunger that I sat on a rock and buried my face in my hands. I shouldn't have shown my weakness. When I looked up, they were watching me with a calculation that sent a chill over me. I waited for one of them to pull a gun and put me out of my misery.

"But they evidently didn't want to waste a bullet, so instead Black simply said, 'Good-bye kid. Good luck.' He tossed me a canteen full of water and the two of them walked back the way we'd come, taking with them the rifle. I only had a pistol tucked in my belt with three shots in it.

"Total quiet descended. I was full of relief at no longer being with them, but also filled with the hopelessness of being injured and with no supplies. I found shelter in some rocks among the trees and days passed slowly as I nibbled berries or tree bark, hoping for the energy to climb the mountains at the back of the canyon. I had water from a stream, but I was almost crazy from hunger.

"It was twelve days since we'd left the prison and it seemed like months. I sat and thought about what had happened during that time and asked myself what I could have done differently along the way. It was a long list.

"Around noon on the fifth day I heard the posse. They got very near, but stopped downstream where they set up for lunch. The smell of boiling coffee hit me like a stab to the heart. Finally, with almost no conscious thought except I wanted the misery over, I stood near them in the willows by the creek and fought back tears of self-pity.

"A voice called out, 'Come forward with your hands up. Surrender without a fight and save yourself.' And I did.

"They stood all around me with their guns drawn, but all I could focus on was the coffee and pots on the fire. I told them, 'You can kill me if you want, but can I have a swallow of coffee first? I haven't eaten for five days.'

"They could tell I had no fight in me and were actually kind to me. After taking the gun that I told them was under my shirt, they let me eat and drink while one of the men saw to my wounds. All that's pretty much a blur now, but it was then, too. On Saturday morning I was helped up on a horse, but not handed the reins. They led me out of the canyon and we rode to a homestead at the head of the canyon owned by someone named Birchim, not far north of Bishop Creek. They hadn't warned me and when we walked in, there was Morton sitting at a table with his wrists and ankles bound and a guard near by. He glared at me, but said nothing.

"'Thought the coyotes would have gotten you kid.' I turned towards Black's voice and saw him on the bed with his head bandaged.

"I found out later that when Bart McGee had found Black and Morton near Silver Peak, they threw up their hands to surrender, but the Indian guide with the group had misunderstood the movement and had shot Black. Then they'd been taken to a blacksmith who'd made shackles for them. Morton had even helped make the ones he'd be wearing." J.B. snorted and shook his head.

"I hobbled over to Morton who was still silent, and said, 'I shouldn't have been surprised when you left me in the canyon to die, not after seeing you two kill that kid and that man by the lake. But I was. I did everything you demanded, and you repaid me by abandoning me.'

"The look on his face was hard to read, but a good part of it was hate. Some of the members of the posse were mumbling behind me. When they stopped, two of them helped me outside to a tree stump where they sat me down. One man slowly walked over to me and introduced himself as Mr. J. L. Sherwin, captain of the group. He said, 'Who are the two men inside? They won't say.'

"'The one on the bed is Moses Black and the other is Leander Morton. I'm J. Bedford Roberts.'"

"'How old are you kid?' he asked gently. I liked his voice.

"'Seventeen,' I answered. Okay, so I took off a couple years. I thought the younger I was, the more likely I could work their sympathy.

"Then he told me, 'Morton said you killed that man back at the lake.'

"I started to jump up. 'That's a lie!' I yelled. He pushed me back down on the stump. 'I was already wounded by then.'

"He asked me to tell them the whole story and I asked them where I should start. They told me to start from where we left Wellington.

"I said, 'You want to know about that poor kid, don't you? You must have found the body.'

"Disappointment flooded his face. 'No, we haven't. We hoped he was still with you and alive. Where should we look for him?'

"I told them, 'About a half mile south of Sulphur Springs and a couple hundred feet west of the road.'

"Then I told them everything. I left nothing out, hoping it might purge some of the horrors. A few of them didn't look like they were ready to be generous, so I told them I'd been forced to go with the others because I knew the layout around Long Valley. I stopped just this side of whining.

"One of the men in the posse was sent to Bishop with word of our capture. While there, he planned to telegraph Wellington for someone to go to Sulphur Springs and retrieve Billy Poor's body so they could take it to his parents in Aurora.

"By Sunday evening, October 1, they felt Black could stand the ride in a spring wagon commandeered from Mr. Birchim. Black and I were loaded in the back, with Morton next to the driver. The goal was to get us back to Carson Prison, but we'd just passed Pinchower's store on the north end of town when the whole group of us was surrounded by dozens of men, some wearing masks and some not, but all carrying powerful rifles.

"Morton whispered, 'Vigilantes. We're in for it now.'

"The resignation I'd felt when thinking about going back to prison was replaced by numbing terror. One of the riders, a Mr. Mallory, demanded, 'Who's the captain of the posse?'

"'That'd be me,' Mr. Sherwin answered, adding, 'Just turn around and let us get on with our job.'

"But Mr. Mallory said, 'You all just take the road back.' Finally, after several minutes of considered thought, our guards turned their horses and started away.

"I called out, 'You can't leave us with these men. I didn't kill anyone. At least take me with you.'

"No one stopped. I suppose they knew it was useless to protest on my behalf.

"'Give it up Roberts,' Morton told me with a growl. "'We're done for.'

"The wagon's driver, the only one of our original guards still with us, was so nervous he couldn't handle the horses. Morton, next to him on the seat, said with a calm I couldn't fathom, 'Give me the reins. I'm a pretty good teamster.'

"So we followed the vigilance committee across a big unfenced meadow to a deserted cabin about a mile northeast in what someone called Jim Shaw's field. Black and I had to be carried inside the cabin because of our wounds and bindings. Morton walked in with a swagger, only his wrists bound, without protest or prompting.

"They sat us on rickety old chairs against the wall. There were a few other chairs, and the obvious leaders sat on them across from us while the rest either sat on the floor or leaned against the walls. There was a boy a few years younger than me that had tagged along and was hunkered down in a corner near Mr. Mallory. Realizing they were planning to hold a mock trial, I watched the posse form a jury and one by one we were questioned. It went on for several hours before they took a vote. I told them pretty much the same story I'd told the other group of men. Morton told them that Jones had claimed to have friends in Inyo County that could help us, and that Jones had killed Billy Poor, leading us into a hornet's nest of trouble. Before I could cover my expression, several had seen my look of surprise and confusion.

"It wasn't difficult for them all to agree that Black and Morton should hang, but they argued for another 15 minutes over whether or not I should swing too. While my mouth got drier by the second, I listened to them argue my fate. One of the men asked me how old I was and I reduced it by another year, which they bought because I was even more slight of build than usual after so long without food. After a few more arguments among them, they decided to return me to prison if I swore to all I'd told them. I'd never heard better words.

"After that we were left tied up with two guards to watch us, while the rest went outside and began building a scaffold. We listened without talking for some time, then Morton who was looking up at the ceiling, asked, 'Black, you ready to die?'

"'No!' His voice sounded tight and angry. 'And this isn't the crowd that'll hang us.'

"Morton's bark of laughter rang off the walls. 'Yeah they are. Don't you hear them building the scaffold, you fool?'

"After a moment, Black turned his dark evil eyes on me and smiled. 'Well, if we're to swing, I mean to have you swing with us. We want company,' he chuckled.

"I kept my mouth shut. I wasn't too sure what he had in mind, but I didn't want to play into his hands by having the men standing guard over us change their minds about me.

"Soon the door swung open and I had a clear view of what they'd been doing. They'd built a single beam scaffold, one end resting on the top of the chimney and the other lashed to the peak of a tripod of small tree trunks. A wagon stood beneath the cross beam, just below two waiting nooses swaying a little in the strong breeze.

"Two of the vigilantes carried Black to the wagon and stood him under one of the ropes. Morton walked with his customary swagger from the cabin, although as he passed me, he looked down and mumbled, 'You'll get yours, kid.'" He climbed unaided into the wagon next to Black, slipped the noose over his own head and said to the man who was keeping watch on him, 'Better tie my hands behind me so I can't jump up and catch the rope.' And they did. When Black asked for some water, Morton snorted with derision.

"Someone near the door mumbled to the man next to him, 'There isn't enough water in the world to dowse the flames where he's headed.' The other man chuckled and a third hushed both of them. Morton then hollered out, 'It isn't right for a man to be hanged without some kind of religious ceremony. If there's a minister among you, I'd like to have a prayer.' There were noises of impatience and disgust, and even Black gave him a strange look, but the man that had shushed the two outside the door stepped forward and spoke a few solemn words. They asked Black if he had anything to say and he just said, 'No!'

"Morton said, 'I'm prepared to meet my God. But I don't know there is any.'

"The acting minister prayed louder, Black sighed, and when the minister said, 'Amen', the wagon moved forward. Black dropped like a stone and was still. Morton actually jumped into the air so his light body would come down heavily onto the rope. I wanted to look away, but couldn't. Urine slowly stained the front of their pants while their still bodies gently swung back and forth. The only sound was the creaking of the stiff rope rubbing on the rough beam.

"My wounds were tended by a doctor in Bishop, but they were afraid there wasn't good enough security there to protect me from a mob. So I was taken to Independence by military guard and spent a week recovering in the county jail.

"When we got back to the prison on October 27, I found out that Burke and Cockerill had been captured a couple of weeks earlier in Fish Lake Valley by the Esmeralda County Sheriff. Burke told me some men had offered Sheriff Helm $500 if he and his deputies would leave them alone with him and Cockerill. Burke offered thanks that the Sheriff had a moral streak and had turned them down flat.

"My father had been notified of my return and he was finding a lawyer to appeal my original case. A lot of good that would do, I thought. One bit of good news was that the old lifer Bob Dedman was alive, and in fact was being pardoned for trying to help the warden.

"We were told that Charlie Jones had been found dead in a cabin near Fish Lake Valley in Nevada where Black and Morton had been captured, but that later proved not to be true. In fact, no one ever heard of Jones again. The guard Isaacs that was shot in the yard didn't die until October 13, and the next day a coroner's jury named 29 convicts responsible for his death."

Alex interjected, "But all twenty-nine that escaped couldn't have been present to stand trial."

"No. But eighteen of the twenty-nine were. Black and Morton were dead and nine were still at large. So eighteen of us stood trial. When that trial was over, there was another for the murder of Matt Pixley, the guy from the hotel.

"The trials took a week and at the end of November the jury found all of us *not* guilty. From all our testimony, much of it substantiated by witnesses, they concluded that most of the gun play had been on the part of Jones and Morton. So Jones was blamed for the deaths of Pixley and Billy Poor, Morton for the murder of Isaacs and Poor, and Black for killing Morrison."

"But that's not exactly true, is it?"

J.B. shrugged. "Close enough."

"Had the Warden survived his wounds?"

"Yeah. He swore nothing would get him out of that job. But after an investigation into the whole affair, the Nevada Legislature voted to bring in the new Lieutenant Governor as warden. Denver died only a few years later."

"How much longer were you in prison?"

"I shouldn't have doubted my father's resolve. Late in '73 I won an appeal to the Nevada Supreme Court on the basis that my first trial hadn't been fair. My father went back to Long Valley, although he shortly moved away from there to Hawthorne, Nevada. I moved to Virginia City, which was about as far removed from the flow of life as I could get.

"I was a good boy and didn't drink. Well, not much anyway. I worked hard at any job I could get, from mining to mucking out stalls. Then one night I had a truly great hand at poker with the pile a big one, and with that money I came here to Big Meadows and started buying land. You know the rest."

Alex said nothing as he slowly stood up. I did the same, ducking into the kitchen and therefore out of sight when Alex walked up the stairs and into his study. Leaning against the table with my eyes closed while fighting to stop the throbbing in my temples, I waited to hear the slamming of the front door as J.B. left the house. Instead, a gasp brought me to attention and I turned around to find J.B. in the doorway to the dining room. He didn't need to ask if I'd heard everything, since I'm sure one look at my face told him that I had.

"Oh, God!" he groaned. "I didn't want you to know."

Gathering my dignity about me, I asked, "Why? Do you think my capacity for forgiveness less than your son's?"

"No." He slumped into a chair at the kitchen table. "Just the opposite actually. Maybe that's why it bothers me more. I'm not sure I want to be forgiven."

"Is that why you gamble so much?"

"What do you mean?" He looked up at me and frowned.

"I'm not sure. It just came to me that there's a connection."

"Funny you should say that." He rubbed his hands over his face, then looked past me to the window over the sink. "Every time I win big, I think to myself that God has chosen that way to show me I'm not such a bastard after all."

"And when you lose?"

"I don't lose very often or very big." He looked at me with a crooked smirk. "Another validation?"

"It's an odd way to assuage guilt." Then I shrugged. "But the important thing is the quality of the life you've led as an adult. That's something you can obviously be proud of, and after all, you didn't do any of the killing."

"But maybe I could have done more to stop some of it." He watched my face carefully.

"J.B., it's over. You did what you had to do in order to survive a terrible situation. You can't blame yourself for what the men with you did, or what you as a kid didn't have the maturity to resist."

He didn't say any more, but a tear rolled down his cheek. Maybe forgiveness is too difficult for some to take. I walked up to him and kissed his cheek, then left the house through the back door. I went for a long walk, not returning until almost dusk.

I didn't tell Alex that I'd overheard the confession. J.B. didn't tell him either. Maybe we both realized that Alex could process such startling revelations better if his feelings were not being examined by his wife. What I had not counted on was awakening the next morning to a note on my dressing table from Alex. He informed me that he was packing up to the high country to hunt and didn't know when he'd be returning.

Seeking out J.B. to ask him how long he thought Alex would be gone, I was informed by Sing that J.B. had also left for parts unknown. So much anger and indignation filled me that my throat started to close up and I coughed for several minutes. Just once, I asked myself, why couldn't someone in that family confront instead of run?

After a long period of fuming and pacing on the front porch, I asked myself why I cared how long it would be before either of them returned. I finally concluded, "If that's the way this family handles things, and I'm part of the family, then I'm leaving, too." It was a foregone conclusion that my decorating plans had also been deserted.

I packed a few things in a leather Gladstone bag and told a surly Parson to get the wagon out, as he was going to take me into Bridgeport. He wasn't happy about it, but when he began to object, he took a closer look at my face and instead asked when we were leaving.

The stage from Bridgeport to Benton was a fast one, and the next day I was settled comfortably on the train to Bishop. Aunt Carrie was happy to see me, and even happier to show me her new telephone, although there were not as yet that many locals who had one to receive her calls. Nevertheless, telephone service was established in part of the Valley and she thoroughly expected people to take advantage of it. She also brought me up-to-date on the town of Bishop since it had incorporated the year before, followed by current politics, and I swear, stories of most of the 540 people then living there.

After one night at her ranch, I determined to be on my way, too eager to be home to relax and enjoy her voluble tales, or even wait for the train the following afternoon. Of course, she argued with me when I asked to borrow a horse to ride on to Lone Pine, but she could see I wasn't in a frame of mind to be stopped. By leaving before dawn and riding hard, I was home late in the afternoon, four days after leaving the Double R.

CHAPTER 10

The worst of the summer heat was over as I headed for home, but I couldn't resist stopping in the deep shade of the locust trees along Independence Creek. After bathing my face in the cold water, I stood next to the horse as it drank its fill. I looked up through the tree leaves above me at the bright sky, two "Sierra waves", huge elliptical clouds smoothed and rounded by high winds, standing out against the blue of an otherwise cloudless sky. Several hours later I neared Lone Pine with every view embracing me in welcome, and the sage-scented breeze caressing my face. When I saw in the distance the cemetery on my left amid green fields, and then the tall trees around the town, my heart began pounding.

Only a few people glanced with curiosity at the female rider entering town riding astride and wearing an old riding outfit with a hat tied down by a scarf. It might have looked odd, but it had been practical while riding hard on the roads of soft dirt.

Eager for the embrace of my surprised and delighted parents, I hurried to the barn to stable the horse. However, by the time I'd finished there and reached the back door, no one had rushed from the house to greet me. Surprised to find the back door locked, I was even more surprised that no one responded to my knocking.

Going around to the front, I slowly walked up the narrow path between rose bushes displaying a few bright, late season blooms. An up-swelling of emotion caught in my throat as I looked up at the house, and I smiled at the familiar creaking of the wooden steps underfoot. Noting the chipped, white trim around the dark walnut door, I recalled Mother's voice gently reminding Father yet again that it needed painting. I was inordinately pleased that he had never found the time to "get around to it".

A gust of wind caught the old wooden swing on the front porch and it squeaked as it gently rocked. It was so overwhelmingly welcome, so familiarly the same as I remembered it, that I had to swallow twice to quell the tightening of my throat. When no one responded to my persistent banging on the door, and I'd shaken off my surprise at finding that door also locked, I made myself comfortable on the swing and settled down to watch the traffic on Main Street. I was immediately struck by how much lighter the wagon and horse traffic was now than when I'd left three years earlier. Three years. How could I have been gone so long?

After only a few minutes of sitting, my muscles began to stiffen. There was not one inch of my body that did not ache or throb with the exertion of the ride home. The soles of my feet, the bend of my knees, my lower back, all was aflame with pain. Although I had to force myself to stretch, it did help.

I had left the Double R in such a hurry, before the anger that fueled the spontaneity of my decision could pass into reasonableness, that I now thought of a dozen things I should have packed. At least I had summoned the presence of mind to bring money, and my parents certainly weren't without resources. As I made a mental list of what I should buy first, the breeze suddenly transformed into a strong gusty wind. Rather than irritated by the stinging sand blowing across the yard, I felt it like the greeting of an old friend, even if a rough one. A flood of incredible contentment swept over me, which only brought to mind the sad realization of how long it had been since I'd last entertained such a joyous sensation.

My thoughts veered back to Alex, and therefore the doubts and frustrations from which I had tried to flee. It was then I saw clearly that lesson in life all must learn--that since you can't run away from yourself, you can't run away from your problems. My situation was not the product of J.B.'s past, Alex's blind idolization of his father, or even Alex's moodiness, but rather my own unwillingness to face the facts of my life as they were instead of how I wanted them to be. In truth, my discontentment with my marriage was the end result of a series of choices I had made, most in avoidance of confronting my true feelings. And starting long before I had met Alex.

It was then I looked up to see the embodiment of my most basic regret. Steven was standing just inside the gate. For a moment I thought it was an imagined reflection of my longing brought to life by my sudden inner clarity. But then Steven removed his hat and ran long fingers through his curly hair while arranging his face to show a calm belied by the sudden flush of his cheeks. He moved forward without once diverting his eyes from mine.

When he spoke, his voice was rough with the effects of his amazement. "This is a nice surprise!"

When I next became aware of my surroundings, I was standing on the first step up to the porch with my arms around Steven and my face buried in his neck. Never before had I felt so overwhelmed with the urgent need to feel a man's arms around me. But when I felt the pressure of his mouth on mine, my responding surge of longing was replaced almost immediately with panic as I realized how public was our view. Pushing away from him, I took hold of his hand and led him to the swing.

"I guess you're wondering what I'm doing here after so long?"

He grinned, the warmth of it stopping my heart as he said, "I don't really care."

"You don't?" I looked into his eyes for reassurance.

"I only care that you're here." Then, with a twist to his smile, he said, "Especially considering the enthusiasm of your greeting." Reaching up to brush from my face a wisp of hair clinging to my damp forehead, he added, "I've missed you more than I can say."

"I've missed you, too." Like water set free by the cracking of a dam, my words poured out. "Oh, Steven, it's more than just missing you. I should never have married Alex. I don't know why I couldn't admit to myself that I had strong feelings for you."

He nodded slowly, looking out to the Alabama Hills. "I know. It wasn't until I saw you with Alex and I felt such strong jealousy, that I realized I'd been in love with you for months. But it was too late. You were seeing Alex." He turned to meet my eyes. "But my feelings haven't changed."

We both blushed, suddenly awkward now that our feelings for one another had been spoken in such an immediate explosion of honesty. We sat on the swing, keeping an appropriate space between us, but our hands clasped together on the seat under the drape of my skirt.

"Our parents are at the town hall," he informed me. "The reclamation efforts for the Valley are being discussed. It's caused a lot of excitement."

"And brought hope back to some of the ranchers that haven't been doing well?"

"Right. It could make a big difference."

"The major shift of our fortunes." He looked at me with a raised brow. "I heard our fathers talking about that many times when I was a child. Do you think this is it?"

"Everyone hopes so. With more water, we could grow more crops and increase our herds. Then more people would settle here, bringing in more jobs. That would mean more growth and stability. Some say it'd make an impact as far as Nevada." After a moment he looked directly into my eyes and said, "I guess I do want to know why you're here without any notice."

My mind raced for a short explanation as I refused to meet the intensity of his gaze. I didn't want to give away too much of the truth, not wanting to put Alex in a bad light, even as irritated with him as I was. But I also wanted Steven to understand why I wasn't happy. He watched me grasping for words and laughed. "This is the first time I've ever seen you at a loss for words!" Then he sobered. "Hey, Alex hasn't been unkind to you has he?"

Knowing he meant physically violent, I quickly reassured him. "No. But he may have abandoned me."

"He left you?" He was incredulous. Then, after a moment's hesitation, "What do you mean 'may have'?"

"He left without telling me where he was going, or when he plans to be back. So did J.B. They ran away from a terrible situation they couldn't deal with, and I got so angry at their leaving without talking to me first that I left, too."

"What happened to bring all this on?"

"Alex found out the truth about his father's past."

"Was it so different than he thought it was? Or so bad?"

"J.B. was the youngest of a group of convicts that escaped from the Nevada State Penitentiary in 1871."

"The Nevada State Pen in 1871?" His face showed the realization of what this meant. "The Convict Lake convicts?"

"Yes."

"Whoa! That's quite a difference from the man whose virtues Alex bragged about during his visits."

"I know. And Alex isn't handling it very well at all."

"But surely he won't stay away forever," Steven reasoned, "or probably even very long. He probably just needs time alone to think it through."

"I'm sure you're right." However, I was oddly disappointed at the prospect of Alex's reappearance, which thought in turn immediately filled me with guilt.

Steven lifted my hand from the swing and held it as though it was a wondrous treasure never seen before. With his other hand he traced the path of each finger to my palm, touching the skin so gently that if my eyes had been closed, I would have thought it the brush of a butterfly's wing. But the quickening of my breathing and the tingle of my senses told me differently.

"I can't believe you're here," he whispered, bending his head to kiss my wrist. "I didn't think dreams ever came true."

"Have you dreamt of this moment?" How hard can a heart beat without exploding?

"Both sleeping and awake." Taking a deep breath, and his voice very low, he asked, "So why did you come here when you decided to run away from home?"

"Because I wasn't running *from* home, I was running *to* it. I've longed to come home for two years, but Alex always came up with a reason why I shouldn't."

Steven cleared his throat and shifted his weight. "I might have some insight as to why he did that."

Surprised, I asked, "How?"

"The morning he left here the first time, I waylaid him at our barn when he came to get his horse. We had a bit of a confrontation."

"A fight?" I was aghast.

"No, no. I just told him I didn't want him coming back here thinking he was going to court you. He asked me if we were betrothed. Of course, I had to admit we weren't. So he told me where I could stick my interference, and that you were the only one that could turn him away."

"Oh, Steven!"

"I know. I should have spoken to you then. But the point is that he's known all this time that I care for you. So, of course he wouldn't want you to come home where I am. I might have gained the courage to speak up, as indeed I have. He's a smart guy."

"Yes." I looked up at the mountains and mumbled, "So many secrets."

"What?"

"Nothing."

"Was there more leading up to this revelation about his father that made you want to get away from the Double R?"

I pulled my hand away. "Things have always been strained between Alex and myself, after we left here anyway. He's not very good at sharing his feelings, or anything else for that matter. Recently things have become very strained between us. He's extremely moody, governed more by what goes on around him than real stability of character would allow. I never know from one day to the next what mood he'll be in."

His voice was tense as he asked, "You're sure he's never hurt you?"

"Oh, no. He'd never do anything like that. No, it's more a slow starving of affection by withholding the nurturing of attention. My body has been fed, but my spirit feels like a thin waif."

He looked down at the body in question and smiled slowly. "I certainly see nothing wrong with it." He quickly looked toward the mountains and cleared his throat.

Looking at him with a myriad of conflicting emotions, words poured from me before I could edit them. "I should never have left here, or tried to live my life without you in it. I had no preparation of how to endure it. But I just couldn't balance our parent's treating us like siblings with so many others expecting us to continue through life as a couple."

He nodded in agreement. "Whatever the reason, the problem comes down to us. We simply couldn't admit the truth of our feelings. It's easy blaming others, but the choice was ultimately ours alone."

"You're right." I laid my hand on his arm. "You've thought a lot about this, haven't you?"

He nodded. "I wanted to understand what I'd done to mess everything up. I figured I'd missed my chance with you and I wanted to be sure I never repeated it with someone else." He looked up at the mountains. "The thing is, I don't want a chance with anyone else."

I looked up to Mt. Whitney, hoping my namesake might inspire me with a solution. Before I could say anything, Steven asked, "Are you leaving Alex?"

The bold question was a harsh slap of reality that I wasn't sure I was ready to address. Divorce was a shameful thing, easily ostracizing a woman from society and even many churches. If I left Alex for anything less than public abuse, chronic drunkenness, or abandonment, even my family would not be welcomed where before they were. I only said, "Probably. But I'm not sure how to do it or how soon it might be."

We heard familiar voices getting nearer and quickly stood up, and further apart. Mother's squeal of surprise announced that she had seen me. But Father moved faster and ran to embrace me, followed closely behind by Mother, Aunt Charlotte and Uncle Vince. Everyone talking at once, we moved inside and settled around the big kitchen table with food and drink. I then relayed to them the details of my life and J.B.'s shocking revelations.

Of course, they were all amazed. But while Steven and Aunt Charlotte remained silent, the others reassured me that this was simply a situation that could be resolved with compassion and understanding. I was told to be patient and loving with Alex, and forgiving of J.B. The latter had been easy, but I wasn't sure I was capable of the former. But I said nothing.

Mother laid a soft hand on mine. "My dear, no marriage is without its trials. Alex will in time forgive his father. Their relationship may change, but if Alex accepts that his father isn't a saint after all, it could bring them even closer."

Squeezing my hand, Mother smiled reassuringly and soon the conversation had moved into other channels, to them the matter of my life and happiness settled. But no one knew of my frustration, its roots spreading far beyond the confrontation between Alex and J.B. If I sat there telling them about my trials with Mrs. Lewis, the long periods spent alone, or the months of boredom where I was allowed to do nothing that challenged my thought except for a few charitable good works, it would be received as childish whining.

As I stood with my parents on the porch watching the Perrys leave for their home, I fought the urge to grab Steven and kiss him good-night. He must have felt the same, because the look on his face as he glanced back over his shoulder at me was one of woeful yearning. Hoping no one had noticed our exchange, I followed my parents back inside the house.

That night as I passed Father on the way to my bedroom, he said, "I want to show you what Carrie gave me for my last birthday."

He led me to his shaving stand in the master bedroom and proudly handed me what he called a Gillette Safety Razor. "It's a new way for men to shave with less nicking of skin. I can even insert a new blade when the old one gets dull. Can you beat that?"

"No more stropping of the old straight-edged razor for you." Looking at my handsome father grinning like a child with a new toy, I felt another wave of inordinate happiness at being home.

Early the next morning I saddled Mother's horse and rode to the far side of Diaz Lake, as far from the main road as I could get. The reeds along the lake's edge were thick and the large cottonwoods lent cover for the many birds sheltering among yellow leaves beginning to consider the coming fall.

After slipping a halter over the horse's headstall, I tied it to a tree and for several minutes stood by the edge of the water just breathing deeply. Returning to the cover of the cottonwoods, I settled myself on the partially decayed stump of a fallen tree. While enjoying the morning breeze that promised a warm afternoon, I listened to the rasp of the ravens in the tree tops and watched ground squirrels tumble over one another in play. However, I soon became aware that tears of despair were rolling down my cheeks.

Over and over I thought, "This is where I belong. I'm a different person here--open and relaxed and alive to who I really am." In one moment of startling conviction, I determined that all my plans from that point on would be preparation for returning to Lone Pine.

A horse whinnied nearby and I heard it coming closer, the ping of its shoes on rock alerting me to the fact that it wasn't one of the loose horses in the pasture not far from me. I was surprised anyone else would be riding this way so early in the day, but when I saw the rider, I was even more surprised. Steven smiled at me as he dismounted.

"Mother said she'd seen you ride south out of town, and I knew you'd end up here."

We spent the next hour talking about my intention of leaving Alex and returning home, and what Steven and I would do then. But not wanting my parents to question why I'd been gone so long, we soon rode back, parting before we reached town to hide the fact that we'd been together.

That afternoon spent with my parents was the most fun I'd had in a long time. We worked in the garden, talked about articles in the newspaper, played cards, and cleaned jars in preparation for making jelly the next morning.

In the cool of evening Father and I walked east along the dirt road toward the old cemetery seldom used any longer, my arm tucked through his as he walked at a pace comfortable for me. Rabbits raced into their holes, lizards darted under rocks, a coyote bounded away into the undergrowth, but the cattle in the pasture watched us unconcerned. The scent of warm sage hung on the cooling air and I breathed deeply, wondering why Owens Valley sage smelled so much better than any other.

After a long companionable silence, Father said, "I heard from the estate attorney for Emily's Uncle Herbert. Your mother always felt a great fondness for him, even if she didn't spend all that much time with him. But he was willing to take her in after her parents died in the Chicago fire. As you know, he traveled a lot on business and that's why she stayed with Carrie's family so much."

"Was there something odd about his estate?"

"Yes and no," he chuckled. "He left her a few hundred dollars, but the attorney revealed what his business was. Want to guess?"

"I have no idea."

"He was a professional gambler! Imagine, Emily never knew that. The attorney wanted to know if Emily would mind." Since I knew Mother's sense of humor and love of the absurd, I merely laughed. "I wrote him back and said she'd revel in it, and to send the money and a full explanation direct to her."

Late the next morning Steven and I managed to get away from everyone by riding through the locust forest west of town and into the Alabama Hills by way of Tuttle Creek Canyon. The steep weathered walls of granite and huge boulders through which our narrow trail meandered cast shadows over us, and I felt myself as in a sanctuary. We were closed off from the rest of the world and wrapped in a cocoon of our own reality--whatever we wanted that to be. Following the trail by the edge of the ravine cut by Tuttle Creek, the trees were showing hints of their fall color, but the profusion of their leaves still partially hid the creek below that was gurgling with summer's light flow.

We watered our horses at one of the few places where there was easy access to the creek, and where the water moved so slowly that it allowed watercress to form across its surface. Standing next to Steven beneath the shade of an old gnarled tree, I lay my head on his shoulder.

"My parents stopped here for a picnic when they were courting," I told him.

"Really?"

"Yes. It was the first time Mother had ever been completely alone with a man. And she loved it."

"She told you that?"

"No." Sitting on a large rock by the water, I told him about Mother's letters to Aunt Carrie back in the late 1800's. I also told him about the mischief our mothers had gotten into while living in Bodie. He laughed with delight, the sound of it filling my heart and replacing any unhappiness I'd brought with me from the Double R.

I closed my eyes and listened to the soft chatter of birds while breathing deeply the fresh essence of the surrounding plants and the rich water-soaked earth. In the distance a coyote howled a soft aria and was immediately joined in a duet by another. Lulled by the all-consuming intimacy of the moment, I forgot myself and said, "I wish the coyotes were singing for us, like they did for my parents on their wedding day."

When I heard the slight intake of his breath, I opened my eyes and turned away from him, fiercely chiding myself for my foolishness. It was surely too soon to say such a thing, not to mention too much of an assumption of his intentions. Placing his hands on my shoulders, and with his body pressing against mine from behind, he whispered in my ear, "Let's pretend it's *our* wedding day, right now."

Turning around and looking up into his eyes for a long moment, I was in no doubt of what he was implying. And because I wanted so desperately the same thing, I refused to acknowledge the possible repercussions of such an act.

We rode silently a little further into the hills to a cave where we had so often escaped as children. Once there, we spread the picnic blanket on the soft earth inside the small cave and then, without words or warning, he pulled me into his arms. Our lips met with an intensity of craving that only years of frustrated yearning and unfulfilled imagination could fuel.

He took his time unbuttoning my waist and loosening the laces of my corset as he savored the anticipation of what he had for so long coveted. With my thought focused on the magnitude of my longing, suddenly the only truth in the universe was our love and that moment in time. With the warmth of his hands on the naked skin of my hips, he pulled me to him, his eyes never leaving my face. I exhaled slowly and relaxed against him with my head on his chest.

After a moment, he cupped my face in his hands and kissed me gently on the lips, and I knew he was giving me an opportunity to change my mind. Instead, I tore at his clothes, helping him shed them onto the dirt before running my hands down his chest and around to his back. The cave walls protected us from the world as we lay down on the blanket, using my folded skirt as a pillow.

The gentle scrape of his rough rancher's hands across my skin teased deeply submerged passions to the surface in a taunt of what I'd felt when with the man I called husband. Steven was rugged cowboy and refined townsman, my childhood friend, and now my lover. When he looked down at me, a corner of his mouth turned up in a soft smile, and I had no thoughts of anyone else, nor the status of my nuptial state. I had come home not only to where I grew up, but to where I belonged. And whether in a bed or a cave, as long as I was with Steven, it felt too natural and right to question.

An hour later our skin gleamed with the sweat of spent passion unlike anything books, marriage, or fantasies had prepared me to expect. As I lay in Steven's arms while he stroked my hair, my conscience still didn't bother me. I sighed deeply, but didn't smile.

He took my hand in his and kissed each knuckle slowly. "Have you been so unhappy?"

"Well, I've not walked upon the moors beneath stormy skies like a brooding Bronte heroine, although I have wandered paths through green meadows. But I dare say I've matched the loneliness in their hearts, and even possibly the sterility of their lives."

"I certainly understand about the sterility of life." He ran his hand down my cheek, kissed me briefly, and then got up to begin the process of dressing. When I leaned on him while pulling on my boots, he said, "I tried to fill my time by long hours of hard work. When that didn't do it, I added community projects. So now I don't have hardly a minute to myself."

Responding to his professed anguish would have necessitated the need of apologizing for his pain, so I chose to keep silent. He seemed to understand and turned to me as he buttoned his shirt. "I know. I could have spoken up before you married Alex. We're both responsible for our situation."

Still, I said nothing, not wanting to analyze the past or remind myself about Alex and the Double R. I only wanted to savor the new intimacy forged with Steven. When we finished dressing, we climbed down from the cave and led the horses to the edge of the rocks where the land became more open.

"I'm so sorry," I said, abruptly breaking my silence as contrition and guilt caught up with me. "If I'd taken more time to know Alex before marrying him, then you and I would be together now."

"Maybe." He sat down on a boulder, picked up one of its smaller cousins, and threw it as far as he could down the hill. "I once overheard a traveling preacher tell one of our ranch hands that 'Life sometimes takes a meandering path, yet still goes in the right direction.' Maybe that's true of us."

The rest of our conversation was about general topics. By the time we returned our horses to the barn on his ranch, we were ready for the lemonade Aunt Charlotte brought to us under the trees. I invited her to join us, and then tried hard to focus as she chatted about the changes in the area and the lives of people I'd known all my life. It would have been easier if Steven hadn't been sitting next to me, his shoulder touching mine.

The following day, after Mother and I finished cleaning up the kitchen, we sat relaxing on the front porch with Father. Steven came by leading the same horse I'd ridden the day before and had liked so much, a big smile on his face.

"Ready for another ride?" he hollered across the yard.

As I ran back outside after having changed my clothes, Mother asked, "Where are you going?"

"Does it matter?" I responded, embraced by pure happiness. She shrugged and returned to her darning of socks, but Father looked up from his paper and gave me a strange, penetrating stare. Finding it odd that Mother's famous intuition had failed her just when Father seemed to have found his, I simply ran more quickly down the path toward Steven.

We rode north and east of town to the Owens River. The horses nibbled the tender grasses at the water's edge while we sat on the welcome sacrifice of a log once a giant cottonwood. Felled by lightening years before, its healthy progeny surrounded us. The translucent leaves fluttered in the cool morning breeze that also rippled the surface of the narrow river as it coursed toward Owens Lake.

Orange butterflies danced from leaf to leaf and ravens called out their rasping call from the top of a near tree, while the horses' strong jaws slowly crunched the grass. Two curious squirrels ran up and sat a few feet from us. With some mysterious invisible provocation, they jumped upon each other and rolled across the dirt in a noisy chattering ball of gray fur that broke apart only when they hit the base of a tree. Barn swallows trailing their distinctive forked tails snapped up small insects hovering above the water, showing the croaking ravens in the trees how graceful flight can be. The ravens spread their long wings and swiftly rose high into the sky, joining a kettle of turkey vultures swirling over the river. Avian one-upmanship.

Our stillness and quiet was a patience learned through years of practice and borne of a desire to be accepted into the earth's natural rhythms. As we began to talk, most of the creatures moved further away or higher into the trees. Only the squirrels, being curious and unafraid, ventured closer as though to eavesdrop upon our conversation. Grateful that it wasn't people watching us, I let Steven take my hand in his and hold it briefly to his lips. Smiling, I laid my head on his shoulder and his arm slid around my waist. Unfortunately, the practical side of my nature took that moment to surface.

"We've a problem to deal with, my love," I whispered, as though afraid that the words spoken louder would reveal a problem too harsh to be faced.

He said nothing for a long time, then surprised me by asking, "Do you call Alex that?"

"What?" I sat up straight and faced him.

"'My love'. You've used it several times with me over the last few days."

"No. I've never called him that." After a moment's reflection, I added, "Actually, I have no pet names for him."

Another long moment of silence followed, broken again by Steven. "Why did you marry him?" I didn't miss the misery in his voice.

"I thought you'd decided to be philosophical about that."

He made a noise somewhere between mirth and self-derision. "I guess not."

I answered carefully because I knew the answer held the importance of a final statement. "It wasn't only because I hadn't admitted my feelings for you, but I also wanted to please my parents. They had certain expectations for my future, and I just accepted that they were right."

"When did you begin to figure it out?"

"It began the morning I left here. When the wagon pulled away from the house, I turned to wave to you but you were no longer there. I was surprised by how disappointed I felt."

"I couldn't bear to watch you slowly roll into the distance. It was too much like the fading away of a happy dream when you're forced to wake up."

"Yes, well, seeing the emptiness beneath the tree was a terrible wrench. And the beginning of a slowly dawning realization."

"Then why did you keep going?"

"I was reminded of the seriousness of the situation when Andy mentioned newly married Alex waiting for me. I was married, and my parents were joyous over the union. Besides, can you imagine the scandal if I hadn't chosen to keep going?"

"I guess I understand that." He tossed a rock into the swiftly moving water. "I've tried to go forward, too."

Walking a few feet away, I turned back to him and asked, "Are you trying to punish me?"

"Of course not." He stood up and walked to the water's edge before turning back toward me. "But I guess I need you to know just how unhappy *I've* been."

"You think that because I've been married and starting a new life that I must have been happy, don't you?"

"Maybe."

I walked to his side and stood so that my shoulder nestled into his side. He put his arm around me and I told him, "There were times when

I enjoyed myself. The country around Bridgeport is beautiful. And I'm fond of Alex too, although he's unnervingly moody. I've enjoyed Irene's company, too. The trip to Yosemite was an adventure I'll always happily remember. But I've also been constantly frustrated by the limitation of my life, intimidated by Mrs. Lewis who hates me, lonely most of the time, bored almost to insanity, a little fearful of J.B. while yet liking the man, and never feeling truly appreciated or respected by anyone. Alex treats me like a casual possession that he can lavish with attention, or ignore completely. But he can't, or won't, understand that I need some degree of independence and purpose to my life, other than just being there when he decides he wants a wife."

After a moment's consideration, Steven said, "So I guess we just have to accept that life hasn't been all we wanted it to be for the last few years and move on from there."

"There's nothing else we can do. Like you said before, we can't change the past."

"Yes, I see that." After a moment, he added, "Damn!"

"What?"

"You have no choice but to return to Bridgeport, do you?"

My stomach lurched. "I suppose not."

"What will you do then?" The muscles in the arm around me tightened as he clenched his fists.

"I lay awake most of last night thinking about that. If Alex doesn't come back, I've been abandoned and I can come back here as the injured party. That way people will be sympathetic and I can go forward with a divorce."

"And we can start our lives together." There was a certainty in his voice that made me smile. But my throat tightened at the thought of how long our happiness might have to wait.

"And if he does return?" He pulled me tighter to him.

"Then I'll have to explain how unhappy I've been, and tell him I'm coming home for awhile to think over what will happen next. Then once I'm here, I can write him and tell him it's over. And hope people don't judge me too harshly."

"As much as I hate to ask this, when will you be leaving?"

"Tomorrow, I think."

"So soon?" His eyes gleamed damp, but he swallowed hard and was immediately in control again.

"The sooner I go home, the sooner I can leave before he returns. That way, I can claim he abandoned me."

That night I confronted everyone about the unhappy details of my marriage, maintaining my courage by holding in mind the picture of Steven and myself in the cave. Not surprisingly, I found everyone caring and sympathetic. Aunt Charlotte was the only one that showed no initial surprise, but to give her credit she said nothing. Overwhelmed by my predicament, Uncle Vince hugged me while patting my back like a colicky child.

We all knew that if the situation wasn't carefully arranged to look as though the marriage was unbearable, I would have a very difficult time entering again into society as a decent woman. The word "divorce" was so onerous that it wasn't uncommon for women to invent dead husbands and present themselves to society as widows. Even if it was suspected otherwise, it gave the townspeople the option of pretending they believed it true.

Of course, no one knew about my relationship with Steven. That would have been more than even Aunt Charlotte's equanimity could have borne, considering that it would mean I was leaving my husband for another man--a sure course that would lead not only myself into ruin, but also my family and anyone claiming me as friend.

Not long before dusk, Steven and I excused ourselves and walked east down the lane to the cemetery. We'd planned to just talk about our future, but one thing led to another and we were soon laying down in the long untended grass, blocked from the seldom-traveled road by a large stone monument to a Lone Pine pioneer. We made love while still clothed, caught up in a frantic effort to cement our commitment and reassure ourselves of the other's love. We spoke only to whisper over and over, "I love you."

As we left the cemetery, I caught my dress on the thorn of a wild rose by the gate. Steven reached down and plucked the last red bloom from the old vine twining along the white picket fence. As he tucked it in my hair, he kissed me gently and said, "I love you rose red."

Smiling, I proclaimed, "I'll never see a wild rose again without thinking of you and our love."

Parting from everyone early the next morning was easier than the last time, because I planned to be returning in a matter of weeks. As the train pulled out of the station, I looked up through the window at the sky and saw one of the familiar smooth, rounded Sierra waves. But lying atop this was an even brighter cloud, windswept into the classic image of an angel's wing spread in flight. I took it as a message from the Valley, waving good-bye and asking me to return soon. I reverently promised I would.

The hours that followed on the train afforded me the opportunity to begin my campaign of separation from the Double R. Eager to get to the ranch so I could pack and get away before Alex or J.B. returned, I was also prepared for a confrontation no matter how unpleasant it might be. Thoughts of my future with Steven gave me strength, and memories of the moments spent in his arms nourished my determination.

CHAPTER 11

It was mid-October, with the Double R drama of 1904 almost over, and three days after my return to the ranch. Packed bags were stacked in my closet so I could leave the next day. That afternoon, however, Alex walked into the house. There was no joyous greeting, but at least he offered a civil apology for having worried everyone. After asking me to be patient, he then ignored me for the next two days.

Since he also stayed out of my room at night, I was even denied that opportunity to have a serious discussion with him. Each morning, I was barely awake when I would hear him leave the house, with no idea where he was going or if he would even be returning at the end of each cool, fall day. I unpacked some of my clothes, resigned to the fact that it would be a few more days before I could tell Alex my plans.

Wandering aimlessly through the house, seeking even a tiny degree of pleasure, I watched Alex's shifting moods and waited for the best time to approach him. As the days passed, my spirit sighed like the last spent ember of a dying fire. I longed to rekindle the optimism I had felt when leaving Lone Pine, and each morning as I swallowed the last of the morning's coffee, there was at the back of my throat a lump of tight unshed tears. A good portion of my misery was the frustration that I couldn't make time move faster toward my freeing confrontation with Alex, but mostly predominant was the misery of being separated from Steven.

The one time Alex ate supper with me in the dining room, he listened without comment to my brief description of several carefully chosen portions of my time in Lone Pine. He was totally unconcerned about why I had gone home when I did, which I thought odd considering his knowledge of Steven's feelings for me.

J.B. had returned to the ranch only the day before my arrival, and other than looking at my return with relief, had stayed in his room or in town, often until late at night. But he was always absent at meals. After almost two weeks, Alex began joining me for supper, and in the morning occasionally even delayed his escape from the house long enough for a quick breakfast with me in the kitchen. Although mostly quiet meals, there were a few polite exchanges so cursory that a stranger would have thought us mere acquaintances. Whenever I summoned the courage to open the topic of leaving, it was as though Alex sensed it and immediately left the house. I unpacked the rest of my clothes.

When a month had passed, I wrote to my parents to tell them I had not yet found Alex in a mood sufficiently receptive that I could follow through with my plans to be home for Christmas. The stress of having to make that admission, and simply contending with the whole unresolved situation, began to affect my stomach. Each morning I awoke in a state of dread and with an unsettled nausea, not helped by Alex's continuing aloofness. After a light breakfast, I would retire to my room not caring if it looked like I too was hiding from the world. Only after I was in bed would Alex leave his study and transfer to his bedroom.

So oppressive was the atmosphere that I continued to wait for a more opportune moment to initiate what I knew would be an explosive confrontation. I began to feel like the patient barn cat that waits for the right moment to pounce on its prey. The depth of Alex's depression became so extreme that I feared the trauma of my leaving might over-balance him. Soon I was no longer sleeping well, and was therefore dealing with a perpetual state of exhaustion. This made the idea of avoiding a showdown even more appealing.

During this unpleasant period, Mrs. Lewis moved through the house like a dark sinister shadow, discussing household business with Sing in a funereal tone. She avoided me whenever possible, refused to meet my gaze, and used Sing as a means of communicating with me. I wondered more than once if she knew the cause of the tension between J.B. and Alex, or was supposing that it was somehow due to me. The one time I caught her watching me as I came down the stairs, there was so much loathing on her face that from then on I added her to my list of things to avoid.

Sing's usual smile was seldom seen, replaced with a puzzled tentativeness that was wrenchingly pathetic. I missed his bright cheerfulness almost as much as I did Steven, my family, and Lone Pine.

But life went on, as did the ranch routine. Lacking comfortable and open communication between us, Alex and I settled instead for an excruciating civility. Finally, spurred by the irritation of being constantly unwell, my patience with him gave out. He had never before been so strangely morose and I wanted to scream at him, "Get over it! What does your father's past have to do with all of us getting on with our lives?"

But before I could tell him that I'd had enough and our marriage was over, a new and unexpected development arose. I realized I was expecting a child. My mood turned from irritation and impatience to carefully controlled terror. One thing I knew--I had to find a way to get Alex into my bed before more time passed, otherwise there would be no way I could pretend the baby's spring arrival was premature.

There had to be no question in peoples' minds that Alex was the baby's father. If even a small doubt occurred to anyone, in no time it would be all over the town. Even more disgraceful than a divorced woman, was a woman who had given birth to a child out of wedlock. And the only thing worse than either of these would be a married woman expecting another man's child. It would be a life-long curse to both mother and child if such a situation was made public, and even marrying the father would not erase the shame. In fact, it would only pass the disgrace on to him. With all of this in mind, I spent the rest of the day in a state of extreme anxiety that lurked beneath everything I did.

Alex came inside late in the afternoon, just as the cool of the November evening began. I was sitting by the fire with a letter of many pages on my lap, staring into the distance and bemoaning my fate, although no doubt giving the impression of deep thought about the letter's substance.

Draping his jacket over the back of a chair, he asked, "Another letter from home?"

Forcing a smile, I said, "You make it sound like I get one every day."

"Well, since you arrived home from your trip, you've been getting more mail than you did before."

Eager to keep the conversation going, I told him, "There's a lot happening in the Valley right now. And they're eager to know if I'll be visiting again before winter sets in."

I omitted telling him that they were wondering why I hadn't yet confronted Alex, or that Steven had asked Mother's permission to include a letter of his own in with hers. That one was in my pocket, as yet unopened.

"Mother says there are some men starting to mine for gold around Tonopah, Nevada. If they're successful and there's a big rush there, the ranchers are ready to ship alfalfa and hay to them. So everyone is very excited about that. Father added a page. Do you remember a number of months ago when he mentioned having met an engineer named Lippincott with the Reclamation Service?"

"It's not a name one easily forgets." He stretched out in his chair on the other side of the fireplace, giving me his attention.

"Just before I arrived there, he'd run into Mr. Lippincott again in Bishop. Evidently, he's well known for having built irrigation systems in the state and they figure he was in the Valley again in that regard. He is, after all, working on reclamation for the area. Anyway, he says Lippincott visited again while I was there, but Father didn't know it at the time."

"Irrigation systems," Alex cut in. "You know about the big Monoville ditch project back in 1860?"

"No."

"Monoville was three-quarters of a mile from any water, and the miners were in desperate need of it to extract the gold from the dry gulches and ravines. So in the summer of 1860, 300 men started the United Water Ditch Company, putting in $50 each. Then they hired 200 men to construct a fourteen-mile ditch. It started at the east fork of the Walker River, flowed down to Dogtown Creek, then southwest five miles to Virginia Creek, and east around to Monoville. It took 40,000 feet of lumber, with construction beginning in June and finished by the end of October."

"My goodness! What an incredible accomplishment." After a moment, I continued. "Anyway, Father says that in late September, only a day after I left, William Mulholland, along with former Mayor of Los Angeles Fred Eaton, came to the Valley. Father says they're both engineers, so he wanted to meet them. But they kept to themselves and drove their own two-horse rig, not even fishing like most visitors from Los Angeles. Then they left as abruptly as they'd arrived."

"All that engineering know-how and they're just there for a short buggy ride? Pretty odd considering how difficult it is to reach the valley from the south, even if they came part way by train."

"It does seem like something's going on," I agreed, "but I can't see what it might be. Why should they be interested in the Valley's reclamation?"

"Doesn't Eaton own ranch land in Inyo County? Maybe they just wanted a break from city life. After all, with the drought they had in most of Southern California this summer, the green river valley and all its rushing creeks must be pretty inviting."

I shrugged and prepared to change the subject. "Oh well, I'm sure we'll find out soon enough."

I had more pressing matters to think about. Not only did I need to figure out a way to get Alex into my bed, I was also preparing a supper party for that night. We had invited Irene, who would come from town with Mr. and Mrs. Sanchez in their wagon. Mr. Sanchez and J.B. had been friends since both had come to the Big Meadows area back in the '70's, J.B. to ranch and Arturo Sanchez to set up as blacksmith and hostler for the freight teams passing through.

Using this as an opportunity to gain a little ground with Mrs. Lewis, I proposed we plan the menu together. She would have none of it. Either she did it all, as was "befitting her position in the household", or I would have to do it alone. I chose the latter, and she chose to visit her sister near the Vining's ranch in the tiny village of Lakeview.

Left to myself, I was determined to provide a sumptuous meal and hopefully gain enough approval from Alex that he'd once again warm to me. Sing's smile when I told him what I had in mind for dinner was encouraging. The centerpiece was a pile of apples in a silver bowl between tall candles in their tiered silver holders, with tendrils of dried flowers beneath. I silently thanked the good taste of the woman who had lost the silver to J.B.'s winning poker hand.

The guests were fed well with clear soup, baked fish, grilled beef steak, molded rice ring, string beans with onion, hot yeast rolls, and lemon pie. Afterwards, we had port in the great room, which I insisted be offered also to the women. With a roaring fire adding light along with the lamps, the inviting warmth of the room encouraged a relaxed atmosphere in which the conversation flowed easily.

I sat back and thought to myself, "Success!"

They left beneath a full moon only slightly less bright than the sun and showing the road clearly. After thanking Sing for all his efforts, I retired to my room where my biggest problem looked to be solved. Alex was sitting up in my bed.

"You look surprised," he said.

"You must admit, it's been some time since you've sought me out at night." I undressed behind the screen in front of the wash basin and slipped into one of my better night dresses.

After a long pause, he said, "I've had a lot on my mind."

"About the ranch or J.B.?"

When there was no response, I peeked from behind the screen. He was obviously trying to figure out how much to tell me.

"This is ridiculous," I told him. Moving to my dressing table next to the armoire, I sat on the bench and began brushing my hair. Glancing at his reflection in the mirror, I noted how tensely he leaned against the headboard. "Alex, I know."

"Know what?"

"I overheard your long conversation with J.B. when he told you about his past."

He stared at me as though I had just spoken in a foreign language. All he managed to say was, "How?"

"I was in the hallway by the stairs." Turning to face him, I added, "I'm not proud of having eavesdropped on the two of you, but after all, I am part of this family. At first, I felt guilty, but when you didn't tell me about it, I realized it was a good thing I'd listened. Why do you think I was so patient with your suddenly leaving? If I'd been ignorant of the situation, don't you think I would have demanded an explanation of your departure the minute you returned? Didn't you wonder about that?"

"No. I never did." He was only mildly puzzled at the realization.

"You just accepted that I wouldn't question you about anything you did? Even if that was to ignore me, treat me rudely, and spend all your time away from home?"

"I didn't look at it like that." He shrugged his bare shoulders. "I just expected you to be here when I returned, and you were."

"Maybe I've misled you as to who I am." I stood up and walked over to the waning fire in the small stove, then turned to face him with resolve. "I'm your wife. Let me tell you what that means, and maybe you can pass it along to your precious Mrs. Lewis."

"Mrs. Lewis? Don't you like her?"

"Oh, my God!" Throwing my hands in the air, I let them fall helplessly to my sides. "We despise each other, Alex. From the day I arrived here, she's treated me like an interloper with the intelligence of a five year old. But it's your attitude I care about."

"What do mean?"

"You've excluded me from your life! I don't know what you think about anything. You didn't let me share your pain at finding out about your father's past. You don't talk to me about ranch business any more, and barely about what goes on in town. I'm stuck out here isolated from other women and friendships I might make if you let me ride into town. But you seem to frown upon that as not befitting my position, whatever that is." When I realized I'd begun to pace, a little voice at the back of my mind kept telling me to calm down before he got out of bed.

"You've never complained," he pointed out, "so I thought you were happy."

The look of puzzled confusion on his face infuriated me, but then again, I had to admit that I was somewhat culpable. Sitting on the bed next to him and taking his hand in mine, I swallowed a sigh of irritation.

"This is a lot for you to be taking in all at once, I know. But lately I've been finding my way through a labyrinth of emotions. I'm living in a house I'm not allowed to change to reflect my personality, discouraged from spending too much time in the kitchen, scowled at if I decide to clean something, criticized if I spend too much time outside riding or walking, and even my friendship with Irene is looked at askance. Worst of all, I'm homesick all the time."

"And your husband is so self-absorbed that he isn't aware of any of this." His old twinkle of humor made an appearance for the first time in weeks. "Whitney, I'm so sorry."

"Me too. I should have been more forthcoming from the beginning. I've tried too hard to be what I thought you wanted me to be, and not enough of who I really am. I can't live that way."

"You don't have to." After a moment, he added, "Should I expect you to be as out-spoken as your mother from now on?"

Thrown by the abrupt question, I laughed. "I don't think so, but if I said out loud all that I think, I'm sure you'd consider me worse."

"Well," he grinned, "your father seems to do okay, so maybe I shouldn't worry. You just be yourself." He slipped the robe from my shoulder and stroked my bare arm. "And I'll make it clear to Mrs. Lewis that this is your house and your decisions are to be respected."

Overwhelmed with gratitude, I leaned forward and threw my arms around him. "Oh Alex, thank you."

That night I achieved my goal, and relieved that our lovemaking had been so brief as to be perfunctory. I was almost asleep when he got up to leave my room. Relaxed and happy at the sweetness of his earlier understanding, I was taken by surprise when he turned at the door to the dressing room and said, "Don't think I've forgotten that you kept from me the fact that you've known about J.B. all this time."

Thrown by the hardness of his tone, I asked with a forced calm, "Can't we just forget about how we know, and concentrate on *what* we know instead?"

After a moment's hesitation, he responded, "I guess that's the important thing, isn't it?"

"Yes." I carefully kept my voice soft. "And after all, doesn't the quality of his adult life count enough to balance out what happened when he was a young man?"

"Maybe. When I was eighteen, I'm not sure I'd have been able to stand up to a group of murderous thugs either."

"So you've come to terms with what happened?"

"All I know is, whenever I try to think of what he could have done instead, I can't come up with much."

"Have you told J.B. how you feel?"

"I should, shouldn't I? It can't be easy for him thinking his son is disappointed in him."

"Are you?"

He shrugged. "Somewhat. I still feel a little like my whole life has been a fraud. But I guess his past has nothing to do with the way he raised me. He never actually lied to me about his past, just left out a lot."

"Why don't you talk to him?"

"I will. Soon."

After I was sure Alex was in his room to stay, I took Steven's letter from the pocket of my dress and read its short content. He told me he loved me still, and hoped I felt the same, encouraging me to waste no more time on sparing Alex's feelings. He just wanted me home. After reading the short note so many times that it was soon memorized, I gently relinquished it to the fire and watched it burn down to ash. I then crawled back into bed and cried myself to sleep.

A light snow began to fall early in December, and I wrote home with the disappointing news that I'd definitely be unable to join them that month. But I still held out hope that I would be home in January.

The Christmas holidays on the ranch were pleasant, but not memorable, and soon after, the snow melted during an unseasonable warming trend. Especially welcome was seeing Alex and J.B. occasionally talking together and relaxed in one another's company. Life was bearable again, which made it particularly awkward to claim to be so unhappy that I wanted to leave my husband and return home. But it had to be faced soon, before my condition kept me from traveling.

However unfair it might have been, since it was necessary that everyone associate the baby with Alex, my big present to Alex and J.B. that Christmas was the announcement that I was expecting. Alex was tentatively pleased, and J.B. seemed more worried than joyous, but I took it as natural considering that his wife had died not long after Alex was born.

I was careful to say that the baby was due in the summer, unless born early "as I had been". Neither man asked for an exact due date, but I could have kissed J.B. when he said that Alex had been born three weeks early.

However, I still had a big problem. I had to tell my parents and Steven about the baby. As the second week of January began, I lay in bed one morning after a night of restless sleep and decided I could put it off no longer, no matter what Alex's mood might be. "Consequences be damned!" I declared to my dark room. Wanting to tell Steven about our child in person, and not feeling free to do that until I'd confronted Alex, my mind was a muddle of things that I needed to do.

Climbing out of bed in a state of excited resolve, I shivered in a cold more pronounced than on any recent morning and quickly pulled on a warm robe. Throwing back the heavy curtains from the window, ready to greet the dawn, my mouth dropped opened in surprise and stayed that way for several seconds.

Snow! Everything that had the day before been familiar was now buried beneath ill-defined mounds of white. The branches of the pine trees were bent low by thick slabs of icy powder, and occasionally a chunk would slide off onto a deep pile already burying the first three feet of the tree's height. Disoriented black birds stood out in stark contrast, frantic quail ran around scratching the unexpected snow in a desperate search for their morning seed, and a rabbit stood on its hind legs sniffing the air while scanning the snow for a bite of something green. Covering the meadows, the foothills and the Sierra beyond was unmitigated white evidence of the night's storm. It had arrived without the gathering of clouds before dark or the howl of wind, but simply the hard and fast snow fall that buries everything within hours.

Dressing quickly, I rushed downstairs to look out the kitchen windows partially blocked by drifts of snow. Sing stood next to me shaking his head.

"Chores very much trouble now."

"Has Alex seen it? I didn't even look into his room before coming down."

"You not know?"

"What?"

"He leave last night with J.B. after you go to bed early. No snow then. He give me note for you."

My hand shook as I grabbed the note from his hand and read Alex's plea not to be upset with him. Not wanting an argument about his leaving, he had decided to save me that by departing while I was sleeping. He wished me good health not unlike a brother might, and made no mention of when he intended to return.

Sing built up the fire in the small fireplace and made me sit on the sofa in front of it while he returned to the kitchen. At first, I was numb with disbelief, but it slowly changed to the panic that attends being trapped with no hope of escape. Sensing that I needed additional warmth to buffer me not only from the increased cold but also the shock of Alex leaving, Sing brought me a large pot of hot sugary tea with my breakfast. Since finding out about the baby, he had treated me like a fragile porcelain doll. Now he acted as though he was afraid the porcelain might crack.

Although there was no sun, the day lightened and reflected into the house a stark white brightness instead of the usual golden glow. Finally, the snow ceased falling after burying the bottom half of all buildings and leaving the vegetation bowed down in humble poses of submission. In the calm that presaged the winds to follow, a fragile peaked ridge of white ran along each top strand of barbed wire encircling the pastures, interrupted only by a knob of ice atop each post. It was stark and beautiful, and as much of a barrier to my leaving as a locked door would have been. Even a letter could not get through to the south now.

A few days later, after a ranch hand cleared the porch of snow, I stepped outside for a little fresh air. The bushes were anonymous mounds with a few bare branches protruding through, while the pastures were an endless desolation of white without character or shape. While I could detect vague piney smells in the damp freshness, the only sound was the sharp crack of a twig snapping or the soft thud of snow falling from a branch. All normal sounds of animals, nature, or man, were silenced.

A gust of wind came up suddenly, blowing from leaves the lighter powder not yet frozen and creating transparent veils of white drifting on the wind before draping on the first thing in its path. The beauty of the scene only intensified my feeling of solitary confinement, and my initial panic reordered itself into a depressed resignation.

As the snow began to melt in early March, I reviewed the two telegrams I had received from Alex, letting me know where he was, wishing me good health, and saying that he would be home *soon*. The snow had reduced enough for a horse to get through, so what did *soon* mean to Alex? It was at this point that I realized he would take the fact of my leaving quite well, since I couldn't believe myself important to him or he would be home with his pregnant wife.

Writing my parents to inform them of their approaching grandparent status was bittersweet, for I knew they would be thrilled about a baby, but disappointed that I wouldn't be home for some time. Three weeks later a letter arrived by a mail carrier on skis. Mother had written me a long letter of jubilance that Alex and I had been able to work through our problems. I didn't have the heart to tell her that was far from the truth, and was filled with a new underlying panic as I realized that Steven must be thinking the same thing.

Many times I started a letter to him, only to throw it into the fire. I dared not tell him the truth about the baby in a letter that could so easily be seen by his parents or someone else. Not being able to travel in my rapidly expanding condition, I wrote and asked him to come to Bridgeport, telling him that I would find a way to get into town. I was prepared for anyone seeing that message to interpret it as they chose.

But well into April, he still had not written back. Then, in one of Mother's letters, she mentioned that Steven had gone to Los Angeles at the end of March. Some of the ranchers had gotten together and decided one of them should go there and find out what was going on with the reclamation plans that seemed not to be progressing. A week after finding out I was expecting, he had volunteered to go and represent them.

In early May, Alex wired me from Bishop to let me know he'd soon be home. He was true to his word this time, and was back with me in less than a week.

While he fortified himself with hot soup and coffee, I sat with him at the kitchen table. He hadn't gone to Lone Pine, but he brought with him news of current events in the Valley. He also greeted me with a kiss on the cheek and no comment about the change in my shape.

Finally setting his cup down, he announced, "Well, the mystery deepens."

"What mystery?"

"About those men your dad talked about in his letters last year."

"What's happened since then?"

"For openers, I saw the men he talked about." He grinned like a little boy revealing a secret.

"No! Where?"

"They were pointed out to me by Carrie when I was staying with her for a few days. There were a number of them, Fred Eaton and William Mulholland being the only ones anyone knew by name. Eaton signed the hotel registry 'Fred E. and friends'."

"What does Mr. Eaton look like?"

"Average height and in his late thirties I'd guess. High forehead, piercing eyes under a shelf of thick brows, strong chin, broad shoulders. Carrie thought him a very nice looking man. It gave me the opportunity to tease her until she blushed!"

"Easy to do. What about Mr. Mulholland?"

"Older by several years. Shorter and thinner, in physique and hair, small intelligent eyes, and a thick dark mustache. I don't think it'd be wise to under-estimate either one of them."

"In what regard?"

"I'm not sure. It's a thought that came into my mind just now as I recalled them."

"I don't know why we should feel uneasy about any of this."

"For one thing, I found out that Eaton purchased an option on the big Rickey Ranch in Long Valley."

"How did you find that out?"

He turned a bit red across the cheeks. "Let's just say I found it out from someone who'd had a bit too much to drink."

"Are you saying its generally not known that he purchased the property?"

"I don't think so, at least not yet."

"Did he buy all of it? That'd be several thousand acres of grazing land and almost 4,000 head of cattle."

"No one knows for sure, but I think so."

"Then you're right. Something does seem amiss. But I can't imagine what it could be."

"No one else can either." And there our speculation ended.

Over the next two weeks, we followed our normal routine of ranch work, social calls and quiet evenings by the fire, eager for the snow to finish melting and all the roads to open even if deep in mud.

Unknown to us, Fred Eaton and his son were at that time buying up properties in the Owens Valley from people desperate for money, or tempted by a quick and profitable sale. But only later did we discover that Mr. Eaton wasn't keeping the properties, but rather transferring the land or the water rights to the City of Los Angeles.

Because of this, people hundreds of miles away were making decisions that would change the lives of those in the Owens Valley forever; decisions that would create bad blood between the City and the Valley that wouldn't find amiable compromise until a hundred years had passed.

On July 28, 1905, in San Francisco, the Board of the Reclamation Service met with J. C. Clausen to hear the surveyor's report, which he had several months before filed with his superior, Mr. Lippincott. Mr. Clausen's report spoke enthusiastically about the fertility and beauty of the Owens Valley, and encouraged the Board to proceed with the irrigation project that would begin the process of reclaiming the land for the Valley ranchers. Mr. Clausen was shocked to hear that the Board was unaware of his report. Lippincott had not shown it to anyone.

When Lippincott spoke, he told the Board he felt the government reclamation project should be abandoned. Instead, he championed the Los Angeles City Water Department's plans for a system through the Valley that would siphon the water from the Owens Valley and transport it to Los Angeles. The project would be headed by William Mulholland, suggested to him years before by Fred Eaton. After consideration, the Board decided to support the reclamation project.

But one thing kept the reclamation of the Valley from proceeding. The City of Los Angeles now owned most of the land under consideration, and since the City wasn't going to use it as ranch land, there was no need to reclaim it for irrigation.

The day after the San Francisco meeting, on July 29, 1905, all hell broke loose in the Valley. The *L.A. Times* published the news of a project to build an aqueduct through the Owens Valley so the waters of the Owens River could be made available to the citizens of Los Angeles. The headline read *"Titanic Project to Give City a River"*. The City could do this because it now owned most of the land in the Valley, purchased by Eaton and others before the true reason for the purchases was made public. The Times dispassionately, and inaccurately, declared, "Everybody in the valley has money, and everyone is happy."

The truth was that many land owners had sold their water rights thinking they were opening the door to growth in the area through reclamation. Other ranchers sold portions of their land to speculators who knew about the coming project, thinking these buyers were people wanting a new life as ranchers who would contribute to the Valley's growth. But some sold marginally supportive farms for a figure they had never hoped to see, and were happy to move on with their pockets full of cash.

Telegraph wires chattered throughout Inyo and Mono counties until there wasn't a man, woman or child unaware that a large, far distant city was planning to "take from us our life-giving water". Those in Los Angeles read about the proposed project with relief and jubilation while speculators rushed to buy up land in the San Fernando Valley. Los Angeles was set to expand its borders by sending to the San Fernando Valley the water the aqueduct would deliver that was beyond what the City currently needed. Those in our Valley heard the news with confusion followed by either fear-based denial or fear-based anger.

Owens Valley property values rose higher than anyone could ever have imagined, making the land speculators unhappy. However, some of the local farmers that were barely surviving were now thinking they could sell out for a big profit. But for many ranchers this set up a moral dilemma when they realized that selling would give more land to the City in support of what they needed in order to proceed with their aqueduct project. Those that took the money had to deal with their neighbors, who were not always understanding. It was a very confusing time.

In Aunt Carrie's first letter after we heard of the aqueduct project, she told us about Fred Eaton and his son being caught by surprise when the *L. A. Times* broke the news so quickly. As father and son checked out of the Clark Hotel in Bishop, people stood outside in the street yelling threats. The Eatons were followed and harassed all the way to the livery stable, where they had to hitch the horses to their buckboard because the hostler refused to do it for them. To their credit, they didn't race out of town, doing an admirable job of maintaining their dignity. But they came uncomfortably near to falling prey to mob violence. As Eaton left on the train, several men on the depot platform yelled threats that included promises to drown him in the river he wanted to steal for Los Angeles. Mr. Eaton quickly wrote a letter to the Independence newspaper denying that he had done anything wrong, and vowing he would be a good neighbor in the future after "clearing away all unhappy recollections".

But it was Mr. Lippincott with whom everyone was most angry. He had been heralded as a savior of the land and in the service of a government department set up for that purpose. Why had he rejected those plans in favor of the City? This was one of the most asked question in those early days. True or not, most people assumed there had been a lot of money involved to sway Lippincott to "steal the Owens River" for the City of Los Angeles.

From that time on people spoke only of "the City", "the River", and "the Valley". There was only one of each that mattered--the City of Los Angeles versus the Owens Valley, with the prize being the Owens River.

One of the first to put forth practical effort to quell the advance of the project was the land registrar at Independence, the county seat of Inyo County. His letter to the Secretary of the Interior and President Theodore Roosevelt explained that everyone in the Valley knew of Eaton's friendship with Reclamation Chief Lippincott. He explained that ranchers had willingly optioned their land to Eaton because they thought he too was an agent of the Federal government, working on behalf of Valley reclamation. The Registrar's letter beseeched these august political personages to give justice to the people in the Owens Valley, pleading, "In the interest of fairness and of the honor of the Reclamation Service, I appeal to you not to abandon the Owens Reclamation project."

Large committees of citizens throughout the Valley wrote to the Secretary of the Interior demanding that they investigate the Reclamation Service men who had misused their positions and turned their backs on the people of Inyo County. The *Inyo Register* called it "the greatest water steal on record", and accused the City of "plotting destruction".

When the Reclamation Service ended its investigation, they couldn't deny that at the same time Lippincott was acting as an officer in the Reclamation Service, he had also been receiving money for consulting work by the Los Angeles Water Department. This conflict of interest was forbidden by Federal law. To the disgust of many, Lippincott was not charged. Instead, he was "encouraged to devote his time to private practice". This he did, and immediately after resigning from the Reclamation Service, he accepted a $6,000 a year job on the Los Angeles Aqueduct project. Justified or not, there was then no doubt in the minds of Valley residents that "the fix had been on for a long time", and the pioneer blood of several thousand angry citizens was now on the boil.

Just as all this was beginning, I went into labor on May 25, 1905. After six hours of hard effort, with one final push demanded of me by Irene and the elderly mid-wife she had brought with her, I introduced to the world a beautiful girl child.

When Alex was allowed in my bedroom and I handed him the baby, he blushed and said, "I guess I shouldn't ask this, but is it a girl or boy?"

"A girl."

It was only there for a moment, but no one could have missed the look of disappointment on Alex's face. However, it disappeared quickly as he continued to look down at her, and eventually he smiled.

J.B. stuck his head in the door and asked, "Can Grandpa come in?"

"Of course." I refused to acknowledge the stab of guilt his request triggered. What a web of secrets we had woven through our lives!

J.B. picked up the baby and I waited for the same look of disappointment when he found out he didn't have a grandson. Instead, I was surprised to see on his face pure, naked relief. Puzzled by the men's reactions, I nevertheless chose not to think about it right then.

Before anyone could raise the subject of names, I announced that she would be named Rose. It was a statement, not a suggestion. Her name would be a constant reminder of the rose that Steven had given me in Lone Pine's Pioneer Cemetery, and which was at that moment pressed between the pages of my Bible. In any event, Alex made no objection to the name. Of course, I would have preferred to call her Stephanie, but that might have been a little too obvious.

CHAPTER 12

While I was adjusting to motherhood and the frustration of being so far from Steven, my family and friends in the Owens Valley were dealing with a battle of their own as they speculated about how the "big ditch" would affect their lives. This is what they called the aqueduct. Mother's letters during this time were grim, and it made me all the more determined not to give them more distressing news.

But in August of 1905, when Rose was three months old, I wrote to mother: "*I had very much intended to bring your grandchild to you this fall, but she has not been feeding well. The doctor has me make a special formula for her and says I must be very careful with her until she gains more weight, especially since she was a little premature.*

"*Her hair is still dark, but slowly getting lighter, and her eyes are losing their darkness and are turning green.*

"*There are so many things I wanted to discuss with you, and so much of Rose's infancy I wanted you to share, but that cannot be for now. My disappointment is deep, as I know yours must be, but the needs of Rose must come first. I will let you know when I can leave here, but probably not until next spring.*

"*Give my love to all the Perrys, and let them know that I hold them close in my heart still, and forever will. Be sure they all know that I named the baby Rose.*"

I could only hope that Steven would read that request and know what it meant, even if everyone else thought it odd. There was no other way to communicate with him. A letter addressed only to Steven would be thought of as one to a brother, and therefore expected to be shared. Consequently, nothing intimate could be written to him, and certainly no explanation about Rose. But I thought that if I only sent him a polite "sister to brother" letter, he might interpret it as an indication that I had changed my feelings for him. Only years later did I learn that he had instructed his parents that under no circumstances were they to open any letters from me. He had ignored their poorly disguised curiosity.

During the weeks following the birth, I was mostly unaware of Alex and J.B.'s activities. Alex spent little time with me, and never when I was feeding the baby. It wasn't that the intimacy of it embarrassed him, but he said I couldn't feed Rose and at the same time listen properly to him. He seldom held Rose unless I asked him to, and then he would quickly hand her back. His lack of fatherly feeling didn't surprise me as much as it gave me tremendous relief.

From what few things Alex did tell me about his daily routine, I realized that he and J.B. had slowly resolved any residual tension between them. I was sure of it when they referred to several of "our projects" related to "our ranch".

During one of my daily walks, I went to the barns where I fed a carrot to each of the horses. While chatting with Mort as he worked on a wagon, Hank walked up and began extolling the virtues of a new brood mare. After watching him count bags of grain, I commented that it was good to see Alex and J.B. getting along so well now. He didn't pretend that he didn't know to what I was referring.

"Do you think they discussed the situation?"

He laughed. "No."

"But everything seems to be settled between them."

"Sure it is," he agreed.

"Well then, they must have talked about their feelings," I rationally persisted.

He smiled slowly while gently shaking his head. "They met up in the horse barn. Alex asked J.B. what he thought of the new mares he'd brought back from Gardnerville. J.B. told him it was a good purchase."

When nothing more was forthcoming, I asked, "That's it?"

He looked at me with a puzzled frown. "What else was needed?"

As I thought about it, I had to agree. Unspoken in Alex's question had been his acknowledgment of respect for his father. J.B.'s response was an acknowledgment of his continued approval of his son, and not just in regard to the running of the ranch. So in that enigmatic code of simplicity that men are so good at conveying among themselves, all that was necessary had been expressed.

But no matter what was happening on the ranch, what conversations I might be having with others, or the many details of life in which I participated, underlying everything was an almost overwhelmingly intense awareness of my baby. It was mixed with a strange balance of joy and anxiety, and I found it almost physically painful to be apart from her even when only downstairs.

I saw Rose not as a child of flesh and blood, but as a beautiful expression of love, although she had a definite emerging personality of her own and was already expressing it in small ways. How I wanted to tell Steven of the life we had created! But I could only look forward to the fall, determined that nothing would keep me away from Lone Pine longer than that.

Mother wrote back her understanding and best wishes for the continued prospering of Rose. She also told us that rumors kept reaching the Valley regarding the City's plans for the aqueduct. People gathered together at the town hall, in each other's parlors, around tables in the cafes, and in the churches. They railed against the perceived invasion while leaning against saloon bars, hanging over fences, shopping in the stores or standing on sidewalks. The predominant focus of the ranchers, homesteaders and business people was on finding a way to stop this march of progress for a city several days travel away, at the expense of what the Valley held most sacred—land and water. Most of the delaying tactics were along the lines of working within the legal system, but some were not, and mention of dynamite occurred in conversations more often than many people found comfortable.

After I read aloud Mother's latest letter, J.B. commented, "That's what we get for taking our blessed isolation for granted for so long."

"I don't know if 'blessed' is the right word," Alex said. "After all, being so far from the rails only makes shipping our meat and produce more difficult and costly."

"True. But you have to admit that part of the benefit of living here or in the Owens Valley is being free of the crowds and noisy bustle of a big city."

J.B. came over to me and lifted the baby from my arms, then walked up and down the long length of the great room while holding her close and looking into her face. I suddenly wondered if J.B. was happy that his grandchild was a girl because he thought life too full of evil temptations for boys. Considering what he'd been through as a young man, who could blame him? Sitting there with both men, it occurred to me that Rose seemed more a grandchild of J.B. than a daughter of Alex. Of course, they didn't know that she was neither.

When J.B. laughed as Rose reached out for his finger, guilt gave my conscience a swift kick. Soon I would be taking J.B.'s grandchild from him. But at least until then we could each in our own way be happy, and at least now J.B. could realize that he had acceptance and love in his life, and had no need to run from a past that had just been a difficult period in the maturing of a troubled boy. Holding to this was partly selfish on my part, of course. It made it easier to convince myself that leaving would be made less traumatic because the two men would have each other.

In the middle of September, a rig from one of the town stables rattled down the long drive to stop before the front door. No one was expected, but Sing went out to welcome the visitor. Both Mrs. Lewis and myself were downstairs, so we followed him onto the front porch in a state of naked curiosity. But only I let out an excited squeal when Mother was helped down by the driver.

As we embraced, she declared, "I wasn't going to allow another month to pass without meeting my grandchild!" Stepping back with a smile, she lay her hand on my cheek and added, "Or spend another day missing my beautiful child. You look well, Whitney."

Introductions were made while a knot of tension grew in my stomach as I wondered how Alex and J.B. would react to Mother's sudden insertion into the household's fragile balance. Looking at her luggage being unloaded from the wagon, I knew this was not going to be a stay of only a few days.

Sing, of course, was all smiles. Mrs. Lewis made fussy efforts to be gracious and welcoming, and Mother accepted it as given, warmly shaking the housekeeper's hand. As soon as we were all inside, I rushed upstairs and retuned with Rose. The moment baby Rose saw Grandma Emily and held out her arms, the two were instantly linked by a deep affinity from which sometimes even I was excluded. In fact, when it was time to feed Rose the supplemental formula, she preferred Mother giving it to her and drank more than she ever had before. Delighted that three generations of Eastman women were together facing Life's challenges, I didn't even resent it.

As we sat in my room, a tray of tea and cookies on the small table between the rose velvet chairs, I said, "I feel so bad that my milk can't give her all she needs. It's like I'm failing her."

"Oh, fiddle!" Mother exclaimed. "You gave her life, didn't you? So what if she isn't getting enough enrichment from you? Be thankful she can digest cow's milk and commercial formula."

"It'd just be so much easier if I could nurse her. I have to make the semolina early each morning because it has to boil so long before the milk, sugar and egg can be added."

"Aren't the commercial flour food packets easier to make?"

"Yes, and that's part of what she eats. But Mrs. Beaton's book says to change the food occasionally."

"Mrs. Beaton? You've been using her book as your guide?"

"Why not?"

"No reason. She was a delightful English lady, and considering she was only twenty-eight when she died, she wrote wonderful books on cooking and running a household. But I often found her references not all that pertinent to what we have available here."

"Her book on household management was on the book shelves and the closest advice to what I needed. The doctor wasn't sure what to do."

"Well, it seems to be working." She wiped Rose's chin and offered her the bottle again.

Such was our preoccupation as we enjoyed for the first time a conversation between married women instead of mother and daughter. So enjoyable was it in fact, that I didn't care if Alex was displeased with Mother's arrival. Of course, I reminded myself, he might respond by ignoring me, but there was nothing unusual about that. And there it was. For the first time I saw clearly that whenever Alex withheld his attention from me, he was trying to punish me for something I'd done or said that displeased him. Instead of being angry, I was only surprised that it had taken me so long to figure it out.

When Alex arrived home from town, he greeted Mother fondly, if somewhat distantly. His first response was the formal comment, "You'll be such a help to Whitney."

But later, after watching Mother and J.B. chatter away like old friends, his mood lightened considerably. In fact, both of us relaxed after that, and I wondered why we always cared so much about J.B.'s reactions. Of course, neither of the men cared one jot about what I thought or felt.

During their long talks on the porch, in front the fire, or walking around the ranch, J.B. brought Mother up-to-date regarding many of the people both had known in Bodie, Lundy and Lakeview. Mother laughed happily and asked question after question while J.B. answered each one with more detail than I'd ever heard him share with anyone.

They also debated both sides of the Owens Valley water issue, each of them showing a remarkable compassion for the citizens of Los Angeles, while yet never veering from their loyalty to the Valley. They were, after all, both ranchers.

For a whole week I didn't see J.B. cast a longing look out the window. At last there was present in the house a feeling of domestic tranquility, and I should have been jubilant. Instead, I felt even more like a fraud. A dozen times I started to tell Mother the truth about Rose and my relationship with Steven, but each time I simply lacked the courage. I came closest when she mentioned that Rose's eyes were not at all like mine or those of Alex, although something about them seemed familiar.

It was right after such a comment that Sing bustled into my room where he proceeded to tend to Rose's diapering. He put her back into the cradle and said, "She big girl now. But she big girl when born month early. She eager to meet her pretty mama and grandmamma." He laughed and hurried from the room.

"Whitney?" Mother turned to me slowly. "She was a whole month early?"

"Yes."

"But you said she weighed seven and a half pounds." She looked down into the cradle, then up at me with a teasing smile around her mouth. "Alex must have been happier to see you when you first got home than you thought he'd be."

I smiled with great effort, trying hard to seem casual. "Of course, we still have problems that we may not be able to solve."

"You sound like you're still thinking of leaving him."

"I'm just not sure." Turning my back, I began folding diapers earlier brought in from the clothes line and piled on the bed. But she wasn't so easily distracted.

"Don't you think Rose needs her father as she grows up?" She didn't sound judgmental, just prepared to calmly discuss the situation. It would have been easier if she had been outraged and disapproving.

"Every child should have both parents," I answered with feeling. I may have sounded a bit too forceful, because she looked at me in surprise when I abruptly said, "I'm hungrier than just tea and cookies. I'll go get us something else." And I left the room before she could stop me.

When I returned, Mother was standing over the cradle looking down at Rose with a strange unreadable expression playing across her face. After I put the plate of cheese sandwiches on the tray by our chairs and turned to her, she placed her hand gently on my shoulder and spoke softly. "It's the curl of her long lashes and the brown flecks in her green eyes. They're just like Steven's. I must be either blind or terribly naive."

"Of course you're not," I managed to whisper.

She looked at me closely. "You must have been terribly unhappy."

"Yes." I had to sit down. "Even more, I've been so confused. But when I was alone with Steven in Lone Pine, I felt like everything was suddenly clear for the first time in years. And I remembered what it was like to feel real happiness and love."

Expecting at least some form of a lecture, or a warning to be cautious in how I proceeded next, instead she merely stood next to me with a hand on my head. Like the child I suddenly felt myself to be, I wrapped my arms around her legs and pressed my cheek against her hip as I looked beyond her at Rose sleeping in her cradle. Mother gently patted my back and without warning I felt the wet of tears sliding down my cheeks. Mother neither moved nor spoke. She just held me tighter. The realization that I was no longer alone in the world carrying the burden of my fearful secret overwhelmed me with gratitude and relief, and I cried harder. But eventually I blew my nose and gulped the cold tea in my cup. Mother calmly ate her sandwich and poured us more tea.

"What should I do?" I asked, sure she would have a logical solution that would give me a clear next step.

She shook her head. "I don't know. And if neither of us knows, then we should just wait a bit longer. Life has a way of showing us the right path if we don't force it."

She was right, and our journey down that path began the next evening when Mother and I joined Alex on the front porch after dinner. He was sipping a whiskey and staring off into space.

"You seem pre-occupied," I commented to him.

Alex had spent the day in town, while J.B. planned necessary purchases with Hank in the barn. and then went to a nearby ranch for dinner and poker. Usually when Alex returned from town, he would bring me bits of gossip. But tonight he was sitting silently, staring unblinking at the far mountains. Afraid that another one of his morose moods might be settling upon him, I was determined to head it off for Mother's sake.

However, after several minutes relating to him the playful antics of two young bobcats Mother and I had chanced upon while riding, I realized he had heard very little of my story.

"Did you hear any of what I said, Alex?"

"I'm sorry, my dear." He sighed deeply and smiled at us, so I knew it wasn't a bad mood, but rather one of deep contemplation.

"Did something unusual happen in town?" I asked.

"It wasn't exactly ordinary. I'm more surprised at my response to it." He frowned and shook his head.

"Why don't you tell us about it?" Mother suggested.

After a moment's hesitation, he said, "I was having a beer at the saloon before starting out for home when a man walked in. Nothing unusual in that, but the way he looked around made me uneasy."

"Why?" Mother asked him, a small frown furrowing her brow.

"He was scrutinizing the faces of everyone in the bar, obviously looking for someone. My first thought was that I pitied the poor bastard when he was found."

So engrossed was he that he failed to apologize for his language. "Why?" I asked. "Was he physically threatening?"

"Not any more than a rabid dog." He smirked and shrugged. "He was only about my height, five-ten or so, but his small eyes were like hard, polished stones. There was no warmth in him, and I got the impression he was wound really tight. When the girls hanging out by the bar disappeared into the back room, I knew I wasn't the only one repelled by him."

"Good heavens," Mother responded. "And they've been with all kinds of men."

He turned upon her a raised brow and I couldn't help but laugh in response. "Do you think us so little of this world that we don't know about prostitutes?"

"Of course not." But his face was pink.

"Was he big and muscular?" Mother asked.

"Not at all. Thin, wiry, very fit looking, like he'd done a lot of hard physical work for many years. His dark cotton shirt was worn and dirty, and so were his pants." His sudden smile was sardonic as he added, "He was also wearing two huge side arms."

"Really?"

"No. But they seemed that way to me, since I didn't have a gun with me."

"You usually don't. Most of the men around here seldom carry a gun." Then I amended myself. "Except for J.B. He always carries a gun when off the ranch, doesn't he?"

"Yeah. But not like these." He sat forward and drained the whiskey in his glass. "If it weren't for what happened next, I'd probably have forgotten him by now."

"What happened?"

"He asked the bartender if anyone named Roberts lived in the area." A chill pricked over my skin and I swallowed with an effort as he continued. "The bartender looked over at me, then thought better of it and looked back at the stranger. But it was too late. The man turned toward me, looked me up and down, and slowly shook his head. He said I couldn't be the man he was looking for because I was too young. Then he asked me if I had a father."

"I told him everyone has a father." Alex gave a snort and shook his head. "He took a step closer with his face contorted in irritation and asked me if my father's name was Bedford. When I told him no, it was James, he was obviously disappointed."

"Oh, my God!" I breathed out. Mother was very still.

"I left right after that. He was buying a bottle the last I saw of him."

While Mother reassured Alex, I carried my cup to the kitchen and was surprised to see J.B. standing by the chopping block. I've never seen anyone so sickly white, and I knew immediately that he had overheard our conversation. As though unaware of my presence, he turned and rushed out the back door, stumbling on the sill and leaving the door wide open.

Following J.B. as far as the back porch steps, I watched him lurch across the yard toward the hogs. He stopped and leaned against the railing of the pen as though for support, one hand over his mouth, and I wondered if he was ill. Alex pressed into me from behind and I turned around to see an expression of horror on his face. Slow to catch on, it was then I realized that J.B. wasn't ill, but rather stricken with a terror that was close to incapacitating him.

What terrible thing had J.B. done on one of those long periods of absence from us? Associated improperly with the man's wife or daughter? Stolen something from him? Or won too much of the man's money during a poker game?

"What should we do?" Alex asked me.

That's when I knew how truly afraid he too must be. Never without a plan of action or an opinion of the right thing to do, Alex certainly never treated my ideas as valid.

"Leave him be for now. He's obviously distressed." That was an understatement. "Maybe he'll come to us."

Alex shook his head with so much vehemence that strands of hair fell across his forehead. "No. He'll hope the whole thing blows over. He won't do anything unless circumstances force him."

"Let's go back inside. Maybe the man will give up his search and move on."

The next morning, the four of us sat around the table in the dining room forcing down a breakfast of pancakes, more to show our respect of Sing's efforts than from hunger. The tension was so disturbing that not one of us knew how to break it. I watched Alex stare at J.B., while J.B. looked down at his plate, and Mother looked out into the great room. We were brought out of our individual musings by the single loud whinny of a horse outside, followed a minute later by the loud banging of the heavy brass door knocker.

We sat as though frozen, overwhelmed by a sense of doom. Sing, who had just entered the great room, moved swiftly to answer the door. Alex and J.B. rose up at the same time, preparing to stop him. But they were too slow to act.

A voice said, "I'm here to see Mr. Roberts, senior."

"He at breakfast now," Sing responded in his typically pleasant manner. "You sit on porch to wait and I bring coffee."

"That's okay," the voice reassured, "he won't mind my interrupting him. I'm an old friend." The man pushed past Sing and hesitated as he looked around. When he saw us assembled in the dining room he walked forward.

Glaring at us was a small. hunch-shouldered man with a leathery face blasted by too many cold mountain winters and hot desert summers. He wore an old gray hat crusted with spatters of dried mud that also showed a dark stain of sweat permanently absorbed into the band. His clothes were the same as Alex had described to us the day before. Hard green eyes riveted on J.B. as though they were iron and J.B. the magnet.

A sly smile turned up one side of his mouth, and yellow teeth glowed in the early light above the rough stubble of his chin. "There you are, old friend. Glad to see me?"

He walked slowly into the dining room, one hand resting lightly on his side arm while his eyes darted into all the corners of the room. All of us by then were standing next to J.B., a united front of protection against an undefined threat. The man extended his hand and after hesitating a moment, J.B. took it. A spasm of pain passed over his face just before the stranger released his grip.

"Aren't you going to introduce me to these folks?" His slow drawl held an undertone of playful sarcasm more menacing than an open threat.

With an obvious effort to breath evenly, J.B. cleared his throat and turned to us. "This is Charlie. Charlie, this is my son and daughter-in-law, and her mother. Would you like some coffee?"

After a curt nod in our direction, Charlie said, "Sure."

Sing shortly returned with a full mug and a piece of apple pie for the visitor. As he chewed slowly, we all returned to our seats and I ventured to ask, "Would you like something more substantial, Mister...I'm sorry, I didn't get your last name."

"Jones. Charlie Jones. No ma'am, this is fine."

He ate his pie silently but with contentment, in no hurry to clarify the reason for his presence. J.B. meanwhile had sunk into his chair as though the man's name finally being spoken was a weight he couldn't bear.

"How long have you been looking for my father-in-law?" I asked, bringing the inevitable out into the open. I didn't need to ask how he knew J.B., because whether or not Alex and Mother recognized the name, I sure did.

"I've kept my eyes and ears alert for most of the last thirty years." He turned to J.B. again. "You haven't changed that much old friend, just matured the kid and added a few gray hairs." He grinned, showing food between his teeth. "Have I changed, J.B.?" He rolled out the "J.B." with a hard emphasis of scathing mockery.

"No. Very little." They stared at each other like I imagine an angry cobra would meet the eyes of a wary snake charmer, although I wasn't sure who would assume which role. J.B. added, "I would have recognized you anywhere."

Charlie Jones laughed. "And probably run the other way if you had."

J.B. responded without hesitating. "Yes. That part of my life is over." With more energy in his voice, he leaned forward and looked Charlie Jones straight in the eyes. "If you think you can scare me by alluding to the time we were in prison or the escape, they know all about it."

So J.B. assumed I had told Mother. Either that or he and Mother had spoken about it between them.

"And you're still the beloved papa?" The incredulity in Jones' voice was not feigned.

Alex and I spoke together, "Yes." Then Alex added, "He was young, impressionable and caught up with intimidating older men."

"*Men*, hell." Jones shook his head. "Among the six of us in our group, most of us were in our early twenties. Only two were in their thirties. I was only twenty-two."

Alex and I sat silent and stunned. How did we both end up with the impression that the others involved were much older than J.B.?

Alex said, "You're the one that was never captured."

"That's right."

J.B. spoke up. "Where did you get to then?"

"I just kept going south. I raided a few houses in the Owens Valley and then made my way around Owens Lake and up to Cerro Gordo. I got work there, and eventually got on with a freighter going to Los Angeles and the ports. Then I just leaked out of the landscape."

"Why did you come back?" The men looked at me, surprised at my directness. Mother sat very still with her eyes riveted on Jones.

"Right to the point, huh? I got a job working on the big Rickey ranch."

Mother surprised us all by asking, "What were you in prison for, Mr. Jones? Back in '71?"

"I stabbed a man. Right in the heart." He chuckled. "It was just a regular saloon brawl until we took it outside. Then it got personal. That was in Hamilton, Nevada." After a sly glance at J.B., he turned to Mother. "I should have had ole Bedford with me then. I might have gotten away before the sheriff came along." He grinned and leaned back in his chair, staring at J.B. "You were the good one for that."

Alex leaned forward. "I don't understand. Good at what?"

Jones turned a look of surprise on him. "Why, escaping of course. I thought he told you what happened back in '71."

We just stared at him in confusion. Mother was the first to put it together. "Are you saying that J.B. planned the escape?"

"Well, not the whole thing. But it was mainly his idea. Him and Clifford. We all did the planning."

He could tell from our expression that this was news we hadn't heard before. It was then that his initial sly enjoyment of our discomfiture returned.

"I see." He turned to J.B. "You told them your own version of what happened, didn't you?" He laughed long and hard, but there was no mirth in it, only a perverse delight. "I should have known. You're too smart to expect them to accept what really happened."

Alex gripped the table cloth on either side of his plate with both hands, bunching it between his fingers. I thought for a moment he was going to drag everything on the table off onto the floor. But instead Alex took a deep breath and sat back in his chair, smoothing the fabric neatly. With a carefully controlled voice, he said, "We've heard as much as we need to know. The fact that J.B. might have suggested the escape is beside the point. I'd like you to go now."

Jones didn't look ready to leave. "What's the matter, sonny? You afraid to find out that some of the other things he said weren't true?"

"No." Alex didn't take his eyes from Jones. "I just don't think we need to know more."

Charlie Jones looked at him for a long moment before saying, "I think you *do* need to know more. Did he tell you he was the first one to kill a guard?"

Even if I'd known how to stop whatever was coming next, I was too paralyzed by shock and fear to have acted. Whether it was of this horrid man, the true facts of the escape, or how all this was going to change the fragile harmony of our lives so recently restored, I didn't know. But the landslide of truth was upon us, and none of us knew how to avoid being completely buried beneath it.

"Right from the start we all thought Roberts was a scary little bastard. Always pacing, like a caged cat with a sore tooth. So we weren't surprised when he said we should break out of there on a Sunday when they were least prepared to stop us.

"Once we started the breakout, Roberts here kept yelling 'Let's go, let's go.' He kept us all focused and pressing forward."

Looking at J.B., I saw a different man from the one that had been sitting there only moments before. Alex looked from J.B. to me and shrugged, as if to say, "So what if it was his idea?"

Jones leaned back in his chair and rubbed a rough, callused hand over his face. "Yep, Roberts here was a tough one. Hell, he even yelled for us to grab the warden's kid when she ran into the yard."

"Why?" Mother asked, unable to hide her surprise.

"So they'd stop shooting at us, of course. But old Ed Goyette wasn't having any of that. He didn't want to come with us anyway, so he ran with the kid into the old hotel next door." He grinned at J.B. "Boy, that made you fit to spit, didn't it?"

We all turned toward J.B., incredulous and shocked. But he sat with his eyes closed, and as still as if he were almost dead. If so, it was going to be a slow and torturous death.

Jones ignored him as he told us, "It was ole Roberts here that kept pressing us to move faster and even travel at night. It was a good thing we listened to him."

"You mean because the posse had an Indian tracker with them?" I asked.

"Yeah. He could find a whisper in a big wind."

Alex spoke quickly, interjecting a new subject into the conversation. "But when you found the Dutchman's cabin, it was J.B. who calmed the man. He saved the man from Black and Morton. That showed his compassion, his humanity."

"Listen to you, sounding like a fancy courtroom mouthpiece." He smirked and shook his head. "He calmed him all right. With the back of his hand. After that, the guy let himself be tied up and knew better than to make a fuss."

Alex said, "But the man came after you, didn't he?"

"Oh, sure. After all, we'd stolen his horses. But we didn't kill him, only tied him up. If Roberts had had his way, we'd have killed him right then. He later convinced us that we'd left behind someone who could tell which direction we'd headed, so we agreed not to leave anyone else alive. If our horses hadn't gone loco over a snake on the trail, a couple of people in a wagon we passed would have gotten plugged for sure."

Alex looked at his father. "You twisted everything in a very imaginative way. You should have been a writer of stories." There was no heat back of Alex's words and I found that more frightening than if he had shouted.

Mother cleared her throat. "I'm sure J.B. was just trying to show those of you more hardened than himself that he could keep up."

Jones's bark of laughter had real humor in it. "I never met a molting sidewinder so nasty as him. We couldn't figure him out. We were worried about his lack of caution, hoping it wouldn't be the end of us." He passed his eyes over J.B. and said, "He doesn't look it now, but he was one dangerous kid, always playing with his gun like it was a favored lady. I never saw so much energy in a man, but he kept us moving more than we'd a done otherwise. That's probably why he talked us into leaving behind those that were injured during the breakout."

"You didn't think they'd slow you down?" Alex asked.

"Of course," Jones admitted. "But some of 'em weren't that bad off. Roberts talked us into leaving all wounded behind. It wasn't a bad idea, mind you."

We sat in silence for several minutes. I was hoping that was the end when Jones startled us with his next question.

"Ever wonder where your Daddy got that gold snake-head ring he's wearing on his pinky? He took it off of Morton after he was hanged. Must have, 'cause I have the other one."

"Other one?" I asked.

"Yeah, they belonged to Billy Poor, the mail rider we waylaid. He tell you about that?"

Alex stared at Jones with a concentration of loathing. In a voice so low I almost didn't hear him, he asked Jones, "What do you want?"

Jones leaned forward and pushed his coffee away, his face losing all traces of civility. Until that moment I'd never seen what is called a look of naked hate. "I want to make sure that Roberts here hasn't fooled everyone. He managed with the law, but those of us that were with him for those six days weren't fooled." He turned to J.B. "All this time, my name has been the one most hated because Morton and you convinced everyone I shot Billy Poor."

J.B. startled us by shouting, "Morton did shoot him! He admitted it."

Alex added, "It was more than that. It was you and Morton putting the kid's head in the fire to disguise him that makes people disgusted!"

"Yeah, we did that. But it wasn't our idea." He turned to J.B. "Was it?"

The last vestige of desire to defend J.B. died right then. From that point on, Alex, Mother and I said little, simply staring at Jones and letting the situation play out between J.B. and this horrible man. Whenever I was tempted to defend the teen-age J.B., I looked at the gold ring he was wearing that I had once admired and instead said nothing.

J.B. was not unaware of the effect all this was having on us. He told Jones, "You can go now. You've accomplished what you came to do."

Leaning back in his chair, Jones picked up his coffee cup and found it empty. "Where's that farm cookie of yours?"

J.B. and Alex both made to rise out of their chair in a spontaneous burst of protest at this denigrating reference. At the same moment that Jones' hand fell to his gun, Sing appeared from the kitchen with the coffee pot.

Although I knew he must have been listening, Sing smiled cheerfully and announced, "Time for more coffee, I bet." After briefly stopping to pour a little coffee into Mother's cup, he poured more for Jones, smiling at him in a friendly manner. As he approached me, I shook my head and he winked before retreating to the kitchen.

Everything settled back down as Jones sipped his coffee. He then surprised us all by saying, "Sorry. He does seem like a decent sort."

Hoping this heralded a change in the tone of the visit, I said, "How did you find J.B.?"

"By chance. I ran into Hank in Bodie last month."

"Hank?" Alex asked in surprise. "How do you know him?"

Jones flashed a pleased smile at J.B. "Another surprise for them? Oh, let me tell." How can a chuckle sound so wicked? "Old Hank is one of the prisoners that broke off from us, following the Carson River toward Dayton."

I sat back in my chair and nodded. "And then he lost himself in the mines around Virginia City." Everyone looked at me in surprise and I told them, "He talked to me once about mining there in the early '70's."

J.B. spoke up. "I saw him there shortly after Alex was born and offered him a job here. He did none of the shooting and was only in jail for robbing a store to feed his sickly wife. She died soon after his arrest." He turned to Alex for the first time. "So don't go hating him like you do me."

If he was fishing for reassurance for himself or Hank, he didn't get it. Alex said instead, "I'm more disappointed than anything." Their eyes met for a moment before they both looked back to Jones for whatever came next.

With a smile that couldn't have expressed greater satisfaction, Jones stood up slowly and stretched his back. "Well, my job here is done. I can move on knowing I've done a good work."

"No!" Alex barked. All eyes turned to him in surprise and I heard Sing gasp in the kitchen. "I want to know what happened at...at Convict Lake as it's called now, after the posse arrived."

Jones sat back down. "Oh, yeah. I bet he cleaned that up, too. And he probably didn't tell you anything about what we did to Mrs. McLaughlin on Dobey Creek on our way there."

J.B. shot out of his chair, passed from the room, and walked up the stairs. At first I thought Jones might stop him, but he let him go, merely shifting around to J.B.'s chair where he could see the door to the kitchen, the expanse of the great room, and the door to J.B.'s room upstairs.

Alex told him, "What happened at the McLaughlin ranch? Didn't you get a meal and supplies from her?"

"The woman gave us more than that," he chuckled. "Or I should say we took more than that from her."

Mother and I exchanged a glance just before my stomach lurched. It wasn't the time to be sick and I took a deep breath as I leaned back in my chair. Mother continued to sit very still and rigidly straight, her hands folded in her lap.

Alex leaned toward Jones. "You can't convince me that my father ravaged an old woman!"

"She wasn't old. But you're right. He didn't touch her. It doesn't matter who did, but what matters is he didn't try and stop it."

Alex returned to his original question. "What happened at Convict Lake?"

"I suppose he told you he hid while the rest of us shot it out?"

"How did you know that?"

"I had a drink with one of the men in the posse that Roberts first told his story to. That day was a big one in the life of this guy and he liked to talk about it to all who'd listen. So I know what Roberts told them. He did hide in the willows all right. But when the shooting started, he darted forward and hid behind a big tree."

"How do you know? You weren't there. You went down to the lake with Burke and Cockerill."

"Yeah, but when we heard horses coming, we headed back to the creek to pitch in. Then we saw how big the posse was that was sneaking up on them. We knew we didn't stand much of a chance even if we could get back to the others without getting shot. So when those three immediately killed two of the posse's horses and wounded a few of the others, we took off and hid where we could watch.

"A couple of the men in the posse were bleeding from small wounds. Then one of them broke from the others and took cover in a thick stand of willow. This guy headed toward Black, Morton and your dad from up the canyon, not realizing that Morton and Black saw him trying to sneak around them. It was then that Roberts ran out and hid behind a big tree near where the posse fella would pass. Of course, we know now it was Robert Morrison, a Wells Fargo Agent from Benton.

"Black moved forward to waylay Morrison, but in the thick of the bushes Black missed him and passed by where he was hiding. Morrison saw Black and took a bead on him. But his gun didn't work. Black twisted around to get off a shot at Morrison, but missed. A second later Morrison went down with a bullet in his side. That's when I noticed that Roberts had stepped out from behind his tree and was just putting his gun away with a satisfied look on his face. Black finished off Morrison by shooting him in the head. That's the part the posse witnessed. They spooked then and took off out of the canyon.

"It wasn't difficult for me to talk Burke and Cockerill into gettin' the hell out of there. That way, if we were captured, at least we'd have separated ourselves from that shooting. Be sure to tell J.B. that I later found out Morrison was due to be married within a few days."

"Where did you go?" Mother asked him, refusing to rise to that bait.

"We headed south along the Owens River. Near Bishop the other two headed over the White Mountains to Fish Lake Valley. I kept on going south."

Barely realizing I was speaking aloud, I said, "Now I realize what was odd about one part of J.B.'s story. He said when he was left behind in Pine Canyon by Morton and Black that he had only three bullets left. I vaguely wondered why."

"Well, he shot a guard the day we broke out, and put one in Morrison. I heard tell that Mono Jim, one of the posse's Indian guides had been shot and killed by the three of them as they left the lake area. Maybe he had something to do with that. You'll have to ask him."

Alex turned to look at me like I was no better than Jones, but I continued on anyway. "I also wondered why Morton should be so full of hate toward J.B. when he saw him in the cabin at the time of their capture. But J.B. had accused them of the Morrison killing before they could say anything. And they must have heard J.B. tell the vigilantes his version of the truth at their mock trial."

"Yeah, the guy from the posse told me that's when everyone tried to put the killing of Billy Poor off onto me, especially Morton. Didn't do any good. They gave him a hemp massage anyway."

"But you did shoot the kid," Mother pointed out.

"Yeah, but mine was the second shot," he reminded her. "Morton's bullet killed Billy Poor. And J.B.'s bullet probably would have been fatal for Morrison eventually, even if Black hadn't finished him off. Dress it up, excuse it, whatever. It all ends the same."

"No wonder Morton told J.B. he'd get his in hell," Alex mumbled.

"Did he now?" Jones laughed. "And I guess I've given him a push in that direction."

"Yes," Mother agreed. "And pushed us there after him. Are you happy?"

"Happy don't have nothin' to do with it." He glared at her. "It's about justice."

Not bothering to hide the repugnance I felt for him, I said, "If hell is a state of mind as some say, I'm sure J.B. has been there before. So now that you've accomplished what you set out to do, please leave."

He settled his malevolent eyes on me, then stood up and leaned in my direction, raising his hand as though to strike out. "I'll leave when I'm damn ready to go."

"No," Mother said, "you'll leave now."

Jones froze in place when he heard the cocking of a gun. "What was that?"

"It was a gun," Mother told him calmly.

She had not been sitting with her hands in her lap all this time because she was a proper lady, but because along with more coffee, Sing had passed her a small derringer. She raised the gun above the table and pointed it at his face, holding it remarkably steady as she slowly stood up. "I suggest you leave now."

My peripheral vision took in the startled reaction of my husband. But he didn't stand or back up Mother in any way. He just sat with his eyes on Jones.

Jones turned to Alex with a sneer. "At least your in-laws have guts."

Alex still said nothing.

"You've done enough damage to this family," Mother told him, using a voice unlike any I had heard from her before. The hardness of her tone and her expression conveyed a resolve that left no doubt of her willingness to do whatever was necessary to end our torture.

"Don't say another word," she directed him. "Just get up and walk out. If you come back, you'll end up an unusual treat for the hogs. Sing has gone for the sheriff, so if you want a chance to get away, you'd better get going."

Jones started to argue, then looked again at the gun in Mother's hand and changed his mind. After the door closed behind him, we continued to hold our positions. Eventually the sound of his horse galloping down the drive and onto the road could no longer be heard.

Sing opened the kitchen door. "Do I go for Sheriff now?"

Mother looked at our amazed expressions and laid the gun on the table. Turning to us with a smile, she asked, "Was it a good bluff?"

Despite the fact that he must still have been reeling from the shock of the last few hours, Alex told her, "Remind me never to play poker with you."

And we laughed. We laughed so hard that when we found ourselves suddenly in tears, we looked at each other and stopped, gasping with both surprise and embarrassment. Following that, we were overcome by spent emotion, exhausted in mind and body. But I was also motivated to hope that Alex would, after all, rebound from the crushing blow of the day's reality heaped upon him so brutally.

I stayed behind in the dining room for a few minutes after first Alex and then Mother retired to their rooms. When I finally dragged myself up the stairs, I passed a pale and drawn J.B. coming down. He averted his eyes and started to hurry past, but I laid a restraining hand on his arm. "You once told me that you never lose very big when you gamble. Well, today you did."

He slowly raised red-rimmed eyes to mine. "I know."

The rest of the day is a blur to me now. But that night, expecting it would take me hours to fall asleep, I instead fell immediately into a deep, dreamless state where at least for awhile I hid from the horror of the day just past.

CHAPTER 13

The morning following our terrorizing by Jones, the house seemed unfriendly and cold, even though the temperature outside was nearly ninety. Mother and I had just completed our breakfast when Alex walked into the dining room, pulled out the chair at the head of the table usually reserved for J.B., and sat down. With a glance at Mother to his left, he glared down the length of the table to me, daring me to protest.

Instead, I buttered the last piece of toast and carried it to him, placing it on his plate as I patted him gently on the shoulder. Mother turned to Sing as he entered the room. "Alex is ready for his breakfast, and we'd all enjoy more toast if it's ready."

Sing hesitated, looked at each of us in turn, then retreated to the kitchen minus his usual smile. We tried to make conversation, but it was forced and unnatural. The weather took up far more of the conversation than it ever had before. Sing returned with a plate loaded with toast, a slice of ham, eggs, and coffee. After setting it all in front of Alex, he hesitated as though waiting for some word of acknowledgement. When none was forthcoming, he hurried back to the safe familiarity of his orderly kitchen.

No one said anything while Alex picked through the food on his plate. When he pushed most of it away with a sigh, I summoned my courage. "Alex, I know you don't want me to bring up what happened, and I won't." He relaxed noticeably. "But you should talk to J.B."

As he started to argue, I raised a hand in protest. But before I could speak, he picked up his coffee mug and stomped up the stairs to his bedroom. I followed him undeterred, finding him slumped in a chair by the window. When I entered, he got up and reached for his outdoor boots, probably thinking I'd retreat if he was heading out. Instead, I walked all the way into the room. He wasn't pleased, but I didn't care.

"We need to talk."

He shoved his feet into the boots and mumbled, "Later."

"No. Now!"

His sigh was purposefully loud to show his irritation. "Fine. What?"

"If you think your rudeness will put me off, it won't work this time."

"I'm listening," he barked. "Get on with it if it's important."

"Well, do you think this ranch important?" I couldn't keep the irritation out of my voice.

"What are you talking about?" He finally looked up at me.

I sunk to the floor by his low chair, the skirts of my morning dress billowing out around me. "Alex, I know this latest revelation has thrown you considerably."

"Of course, it has." He shrugged. "So?"

"But you're not accepting, or forgiving."

"Are you insane?" he snapped at me. "I did that once and look what happened. It was all lies."

"Not totally. Yes, he left out a lot and put his own twist on things. But maybe his version was the way he's chosen to think about it so he can endure the knowledge of who he used to be."

"He still lied to me," he pouted. "Even when he had an opportunity to set it all straight."

"Isn't it natural that he wouldn't want his son knowing him as he was back then? It isn't like he's capable of those acts now."

He turned to me then, a look of agonizing doubt on his face. "Isn't he?"

After I recovered from my surprise, I asked, "Alex, where does he go when he suddenly takes off for weeks at a time?"

He looked at me for a long moment. "He says he goes to stay with friends for private poker games."

"'He says'?"

"It's rather difficult to believe anything he says now, isn't it?" His eyes began to mist over and he turned his head to look out the window.

"Where does he get his gambling money?"

"From me." He swallowed hard. "When he started staying away so much a couple of years ago, he also started making bad business decisions regarding the ranch. Well, uninformed ones anyway. I told him if he wasn't going to pay attention to the ranch, and was so willing to leave it all up to me, it might be best if he just stayed out of ranch business altogether. Whenever he wants money, if it doesn't put a strain on our finances, I give it to him."

"That demonstrates his willingness to be reasonable, doesn't it?" I put a hand on his shoulder. "You need to talk to him now. The longer you wait, the more of a gulf there'll be between you. Until you both know where you stand with each other, neither of you will be able to come to terms with the situation and move on to what comes next. Whatever that might be."

Reaching for his coffee cup on the table next to the chair, he gripped it tightly while running the forefinger of his right hand around the rim. This went on for some considerable time, until finally he mumbled, "He'll probably stay in his room all day." Then he looked at me with a wry lop-sided smirk. "Oh, okay."

At that moment Sing knocked and entered with a pitcher of fresh water. Alex asked him, "Would you go tell J.B. that I'd like to talk to him? Ask him if it'd be okay for me to come to his room."

Sing hurried off, relieved that all this tension was soon to end. He was back almost immediately, announcing, "He not there."

"He's probably outside somewhere," Alex said.

"I hope so." But Sing sounded uncertain as he held out an envelope to Alex. When it was grabbed from his hand, Sing stayed where he was. In that house notes left in a room never meant anything good. I stood up and waited next to Alex's chair.

He held the unopened envelope in his hands, his face dangerously red. and the small vein at his temple twitching. With a quick ripping of paper, he opened the envelope and began to read. Animation and color slowly faded from his face, replaced by a blank tension of unreadable stillness. When he was finished, he wadded the single piece of paper into a ball and threw it at the trash can where it bounced off the rim onto the floor. When Alex abruptly stood up, Sing barely caught the chair before it fell over backward. The stomping of Alex's boots on the stairs and the slam of the front door echoed through the house.

Having heard the commotion, Mother rushed into the room just as I retrieved the note and smoothed it out. Over my shoulder, Mother read aloud.

"Alex: I could live with your anger, but not your disappointment and the loss of respect that must follow. It is easier to spend the rest of my life without you than to live with unspoken accusations creating a widening gulf between us, all the while trying to pretend it is not. Inevitably, one of the times I would leave the ranch, I would probably not return. Leaving now and in this way is more honorable. I have places I can go. And you have Whitney and Rose. But no matter what kind of man you may think me, please know that I always told the truth in my affection for you and your mother." J.B.

"How could he sign it with his initials?" Mother gasped.

"It's just so awful," I wailed.

Sing raced down the stairs and into the kitchen, beginning a noisy and obviously emotional cleaning of the house.

"Poor Alex," I murmured, looking out the window at the barns in the distance.

Mother took my hand. "Poor you."

I turned to her in surprise. "What do you mean?"

"I know you, Whitney. You have a kind heart. You'll hesitate to leave him now. But you have a daughter that deserves a life with both her parents. Her real parents. And you and Steven have a right to your happiness, too."

"Yes. But leaving now would be kicking Alex while he's down."

"Well, wait a bit then." She patted my hand as she held it gently between hers, then added softly, "But don't wait too long."

I looked into her eyes. "You're wanting to return home, aren't you?"

"Not while you need me here."

I smiled. "That's an evasive answer. Of course you must return home to Father. I'll be quite all right. Once Alex has worked hard around the ranch for awhile, he'll accept what's happened and I'm sure will adjust. People do."

"Yes, people do," Mother agreed, looking sadly down at the note. "I'll go pack."

"Sing will drive you into town early tomorrow morning. The stage leaves just after dawn."

That evening as I watched Mother finish her packing, I asked her, "Why did Sing give you the gun instead of me?"

"Because you would have hoped you could pull the trigger." She looked at me and smiled. "I knew I would."

"And Jones would have been able to tell the difference, wouldn't he?"

"Yes. He may act like a predator, but he's stayed alive and free all this time only by developing the instincts of prey. He'd never believe that you could kill in cold blood."

"But you really would have done it?"

"To protect my daughter?" She put her hand on my cheek. "Without a qualm."

Feeling my heart lurch as I pictured Rose sleeping peacefully in her bed, I didn't dispute her words.

In the black stillness of early morning, with the stars still lighting the sky, Mother and I parted amid unashamed tears and promises to be together again soon. The wagon rolled toward town down the long winding road that cut through meadows turning brown under the late summer heat. When I could no longer see the wagon, I fought the tight lump in my throat and sudden waves of desolation grinding in my stomach. Finally returning inside, I was presented with Sing wringing his hands in the kitchen doorway.

"Oh God, what now?" I asked, wondering if I should run after Mother. But I quickly determined that this was my mess to clean up and I'd have to face it alone.

"She gone!"

"Mother had to return home eventually. Why are you so upset?"

"No, no! Mrs. Lewis. She gone and her things with her."

"She's been in Lakeview with her sister. Are you saying she returned and has left again?"

"Yes, she return soon after Jones leave. She talk to J.B. outside on porch long time. After that she in her room. All day yesterday, too."

"Why didn't I know?"

"She make me promise say nothing to you. She say she want to tell you. But you upstairs with mother."

"You didn't hear her leave?"

"No. She leave during night. Maybe with J.B.?"

I sat down heavily in the chair by the writing desk in the middle of the room. "Are you telling me they had a, well, a relationship?"

"Don't know." He stopped to consider, then looked even more distressed. "I never think so. Maybe she just not want to stay here with things so bad."

"J.B. must have told her what happened with Jones. Does that mean she knew the truth of J.B.'s past?"

"I not know answers. Just know Mrs. Lewis gone. J.B. gone. Everything different." He began wringing his hands, declaring, "I hate this!"

"Oh, Sing, I'm sorry. Your whole world has changed over night, hasn't it?" He just looked at me in misery. "Don't worry. No matter what happens, I won't forget to consider your needs."

He calmed himself with an effort. "Thank you, Mrs. I start breakfast."

Heading upstairs, I found the door to Alex's study open and boldly walked in. Looking up from his desk, he told me, "He wrote a check to himself for half the ranch funds." Then, startled by a sudden thought, he jumped up and walked to the wall safe hidden behind a large painting. He opened it with a shaking hand, reached far to the back of the gaping iron enclosure and removed a leather bag. After stacking several small bundles of cash on his desk, he turned back to me. "And he took exactly half the cash on hand. Is this his idea of the honorable way?" He threw each bundle back into the bag, threw the bag into the safe, then slammed the door and twirled the dial. "Of course, if we want to discuss his ethics, we could talk to Billy Poor's parents."

Ignoring his last bitter comment, I said, "Maybe it's his way of trying to honor the fact that the Double R was built by him, but left to you."

"You're reaching for that bit of positive thought." He sank down into the chair behind his desk and covered his face with his hands.

"Well, I have more bad news," I told him. "For you anyway, although I'm rather pleased about it."

"What?" He looked up at me and waited.

"Mrs. Lewis has left. She came home from her trip, packed and left, all without our knowing about any of it."

"Did she leave with J.B.?"

"I don't know. Is that a possibility?"

"Whitney, at this point I think we have to assume anything is a possibility." Then, after running his fingers through his hair, he looked at me and said, "I suppose you feel it's good riddance."

"I won't deny it."

We discussed some ranch business, how to word a polite denial to several social invitations, and what I needed to purchase in town on my trip in with Sing. As I rose to leave the room, I noticed a long white envelope on the corner of his desk.

"Is that part of yesterday's mail? Sing must have put it there."

As soon as I handed him the envelope, he opened it without hesitating. Inside was a legal looking document and a letter.

While he read it, I watched him carefully. Over the past several days, he had undergone an extreme transformation. Instead of sitting tall and proud as he always had, he now slumped in his chair, shoulders rounded forward as though carrying a great burden. The skin of his face was gray and tight, eyes red and sunken. I forced myself to turn my attention to the document in his hands.

"Is that a deed?"

When he said nothing, I came around to his side of the desk and picked up the paper. It was a lease agreement accompanied by a letter from a law firm in San Francisco, directing J.B. and Alex Roberts to review the enclosed before further discussion could commence.

"What does this mean? What did J.B. lease?"

"The ranch lands."

"What?" My mind raced to understand. "But J.B. bought the land back in..."

"Another lie," he yelled. Then, under his breath, he added, "Probably the one he was really running away from."

He stood up and walked to the window overlooking the back of the ranch. "We don't own this land. We only own the buildings and equipment. The rightful owner can come and claim it at any time."

"Not if you have a lease," I reasoned.

"Look at the dates."

The lease had expired two months before.

"But who's the owner? Do you recognize the name?"

"No. It isn't the name of anyone here in town."

"But the letter is directed to you as well as J.B. If you don't know about this, why is it addressed to you, too?"

"I have no idea."

It was then that I was joined by the oppressive companionship of impending doom, and a dull pain at the base of my skull. Would the owner give Alex a lease extension? Would he want to do that with Alex instead of J.B.? Would he want us off the land, and would that be my opportunity to go home? These questions and more crowded my mind, but I didn't dare broach them to Alex. No doubt most of them had already occurred to him anyway.

"Please close the door when you leave." He didn't turn toward me, just stood by the window looking out at the ranch that suddenly was no longer his. I'd never before seen such an image of total defeat. Dismissed from the room as well as his thoughts, I simply turned and did as I was told. As I walked toward my room, I heard the door's lock tumble into place, and I clenched my jaw.

Alex sent Sing into town later that day to telegraph the lawyer with the news that J.B. was gone from the ranch and only he was in charge now. The next day a telegram arrived from the lawyer saying he would be arriving in Bridgeport on September 25. He asked that Alex meet him at the Leavitt House early in the afternoon. My first thought was to wonder why the attorney had to come to Bridgeport, when he could either send a renewal or notify us to move, all by mail?

Mr. Alfred Tyler, Esquire, greeted us in the front parlor of the hotel, whereupon we immediately removed to a smaller side room. No one could have looked more ordinary than this man of average height, bland features, conservative dark suit, well modulated voice, and just the right degree of deprecating manner. He also had the most wonderful head of thick white hair I had ever seen.

"Mr. Tyler," I began, "until we heard from you, we had no idea the land was leased. J.B. kept everyone in the dark regarding that. You can imagine the number of questions we have."

"Yes, indeed." He thought a moment. "Let me start at the beginning then, and tell you all I know. The land was originally owned by Daniel Brookstone of San Francisco, back when J.B. moved onto it with his new wife."

"My mother's maiden name was Brookstone," Alex exclaimed.

"That's right. Daniel was her brother. Even after your mother left your father, Daniel continued to lease the land to your father for ranching. Not long after your parents' divorce was final, Daniel died and the land was left to his sister, your mother."

"Left him?" Alex shouted. "Divorced?" He stood over the lawyer in such a threatening manner that I quickly pulled him back onto the sofa next to me.

Alex mumbled, "Oh God, more lies."

Poor Mr. Tyler was obviously alarmed, so I explained. "Alex had been told that his mother had died when he was an infant."

"Oh, dear." The lawyer frowned and shook his head. "I'm so sorry to have brought you such shocking news. The way I understand it, upon returning home from a long trip, your father found that she'd run away from him. She told him in a note that she'd left you with him in exchange for his promise not to pursue her. She told me that she'd discovered something about his past that frightened her and made her feel unsafe around him." He looked intently at Alex. "Oddly, she had no fear of harm befalling you. I also gather that he had alternated between neglecting her needs to overly regulating her movements. So much so that she felt she was being held prisoner. Because of what followed in her life, I believe now that much of that thinking was due to the beginning of a developing instability."

"Not necessarily," Alex mumbled.

"You seem to have known her quite well," I quickly commented.

"Yes. We had an avuncular relationship for years."

Alex had calmed down, and now asked, "Where has she been all this time?"

The man began to sweat. "After leaving your father, she first lived with her brother. He was a widower and she planned to take care of him."

"Planned to?" I asked.

"Yes, well, several things happened very quickly." He took out a handkerchief and mopped his brow before turning to Alex. "First your Uncle made out a will leaving the Bridgeport property to your mother in the event of his death. Then your mother began to show signs of, well, instability. Your uncle sought treatment for her in Sacramento, where it was determined that she, well, was slowly fading into paranoid dementia."

"What's that?" Alex demanded.

I put my hand on his arm and said gently, "She was going insane, Alex."

"Oh, my God!" The vein in his right temple twitched.

"Yes," Mr. Tyler agreed with a frown. "It seems it had occurred in the family before. Then, on the way home from Sacramento, the stage overturned and your Uncle was killed. Your mother was only slightly injured, but the point is that she then inherited your ranch land. Your uncle wasn't extremely wealthy, but he had some money set by.

"She wrote your father and told him everything, and that our firm had been put in charge of the land lease, which would be renewed every ten years at the same rate. She then voluntarily admitted herself to a private sanatorium, with our firm having Power of Attorney. The lease payments were enough to keep her comfortable, and I checked on her twice a year to be sure they took good care of her."

"Oh, my God," Alex muttered again. Then, as a new thought occurred to him, he added, "But I never wrote a check to you."

"We always received the annual payment as a bank draft from Mr. Roberts. He specified that nothing be sent him as a reminder."

"He must have paid it from his gambling winnings," I said. Alex nodded and Mr. Tyler looked surprised. Feeling that we needed to get to the point, I asked, "So why are you here now? Just to renew the lease?"

"No, Mrs. Roberts. Her will was set up so that at her passing, the land would go to her son. Not to Mr. Roberts." He turned to Alex. "I'm sorry to tell you that she passed away last month. I'm here to give you the deed to the ranch property."

"Why couldn't all this have come in a letter and the deed mailed to us?" I persisted.

"Because there was one condition in her will that I had to check in person."

"What?" Alex asked, his tone a bit leery after all the revelations.

Mr. Tyler drank some water before answering. "She wanted to be sure that you showed no signs of mental deterioration. That you were a normal, stable man."

"Ha!" Alex's bark of laughter startled us both.

"Mr. Tyler," I moved to quickly explain, "Alex has had a number of shocks lately. I think the irony of your statement was back of his outburst." Mr. Tyler paid close attention as I briefly told him about J.B.'s unsavory past that had just come to light, and the news that J.B. had left the area, quite possibly for good.

"I can see why this news would be so unsettling then." He smiled reassuringly. "But you're obviously handling it all, so I can attest to your strong mental state. Hopefully, the fact that you now own your land after all this time of leasing, will be somewhat of a positive happening for you."

Neither of us bothered to remind the confused lawyer that until his contacting us, we hadn't known the land was leased. Alex walked to the hotel's front window, standing with his back to us as he looked out at the passing traffic on Main Street.

Mr. Tyler cleared his throat. "Maybe we should just end this meeting so you can go home." He handed me an envelope containing the deed to the land, Mrs. Robert's birth and death certificates, and a check for $1,000 which was the remaining funds in her account.

There was also a faded photograph of a beautiful, dark-haired woman standing next to a much younger J.B. on the steps of a church. She was holding a baby in her arms, long white lace hanging from its Christening gown. J.B. was smiling, but the woman offered no smile to the camera, just an expression of incredible blankness. Looking closer, I realized that her expression was simply despair accepted, with no hope for anything better in the future.

Alex came across and glanced at the picture. "I was once told there were no records of my being baptized here in Bridgeport."

"There wouldn't be," the lawyer commented. "You were baptized in Aurora."

As Alex walked back to the window, Mr. Tyler watched me as I examined the picture. "Yes," he said, agreeing with my unspoken thoughts, "his mother was quite lovely. I was very fond of Jessica Brookstone. She took back her maiden name immediately upon leaving Mr. Roberts."

"Another J.B. Good Lord," I exclaimed, "imagine being known by the same initials as the wife who deserted you."

His comment surprised me. "Men find many ways to remind themselves of their sins."

"Who wants to be continually reminded of their sins?"

"Someone seeking redemption possibly?"

Recalling J.B. saying that when he won at poker he took it as validation that God had forgiven him, I wondered if he now thought that God was reaping delayed punishment for a long list of sins: the violence of the prison breakout, the manipulation of others to do their worst and then letting them hang for it, driving away his wife by his treatment of her, years of perpetuating familial myths as fact, and whatever other ugly things he might have done.

For all this, J.B. was to suffer that which for him was the ultimate reckoning. He was to be deprived of his son, his new granddaughter, and his ranch--the only things good in the whole of his life. Sheriffs, the courts, J.B.'s father, people wronged, and vigilantes had been unable to make him pay for what he had done. But Life had. It always does.

"Alex," I asked gently, "do you have questions about your mother that Mr. Tyler might be able to answer for you?"

He turned back to me and glared. "Like what? Did she ever wonder about me? Did she even remember that she'd had a son?"

"Well..." Mr. Tyler began.

Alex turned on him. "I don't care!" he yelled. "She cared nothing for me, and I don't care anything about her. She's a closed chapter in my life!"

Mr. Tyler nodded his head and stood up, gathering his things without further comment. As we climbed into our wagon, I watched Mr. Tyler head across the street to the Kirkwood Saloon. He looked like a man determined to be there awhile.

For several days Alex stayed almost exclusively in his study. Sing brought a tray of food and coffee to his door each morning and afternoon, but more often than not he took the trays away untouched except for the coffee. Even if Alex briefly went into his bedroom, he would always return to his study with a slam of the door. The inevitable isolating sound of the key turning in the lock seemed to echo louder each time I heard it.

Sometime during the fourth night after our meeting with the attorney, I awoke to hear Alex moving noisily through the house. There was no indication what he was doing, but eventually the front door banged shut. I refused to get up to investigate, thinking it better to let him work off his frustrations alone. Almost reluctantly, I eventually fell asleep.

The weak glow of the sun was only just visible in the distance when I awoke the next day. Dressing quickly in a split skirt and leather jacket, I hurried downstairs looking forward to an invigorating ride before breakfast.

Sing approached cautiously from the kitchen and met me at the bottom of the stairs.

"Good morning, Sing. Is Alex out of his study yet?"

"He just leave. He tie riding horse to back of wagon and leave."

"He took the wagon?" There was something wrong with all of this. "Was he hauling something?"

He looked around the great room. "Oh boy, yes. He take everything with Double R brand and throw it in wagon."

The first thing I looked for, the large iron brand over the fireplace, was gone. Its removal had revealed a light duplicate pattern where the rock had not absorbed the years of rising smoke to the same degree as the surrounding area. Over this, Alex had splashed the contents of an ink bottle, now laying on its side on the rug in front of the hearth.

I picked up the bottle, set it on the game table with a shaking hand. and stood by the front windows where I breathed deeply for several minutes. Forcing myself to walk onto the front porch, I slowly looked toward the road and was hit by the shock of confirmation. The entrance arch was naked of the matching medallion that had for years hung over those arriving or leaving the ranch.

Sing told me, "I take care of Rose. You go do what you must do."

Thankful that I was dressed for riding, I rushed to the barn. Hank and Mort were busy at the forge and didn't look up until I spoke to them.

"Have you seen Alex?" I asked.

"Not since he woke us up just before dawn." Hank wiped his hands on a grimy towel while looking at me with a frown. Mort continued to work.

"Why did he wake you?"

"He had us gather up all the branding irons and put them in the back of J.B.'s old wagon. Then he told us to start making new irons."

"What for?"

When he hesitated, I urged him, "Please tell me."

"I'm kind of worried about him. He wasn't his usual self."

"He's acting crazy is what you mean," I told him bluntly.

"Yes, that's exactly what I mean." He appeared relieved at my forthright words and wiped the sweat from his forehead. "When he left, he said to gather some men together to rebrand all the cattle."

I was aghast. "That'll take weeks."

"That's what I told him." A hot, newly made branding iron hissed loudly as Mort plunged it into a bucket of water. Hank pulled me aside and lowered his voice. "He said he didn't care how long it took, and to tell the men there'd be a bonus in it for them." He laughed shortly. "We won't have any problem hiring hands to get it done."

"Has he designed a new brand?"

"No." He spat on the ground and once again looked uncomfortable.

"What is it?" I asked, braced for whatever was to follow.

He pointed to the new branding iron Mort was holding up. It was a large X. "He said this burned over the Double R brand would say everything he wanted to say."

Not wanting to show my distress, I merely asked, "When he left, which way did he go?"

"He turned left toward the mountains. He wasn't going fast. The wagon was too heavily loaded for that."

"You know about Jones coming here, don't you?"

"Yeah. J.B. told me before he left, in case I wanted to go with him. But I'm through running. This is my home now." After a moment's hesitation, he asked, "Are we okay?"

"You and me?" I asked. "Oh, of course, Hank. You did what you had to do. Besides it was so long ago." I laid a hand on his arm. "I'm so sorry about your wife."

He looked at me and almost produced a smile. "Thanks."

Once mounted, I rode as fast as the old road would allow before cutting across a large marshy meadow, something the wagon would not be able to do. After an hour of this hard riding, I could see the dark blue waters of the first lake above Bridgeport. Alex was not that far ahead, the horses pulling hard up the steep road along the lake edge.

Instead of catching up with him, I pulled up and dismounted, tying my horse near the trail before following on foot. When Alex stopped the rig close to the lake, I stayed on the slope above, hidden by a large boulder surrounded by trees.

He got down from the wagon and immediately began to unhitch the two heavily breathing wagon horses. While he did that, I took note of the wagon's contents. The large decorative iron medallions were there, but so were dozens of branding irons, belt buckles, papers, two flower vases, an album of photographs, an oil painting of J.B. and Alex when he was a young boy, and several things I couldn't see clearly.

When Alex led the wagon horses to a tree near his riding horse, I noticed that the rear of the wagon was precariously close to the edge of a short, steep drop down to a deep part of the lake. He stood next to the wagon for a long moment, his head bowed as though in prayer. I thought maybe he was rethinking his initial plan, but he reached into the wagon and lifted out one of the iron medallions. With a strength born of rage, he threw it out into the lake, and followed it with the branding irons that he threw two at a time. There was no look of anger or even relief on his face as he did this, but only grave determination.

When most of the items were submerged, he got behind the wagon and applied his shoulder to it. The wheels turned only a half rotation before the wagon tipped and plummeted into the lake, slithering on the rocky bottom several yards out into the water before sinking quickly.

I returned to my horse, mounted and rode quietly on the soft earth along the edge of the dirt road. Only when I was sure Alex couldn't hear did I switch to the hard road for the fast ride back, thankful it was downhill. Alex too would be riding back, but he wouldn't be in a hurry and would be leading the wagon team, so I knew I could reach home well before him.

Indeed, by the time he returned, my horse had been put away and was eating a small grain reward. When Alex arrived at the house, I was in a dress and seated at the dining room table with a book and a cup of tea in front of me. I looked as though I'd been there for hours. He said nothing, merely striding past me and straight up to his study. I was really beginning to hate that room.

The next day I awoke to find him quietly sitting across the room from the foot of my bed, sprawled in one of the rose velvet chairs and watching me intently. He was haggard, dirty, and unshaven, with long tendrils of hair unwashed for many days hanging almost into his eyes.

"Alex!" I sat up in bed, my heart beating with alarm, but trying to sound casual. It passed through my mind that I was glad Rose was no longer sleeping in my room. "Are you all right?"

His face was sober and brooding, with cheeks and eyes cadaverous. In a harsh rasping voice, he asked, "Why didn't you come to me?"

Somewhat sleepy still, I was slow to comprehend his meaning. "What?"

"Why didn't you come to comfort me?"

"You told me to leave you alone," I answered reasonably, trying to keep the bite of rising irritation out of my voice. "You locked me out of your rooms and you avoided me whenever you briefly emerged." I slipped out of bed, pulled a robe over my long, high-necked cotton gown, and sat in the other chair close to him. "Those are not the actions that say to me that my presence is wanted."

Dismayed by Alex's erratic state of mind recently, I had the day before agreed with Sing's suggestion to turn the room next door to mine into Rose's room. Mrs. Lewis' old room downstairs was now the guest room. Rose was therefore asleep next door and undisturbed by our voices, or the tense atmosphere of simmering rage.

"You should have persisted," he mumbled, his petulant words a little slurred.

Struggling to remain calm, I said, "Alex, you're not being reasonable. You haven't slept for several nights. Why don't you go to bed and get some rest? You'll think clearer after that."

When I took hold of his hand, he submitted without protest and allowed me to lead him into his room. With barely any help from him, I removed his clothes and got him into bed. When I moved to leave, he grabbed my forearm in a grip that made me yelp with pain. Looking up at me with overly bright eyes, he whispered loudly, "That man's name will never be uttered in this house again!"

"Yes, I understand." Only then did he release me, falling back and closing his eyes.

Whether or not he slept soon, or soundly, I have no idea. I heard nothing from him until late that afternoon when he asked Sing to bring him a tray of food. Eating a light and lonely supper by myself in the dining room, I watched as Sing returned to Alex with a large kettle of hot water. But still he didn't emerge to join me.

Late that night as I crawled into bed burdened by the weight of emotional exhaustion, Alex appeared in the doorway between our rooms. He was freshly shaven, scrubbed clean and wrapped in a long brown robe. This he dropped to the floor without a word of greeting, boldly revealing that he was wearing nothing beneath. And also revealing that he was ready for more than sleeping.

Without greeting or fond words, he jerked back the covers and tossed them to the foot of the bed. He then fell upon me with a ferocious impatience, tearing my cotton gown as he pulled it up from around my resisting legs. When the pressure of his mouth split my lip and I tasted blood, I felt a rush of panic that escalated as he forced his body between my legs. With no care as to my willingness or comfort, he neither stopped nor even slowed when I cried out in pain. When he mauled and pinched my breasts, I put my hands on his shoulders and tried unsuccessfully to push him off. But I was forced to accept that he was in command, and could only stoically endure the tearing punishment to my body. While silent tears ran down my cheeks and back into my hair, Alex continued his silent assault in an effort to control the last thing J.B. had liked--me.

When he left immediately after completing his act of domination, I rolled onto my side and lay there a long time, shivering with the shock of what had happened. Gone completely was the last surviving fragment of tenderness I'd ever felt for my husband. Eventually, I fell asleep, sobbing Steven's name over and over.

For the next few nights I lay awake tense and wary as I waited for his approach, determined that I would never again allow Alex in my bed. A lead pipe was under my pillow just in case he wouldn't listen to reason, even if it meant dealing with a legal system that would consider only that he was my husband and had "his conjugal rights". But I needn't have worried. He not only never again came to my bed at night, he showed me no affection of any kind, although he was from that time on always scrupulously polite.

He showed even less interest in Rose, an adorable seven months old. But I didn't try to change that. When I was ready to leave, I didn't want an attachment to Rose to be a source of objection from him. More than once I recalled lawyer Tyler's words that instability "had occurred in the family before".

Over the next couple of weeks, I heard Alex laughing with the men as he handed them their pay packets, and listened to his whistling as he shaved in the morning. Resentment and anger burned in my stomach. At meals, he readily discussed articles in the newspaper as well as any other topic of ranch or local interest, seeming to be unaware that I spoke very little about anything. One night during the holidays, we played cards with a couple from town that Alex invited for dinner. He ate with gusto, and finished most of the five bottles of wine served with the meal.

Although I was encouraged by his participation in such normal activities, this uncharacteristic cheerfulness that seemed to increase along with the amount of drink he regularly consumed, in no way pleased me. Although I wanted to confront him about my leaving, something held me back. It wasn't a lack of courage on my part, but rather an underlying fearfulness that all was not quite right with him.

As the weeks moved forward through a cold, snowy winter into 1906, Alex seldom was seen without a glass of whiskey in his hand, and it was never less than half full. Most nights I led him with great difficulty to his bed, or at least a sofa where I could cover him with a blanket. For the first few weeks of this, he would arise at seven o'clock and go outside to work. Then it became eight o'clock. On the morning I struggled to awaken him at nine o'clock, he took a swing at me. He missed, but that was when I realized he wasn't going to improve on his own, and that something had to be done.

Before I could think what that might be, I received a long letter from Father. He was full of news regarding the Valley and the "trouble" with the City. While I was enduring my personal troubles, the people of the Owens Valley were enduring their own.

In January of 1906, Congressman Sylvester Smith took into consideration the needs of the City at the end of a ten year drought with its reservoirs almost dry, but also the needs of the Valley whose existence hinged on its agricultural production. Although some claimed the Los Angeles reservoir levels were artificially lowered by the City dumping the water through the sewer system, such could not have happened since the one was not connected to the other. But it was evident the City was in desperate need of water. Keeping the needs of both City and Valley in mind, Supervisor Smith felt that a reasonable compromise could be reached.

Claiming that if the aqueduct went through, the Valley would be decimated, he proposed instead that the Reclamation Service proceed with its reservoir project, with the water first being sent to farmers along the river and then to the City for its domestic use. Also, if there was any water left over, it should go to other irrigation in Inyo County.

But the City's attitude was clearly reflected in a *Times* article after the passing of the September 1905 bond issue to pay for the building of the aqueduct. "*The Owens River is ours, and our business now is to hustle and bring it here, and make Los Angeles the garden spot of the earth and the home of a million contented people.*"

The City was looking to the future, which was defined as not just satisfying the current population, but the growth of a greater Los Angeles area that would include cities not yet in existence. Consequently, in order to hold title to the water rights that the City had acquired in the Valley, it would have to show consistent use of that water in Los Angeles. Otherwise, when they wanted it for the City in the future, it could be argued that they really didn't need it. So the City decided to pour any excess water received from the Owens River into the agriculture of the San Fernando Valley, next to the currently developed Los Angeles area, until it too became developed. But this doomed our Valley ranches, or at least promised to drastically reduce their production.

Those in the Valley objected to this as going beyond the City's original plea for water to slack the thirst of the existing population. Inyo citizens, and not a few newspapers across the country that were against this San Fernando irrigation, took up the chant, "Not one drop for irrigation!" In letters written to newspapers near and far, local businessmen and especially local Inyo editor W. A. Chalfant, made it clear the Valley was perfectly willing to "accommodate need, but not greed."

In preparation for the aqueduct construction, Senator Frank Flint proposed a bill to allow the City a right-of-way for the aqueduct across public lands. But Congressman Smith asked that an amendment be added prohibiting the use of the water for irrigation by the City, using it only for drinking or domestic use. After a meeting with Mulholland and his associates, they told Congressman Smith that they would agree to the amendment if he would support their right-of-way bill. After they all met with the head of the Interior Department, and the amended bill had been sent back to the House committee, Smith returned to the House Public Lands Committee with the good news of a compromise.

But while Congressman Smith was returning to the Valley, Mulholland and his associates were on their way to Washington. There they convinced President Roosevelt that because of the existing laws, it would be necessary for the City to have continuous use of the *whole* supply of water, even if it meant some of the water would irrigate the San Fernando Valley. Otherwise, they could not protect their right to the water. The President listened to Senator Flint's argument that it was "a thousand-fold more important to the state and more valuable to the people as a whole if used by the City than if used by the people of the Owens Valley." The President agreed, and removed the irrigation restriction.

In his letter directing this action, the President wrote that regarding the opposition to this by the "few settlers in the Owens Valley", that "their interest must unfortunately be disregarded in view of the infinitely greater interest to be secured by putting the water in Los Angeles."

When the bill came back to the House Committee changed by the President, Congressman Smith realized that it was futile to fight further, and bitterly accepted what was seen by the Valley citizens as another betrayal by the City. In June of 1906 the bill passed and Los Angeles was given title to the public lands in the Valley for whatever use they wanted, without restriction.

It was then that Valley ranchers began to feel that a great conspiracy had been set against them. How to stop it became the all-consuming subject for every meeting between people. Much of the talk, even as far north as Bridgeport, was the lament of unfairness and lack of appreciation for the Valley ranchers and business owners. As one man said, "We're after all the sons and daughters of pioneers that opened the West to the rest of the country, and those that mined the hills and sent their ore to the ports of Los Angeles so it could grow into a big city."

This sense of their place in history may have contributed to the recriminations some ranchers heaped upon their neighbors who sold their property or water rights to the City. But the criticism by those who could afford to hold out was balanced by their compassion for those who needed to feed a family, even if it meant selling a beloved homestead to those who were the enemy of your friends.

Over the next few months, Father sent letters with newspaper clippings recounting the Valley's continuing efforts to fight the City's determination to take the Owens River. Father wrote that some men were mumbling that if even the Federal Government had abandoned them, then they might revert to the old pioneer attitude of self-sufficiency that decreed it was acceptable to do whatever was necessary to protect your own, even if it included violence.

To be fair, it was seldom acknowledged that having won the fight, the City did propose to share some of the water with the ranchers. Of course, this was accepted grudgingly by the citizens. No one likes to be condescended to, and that was the way most of the tough, independent citizens saw it. As Uncle Vince sarcastically commented to a City representative, "Magnanimous of you to let us use water that already belongs to us." The City's man just smirked and responded, "Not any more it doesn't."

The City was set to control water distribution for most of the land between Bishop and the Owens Lake. And, in actuality, although the City could take any quantity of the water whenever it wanted to, at least until the 1920's much of the water would be left for the ranchers' use. The real problem for many was that the City would own the land, and the ranchers would have to lease it back from the City if they wanted to stay and work it, knowing that the City could kick them off at any time. Land was real wealth and real independence. Without the land as their own, the ranchers felt they had lost both.

Full of frustration and anger over the loss of their ranches, future availability of water, and the overall fate of the Valley, the townspeople focused on little else and waited to see what would happen next. Consequently, few people gave thought to what all this meant to the local Paiute tribes. They had lived lightly upon the land for thousands of years, gently coaxing their sustenance from native plants and grasses that were watered by an abundance of creeks, and a high water table. Living in small groups throughout the foothills where water, grass, trees, wild game, and fruit-bearing vines and bushes were abundant, they also continued to be an important labor force for the town.

Some of the Paiutes still lived in grass, reed and brush dwellings in the foothills of the Sierra and along the Owens River. Although substantial enough for their needs and comfort, the structures were considered by the townspeople as trash dwellings. Other tribal members had built small cabins with planted gardens and pens for goats, chickens and other farm animals. Unfortunately, some of these were near or on the aqueduct right-of-way. "In the way" and "of no value" are not good phrases to have connected to your home, especially when dealing with whites so powerful even other whites can't fight them. This meant that the Owens Valley tribes waited along with everyone else, although owing to their past treatment in the Valley, considerably less hopeful of a positive outcome.

Along with Father's letters and our own newspapers, the news from those passing through Bridgeport helped to keep us informed of all that was taking place. The Valley residents had quickly become the pioneers that had "provided for Western expansion of this great country of ours", and therefore deserved better treatment. The City had been assigned the role of thirsty, evil giant with no respect or concern for any need but its own.

But *its own* was thousands of people who had suffered through years of drought. I often wondered about the men and women in Los Angeles whose water was rationed during the hot summer months at the same time they saw even more people settling around them. Of course, that might have slowed if the City had not continued its campaign to attract people to the area, and fewer swimming pools had been installed. But whether long-time resident or newly arrived, few of them probably gave any thought to where the water came from that flowed so readily from their taps and garden hoses. In any event, the Owens Valley was being represented as a great desert with a small population of people in a few little towns that would be left with enough water for their needs--so why not take what the City wanted from those few hundred for the benefit of many thousands? This, however, was a justification that ignored the reality of the broader picture.

There were hundreds of acres of cultivated fields and grazing cattle that relied on the abundance of water flowing from the Eastern Sierra, allowing the desert and mountain foothill communities to thrive. The wide range of produce along with beef, mutton, honey, alfalfa, wheat and barley raised in the area was sent out to towns throughout California and into Nevada, Arizona, and beyond. But more than that, there was the natural landscape, the experience of which was even then enjoyed by hunters, fishermen, and nature enthusiasts. Below the Sierra, hiding in its thousands of folds and depressions with its uncounted small lakes and seasonal streams, lay the unique expanse of the Owens Valley itself.

To the north, ancient volcanoes loom whose eruptions millions of years ago scattered over the valley floor quantities of lava rock reminiscent of chocolate crumble under the children's table. Within easy travel to the east and anchored to the fragile earth are the oldest trees in the world, some almost 5,000 years old. In the Valley's southern range, the Alabama Hills with its huge boulders and natural arches give shelter to petroglyphs created by ancient peoples, but viewed regularly only by a wide range of wildlife. Green riparian richness overflows with plants, some found no where else, and edge cold rushing creeks cascading down to the Valley floor where they water stands of willow, pine, birch, aspen, cottonwood, locust and a scattering of rare oaks. All of this shelters and nourishes hundreds of birds, reptiles and mammals. Beyond this abundance lies the broad sweep of the open desert covered in wildflowers unique to the Sierra foothills, silver-gray sagebrush, brittlebush, yellow rabbitbrush, rare cactus plants, and acres of Joshua trees. This is the *barren* land considered of such little value that it was permissible to let it die for lack of water.

Father, along with dozens of other citizens, wrote to the newspapers across the state to prophesize the inevitable destruction of this bounty if the *big ditch* was allowed to snake its way through the Valley. But public outrage, the pleading of County politicians, news media sympathetic to the Valley, citizen groups sending challenging letters to all who would listen— nothing checked the progress of what had been set in motion. There was to be no reprieve.

Set to disappear were the livelihoods of those who had spent years of effort coaxing acres of alfalfa, barley, wheat and corn, fruit trees, grape vines, private vegetable gardens, bee hives, and herds of cattle, sheep and horses into flourishing enterprises. Fed by 2,800 square miles of watershed, the Owens River had for 35 years been the source of water for 300 miles of ditches dug by ranchers from the river to their fields. But late in 1906, the men, women and children living in the Valley looked at this abundance, both cultivated and natural, and had but one united realization. *"All this is to be taken from us by a city most of us have never seen, and still fewer of us even want to see."*

But this ruination was an anticipated future. The ruin of my personal life was already upon me. Through that winter and into the summer of 1906 I stood by and watched Alex fill himself with drink day after day and night after night, seldom sober enough to carry on a short substantive conversation. Having no idea how best to stop him, I received a stony glare whenever I tried. Afraid of his increasing volatility, I hesitated to approach him about my leaving. I had not forgotten his attack the last time he was in my room, and I still slept with the pipe under my pillow.

I spent almost all of my time with Rose. Sing was an angel, caring for her whenever I had to get out of the house or scream from the confinement. Whether riding across the spring meadows covered in a gay profusion of color or the green early summer grass, I would set a course toward the mountains. My simmering anger and growing loneliness would recede along with the meadows left behind as I exchanged them for the sweet smell of mountain air. On one such ride, when finally immersed in the yellow of rattling aspen leaves excited by the cool breeze, in a grove so dense that the bright sky almost disappeared, I dismounted. While the smell of damp earth calmed me, and my horse pawed a mud puddle, I sank to the ground beneath a large pungently scented pine and pressed my back against the rough bark, welcoming the discomfort of it. It was pain I could understand. Leaving such restful beauty and returning to the ranch was possible only because I knew Rose would be there to greet me, now a little over a year old.

As things became harder to bear at the ranch, several times I ended up at Irene's house, pouring out to her my anxieties and frustrations. She would spread a fine linen cloth over the small table in the kitchen, make for us savory delights and pots of tea, and serve it all on translucent thin white china. Surrounded by the pristine cleanliness of her most feminine house and filled with tantalizing food, I would relax and listen to her chat about local gossip and feminine interests. I could then return home, energized for the ordeal of tolerating my sterile and volatile life.

On one such visit to Irene, I brought up two subjects that I still recall clearly.

"How in all the world," I lamented, "did two people like my parents find each other? They fit together so perfectly. Why didn't I find such an alliance?"

"But their type of marriage is the exception," she pointed out. "You actually have a good marriage compared to some I've seen."

I then told her about his attack. She listened without comment, but her eyes narrowed for a moment and her jaw tightened. "You must leave him as soon as possible."

"I know." Carrying my plate to the sink, I looked through the small window there. "But neither of my parents ever considered such a thing."

"So what?" she responded sharply. "Why is it so important to you what they would or wouldn't have done?"

"Because for a long time I relied on the faith that my marriage would eventually work out, and I'd end up with what they have."

"You were foolish then, weren't you?" she asked.

"Evidently."

"I know I was blunt." She poured more tea into my cup and I returned to the table. "But until you stop grieving for something that's so rare as to be practically non-existent, you won't begin to see what you must do next." Of course, she was right.

We then discussed a "*Ladies Home Journal*" article on patent medicines full of cheap alcohol and laudanum, an opium solution. It upset me because I myself had used Dr. Bull's Cough Syrup, which was found to contain these ingredients. The article described what it called "the poison trust", the patent medicine industry's use of pressure to prevent any unfavorable criticism of their practices by newspapers.

Irene said, "I'd much rather drink the new beverage being sold in town. It actually settles the stomach."

"Really?"

"Yes, it's called Coca-Cola. It's quite tasty when mixed with fizzy water. They charge five cents at the drugstore, but it's well worth it."

"I'll have to try it some time."

During every visit with Irene, I longed to tell her about Steven and my eventual return to Lone Pine, but I could never call up the necessary courage. It would have seemed an intrusion into the pure little world she had created, and I would have more willingly tracked mud onto her clean floors. So I sipped tea, kept silent, and waited for the right time to tell her I was leaving. After, of course, I found the right time to tell Alex.

CHAPTER 14

The fall of 1906 blazed through October with the willows and cottonwoods rattling their yellow leaves among the orange, brown and red of their neighbors. The rippling oceans of long green grasses had been replaced with withered brown wisps of vegetation. Each day the sun gleamed less bright and the mountain shadows stretched longer, with dusk appearing earlier every evening. The languor of long sultry summer days gave way to the energy of shorter autumn days hinting of the winter chill soon to follow.

The newspapers were still filled with details of the catastrophic earthquake in San Francisco, the fires that followed and the thousands of people displaced from their homes. The older Lone Pine residents felt a special kinship with those displaced and living in makeshift shelters, remembering their own devastating tremor that had leveled Lone Pine in 1872.

Several times that summer I tried to open a conversation with Alex about the state of our marriage. Possibly sensing where any private conversation would lead, he had either refused to sit down with me or had shown a meanness of attitude that kept me from insisting.

Then, late in October, I awoke to find Alex across the room from my bed, standing over Rose asleep in the crib. I kept it in my room so I could have her with me when she was unable to fall asleep in her room. His face was just visible to me in the weak early light, and his expression was more animated than any I had seen for some time. His color became heightened as he chewed on the inside of his lower lip. I found the intensity of his concentration disturbing and my hand crept beneath my pillow for the cool reassurance of the hidden pipe. But it was Rose that he was staring at with rapt contemplation. Why had he gone from ignoring her to studying her with such intense interest?

Hoping he had not been occupied in this way for long, I spoke quickly. "Good morning, Alex. I hope you got some rest last night. I heard you come to bed late, so I'm surprised to see you up so early."

He finally forced his eyes from Rose and focused on me, speaking slowly, and giving away nothing of his true feelings. "She's very pretty, isn't she?"

"Yes, she is. She's almost a year and a half now and growing fast." To avert the discussion, I asked, "Are you headed outside now?"

"Yes." He was obviously preoccupied with a deeply puzzling thought as he walked toward the dressing area between our rooms. There he stopped and turned back to me. "Did I tell you that I saw the doctor yesterday about the cut on my hand?"

"No, you didn't."

"You were right. It needed a few stitches."

"I thought the bandage looked new. I hope it didn't hurt too much."

"It didn't hurt much." He started to move away and then stopped, once again turning back. "He kept me talking while he did his work. I got to telling him about my childhood injuries and illnesses. It kept me from paying attention to what he was doing." He shook his head a little and with a small shrug, he left my room, closing the door between us. Puzzled by his behavior, but thankful that he was in a calm mood, I dressed and had breakfast without considering it further.

At supper, Alex announced that he was taking Hank, Mort and Parson with him for two weeks to Virginia City. That would leave only a couple of men to care for the horses, since the few permanent hands and any temporary workers recently hired, had not yet returned after moving the herds to their winter pastures. I had never known Alex not to go with the men on that trek, but so much had happened over the last year that when he had decided not to go with them, I had accepted it without question.

But now he was taking his three best hands with him on a trip to Virginia City, something they told me he had never done before. Although the men were pleased, they were also perplexed and even somewhat uneasy. Virginia City may have been greatly reduced from the peak of its prosperous mining days, but it was still a rambunctious town with enough activities both innocent and wicked to occupy any man for many days. I had no idea which it would be for Alex and his men, for as usual he felt no need to explain anything to me about his plans.

After a long walk, I eventually settled on the back porch and stared into the distance at the Sawtooth Ridge as though it could give me the energy or inspiration to make the correct next decision. But I didn't have the same relationship with the mountains that Mother did, and no answers came to me. For a moment my mind cowered in a state of submissive non-thought, afraid to think for fear of feeling.

Finally, however, I had enough of being numbed by the constancy of indecision and fear of Alex's moods. Where was my old fire? Where was the rallying energy I had always felt at the core of my character? Could I be feeling so low merely because I was for the first time in my life really and truly alone with no one to turn to for advice?

Pondering this, I went up the stairs to Rose's room. Picking up my warm and sleepy child, as always my heart beat harder when she opened her eyes, stuck a fist in her mouth and mumbled, "Mommy." When I held her so tight that I felt her little hand smack the side of my head, I suddenly realized that there was an immediacy to my life that took all precedence. I had no choice when I could make my next move. With it already fall, I had no time to delay.

After settling Rose in her crib with her favorite toys, I went to Alex's study and found the door open while he sorted through papers. I told him we needed to talk. He didn't look up, instead putting a stack of papers into a black leather valise.

"Can't it wait until I get back?"

"No. You say you'll be gone about two weeks, but I know from experience it can drift into longer than that. If we have an early snow, it could block the narrow pass south of town."

"So? I'll be coming in from the north."

Taking a deep breath and letting it out slowly, I told him, "I'm going home, Alex."

He looked up, one brow slightly raised. "For how long?"

Although it was tempting to say I didn't know, I swallowed and said, "For good."

He produced a gentle snort. "I've been wondering when you'd get around to this." He continued sorting through papers, showing little change of expression. "I knew our marriage couldn't survive all that's happened."

I moved closer to the desk, but stopped when he took a step away from me. "Alex, I'm not leaving you because of J.B. I'm leaving because it's never been really good between us, especially for the last couple of years. And it's not like you're overly fond of Rose."

"Why should I be? You've done a good job of keeping us apart."

"How did I do that?" Hearing the shrillness in my voice, I took another deep breath. "Alex, you could have cared for her or played with her any time you wanted, but you never showed any interest."

"I was kind of busy, you know." He glanced at me with a frown before adding, "What with running the ranch alone and J.B.'s little revelations."

I continued speaking as though he hadn't said anything. "I'll always let you see Rose whenever you want." Of course, I knew he would never want to see her, but if by some odd chance he did, Steven would never allow it.

He secured the latch on the bag and put it on the edge of the desk before speaking. "I don't suppose I can keep you from leaving while I'm gone, but I'd prefer that you wait until I'm back so we can talk. We'll need to decide how much money you'll need for you and Rose. I can send it to you each month."

And keep me tied to you that way, I thought. But I only said, "That's very thoughtful of you, Alex."

Taking it for granted that I'd wait until his return because of the money, he said, "Good. I'll only be gone about two weeks, maybe even less. My business won't take long, and the men will have a decent break. When I return, we'll resolve all this."

"Fine." I took a deep breath. "But know this. If you don't return by the end of two weeks, or if the snows come early, I'll be gone."

"Okay. Fair enough." He picked up the satchel of papers and walked from the room, giving me not one backward glance.

Relieved that the discussion had after all been so dispassionate, I spent the rest of that day sewing a dress for Rose. Playing nearby, she watched me carefully, laughing whenever my ineptness led to a pricked finger that I greeted each time with a yelp.

Late in the afternoon of the next day, just as Sing began serving me dinner, a telegram arrived from Bodie. One of the hotel owners was reminding Alex to be sure and deliver on time the pre-paid hams destined for the town's Thanksgiving festivities at the Occidental Hotel. That meant the dozen hams in the smokehouse had to be in Bodie soon or the town's plans would be ruined.

After thinking it over, I decided to bring the meat to them myself in one of the wagons. Sing agreed to watch Rose only after I convinced him that he couldn't talk me out of going. We then loaded the wagon with the expected bounty, and just before dawn the following morning I kissed Rose good-bye and climbed onto the seat of the loaded wagon.

My first stop was at Irene's house to tell her where I was going. I rapped on her door just as a hint of light began to shine on the mountains. Following a twitch at the curtain as she peeked out to see who could be so rude as to awaken her that early, the door opened and I quickly stepped inside.

"You're dressed for riding," she noted, "but I only see the buckboard."
After looking me up and down, she yawned and said, "Are you okay,
Whitney?"

"Regardless of my odd behavior, yes I am."

As she prepared to stoke the stove, I stopped her, making her sit down
at the little table in the kitchen. "I don't have time to wait for the fire to get
up." I then explained to her what had happened between Alex and myself,
and the need for me to deliver the hams to Bodie.

"After all that's happened, you still care about the ranch's reputation?"
She didn't even try to hide her surprise.

"Well, yes. But even more, I care about that poor man and all his
guests that'll be disappointed. The Double R hams are wonderful and a
long tradition at his hotel. There isn't anyone else at the ranch to do it or
I'd never venture there by myself. But I'm sure I'll be fine. I'll make it
clear who I am at the stations right away, and since they all know Alex and
J.B., I'll be treated well. I should be back in about three days, allowing a
day to get there, one full day there, and a day returning. If I can't stay at
Murphy's Station, I'll just camp out. I put gear in the wagon for that, along
with some food."

"Whitney!" Alarm suffused her face. "A woman alone on that road,
especially one as pretty as you! You must be insane."

"I also have this." She stared at the gun I pulled from my pocket. It
was the same one mother had previously shown to Charlie Jones with such
efficacy. When I added that there was also a rifle under the seat, she shook
her head. Then an attitude of sudden resolution straightened her spine and
she declared, "I'm going with you."

"What? Oh, Irene, I didn't stop here to have you do that."

"Nonsense. I'll be dressed and packed in half an hour. Get the fresh
bread on the counter, and there's a small block of hard cheese in the larder,
too." She then disappeared into her bedroom. Although she hurried, it
was still an hour later when we left.

After leaving the valley, we veered onto the canyon road to Bodie. It
was steep and covered with deep ruts cut by the iron wheels of heavy freight
wagons, hundreds of which had passed over that road since the boom of
1878. Recent rains washing across portions of the road had carved into
it a washboard surface, and the hard shaking of the wagon as we rattled
along caused me to fear losing a wheel. However, the trip had its pleasant
aspects.

For the first half of the trek up the canyon we admired golden fall color sweeping up from the road and covering the hillsides. Rust and amber and sunny yellow leaves blew from the trees over-shadowing our progress. Hawks screeched as they floated overhead, rabbits flashed white tails before disappearing beneath bushes, and a coyote loped unhurried across the road in front of us. We passed two freight wagons and several riders, but they merely looked at us with curiosity and nodded in respectful greeting. Nevertheless, as each approached, I felt for the gun in the pocket of my dress, and didn't relax until they were well past.

That night we set up camp not far from the road, blocked from anyone passing by thick stands of trees and brush. Early the next morning, with the horses fresh and eager, we started up the steep and barren last few miles of the road, its condition even worse than we had experienced up to that point. Weathered cliff walls of rock and crumbling dirt rose to our left, while to our right was a steep drop down to miles of treeless scrub-filled rolling terrain. The horses strained upwards under the bright sun, the air cooled by a light breeze that also blew over us the dust of passing wagons. The largest of these rigs pressed us to the edge of the road and my heart thudded as our wagon's wheels turned perilously close to the precipitous drop-off.

As we crested the last rise in the road, the old town lay before us a very welcome sight. But this sense of euphoria lasted only a moment. Although I knew we were going to be presented with a town reduced from its past glory, I hadn't expected so many buildings in partial ruin and dilapidation, or the remaining evidence of fires that had ravaged areas between buildings. For a town with only a few brick buildings, and the rest old dry wood, fire was both its worst enemy and its frequent visitor.

The road up the canyon continued straight into town, past deserted buildings falling into ruin, weeds poking up through the boards of the sidewalks connecting them. Filling the air as we rolled down Main Street was the rattle of four wagons accompanied by shouts and whistles and the crack of the driver's whips. Men and women walked down the wooden sidewalks, each casting a curious look in our direction. Each time we passed a saloon, a burst of male laughter reached us, and occasionally even the jangle of an old piano would assail us. But it was the thumping jar of the stamps crushing ore that never ceased, echoing over the hills and heard even in town. As intrusive as were these few stamps, I couldn't imagine how disturbing the additional dozens would have been during the town's boom years.

We passed the Miners Union Hall on our left, still the center of the town's activities, then crossed Green Street. Picturing Mr. Boone in my mind as we passed his old store, I smiled and encouraged the horses on until we reached the Occidental Hotel.

We were greeted by Mr. Boyd with both surprise and gratitude, and invited to stay in one of his best rooms without charge. Assuring us that his employees would unload the wagon and deliver our rig to the livery stable, we were led to our room where we washed off as much of the road dirt as possible without being able to bathe. Taking time for little else, we eagerly made our way downstairs and onto the front walkway.

Having all my life heard stories of the glories of Bodie, it was sad to see so much of it now slowly deteriorating. Some of the deserted houses were stripped of their doors, window glass and fancy decorative trims, all of which had no doubt been used elsewhere. Many of the finer wooden structures had been moved from the edge of town to the active business center where they were grouped together to more efficiently service the 800 still calling the town home.

After we returned to the hotel for a delicious meal, we walked up Green toward Woods Street in the fading light, wrapping our shawls around us as the temperature dropped rapidly. Soon I was standing in the middle of a narrow road in front of my parents' old home, which looked unbelievably tired and neglected. It was difficult to say how long it had been deserted. In Bodie's harsh atmosphere, with snow to the roof tops alternating with searing heat, it could have been months or years.

The once white curtains at the windows showed numerous tears, and the bricks Father had laid down for a path from the street to the door twenty-five years before were scattered into the surrounding brush. None of the rabbitbrush Mother had planted along the walk for its yellow fall color had survived.

I walked carefully across the square wooden porch so loved by Mother, loose boards squeaking beneath my feet and the low railing slumping in the corner. Finding the front door unlocked, I entered eagerly, but stopped for a moment to accustom my eyes to the dark interior. Looking at the front window's torn shade, I walked over to it and rolled it up. Each step left the pattern of my feet on the unswept floors and caused puffs of dust to rise around me. I ducked my head when I brushed against old yellowed newspaper hanging from the ceiling where it had once been used as insulation. Wallpaper had also come loose and showed lacy brown stains created by leaks during wet weather. In several places it was hanging from the walls in limp strips. But even more than the disrepair, I was surprised that the house was so cramped and small.

While Irene walked around outside, I stood framed in the front window looking out upon the bare hills rolling toward Bodie Bluff. It was difficult to imagine myself living there, although my parents had certainly managed quite well. Having been raised in a large, comfortable house, and now living in another, I found it difficult to picture myself cooking on the small two-eyed iron stove in the sparsely furnished kitchen, or sleeping in a bedroom where there was barely enough room to walk around the bed. But heating such a small house during the long and severe Bodie winters could only have been an oft counted blessing.

As I walked outside to stand on the front porch, the decaying interior of the once loved home behind me, I felt a sudden shock of loneliness. Whether it was the brittle desolation of the town's location, or the anticipation of returning to the Double R, I'm still not sure.

As we walked down the road in front of the house, Irene commented on the total deficit of trees. Only the pale green of sagebrush scrub covered the golden sand and a few even grew in the middle of many once busy side streets. Picturing the area blanketed in deep snow, I felt a great respect for the perseverance of every Bodie citizen that had ever endured such incredible frozen barrenness.

Throughout California and Nevada, thousands of people in the late 1800's had lived and worked through times of boom and bust in numerous mining camps. Mother, however, never liked it when people called Bodie a mining camp. To her it was a town. She once said that because of impatience, greed and a great want of forward thinking, Bodie missed becoming a sprawling great city. She blamed more than the failing mines. She blamed stubborn men of little imagination who were in charge and made the decisions, ignoring the suggestions of the women and men who wanted social and financial stability that could have produced sound reasons for people to stay. Consequently, although the town in 1906 had good schools and good water, and a second church, it had little hope of growing without the discovery of more ore.

We crossed over Green and walked north on Woods Street. Before us loomed the huge buildings encasing the Standard Mill, with its large tailings pond spread out before it near the road to Aurora. It wasn't the same mill where my father had worked as an equipment engineer. That giant wooden structure had burned down in 1899. In its place was a large, corrugated iron building, its peaked roof and gray bulk absorbing the last rays of the sun, and reflecting into the water of the pond.

Inside was the 20-stamp mill where ore was crushed, then passed along to another area where a process using cyanide separated the gold from the rock. Before 1895, the miners had mixed the crushed ore with mercury to separate out the gold. Both processes, along with the ear-splitting pounding of the heavy iron stamps, affected the men's health in dire ways. And yes, they knew it was dangerous even back then.

A few years before, brothers Warren and Ed Loose had formed the New Bodie Mining Co. and had driven the 1400 foot Whitney Tunnel into the Ritter Range to the west of the Bluff. This was the ore that the 20-stamp mill was now churning into pieces, the loud ringing clang filling the air for miles around and causing everyone near the bluff to speak much louder than otherwise would be necessary. But it was proof that the mine was still producing, and for investors, miners and local business people, it was therefore a welcome sound. However, on the once busy south end of the bluff, only the Red Cloud was taking out ore.

This didn't look like a town set to burst forth in a rush of renewed success. The buildings had once seen coats of fresh white paint, but most of that had been blasted off by howling winds full of grit. More than a few of the wooden buildings listed sideways, reminding me of an old miner who often sat on the bench outside the Meysan's store in Lone Pine, so life-worn he could barely hold himself upright even with the help of a cane.

The Bodie streets were wide, once accommodating dozens of freight wagons trundling supplies to the stores and warehouses. There was now so little wheel and horse traffic grinding into the muddy streets that weeds had started growing along the edges near the sagging planked walkways. But although the population may have waned, we saw a mule train carrying wood to those who were storing it up for the coming winter. Wood was still a necessary and sometimes scarce commodity for the households, even if the mills now had electricity.

We made our way down Mill Street, passed around the huge rocky dump of the Bulwer Tunnel, and arrived back on Main Street. Two stagecoaches passed us, only a few passengers inside. During the 1879-81 boom, there would have been dozens of coaches with nine or more inside, and even some hanging on atop the roof.

The walkways were so clear of people that we made our way easily, except around the saloons, once numbering close to a hundred but now less than half a dozen. However, as we approached the Occidental, a group of cowboys tied their exhausted horses to the hitching rail in front of the hotel before walking toward the saloon and chop house next door. They were men of indeterminate age with weathered faces glaring from under dirty hats, and showing exhaustion after hours riding horses matted with sweat-caked hair and lathered drool.

So recently had they left the trail that they were still wearing the leather chaps that protected their legs against the sharp spines of cactus and scrub. Their multi-colored shirts showed heavy grime, as did the well-used "neckerchiefs" tied around their necks. Boots caked with mud and horse droppings sported spurs that jangled rhythmically with each step on the loose boards of the sidewalk. But they nodded to us with polite respect, and one tipped his hat. Still, as they passed, Irene and I fought the urge to reach for a lavender-scented hanky to press to our noses.

We spent the rest of the day immersed in the atmosphere and routine of the town. We chatted with women in the shops, listened to the raucous laughter and music coming from saloons, smelled the pungent fried onions emanating from the chop houses, smiled at the laughter of children skipping down the street, pretended not to hear three cowboys swapping ribald jokes as their horses slurped from an old tin trough, and even helped a man trying to load groceries into the back of his wagon with one arm in a sling. So we were content to enter the hotel, sip a sherry in the parlor near the smoldering fire in an old black stove, and enjoy one another's company. It took us no time at all to fall asleep in our room after that, each in a narrow but comfortable iron bed.

However, fatigue and unfamiliar surroundings contributed to a strange dream. Even today the memory of it is vivid in my mind, probably because of the considerable time I spent pondering its significance. It started with me in bed with my husband there in Bodie, where we had lived for a long time. But my husband was Steven, and he asked me softly, "My darling, what are you thinking?" He never stopped stroking my hair as I lay naked in his arms, in the middle of a bed with a dark mahogany headboard. Instead of answering him, I kissed him and we began to make love. But he suddenly stopped, got out of bed somehow fully dressed, and walked out of the room without looking back. I woke up with Irene shaking me. "Whitney, wake up! You're having a bad dream."

As I sat up in a lingering haze of deep sleep, I wondered vaguely how she knew. Only when she handed me a handkerchief did I realize that

I had been crying. The fear I felt when I recalled the picture of Steven walking away stayed with me for several hours.

After a satisfying breakfast, we had our bags brought down and started for home. Seeing the cemetery off to our right scattered over the low rolling hills on the edge of town, I wondered about the thousands of people who had lived here over the last fifty years. I wished for a moment that I could stay longer in the fascinating and mysterious old mining town, but a yearning to once again feel the softness of Rose in my arms replaced that desire with a stronger longing, along with a sense of urgency that settled at the back of my mind and wouldn't let go.

After camping near Murphy's Station that night, we started out again early in the morning. I was so busy watching the progress of the horses on the rutted road that I was startled to attention by an exclamation from Irene.

"It's Sing!"

"Where?" I brought the horses to a halt.

"Ahead, riding toward us."

Sure enough, a dirty and sweating Sing pulled up by the wagon. The old mare he rode, the only horse on which he felt safe, was breathing hard.

"Sing, what's the matter?" I asked. "Who's watching Rose?"

"Very bad. Very bad. Mr. Alex come back yesterday."

"He's home?"

"No. But he come home, take Rose and leave again. I try to stop him. He knock me down."

While I fought to breathe, Irene asked, "What do you mean he took Rose? To Virginia City with the men?"

"Don't know. He not say."

Irene suggested we pull off the road in the shade of the trees so Sing could tell us in detail what happened, but I didn't care about the details, and instead said, "No! We need to get home."

"Of course," Irene agreed. "But go carefully, Whitney."

With shaking hands that I hoped would not communicate down the reins to the horses and spook them, I managed to get us home safely. Sing followed along behind the wagon. All the way I held onto the hope that we would find Alex and Rose at home, the whole thing a weird misunderstanding.

But the house was filled only with the silence of emptiness and early evening shadows. After Sing built a fire in the small fireplace, I curled up on the end of the sofa in front of it and stared at the flames, trying to figure out what had happened and how to begin to get her back. In the kitchen, Irene helped Sing make us tea.

When Sing brought me the tray, I ignored the refreshment and instead told him, "Sit down, Sing. Tell me exactly what happened."

He hesitated at the unfamiliar invitation, but did so, mostly I think out of exhaustion. Irene spread a light throw over my legs and sat next to me.

"I surprised when he come in front door. He ask where you are. I say gone to Bodie with ham. Then he go upstairs and into room of Rose where I just put her for afternoon sleep. I hear him say, 'Just who are you?' That make no sense, so I immediately afraid."

A wave of dizziness hit me, and I wondered if I as going to fade away like the heroine in an old novel. But I shook off the temptation and took too large a swallow of the hot, sugary tea in my cup. The burn on my tongue brought me back to my senses quickly, and I wondered what had given Alex the idea that Rose wasn't his.

"Then what happened?" I asked.

"He wrap her in blankets and I ask him what he going to do. He say, 'I'm taking Whitney's baby.' I say, 'She your baby too.' He say, 'No. I can't sire children.' He say doctor tell him it because he have bad case of mumps disease when young man."

Tears began to drip down my cheeks, but Sing continued to speak. "I tell him doctors wrong many times. He say, 'Not this time.' What do I think?"

Irene gave me a quizzical and hurt look. But I had no patience for their judgments or hurt feelings. I was so close to being overwhelmed by my fear for Rose that I wanted to scream at them. But I only said, "You're right, Sing. Doctors are often wrong. More importantly, right now we need to find out where Alex has taken Rose."

Although I knew they would both interpret my response in their own way, they now obviously had doubts about me where before there had been only blind trust. It was a test of the steadfastness of their loyalty and friendship that they didn't press the issue further.

While Sing prepared a light meal for us, and I tried to decide what to do next, Irene said, "Whitney, I know how unhappy you've been for a long time now." She dropped her voice to barely a whisper. "If Rose is Steven's, I understand. I may have chosen to not include a man in my life, but I do understand what it feels like to be in love."

"Oh, Irene." I squeezed her hand and felt a stab of contrition. "I should have told you before, but I was so desperate to have your friendship and respect. I wasn't sure how you'd feel about my cheating on Alex."

She snorted with derision, and her pale skin was suffused with color. "If there's been any cheating on the Double R, it was by J.B. and Alex. They both cheated you out of the kind of love and married life that you had every right to expect. It was their web of lies and campaign to exclude you that prevented that."

"But now what am I going to do? How am I going to get Rose back?" I felt myself choking up again and dabbed at my eyes.

"You must wire your father and tell him what's happened. He'll come and help you. You know that."

"Oh, God. What will he think of me? Mother would never have been unfaithful to him, or he to her."

"Whitney!" She was the picture of indignation. "This isn't about *their* marriage. This is about *yours*. Anyway, you aren't going to tell him the whole story in the telegram. Just say Alex has left you and taken Rose, and you need his help."

"You're right. I'm an idiot." I rubbed my eyes and took another swallow of tea, trying to reduce my fear so I could think more logically. "I'll write out the message, and then Sing can go into town and send it. We can only hope the telegraph operator respects his oath and keeps his mouth shut."

"Whitney." She hesitated, then asked, "You don't think Alex will harm Rose do you?"

"Oh no, he'd never harm an innocent child. It's me he wants to punish, hoping I'll suffer like he thinks he is." I looked into the flames and tried to generate some compassion. "The foundation of all he thought his life to be has been knocked out from under him, and the realization that his daughter isn't his after all must have been the final shock for him."

But it wasn't Alex's state of mind that was my concern. I worried about Rose--what she was eating, how he was carrying her on his horse, if she was warm enough, and if she was frightened. Through all the conversations with Sing and Irene, while writing the telegraph message and giving Sing his instructions, while nibbling at whatever food was put before me, was the urge to stand up and scream at the top of my lungs until the plaster cracked and the windows shattered--and someone gave me a sock on the jaw that would put me out of my misery.

CHAPTER 15

As soon as I saw Father's face so full of love and concern, I rushed forward. Barely giving him time to dismount and tie Noble to the hitching rail, I threw my arms around his neck. Relief flooded through me as soon as I was wrapped in the warmth of his arms, and for a fleeting moment I felt again the comforting security of a child loved by a protective and caring parent. But this was more than the occasion of a lost doll. I pulled back and resumed the role of woman, and mother.

Turning to Uncle Vince, I gave him a quick hug and said, "Thank you so much for coming."

When he saw me looking beyond his shoulder searching for someone else, Vince correctly interpreted my action. "Stephen is in Los Angeles on town business."

"Oh." I swallowed my disappointment and invited them inside.

Giving an anxious glance at the sky and what looked like an approaching storm, I offered a quick prayer that it would hold off. Noble stretched his head in my direction and nickered softly, and I gave him a quick pat on the nose before gathering my skirts and hurrying up the split log steps.

Even with the tension of the situation, I had to smile when the men gaped at the dramatic vastness of the large great room crowned by the upstairs balcony. Both men were puzzled by all the furniture arranged as though a party had just broken up. I explained that it was the way Alex and J.B. had always wanted it, and left it at that.

Sing brought coffee to the dining table, so we gathered there. When I introduced the men to Sing and Irene, Father expressed his gratitude to them for standing by me at such a trying time. Sing served the men large meat sandwiches before retreating to the kitchen where he suppressed his worry by cleaning it beyond its need.

Irene excused herself and went out to the back garden to harvest fall vegetables, and weed between the rows. It was her way of coping and leaving us to our privacy at the same time.

The moment of explanation being at hand, I started by telling them of the visit from the lawyer and the truth about Alex's mother. As they shook their heads in wonder at this latest passel of lies, I followed up with a description of my confrontation with Alex about our separating, and then my trip to Bodie and meeting Sing on the road back.

Called in from the kitchen, Sing told them about Alex's return to the house. He looked down at his toes and said, "When I try to stop him leaving, he knock me down." It was obvious that his feelings had been hurt more than his body. He went to his bedroom and closed the door.

I knew that Alex's comments to Sing about Rose would necessitate either my lying to them about Rose's parentage or telling them the truth. I faced their surprised and questioning gaze and simply said, "Alex's conclusion from what the doctor told him is correct."

Father was of course shocked, but tried valiantly not to show it. Uncle Vince felt it and showed it. Father licked his lips and said, "Whitney, I've always trusted your judgment, but this, well." He ran his fingers through his hair. "Granted, you must have been very unhappy, but to risk your reputation like this." He left off talking and simply shook his head. After a moment, he added, "I assume you're in love with the father?"

"Yes, very much."

"Do you plan to marry him?"

"Yes. We've talked about it already."

"Then eventually this will all be sorted out, I guess." He looked only marginally relieved.

Vince told him, "Look at it this way, Frank. No matter who the father is, you're still her grandpa."

Before I thought it through, I said, "I'm glad you feel that way, Vince, because you're her grandpa, too."

It took a few confused seconds for both of them to put it together. When they did, it was almost comical to see how they tried to arrange their faces—surprise, realization, then thoughtful calculation followed by a number of questions swallowed. Vince was the first to speak.

"When you were in Lone Pine, right?"

"Yes."

He nodded his head. "I told Charlotte I sensed a change in the two of you, but I had no idea you were in love." He sat back and took a deep breath. "I suppose eventually we'll hear more of the story, but right now we have more pressing things to do."

All we had to go on was the direction in which Sing had seen Alex ride, which was only back toward town. But we also knew that his original intention was to go to Virginia City.

Father said, "That's why I think he'll go in the opposite direction."

They quickly stocked their saddlebags with supplies, then made secure the tie-downs on their bedrolls and slickers. It was when they checked their supply of ammunition and strapped on side arms, something seldom worn by either of them, that I started to tremble deep inside.

Soon they were only a speck in the distance and I was left behind, trusting that the two most steadfast men in my life would find my daughter. I was thankful to note that the earlier clouds had blown over and the sky was clear. But that meant a cold night, and another reason to worry about Rose's comfort. I returned to the warmth of the fire, and I pictured Father and Vince speculating about my relationship with Steven.

Restless and unable to settle down to anything, I started up the stairs to my room. A noise from the guest room stopped me, and I realized I'd forgotten about Irene. Thinking I would check to see if she needed anything, I walked down the back hall and raised my hand to knock on the guest room door. It opened before I made contact with the wood. I was facing Mrs. Lewis.

"What are you doing here?" I demanded. "Why have you come back?"

"I thought you might need me. I was only in town." Her face was stoic, but her eyes were bright. "It seems my room is occupied by someone else."

"It's no longer your room. And don't even suggest that you're here for any decent reason." I stepped toward her until we were only inches apart. "You're here because Alex went to you in town and told you he'd taken Rose, and why. You returned because you wanted to see my misery when I found out." She didn't bother to deny it, but the subtle twitch at the corner of her mouth made clear the accuracy of my accusation.

"You wretched bitch!" I screamed. All the frustration and anger I'd so often felt because of her treatment of me, coupled with my current fear, coalesced into a fury that overcame control. I slapped her across the face so hard she fell against the open door. "Get out! Now!" Unused to screaming at such a high register, my throat constricted to the point that I thought I might choke. Clenching my fists, in a harsh whisper I told her, "Your things are packed in crates and stacked in the corner of the room. Sing will help you load them in the wagon. Anything you leave will be burned. And if you're not out of here in half an hour, I'll have one of the men drag you out."

With her hand on the hot red imprint left by my hand, her sudden shrill laughter dripped with scorn. "Most of the ranch hands have left.

None of them would help you anyway. They wouldn't put their jobs on the line like that. They know Alex is angry with you and has chosen to leave you."

"Well, while Alex is gone, they work for me. So it's me they'll be wanting to please."

"They won't work for you." She couldn't keep her lip from curling. "When they realize Alex isn't coming back, those still here will leave, too."

Her words hit me like a knife stab to the gut. Was it possible that Alex wasn't intending to return? Did that mean he'd taken Rose too far away for Father and Vince to find them? Up until that moment, I had supposed it would only be a short time until they'd all be returning together.

Aware that she was reading my thoughts from my expression, I turned my back on her and walked into the great room to stand before the front windows. The brown meadows, now empty and ready to receive the first snows, were so peaceful as compared to the turmoil taking place in the house. I longed to ride across them and feel the breeze blow away the hell of my conflicting emotions. Mrs. Lewis had followed me into the room, unable to hide her gloating smirk. Her presence was a grating reminder of the unpleasant facts that needed to be resolved.

With a straightened spine, I turned to her, clasping my hands in front of me so tightly that the nails of one hand cut into the other. "I'll deal with the men. Start loading your things. Your half hour has started."

For a long moment she stood glaring at me, but finally with a swish of her black skirts she retreated to her old room. As she stepped into the hallway outside the bedroom with her valise and a small hat box, it was to be met there by a scowling Hank. Sing stood behind him in the doorway to the kitchen, his face showing the resentment toward her he had so long concealed.

Hank's voice when he spoke was low and clear. "I heard what you said as I came in the back door." He turned to me. "I came back with Alex. I had no idea what he intended to do or I'd have stopped him."

"I'm sure you would have."

Turning back to Mrs. Lewis, he said, "And you're wrong about the men. Several of us will gladly stay with Mrs. Roberts. If that means Alex fires us, then so be it." He picked up her cases and walked with them toward the front door. Over his shoulder, he told her, "Sing and I will take you into town."

She followed without a glance in my direction, waiting by the wagon while Hank and Sing loaded her things. Listening to the retreating crunch of the wagon's wheels on the drive, I continued to stand by the front windows of the great room until there was nothing more of them to see or hear. Irene appeared at my side and slipped an arm around my shoulders as she led me to the kitchen where it was warm. There she forced me to eat, but when I found out she had a bad headache, I made her go and lie down.

The silence enveloped me like the smothering of a wool blanket thrown over my head, and I didn't know how to fight my way out from under it. I sat on the front porch waiting for Hank and Sing to return, even though I knew they might stay in town for a long time. Which they did--Sing to shop and Hank for unknown reasons. Sleeping was fitful and brief that night.

Irene had to return home some time, and I encouraged her to do so the next day. After a long hug, she allowed Sing to drive her home, to her pure white world where she was tightly in control of everything. This left me to face the waiting alone until Sing returned.

I walked through the rooms and let the silence wash over me, forcing myself to remain calm. It wasn't difficult until I entered Alex's study. After going through the drawers of his desk, the cupboards and the book shelves, I knew that all the important papers regarding the ranch were still there. But I found no records of bank accounts or investments. Would Alex have left me without funds or money to run the ranch? Yes. He had shown the depth of his anger when he had kidnapped Rose. I dropped into the chair behind his desk and buried my face in my hands.

My rage resurfaced with a suddenness that gave me no time to back it off, and with the scream of a wounded animal, I reached out and swept everything off the desk onto the floor. Ignoring the broken glass of the lamp and the oil seeping into the rug, I stepped around the mess and left the study. I purposely left the door wide open, grimly satisfied that for once I was leaving that room without hearing the click of the lock behind me.

Escaping the oppressive silence of the house, I went outside into the sunshine. Breathing deeply the scent of the stables, the fields, and the mix of pine and sage, I tried valiantly to rid myself of dark thoughts. But no matter what I did or where I wandered on the ranch, I was playing a waiting game with rules I didn't understand.

Sitting in the great room where I could see the road, I turned the pages of the book on my lap without seeing the words. A sense of fathomless dread lay over me with a warmth that made my face hot while yet my hands felt like ice. More than once I questioned how I would go on in life if anything happened to Rose. That night there was no sound but the gusting howl of wind and the whipping of tree branches. I curled my legs beneath me and sat at one end of the sofa watching the fire in the small fireplace slowly die. Having no energy to throw another log on the glowing embers, I moved closer to the comfort of the flickering candles on the end table. After I fell asleep, Sing covered me with a quilt and built up the fire, then himself retired for the night.

What took place between Father, Vince and Alex I can only relay from what I pieced together from the men's story upon their return, and questions I posed to them over the next several months.

Frank and Vince knew they needed to find someone who had seen Alex and had observed in which direction he had traveled when leaving town. They didn't get their information at any of the saloons, the livery stables or the mercantile. It was from the post mistress at the Post Office where Alex had called to ask that his mail be forwarded to the Lakeview Hotel at Lake Lundy. While the postmistress had fussed over Rose, he mentioned that he was staying at the lake for several weeks while 'the wife' made extensive renovations to the house. She had thought it odd that Alex would allow such a thing while he wasn't present to supervise, but she understood the urge to remove such a young child from the dust and mayhem. She had suggested leaving Rose with her, but he had said he wanted her with him.

Once the men reached the Lundy road, not far from the north edge of Mono Lake, they rode steadily toward the old lumber mill and mining town five miles up canyon and on the far shore of the long blue lake. It was once a busy town crowded with hundreds of miners, shopkeepers, girls referred to by the good women as soiled doves, and mill workers. But like most such mountain mining towns that had sprung to life in the late 1870's, it had slowly fallen prey to failing mines, fires and avalanches.

Only the hotel, a mercantile store, a few scattered cabins and a small power plant remained. In fact, there were so few people present in the charming little village that it didn't take the men long to find someone who had seen Alex ride up Mill Creek toward the old Wasson town site. But there had been no child with him, of that the witness had been certain.

A miner in Wasson told them the only stranger he had seen in weeks had been a man on a horse going up the narrow trail behind the mill site. He was carrying a bundle that he guessed could have been a child. Following his directions, they walked their horses up a steep narrow path that climbed the mountain to a number of old mine openings. Alex was easily found near the Little Chief Mine, sitting on the far side of a campfire outside a small tent.

Night had come on quickly as they climbed up the mountain, and the bright glow of the campfire between them kept Alex from seeing who his visitors were. Walking forward, their guns drawn, they found that Alex hadn't taken on faith that whomever was approaching him meant no harm. He had a rifle braced across his knees and his hand ready at the trigger.

Frank was the first to speak. "Unless you plan to use that and stand trial for murdering your father-in-law, you'd best put it down."

After a moment's hesitation, Alex did just that.

Vince looked around and asked, "Where's Rose?"

"She's safe."

"Where?"

"With a woman I know."

"Again," Vince growled, "where is she?"

"She's safe. That's all you need know."

Frank spoke up quickly. "How could you take your daughter on such a rough ride?"

"She's not my daughter. I can't have children." Alex made a strangled sound in the back of his throat. "Knowing now what I do of my family history, that's probably not a bad thing."

"How do you know you can't have children?" Frank asked.

"I had mumps when I was a kid. The doctor said they now realize it makes a man sterile."

"That can't always be the case. He can't be sure that's true of you."

"Well," Alex drawled sarcastically, "he was under the impression that he was."

"Okay, let's accept the premise that Rose isn't yours," Vince reasoned. "She's still a very young child that needs her mother."

"And," Frank added, "her mother needs her."

Alex smirked. "That's the point, isn't it? I don't take well to being a cuckold. I just can't figure out who Whitney got with or when." He shook his head. "I never would have thought it of her."

"It hasn't been established that Whitney cheated on you," Frank pointed out. "The doctor could still have been wrong, and you're endangering your own child."

Vince took a step forward. "The point is, we're here to get Rose back and we mean to have her."

Alex stood up slowly. He looked first at Vince and then at his father-in-law, locking eyes with him before saying, "Over my dead body."

"That can be arranged," Frank snapped out.

Vince took a step closer, at the same time cocking his gun, but Frank grabbed Vince's jacket sleeve. Desperate to avoid bloodshed, Frank told Alex, "Don't make us force the information from you."

The only response Alex gave them was a short bark of contemptuous laughter to make his disbelief evident.

Frank removed his hand from Vince's arm. "Don't think we won't do it. We won't like it, but Rose is my granddaughter, and that'll give me a hell of a lot of motivation to continue even when you're screaming." He looked calmly at Alex, clearly indicating that it was his choice.

A second after Alex laughed again, Vince kicked him in the knee. Alex fell to the ground with a yelp, the hand he put out to break his fall stepped on by Frank. Surprised, Alex looked from the boot on his hand up to the merciless stare Frank had fixed on him. He quickly, and accurately, realized that they wouldn't stop at hurting him badly to learn Rose's whereabouts.

"Okay! Now that I know you mean business. She's with a Mrs. Smith. She has a cabin near the old Mono Diggings."

Frank removed his boot from Alex's hand and Vince stepped back, saying, "There's a lot of so-called Mrs. Smiths. We'll all leave first thing in the morning, and you can take us to her."

"I'm not going back with you." Alex looked at his hand and carefully felt for broken bones. "There's nothing there for me now."

"You're going back all right," Frank told him. "You have business to settle with your wife, a ranch to run, and people depending on you." Then, losing all patience, Frank yelled, "Grow up, damn it! Deal with what's in your life and stop moaning over what you can't change. Your father made his choices, now it's time for you to make yours."

"You don't understand," Alex pouted. "My whole life is a lie!"

Frank got in his face. "Your father's life is a lie. Your life is ahead of you and can be anything you want it to be." Raising his voice to a shout, he hollered, "Damn it, be a man!"

For the rest of the night Alex sat staring into the flames deep in thought, with his bedroll wrapped around his shoulders. Not knowing if Alex was contemplating a way of escaping, or preparing himself for his return to a ranch and a wife no longer his comforting refuge, they didn't know nor care. But they weren't taking a chance of his getting away before they found Rose, so the men took turns sleeping.

At first light, the fire was put out and the hot coals drowned in water and dirt until only a muddy residue was left to show anyone had been there. The ride through Lundy, just awakening beneath towering Mt. Scowden, was a quiet one. They saw no one, and if anyone saw them, they chose not to make themselves known to the three surly men riding out of town before the light was much burnished in the sky.

Mrs. Smith must have spotted Alex through her window because she greeted them at the door with Rose in her arms. She was a haggard, plump woman somewhere in her sixties, wearing a faded dress covered by a dingy, once-white apron. Wisps of gray hair straggled over eyes red from too much drink, and which now stared at them in surprise. When she opened her mouth to greet Alex, her foul breath made it clear the status of a sour stomach and bad teeth. Frank wasted no time with introductions, but rather walked straight up to the woman and reached for Rose with a curt demand, "Give her to me. I'm her grandfather."

When the woman looked to Alex for permission, he merely shrugged his acquiescence. While Vince looked at Rose over Frank's shoulder, caught up in the emotion of realizing that this child was his granddaughter, Alex thought he could sneak away. But without taking his eyes from Rose, Vince reached for his gun with a speed that surprised everyone. Pointing it at Alex, he told him, "Don't even think about it. You're coming back with us."

Frank got Rose's blanket from the woman, wrapped her tightly, and handed her to Vince while he mounted. Vince handed her back, somewhat reluctantly, and the three of them rode on to Hector Station north of Mono Lake where they spent the night in one room with Vince sleeping in front of the door.

By leaving early the next morning and riding at a steady but easy pace, they were back at the ranch at dusk. My skirts raised to my knees in my rush to reach the bottom of the front steps, I still almost tripped in my eagerness to reach them.

After Father lowered Rose to me, I smothered her with so many kisses that she finally stopped laughing and began to fuss. Sing came forward and took her from me. Although he too held her close, she merely laughed and made a grab for his long braid. Catching her hand and kissing it, Sing took a moment to glare at Alex standing by his horse, then carried Rose to his room where her things had been transferred. He wasn't letting her out of his sight.

Of course, Alex immediately went to his study. Only this time he quickly discovered that the lock on the door had been disabled. When he rushed back out and stood on the landing yelling for Sing, I answered his bellow instead and walked half way up the stairs.

"What the hell's happened to my door?" he shouted at me from the doorway to his study. "It won't lock."

"That's right." I walked within a few feet of him and stared him directly in the eyes, something I hadn't done since the night he had raped me. Freed from the need to suppress my anger, I boldly announced, "We have things to settle between us, and you're not going to avoid it by hiding in your damn study!"

He turned around, went back into the room and slammed the door, against which he promptly began dragging furniture. Behind me Uncle Vince spat out a crude invective and raced past me up the stairs, one broad shoulder slamming against the study door with a thud that shook the wall. He continued to push until the door was open far enough for him to step through.

When I hurried into the room, it was to find Uncle Vince grasping Alex's shirt front and bending him back over the desk. Although Vince's words were indistinct, it was clear that he was mumbling instructions to Alex on how he had better treat me in the future. The word "respect" was clearly repeated several times, while Alex's face turned a dark red beneath the hands around his neck. Before his face changed to blue, I said calmly, "Uncle Vince, please let him go."

Vince turned him loose and stepped back, but before leaving the room, he told Alex sternly, "Just remember what I said." Vince met Father on the stairs and led him away. It was a side of Vince I only saw that once, and I shudder to think what might have happened if I hadn't stepped in when I did.

Alex straightened his clothes and grunted, "That Uncle of yours is crazy."

"All this could have been avoided if just once you'd been willing to be open with me. If you'd told me about your conversation with the doctor, I could have explained that what he said is only sometimes the case." I took a deep breath. "Whether or not his diagnosis is correct in your case, I don't know. But I do know that Rose is indeed *not* your child." Even though he claimed to have known this, my affirmation caused him to flinch. "I won't make excuses. Anyway, I don't owe you one after the way you've treated me."

"I thought you weren't going to give an excuse," he glowered.

"That wasn't an excuse." I gentled my tone before saying, "But I am sorry to be another cause of distress for you, although the hit to your pride is probably what's really bothering you. You were never that interested in Rose, a girl."

"I needed time. I needed to. . ."

"I had needs, too!" Forcing myself to remain calm, I continued. "But you didn't care. So I took charge of my own needs."

"Who did you take charge of them with?"

"It doesn't matter."

"It does to me." His eyes penetrated into mine and I fought not to turn away from him. "What I can't figure out is when. You were here at the ranch or at Irene's most of the time." I said nothing. "The only other time possible is when you went to Lone Pine." He stopped abruptly and turned red, yelling, "Steven!" When I still said nothing, he added, "That son of a bitch!"

"You have no right to pass judgment on me or Steven!" I walked to the window and fought to show a calm I didn't feel. Turning to face him, I expected to see anger, but instead was facing a hard, blank expression that I'd never seen before and couldn't read. I told him, "The sum and substance of all this is that I'm leaving immediately with Father and Vince."

"I hope you're not expecting any financial support from me."

"No. I expect nothing from you."

Evidently not taking me at my word, he said, "If you try to get money from me, I'll contest the divorce. I'll charge you with adultery and ruin you!"

"I'm not asking you for anything, you bastard!" I yelled back. "And don't start threatening me with what you will or won't do. You can't prove Rose isn't yours, but I can prove who your father is."

He looked at me in shock, and yes, fear. "You wouldn't expose that!"

My voice was as hard and calm as when Mother threatened Charley Jones. "Not unless you try to hurt my reputation, and by extension Rose, by claiming she isn't yours."

After a moment, he said, "I guess we're at a stand-off."

"Or an agreement of self-preservation."

He sat down heavily at his desk. "Yes."

"We'll talk more in the morning and you can tell me then how much of a settlement you'll make me. And I expect an uncontested divorce. But don't worry, I only want enough money to cover Rose's expenses until I get settled."

As I turned to leave, his next words stopped me at the door. "You've become very hard, Whitney."

Keeping my back to him and saying nothing, I simply opened the door and passed through, closing it securely behind me as I knew he wanted it. Only this time it was my decision to put the barrier between us, and he knew it was final.

I hurried late to breakfast the following morning, surprised that I had slept so soundly. Arriving in the dining room just as everyone else was finishing, I grabbed the last piece of toast and accepted when Father offered me the last slice of bacon on his plate. Sing was in the kitchen feeding Rose, having decided to keep her with him even while doing his work. Nothing could have pleased Rose more.

"Alex hasn't come down yet?" I asked.

Father answered. "He went outside awhile ago and headed to the barn. Hank said he'd tell us if Alex tries to leave the ranch."

"Were you comfortable on the sofa?"

"Surprisingly, yes."

"What about you Uncle Vince?"

"Yes, dear, I was fine, too."

"You both could have had a room of your own, you know."

"Don't worry about us, Whitney," Father reassured me. "We wanted to be centrally located in case Alex decided to try and sneak out."

"When are we getting underway?" Vince asked.

"As soon as I get packed," I told them. "How about tomorrow morning?"

"We'll have your wagon ready and loaded with anything you want," Father promised. "We can leave it in Benton at the station. I'll wire Emily to meet us at the Owenyo Station with ours."

The sound of a horse and rider stopping out front caught our attention and I walked to the door, opening it a fraction of a second before the door knocker could be raised.

Sheriff Kirkwood tipped his hat to me. "Morning, Mrs. Roberts. I just spoke to Alex out in the tack room and he said your father was here. I hope you don't mind my stopping in to meet him."

"Not at all." I stepped back and he entered. "Would you like some coffee, George?"

"You bet," he accepted eagerly.

I smiled and wondered if that wasn't his real reason for stopping at the house, as Sing was known for serving apple pie to guests with their coffee. Only a little older than Alex, George Kirkwood was a good-looking man with intelligent, deep-set eyes and a neat mustache accenting a strong jaw. I wasn't fooled by his casual manner, however, knowing he was a quick-witted law man and a keen observer who missed little of what happened in town.

Following introductions, the sheriff pulled out a chair at the table and made himself comfortable. After the usual discussion about the weather was out of the way, George commented, "I understand from several people in town that you gentlemen were out looking for Alex. Is everything okay?"

The furtive exchange of glances between us probably didn't go far in reassuring him, even though we all mumbled our own versions of reassurance.

The sheriff took a swallow of his coffee and said, "Look folks, I don't hold much stock in rumors usually. But you men showing up here, and then immediately leaving again looking for Alex after asking about his daughter? You have to admit it sounds pretty unusual."

Father told him, "Everything's fine now. Whitney and Alex had quarreled, that's all."

George looked at me. "Didn't you and Irene Baxter go to Bodie last week?"

"Yes, we did."

"Didn't Alex want you to go?"

"He wasn't here when I left. He'd gone to Virginia City with some of the men from the ranch."

He nodded his head, then commented, "Must have changed his mind if he returned before you got back from Bodie. And he took Rose with him when he left? Odd. Where did he go then?"

"Lundy Lake," Father answered him. "Or old Wasson, actually."

Realizing we needed to give him more of the picture, I said, "Sheriff, it's very simple. I'm leaving Alex. That was what our quarrel was about. While I was in Bodie, he doubled back and took Rose with him, then left her with Mrs. Smith near the Mono Diggings." That caused the Sheriff to frown, evidently knowing the nature of the woman. "He then went on to Wasson to brood and get as far away from all responsibility as possible. My father and Vince went after him in order to get Rose back home safely. After talking with them, Alex decided to return and face his problems."

"That's what you call simple, eh?" When my only response was a shrug, he asked, "Did he take Rose to get even for your wanting to leave him?"

I hesitated, then admitted, "Possibly."

"Is everything okay now?"

"I think so. He agreed with me that today everything would be settled, and we'd discuss how much money I'd need for Rose's care. Which shows he's accepted the situation."

He nodded and looked thoughtful, his gaze traveling over each of us in turn before settling on Father and Vince. "I noticed a bad bruise on the back of his left hand, and he was limping a little. You guys know anything about that?"

Vince quickly asked, "What did Alex say?"

"He said it was just the knocks of running a ranch."

"Well, there you are then," Father responded.

We then sat quietly and looked at the sheriff, waiting for his next question. But the sound of a light rig stopping out front caught our attention and again I opened the door to greet an unexpected visitor.

"Irene! You dear thing. What are you doing back so soon?"

"After I got your note telling me Rose was back, I felt like I should be with you to help with whatever might be needed." Dressed in a dark mauve dress with white lace at the collar and cuffs, she looked ready for a festive occasion.

Irene greeted everyone and settled in the chair next to me with a cup of coffee. We then began a discussion of the local economy and the new menu at the Leavitt House. When cattle became the subject, Irene asked Father and Uncle Vince for their assessment of a new udder salve on the market.

While they chatted, I took that time to wonder if the sheriff believed that Alex had been reasonable when found, or if Father and Vince had gotten rough with him. Had the doctor broken confidence and mentioned to the sheriff that Alex couldn't have children?

"Whitney?" Irene's voice broke my reverie.

"I'm sorry. My mind wandered." Smiling, I squeezed her hand resting on the table between us. "It's not the company, just so much to think about and to get done by tomorrow morning. That's when we're leaving."

"Oh. So soon." Irene couldn't hide her disappointment, and her hand clutched at mine as though unwilling to let me go.

I looked into her eyes, wanting to say so much about all her friendship had meant to me, but I only said, "I need to be home now, so I can get my life together and plan my future. But please promise that you'll come spend time with us. Not just a short visit, but to stay for awhile."

Her face lit up. "I promise. But how's Alex taking your leaving?"

"Not well. He's trying to avoid me this morning, although he promised everything would be settled today. Right now, he's out in the tack room, probably straightening everything that he straightened the last time he was trying to avoid being in the house with me."

"I wonder what he was doing as I drove my wagon down the drive to the house."

"Why?"

"Well, I heard some kind of loud noise as I turned onto the drive." She turned to Father and Vince. "Didn't you hear it?"

"No," Father answered her. "What kind of noise?"

"An odd muffled pop. It wasn't loud enough that I could hear or recognize it clearly."

Uncle Vince, always quick to act, rose up and rushed from the room only a few steps ahead of Father and the sheriff.

Irene pressed a hand to her mouth, mumbling, "They can't think..."

Standing up, I lamely offered, "Maybe I should go, too."

"No! Let the men take care of it. They'll probably find that nothing has happened."

Losing my courage, I gave way and prepared to wait, letting the men handle things like women have so often done throughout history. Then I thought of Mother and her pioneer friends, and felt like an ineffectual fraud.

Weeks later Vince described to me what took place, since Father wouldn't speak of it when I asked him. Reaching the tack room, the men opened the door and let the sun's rays shine onto the polished tack and aromatic leather. But also present was the sharp acrid odor of a gun recently fired, and another strangely sweet putrid stench. The sheriff pushed to the front and walked further into the tack room.

"Oh, God," he retched. "He's shot himself."

Vince told me, in what I'm sure was a sterilized version, that Alex must have been standing by the work bench cleaning a hand gun when it went off. The bullet hit him in the throat and severed his spine on the way out. Since it was such an odd place for a person to point a gun if committing suicide, the Sheriff immediately assumed it was an accident. He concluded that Alex was holding the gun up to check its cleanliness and it went off. Of course, that scenario assumed that Alex was so stupid that he'd clean a loaded gun. But as the sheriff said, stupid accidents happen all the time. We all knew the story of how Charlie Day, only a few years earlier, had shot himself in the stomach while cleaning a loaded gun. Thankfully, Charlie survived.

But Alex was dead. A staggering rush of emotions flowed through me at the moment Father walked into the dining room and I saw the look of shock on his white face. But beyond shock and an initial urge to disbelieve, there was no desire to weep. Although the men spared me as much detail as possible, the bare facts and my imagination painted a gory picture my mind fought to reject but couldn't.

The passing of the following days included the mortician arriving and taking away the body; a graveside funeral at the small cemetery in town, attended by almost everyone in Bridgeport and a few from Bodie; people arriving with food of every conceivable variety to see us through *our period of bereavement*; the reading of the Will that left the ranch to me; and my quick sale of it to a neighbor for what he must have felt to be the best deal of his or anyone else's life. Thankfully, Hank and Mort liked the man and agreed to work for him.

Two weeks after what those most tactful of the townspeople referred to *as the fateful night*, I left the ranch for the last time. The best and most important thing I took with me was Sing's smile, which he wore all the way to Lone Pine. He promised to be of use, whether taking care of Rose or helping Mother around the house, which I had described to him so many times. More than anything, he just needed to be with those whom he could trust. The fact that Lone Pine had a small Chinese District also appealed to him.

When the train pulled out of Benton Station and headed south toward the Owens Valley, the beating of my heart picked up speed along with that of the big, black steam engine. A wave of joy surged through me when I thought of once again seeing Steven and telling him that he had a daughter. Closing my eyes, I could almost feel his arms around me. Sing wasn't the only one smiling then.

CHAPTER 16

While on the train headed home (what beautiful words!), I finally allowed myself to look to the future with hope. I was comforted by the presence of Father and Vince in the seat behind Rose and me; our two gruff guardian angels. Sing was allowed to ride with us instead of with the luggage only after Father explained to the conductor that Sing was the only person that would be able to keep the baby from crying all the way. The roll of bills Father slipped the man didn't hurt either.

But I was already missing Irene. She had been such a support during the previous two weeks, especially the day of the funeral in the old cemetery in town. Most of the time I had felt as though floating through a dream. Father and Uncle Vince had also kept near, as had Sing with Rose in his arms. But it was Irene who led me around headstones or tree roots I would otherwise have tripped over, while her calm voice quietly whispered to me the name of the person coming toward me to offer condolences. And it was Irene that handed me her handkerchief, although she did it only when she noticed women giving me odd looks due to my obvious lack of tears. I had used it to remove a bit of dust from my eye, and everyone watching had turned away satisfied.

Most of those present had no doubt interpreted my behavior as the extreme of shock and grief, but it was hardly that. Yes, I was shocked that Alex could be so careless, and was so suddenly gone from my life. I was also disturbed by the fact that I didn't know how to contact J.B. about his son's death, although the way such news traveled from town to town, I knew he'd hear of it eventually. But mostly I was dumbstruck by the sudden change this meant to my life, and the almost overwhelming sense of release.

After the reverend completed his remarks, we had turned back to our buggies preparatory to returning to the ranch. A few flakes of snow fell and people commented on the rapid change in temperature. Consequently, everyone dispersed rapidly, and I was saved the awkward lingering conversations I'd been dreading.

On my last evening in Bridgeport, I had stood outside by the vegetable garden, full of the dry remnants of so much abundance and promise. The snow had only brought a short flurry, but small glistening patches lingered in the cool shadows of bushes and trees. When I looked over at the willows now bereft of their leaves and appearing almost as disillusioned as I felt, I remembered how I had so often sought refuge in their midst. Turning my head in the direction of the long line of mountain peaks, the rising granite of the Buckeye and Sawtooth Ridges had been barely visible in the cover of the encroaching darkness. Soon they had been draped in a mantle of light that was luminous under the moon's glowing influence. Drawing my shawl tighter around my shoulders, my thoughts had turned to Steven, and once again being with him. All this I recalled as I looked out the train window and watched the Sierra peaks fly past as the train headed south.

Mother didn't meet our train after all. One of the hands from Uncle Vince's ranch was there, very solemn and simply saying something had happened that required Mother to be elsewhere. We drew near the town from the north and approached what the locals referred to as the *new* cemetery with its mixture of wooden crosses and granite monuments. Almost twenty years old and established across the road from the mass grave of the 1872 earthquake victims, it replaced the old cemetery southeast of town where the oldest of the Valley pioneers lay undisturbed by new arrivals or frequent visitors. As we approached, a number of people dressed in black were leaving the small, dirt cemetery in buggies and wagons, with even more on foot.

Father suddenly called out, "Emily!" Vince's ranch hand brought our wagon to a stop and Father jumped down. Running up to Mother, she threw her arms around his neck and began weeping.

Uncle Vince quickly joined them, naked fear on his face until he saw Charlotte approaching. She too looked sad. When I walked up, everyone began talking at once, and I found out that the funeral had been for Mrs. Bowman, one of Mother's closest friends.

I explained to Sing, "Louise Bowman was a sweet older lady and the last of the quilting circle that welcomed Mother when she first arrived in Lone Pine in 1878. She and several other women in the group came west over the Oregon Trail."

Looking to Mother, I asked, "Is Constance here?"

"No. Louise hadn't talked to her daughter for some time. I wired Constance about Louise's passing, but received no response."

"I doubt you were eager to see her again anyway."

"No." Mother couldn't help but smile, even as she wiped the last of the tears from her cheeks. "Constance never forgave Frank for falling in love with me, and she resented me even before that, so we never became friends. But her mother was a dear woman, and over the years we became very close."

"I'm sorry. It must be very hard for you, especially after losing Millicent Faber only a few months ago."

A cold wind began blowing and Mother hurried me back to the wagon. "It's a difficult time for us all, for many reasons. Frank wired me with the news of Alex's death."

"Wait until you hear the details," I told her.

"Time for that later. Let's get along home."

She gave my arm a little squeeze and helped me up onto the wagon's seat. "You go on to the house and get settled, and I'll be home shortly." Turning to Sing, she said, "It's lovely to see you again, Sing. Frank wired that you were coming, so I have a room all ready at the end of the hall near Whitney and Rose's room. Whitney will show you." She took her granddaughter from Sing and squeezed her with exuberance, causing Rose to giggle.

After a moment, Rose held her arms out to Sing, and Mother reluctantly released her. Sing said nothing, merely producing a weak little smile while nodding his thanks and holding Rose on his hip like any busy mother might do. The poor man must have wondered what his future was going to be, not knowing if Lone Pine was a town that treated its Chinese with tolerance or abuse. Not sure myself, I said nothing and hoped that his association with our family would pave his way to acceptance.

As we arrived at the house, I looked for Steven on the front porch. When he wasn't there, a wave of disappointment enveloped me. Then I laughed at myself as I realized that the romantic scene I had written in my mind needn't be the reality. After I got Rose settled with her toys in a crib Mother had set up in my old room, Sing insisted on sitting with her until she fell sleep. I then went downstairs to the kitchen where Mother and Charlotte were preparing supper, hoping Steven had finally arrived at the house. But he hadn't.

Mother continued chopping vegetables, but divined my thoughts and answered before I could even ask the question. "Steven is still in Los Angeles, but he sent a telegram yesterday saying he was on his way home.

He should be here within the next few days." She tried hard to hide a smile, but her eyes danced with excitement.

Charlotte scooped up the vegetables and dumped them in the large stew pot on the stove. "Frankly, we expected him home long before this. He's wired twice to extend his stay, but this time he said he had some good news for us."

Vince handed me a small glass of Lone Pine Beer, produced locally at the brewery west of town. "What with all the meetings he's attended, not to mention the City people he's talked to, I'm hoping the good news is that they're not going to take as much water from us as they thought."

"Or at least not dump the excess into the San Fernando Valley," Father mused as he walked in behind me.

"I suppose it's too much to hope that the project has been cancelled?" Charlotte ventured.

Everyone just looked at her, considering the question rhetorical. It showed how much we'd all accepted our fate.

I stepped out onto the front porch the next morning before anyone else was stirring and watched the local light show. The dull, misty glow of pre-dawn hovering over the Sierra rapidly gave way to a warm pink glow that deepened until the jagged ridge was bathed in a vibrant orange. By the time the birds had ceased their jubilant morning chorus, the mountains had achieved their daytime face. Bright blue granite topped by a powdering of snow stood out as a stark backdrop for the contrast of the chocolate brown mounds of the Alabama Hills. Such natural drama of subtle color was a comforting welcome, and I was filled with a surge of renewed confidence.

However, I soon realized that everyone in the town when discussing future plans, did so with an air of tentativeness. Charlotte told me, "It's like we're all waiting for the other shoe to drop." It created an atmosphere of underlying tension that was present no matter what was taking place, even if it was an otherwise pleasant occasion.

But I had my own strained waiting to endure. Steven was due home at any moment and I was having difficulty keeping my thoughts occupied on something other than that. The strain increased when I realized that Charlotte still hadn't been told about her relationship to Rose. I was surprised that Mother hadn't told her, considering how little they kept from each other.

The following evening, we all sat together on the porch watching life in Lone Pine promenade by our house. Mr. Edwards passed by in his old black rig, his dark grey horse looking neither right nor left yet unaided by blinders shielding his eyes. Two of the daughters of Mr. and Mrs. Meysan walked past on the way to their homes, carrying packages in their arms. The Summers boy skipped down the road toward town, probably on an errand. Mr. Spear went by in his small open wagon, two fishing poles laying next to a wicker creel bulging with a bountiful catch.

Each one waved or nodded or called out a cheery greeting to our seemingly serene group. But they didn't see the tightness of Aunt Charlotte's smile or her puzzled frown as she noted Uncle Vince's clenched jaw and low growl while reading the newspaper, the savagery of Father's whittling, Mother's distraction and unusually inept sketch of Mt. Whitney, and my inability to resist furtive glances down the street to the south.

Father suddenly broke the silence to speak to Vince, and Mother jumped. "Did you hear that John Shepherd sold his ranch to George Chaffey?"

"That's over 1,300 acres north of George's Creek," Mother exclaimed with wonder.

"Who's George Chaffey?" I asked Father.

"He's an agriculture developer from Southern California. He's been experimenting with irrigation of citrus groves somewhere east of Los Angeles."

I couldn't summon sufficient enthusiasm to question him further, and just before dusk my parents retreated into the house. Charlotte chose to walk home the two blocks to their house, while Uncle Vince stayed behind to finish his paper. When I was sure the others couldn't hear, I sat next to Vince on the swing and asked him, "Have you told Charlotte about Rose yet?"

"No." He folded the paper neatly. "I told her about how we got Rose back, and Alex's death, but little else. Emily and I thought we should wait until you tell Steven."

I shook my head. "You should tell her. I don't think she'll be as surprised as you think."

"Maybe not."

"If you don't tell her soon, she'll resent your knowing all this time and not saying anything. Your relationship is too open to hold this back from her." I put my hand on his arm. "Please believe me, secrets are horrid monsters. They nibble at the edges of pleasurable moments, whisper nasty thoughts into your ear at odd times, and disavow all knowledge of contentment."

He looked at me with compassion, and said, "You really have been unhappy, haven't you?"

I looked away toward the street. "Yes. These haven't been easy years."

"Well then," he stood up and looked down on me, "if I'm to tell Charlotte about Rose, you have to tell Steven the minute he returns. He'll be so glad to know you two can finally be together, he'll probably be quite reasonable about not having been told sooner." He smiled broadly. "And when he holds his daughter in his arms, he'll forgive everything completely."

"I hope so."

He put a hand on my shoulder and patted me with affection. "I'm sure he'll understand once he knows the whole run of events."

"But you're going to tell Charlotte?"

"Yes, yes. I'll go do it now."

And he did. I knew because she came up the front walk an hour later at a fast walk with her skirts hiked up, threw open the front door, and pounded up the stairs. Having seen her approach from my window overlooking the street, I met her at the door to my room prepared to absorb the scolding I deserved.

"So," she declared with hands on hips, "I'm the last to know, am I?"

"I'm sorry, Aunt Charlotte. I wanted Steven to know before anyone else. Circumstances kind of got in the way of the plan."

"They often do." She pushed past me into the room. "Now, let me see my precious grandchild."

"She's the same child she's always been."

"No, she's not." Cradling a sleepy Rose in her arms, Charlotte whispered, "Now she's my grandbaby. It's just different, that's all. When Rose has a baby, then you'll understand."

Good grief, I thought! What all would happen in our lives before that?

Then I noticed a little tear hovering at the corner of Charlotte's left eye. Looking down at the sleepy little girl in her arms, she muttered softly, "Oh, my. Steven's child!" Relieved she was more eager to be with Rose than focus recrimination on me, I left her alone and went downstairs.

The next two days as we waited for Steven to arrive were days of life suspended. Daily cooking, cleaning, child care and chores were completed, but there was no sense of vitality in their accomplishment. Even our conversations at meals were subdued and consisted of less discussion than usual.

When Steven finally did arrive, it was late in the afternoon. We didn't think it was him at first because we heard an automobile cough and sputter to a stop, a machine only rarely making an appearance in our Valley because of the lack of paved roads. But it was the intensity of Mother's gasp after she rose to look out the parlor window that brought us all to our feet.

My first sight of Steven in two years was that of him helping down from a dusty black auto a woman whose fair beauty was exceptional. He assisted her in the removal of the long, linen duster she wore to keep the road dirt from her clothes and tossed the garment onto the seat along with his own. The part of my mind that was refusing to grasp the meaning of the scene before me focused with admiration on the pale blue suit she wore. Her tiny cinched bodice was covered in a snug fitting jacket tapering down to small hips, and the long skirt just covered her ankles, showing fine leather boots peeking from below the hem.

Uncle Vince was the first to speak. "Look at all those blonde curls."

It was indeed difficult to miss the tangle of shining golden ringlets cascading down the back of her head, falling from beneath a velvet bonnet the same color as the dress, only now covered in a fine mist of brown dust. All this I took in with a single glance before my eyes turned to Steven, dressed in a new suit that could have benefited from a pressing. But as he turned toward the house, he also wore a smile, and a set to his shoulders that broadcast defiance.

This wasn't the way my return to Lone Pine was supposed to play out, and I longed to run away to some place where I wouldn't have to face whatever was to come next. Instead, I stood back from the others as they raced from the parlor into the entry. My stomach kinked into knots, my heart raced in a chest that felt too small, and a thin ringing played in my ears. Before I could calm myself, the door opened and framed there was my beloved Steven and some blonde interloper on his arm, and a beautiful one at that. Her eyes were almost the same color as her dress, and I thought unkindly, "I bet she wears a lot of blue."

After hugging Charlotte and enthusiastically shaking hands with Vince and Father, Steven turned toward Mother. In doing so, he caught sight of me. The frozen tableau that followed must have lasted more heartbeats than the young woman thought proper.

"Steven, you haven't introduced me yet."

Valiantly overcoming his surprise, Steven reached for her hand and turned back to us. "Everyone, I'd like you to meet my wife."

That was as far as he got before Aunt Charlotte yelped, "Your wife? But..."

"Well, son," Vince quickly cut her off, "you're full of surprises, aren't you? How long have you two been married?"

"Four weeks yesterday."

Steven took one glance at my white face and turned away, leading his new wife (even now the word is bitter upon my tongue) through the tightly packed lot of us into the parlor. Mother murmured something about putting on the kettle while Vince and Father hurried out the front door to see the automobile, leaving Charlotte and me with the newlyweds. Steven and his new wife sat poised and uneasy on the sofa. The elegant subject of our shock carefully arranged the expensive skirts of her suit while Charlotte and I perched on the edge of the two large chairs across the room.

"Well, isn't this nice?" Charlotte chirped nervously. She then turned to the obviously self-conscious woman next to her son and added, "I don't think you were introduced to Whitney just now. She's Emily and Frank's daughter."

"Hello, Whitney." She held her smile stiffly, although obviously trying to look friendly. "I've heard so much about you from Steven. The sister of his youth and all that. But I thought he said you were married and living away from Lone Pine."

Forcing myself to smile, I answered her. "I was, but I'm home now to stay." Steven gasped loudly, flushed the color of a new brick, then coughed several times. Ignoring him, I commented, "I don't believe I caught the name of my *brother's* new wife."

"Oh, yes." Her laughter was low and throaty, the amused sound overtly sexual. "My name's Lavinia."

My face must have changed in some way because Steven asked me if something was wrong. I assured him that everything was fine while chastising myself for reacting so strongly to a mere coincidence of names.

"That's not a very common name," I managed to say.

She shrugged. "No, I suppose not, at least here in the dusty wildlands." She chuckled and added with a smile, "But I met another woman with my name when I first moved to Los Angeles. In fact, we were close enough in appearance that we could have been sisters."

Still focused on the earlier part of the conversation, Steven said to me, "What do you mean you're here to stay?" Then turning to Lavinia, he explained, "She's married to a man with a big ranch outside Bridgeport." He looked back at me and asked, "The Double R, right?"

"Yes."

Lavinia frowned and asked, "Where's Bridgeport?"

At the same time, Steven asked, "How is Alex?"

My mouth opened, but I found that my mind didn't know what words to form. Mother walked in with the coffee on a silver tray and placed it on the table with an unsteady thump. "Oh my, I'm so sorry. I've had a bit of arthritis in my arm lately."

"You should have asked me to bring it in, Aunt Emily."

Mother mumbled, "It's fine. I'll get the plate of sandwiches. You must be famished." She left the room with a puzzled glance at Charlotte and me.

"When did you get the auto, Steven?" I hurried to ask him.

"It belongs to Lavinia, actually." He had not as yet met my eyes, his words spoken to his coffee cup, to my right shoulder, or to his mother.

"Really?" I turned my eyes to Lavinia, surprised that a woman would have such a machine.

"It belongs to my brother," she quickly explained. "He moved to Europe and left it with me."

"What a nice brother." I turned to Steven. "Are you going to let me have your favorite horse, *brother*?"

His laugh was dry and without humor as he responded tartly, "You never know, *sis*." To change the subject, if not the tone of the conversation, he handed out the coffee cups and said, "So Whitney, when do we get to see the lovely child, Rose?"

"She's napping right now."

"Can't you wake her?" Lavinia asked.

"No, I can't!" Then softening my voice, I added, "She needs her rest." I was simply not ready to see Rose on Steven's lap, or worse yet held by the woman sitting so close to Steven that I longed to yank her onto the floor by her shining blonde curls. I was only mildly surprised at the violence of such images arising in my mind.

Steven nodded. "Well, I look forward to seeing her later then. But you still haven't answered my original question. What do you mean you're here to stay? Will Alex be arriving later?"

After taking a cup from him and returning to my chair, I sipped the hot aromatic liquid before setting my cup beside me on the polished table. Then, sitting up straight with my hands in my lap, I answered, "There's a reason I'm wearing dark purple. I'm a recent widow."

Lavinia choked on her coffee and recovered enough to say, "You're not married then?"

"No." Then, as though speaking to a child, I found myself saying unkindly, "That's what being a widow means."

Coloring slightly, she then asked where she might find the facilities. Steven showed her to the back door and the new privy just beyond the bath house. It gave me a moment to regret my sharp tongue, realizing suddenly that the poor woman must be worried about the closeness between Steven and myself, although I couldn't imagine he would have told her about our time of intimacy. Probably, I thought, he's talked too much about our growing up together.

When Steven returned to the parlor, everyone else had come back into the room before him. Between myself, Father and Uncle Vince we succinctly told him the highlights of what had happened, leaving out the truth about why Alex took Rose, and saying instead that he just wanted to hurt me, which was certainly true. By the end of the story, we realized Lavinia was standing in the parlor entry, having heard the part about Alex's death in the barn.

She entered the room and told Steven, "I'm sorry. I think the trip has been too much for me." And indeed she was white and perspiring. "Could we possibly go home now so I can rest?"

It was obvious Steven didn't want to leave, but he stood up and bid everyone good-bye. Lingering by my chair, he took my hand in his and looked into my eyes for the first time. "I'm sorry you've had such a bad time. I didn't know. You should have told me." It was all said so quickly and so low that I wasn't sure anyone else had heard. Back of the words, however, I clearly heard the hurt and reproach that had motivated them.

While everyone else followed the departing couple onto the porch with congratulations and solicitations for Lavinia's health, I watched from the parlor window. Vince walked to the front of the car to help start it by giving a hard turn on the handle attached to the magneto under the hood, which was the way of the early autos. Steven sat in the driver's seat gripping the steering wheel as though he was afraid it would fly off if he let go. This left it to Father to assist Lavinia into her seat beside Steven.

We watched them drive away, each of us holding our places like actors waiting for the curtain to fall. The car's engine made a few loud pops and bangs, spooking nearby horses and starting several dogs barking. A passel of excited children ran down the street after them while I tried not to picture Steven and Lavinia arriving at the Perry ranch where they would be sharing Steven's bedroom. Feeling Mother move closer behind me, I knew she was watching the scene over my shoulder.

"Are you all right, my dear?" she whispered.

"I can't believe he got married."

"I'm so sorry, Whitney."

"He just can't be in love with her!"

"I can't believe he'd marry her if he wasn't."

I continued to silently stare out the window, and finally Mother returned to the kitchen. I couldn't shake the image of Steven and Lavinia in his bedroom, and burned hot with hate for a woman that I admittedly didn't even know, but that right then I wanted to take by the shoulders and shake until her head snapped off.

Mother came back in with a cup of tea and handed it to me as I asked her, "Do you think Charlotte or Vince will tell him about Rose?"

"No, of course not." She smiled. "I got them to agree to that on the porch just now."

I looked at her in awe. "Where did you get the ability to think things through so quickly?"

"From experience. Necessity is a great teacher."

I sighed and told her, "I'm going to my room." When I reached the bottom of the stairs, I turned back. "Can you bring me some supper later? I don't want to come down to the table and be with everyone right now."

"No, I won't." Seeing my astonishment, she didn't bother to apologize. "You don't have time to play the retiring lady with the vapors. You have to face all this, and you might as well start immediately."

Slowly nodding in agreement, I started up the stairs. Mother then called out, "Whitney, don't waste too much time feeling sorry for yourself." She moved to the bottom of the stairs so I could see her smile. "But also, don't feel guilty that you do."

Her practical advice helped me more than sympathy would have done, but she did leave me to myself for a few hours. I sat in the chair by the window of my room, next to my baby in her crib playing with her cloth dolls, and gazed into the distance at Lone Pine Peak and Mt. Whitney. I was haunted by the feeling that the Double R curse of betrayal had followed me home, my life contaminated from the moment I smiled at Alex seven years before.

The next morning after breakfast I asked Steven to join me for a ride to Diaz Lake. During the meal, we had all laughed at Rose's attachment to Steven when she didn't want to get down from his lap, even long enough to eat. When he got up and prepared to leave with me, Rose started to fuss until Sing took her and told her to hush.

She looked up at him and declared, "Hush!" As we laughed, knowing it was probably going to encourage her to do it again, Sing whisked her upstairs.

Lavinia wasn't happy about my riding off with her husband, but Mother and Charlotte told her they needed her help with the making of pies. Mother put an apron around Lavinia's neck while Charlotte tied it in back, both talking non-stop about the recipe and where they'd obtained the apples. Consequently, there was no opportunity for Lavinia to pull Steven aside and voice her displeasure.

We rode in silence all the way to the lake. I tried to enjoy the breeze rustling in the cottonwoods along the road, the call of the birds, the bellowing of the cattle in the pastures, and the air scented with sage. But it was difficult to focus on anything other than Steven riding just ahead of me--the length of his strong legs gripping the sides of his horse, the curve of his back and the set of his hips moving in rhythm to the horse's gate.

Once we reached the large old trees by the lake, we dismounted and walked the horses until we reached the stump of an old cottonwood brought down in a storm. Sitting there with a view to a pasture full of grazing pack horses, we should both have been relaxed. But we weren't.

Finally, Steven spoke. "I saw the look of surprise on your face when I walked in with Lavinia." Not knowing how to respond, I said nothing. "How can you feel betrayed by me when you're the one who decided to return to Alex and stay with him?"

"I stayed with him because I had to help him through the nightmare of what he was finding out about his father. He was devastated. And then I discovered I was pregnant."

He clenched his jaw. "So as soon as you returned, you allowed him to..." He took a deep breath. "I thought you were going to tell him right away about us, and then leave and come back here." His voice was going up as he spoke, and he no longer was trying to hide his frustration.

"Steven, please. Let me explain." I picked up his hand and held it tightly. "I was pregnant when I arrived at the Double R, but I didn't know it right away."

It would be impossible to describe the array of emotions that crossed his face as he processed what I'd just said, and needless to say he was flabbergasted. "Rose is *my* daughter?"

"Yes. I wanted to return home immediately and tell you, but Alex was acting so out of control that I was frightened of him, so I made him think it was his child. I was willing to come home expecting, but by the time I felt I could stand up to him and leave, we had an early winter storm and the south pass was closed. Then Rose was born with a weak digestion, and I couldn't travel until she was stable. Then Mother came and Jones showed up and..."

"Who the hell is Jones?"

"Oh, that's right. You don't know about the second act in the nightmare." I took a full hour to tell him about the recent dramas at the Double R, including J.B. fleeing the ranch, Alex's trip to the lake with the items marked with the Double R brand, and the visit by the attorney. I ended with the description of how Alex had departed for Virginia City while I went to Bodie with Irene, and then his return to take Rose. By the time I had filled in more details about our fathers' part in Alex's return to the Double R and his subsequent death, Steven was slowly shaking his head in disbelief.

"My God, no wonder you didn't write me during all that. What would you have said?"

"Oh, Steven, thank goodness you understand."

"Well, I do and I don't." He played with a stone he'd picked up, rolling it around in his hands. "I still think you could've found some way to get word to me." The anguish in his voice made me wince.

"Looking back," I explained, "there were several things I could have done differently. But at the time, I did what I thought was right considering everything that was happening around me. And I thought you might have inferred the truth when I told Mother to be sure to tell you the baby's name was Rose."

"Rose?" He thought a moment, then laughed. "Our last meeting in the cemetery, and the rose I gave you."

I sighed. "Well, it was an attempt to let you know. Maybe not as good as I thought."

"Only because I was so thick-headed. Anyway, something shocking is really best told in person."

"You mean like the fact that you got married without telling anyone, or even sending a telegram?" When he didn't respond, I slewed my eyes around to him and found him watching me.

"You don't like Lavinia, do you?" he asked.

"That shouldn't surprise you." After a moment, I asked, "Are you very much in love with her?"

While I held my breath and he tried to find words, a horse and rider came by.

"Well, hello you two," Mr. Didden said with a big grin. "I heard you were back in town, Whitney. You staying this time?"

"Yes sir, I am."

"Good." Dismissing me, he turned to Steven. "If you're returning to town, I'll ride along with you and get that medicine you're holding for me. I'd like to doctor the horse tonight."

We had no choice but to go along with his plan, since to him we were still just two childhood friends that couldn't possibly care about being interrupted in conversation.

Of course, as soon as I walked in the house, Mother popped out of the kitchen. "Well?"

"I told him about Rose."

"How did he take it?"

"Quite well, actually. He even understands why I didn't write him, what with everything that was happening with Alex and my fear that someone might see a letter if I wrote him. Beyond that, he didn't get much of a chance to react to the idea of having a daughter."

"Did he explain about meeting and marrying Lavinia?"

"I was just turning the conversation in that direction when Mr. Didden came along and asked to ride with us back to town."

"Then wait. Somehow, it'll all come right in the end."

Mother and her optimism. It never failed her, yet I just couldn't be as sure.

A lot had happened locally during the years I had been gone. The general financial mood of the town when I left in 1900 had been somewhat depressed. But by the end of 1904, gold strikes in southwest Nevada in the Bullfrog-Rhyolite-Beatty District, at Tonopah, and at Goldfield, had stimulated the growing of wheat, barley and potatoes. These were items that could stand the long shipping by train and wagon to the mining camps and far-situated towns. Cattle and sheep sales were also booming, along with the smaller farm products like honey, spun cotton and chickens.

In 1902 the Bishop Light and Power Co. had been created to supply the needs of the local ranchers, although it didn't come as far south as Lone Pine until a few years later, and then only for some of the stores. A Colorado power company then purchased the Bishop company along with its rights to reservoirs. After a few years, and several name changes along with the absorption of local water companies, the Southern Sierra Power Company built power plants and transmission lines from the Valley to the new mining towns in Nevada. Owens Valley citizens signed on as laborers during construction and later the maintenance of the plants. It was employment that was very welcome.

All this activity in Nevada stimulated another burst of optimism about the Cerro Gordo mines, and a new smelter was built near Owens Lake with the expectation that silver could profitably be extracted from junk ores that had thus far been ignored. In 1906, men were hired as teamsters to haul the low grade silver ore from the old Cerro Gordo Mine dumps down the Yellow Grade to the new smelter at Keeler. Eventually, like every other surge of effort related to Cerro Gordo, this project failed as well.

Even before the turn of the century, Bishop had established itself as the economic and commercial core of the Valley. The Inyo County Bank was established in 1902 and began a close partnership with the Valley ranchers. The founders, the Watterson brothers Wilfred and Mark, were sons of a large sheep ranching family in the area and were highly respected and trusted. In 1899 their uncle, George Watterson, had established a small store that supplied domestic merchandise throughout the Valley. When it was announced in 1906 that construction of the aqueduct would begin in 1908, many businesses in Lone Pine and Bishop began to build up their inventory. The train brought in carload lots of items that included construction hardware, stoves, farm machinery from the John Deer Plow Company and the Studebaker line of buggies (and later automobiles), cream separators, tractors, guns and ammo, and an extensive line of English fishing tackle.

Knowing from experience the short-lived nature of mining and agriculture, the Valley citizens had since 1903 also advertised the local fishing and hunting opportunities to sportsmen, along with the Valley's fresh air and beauty to those who were looking for a change of pace from City life. The City's plans to take the water that supported the ranches also affected this new bid for tourism dollars. This combination of planned boom and possible bust generated a confusing combination of optimism and dread.

As the start date of construction neared, many of the businessmen and ranchers realized their greatest asset was in the sale of their land. Even Bishop banker Mark Watterson sold 440 of his acres for $8700, although he later opposed sales to the City by other ranchers. Some Valley merchants and notables sold land to the city too: the one-time editor of the Inyo Independent, Irv Mulholland, sold 1,020 acres for $10,120; Lone Pine brewer John Lubkin sold 240 acres for $5,300; realtor and County Assessor Ben Yandell sold 440 acres for $4,080; and merchant and farmer Eibeshutz sold 160 acres for $900. This was a lot of land for what was a lot of early twentieth century dollars.

Altogether there were 192 parcels sold, although most of the 240 miles of the aqueduct cut through land given to the project by the Federal Government. Still, the City needed the ranch lands for the water rights, and the ability to limit the amount of water used for irrigation.

The more radical citizens occasionally protested what many called the invasion by the City with the setting of fires at the construction camps set up prior to the start of construction in 1908. But arson was just a typical citizen protest tradition, and didn't amount to much. Since the 1870's, laborers had regularly set fire to something when they were unhappy with their employer, as did neighboring ranchers in conflict over boundaries or some perceived slight. There was no prejudice to this.

Prejudice in its typical form, however, was very much a part of life in the early 1900's, and was quite simple. It included everyone other than white males. Women were on an equal par with the Mexicans unless the Mexican was male and had assumed the Anglo way of life. That would elevate him to at least the lower rungs of the white, male hierarchical ladder that included the Germans, French and Basques. The Paiutes weren't considered for inclusion on even the lower rungs of the ladder, although some whites considered them friends. The Chinese formed a labor force in roles the Paiutes rejected, and were otherwise ignored until someone was needed to blame for a crime.

With the arrival of the City's advance construction teams, one change in the town happened quickly. In anticipation of the large number of men that would be coming to the area, new prostitutes arrived, gradually increasing the number of cribs already on the northeast end of town behind the feed store.

Mother, Aunt Charlotte and I discussed this one day as we shared lunch in the Perry's small kitchen. Charlotte told us, "Some of the townswomen want to eject the friendly sorority from the town."

Mother surprised me by responding, "Why? We've had them here throughout the town's history. Most even contribute money to help those in need. and they all support community projects."

When I laughed, Mother turned to me for explanation. "Mother, you never mentioned anything of the sort in your letters to Aunt Carrie."

"True, but in the 1870's, one didn't talk about such things in letters to friends."

"You didn't have any problem telling Carrie about such a woman who you befriended when you were in Bodie," I countered.

Aunt Charlotte responded before her suddenly flustered friend could prepare an explanation. "Someone like Kitty fit in naturally in a place like Bodie. Your mother was just discovering Lone Pine and her love for it was a little blind. For her, it was the ideal town, and she wasn't yet willing to see it's dusty underbelly."

"Regardless," Mother added, determined to change the subject, "why are the *good* women now making such a fuss about a few more loose women coming to town?"

"They say it'll cause the construction workers to loiter in town, and consequently around our young girls."

I rolled my eyes. "Do they think the crews are going to be composed of demented ravagers of young women?"

Charlotte chuckled. "I told the complainers that if they felt that way, having the prostitutes here would be the best thing. That way the men have a convenient outlet for their urges. I actually may have won the argument with some of them."

"I think," Mother mused, "that we'd do best not to allow our dislike of the project to influence our assumptions about the men involved in its construction."

So between the eager speculation of profit for the businessmen of the Valley towns, the ranchers selling to the mines as much of their crops and meat as they could, the unreasonable fears of mothers, the giggling expectation of teenaged girls, and the land owners who hadn't yet sold to the City wondering if they should, it was a time of wild speculation and uneasy anticipation. Everyone admitted there would be positive benefit for some people, but also that there would be hardship for others. The immediate concern for each Valley resident was, which would it be for them?

CHAPTER 17

Never could I have imagined such a tense Christmas. The weeks leading up to it had been busy with decorating, cooking, and parties, as well as the purchasing and wrapping of gifts. With Sing's invaluable help, I was able to keep up with Rose's daily needs and the extra work we created in the house. Sing pitched in with an eagerness that fueled the rest of us, and even the normally dour daily girl was heard to laugh. But for me, underlying it all was a degree of acute disappointment and loss that kept it from being the happy holiday I had anticipated.

Christmas Eve, however, was a sweet reminder of so many I had experienced, with all of Lone Pine coming together full of holiday spirit. The activities took place in the upstairs hall of the schoolhouse on Locust Street, with the children providing a program of skits, poems, recitations and songs. A group of young men had taken a six-horse wagon to the wood supply road, through Lone Pine Canyon, and up to where they could cut down two lovely fir trees. Being too tall for the school room, the men had cut off the top and bottom of each tree so they could fit on either side of the stage at the west end of the hall. The piney scent of the trees filled the schoolhouse and everyone entering took a deep breath. These were the only Christmas trees the town would see, and a good portion of everyone's delight was due to the communal sharing of them.

By the time we arrived for the celebration, the tree had been decorated with strings of popcorn, clove-studded oranges, and small glittering toys. On the tip of each bough was tied a small candle waiting to be lit at the last moment, with buckets of sand discretely hidden nearby in case of fire. Beneath the trees were piles of presents brought there in pillow cases, the names of the recipients plainly written on each so Santa could hand them out.

As soon as the program of carefully practiced songs and skits was over, each child was given a big red apple, a navel orange, a colorful bag of candy, and a small bag of nuts. Rose was delighted with these treasures, and would have been satisfied with just that. But when squeals and screams started from the other children, her attention was diverted to Santa Claus bounding into the room, jumping up and down and cracking a teamster's blacksnake whip over the heads of the audience.

His behavior might not have been traditional outside our western town, but his dress was the same red suit trimmed in white fur, tall black leather boots, shiny black belt and floppy red cap with a white ball on the tip. His beard and hair were white and long, and his hands rested on his stomach whenever he belted out a deep "ho, ho, ho"! The little children watched in quiet awe, while the older ones laughed and called out to him, demanding their gifts. He obliged by reaching under the tree and pulling out presents, calling the names of the recipients one after another. When their names were called, the children ran down the aisle, their eyes bulging at the sight of a big box if they were so blessed by Santa. Has any child ever truly believed that good things come in small packages?

While the children ripped into their presents, Santa disappeared, adding to their certainty that he really was a magical being. A few adults turned to each other and inquired if that funny noise they just heard was the jingle of bells on the roof, while another said he thought he'd heard tiny reindeer feet. The younger children reacted with open mouths and big eyes, and even the older ones giggled. If they had been a little more observant, they would have noticed that stage driver Oliver (Ollie) Dearborn had been gone while Santa was there, and returned shortly after he'd left, a bit rumpled and flushed in the face.

Christmas morning, immediately after breakfast, the older children rushed to the E. H. Edwards Store on the corner of Main and Willow. The stately Mrs. Edwards greeted them with an enthusiastic "Merry Christmas" while scattering hundreds of marbles in the street. The children promptly scrambled around in the dirt, each one determined to get his fair share. Immediately after, the children gathered in groups and played each other for more.

While the children were thus occupied, the adults rested up in anticipation of that evening's all-night dance that would end the celebration. No one could have dragged me to that. Watching Steven holding the beautiful Lavinia in his arms while dancing would have been more than I could have borne. Our family, after a big breakfast of ham, eggs, biscuits and gravy, settled before the fire in the parlor with coffee.

Rose, after being told she couldn't play with the gold pin given me by Father that morning, decided to play with her new cloth doll. She contentedly pushed it in the tiny sleigh Vince had made for her from scrap lumber. Our conversation was more relaxed than I anticipated, probably due to the laughter that accompanied the reminiscences of past holidays spent together. Lavinia listened with what I suspected was a feigned interest and said very little.

Charlotte, who had shared more conversation with Lavinia than anyone else, noticed this and announced during a lull, "Lavinia used to live in San Francisco before coming to Los Angeles, where she met Steven, at a mutual friend's party soon after he arrived in town."

My first thought was that I had seldom heard a sentence so replete with information. But I turned to Lavinia and asked, "Did you grow up in San Francisco?"

"Yes." Her voice was so low as to be barely audible. She cleared her throat and added, almost reluctantly, "My parents died when I was very young, so I was raised by an aunt in San Francisco. Then I moved to Los Angeles."

"With your aunt?"

"No." A look of pique crossed her face the moment she said it, and I knew she was wishing she'd answered differently. It would have kept more questions from following, since she was obviously shy and disliked having so much attention focused on herself.

Mother asked, "What brought you to Los Angeles?"

"A friend invited me to move in with her. She was taking care of an invalid father and I thought I could help."

Steven had been watching Rose playing with her doll on the rug, but now turned to Lavinia with a frown. "I thought you said it was her mother that needed the help."

"No, dear, it was the father." Her cheeks were very red, and I felt sorry for anyone so shy that a simple conversation would be so uncomfortable for them.

"Are you practiced in caring for invalids?" Mother asked, her curiosity evidently stronger than her concern for Lavinia's discomfort.

This time Lavinia took her time to consider a response, her blue eyes turning darker as she wet her lips prior to speaking. Rose took that moment to jump up and run to Steven with her doll in one hand and one of its cloth shoes in the other. Pushing both at him, she demanded, "Daddy fix!"

The gasp from everyone was loud enough to startle Rose, who looked around at us with a puzzled frown before returning her attention to Steven. He smiled and kissed Rose on the top of her head, telling her softly, "I'll do my best."

Lavinia said sharply, "Silly child!" She stood up and looked down at Rose. "He's not your father. Your father is..."

"Steven!" I stood up abruptly. "Why don't you use the kitchen table to fix the doll? Rose you go with him."

After only a brief hesitation, Steven picked up Rose and left the room. My whole body trembled with the pent-up strain of months spent dealing with Alex, followed by the disappointment of finding Alex married. Consequently, I no longer cared how embarrassed Lavinia might be. No more than two feet from her, I told her through clenched jaws, "Don't you ever speak to my child that way again! Children often say things that make sense to them, but not to anyone else."

"I'm sorry." She took a step back. "I just thought it wasn't right for her to forget her father."

"What she remembers of Alex is my decision. But especially the idea that he's dead."

She had the grace to blush and stammered, "You're right, of course." She looked down at her hands clenched at her waist. "I guess I was just so surprised that I didn't stop to think."

"We were all surprised. But there was no cause to react as vehemently as you did." Beginning to think she was after all a little unstable in her moods, I walked out of the room, leaving the others to cope with what I knew would be a very awkward scene.

Meanwhile, Steven with Rose on his lap was hosting a pretend tea party at the big table in the kitchen. Rose was laughing and smacking her lips. When I walked in and she realized I'd heard her, she clamped a hand over her mouth and looked at me for a rebuke.

"My goodness, Rose," I told her, "you're a very hearty drinker. Who did you ever see do that?"

"Missus Smith," she lisped.

Steven saw my color change and immediately told Rose, "You've had a very big morning. Don't you think it would be a good idea to take a short nap?"

"No." She clutched her doll and stuck out her lower lip in an exaggerated pout.

From behind me, Mother said, "I think a nap is a very good idea for both of us, Rose. But we need a story first, don't we?"

"Yes!" She jumped down from Steven's lap and ran to the foot of the stairs. However, after looking up at the steep steps, she turned around and held out her arms to Mother. Together they went upstairs.

Collapsing into the chair across from Steven, I responded to his raised eyebrows. "Mrs. Smith was the woman who took in Rose for Alex while he went on to Lundy. She was an old crone, half drunk most of the time, and she would have done anything for money. She had quite a rough reputation. When they told me where Alex had taken Rose, I wanted to tear him apart."

After a moment of quiet, Steven said, "I'm sorry Lavinia spoke as she did." As he continued, his words came out faster with each sentence. "She was about to say something about Alex being dead and I understand that you couldn't let her say that to Rose. But Lavinia's been very tense since we got here. I don't think she's at ease in the country. But in time she'll learn to like the Valley, and even fit in. She's always lived in big cities before, and Lone Pine is such a small town, and with dirt streets too. There's not much for her to do here. It's not like she'd fit into the quilting circle. And she doesn't like to cook, so..."

"Steven, you're babbling."

He stopped and looked at me with surprise. "You're right." He shook his head slowly and ran a hand over his face. "I get with you and feel like I want to share every thought I've had recently about everything."

Thankful he hadn't given me intimate details about his marriage, but needing to know at least if he was deeply in love with Lavinia, I told him, "I need to ask you something."

"Okay, what is it?"

But when I looked into his open, honest face, I only said, "Never mind. I think I know the answer." The kitchen door swung open and Lavinia walked in. I wanted to throw the cream jug at her.

"Steven," she addressed him, ignoring me, "I really think we should go home now. I'd like to rest in preparation for tonight's party."

Standing up, I said, "Of course you do. Have a nice time tonight."

Mother came in just after they had left and reached for an apron. "Did you get a chance to see if he's really in love with her?"

"Oh, Mother, of course he is. He married her."

She turned the crank on the coffee grinder as she commented, "But he certainly didn't know her very long."

"No," I sighed, "but she's beautiful and graceful and probably performs like a pro in bed."

"Whitney, don't be coarse."

"Sorry. But I have to face that their relationship really isn't any of my business. He married her and so of course he's in love with her. So that's the end of it."

"I'm so sorry, dear."

I looked at her kind, gentle face and practically wailed, "What have I done to reap punishment of such Gothic proportion?"

Mother fought a smile, and in spite of my anguish, I too had to laugh at my dramatic assessment. Further comment was cut short by the crunch of buggy wheels stopping in front of the house. The familiar voice of Peter from the Robinsons Stables commanded the horse to "Whoa!", and I rushed to the kitchen window in time to see him assisting a woman from the buggy.

"Who is it?" Mother asked.

"It's Irene!"

Before she had closed the gate behind her, I was throwing my arms around her. "Did you come on Santa's sleigh?" I laughed. "Because you're just about the best present I could get."

"I'm so glad you feel that way." Her cheeks were rosy from the cold and her eyes twinkled. I had never seen her look so pretty, or so vibrant. "I missed you so much and the thought came to me that I could just get out of town before the first hard snow if I left immediately." Peter deposited Irene's things on the front porch and tipped his hat as he passed us on his way back to the wagon. Irene quickly said, "I only hope my being here isn't a bother to your parents." Lowering her voice, she added, "I got your letter about Steven and his wife. How awful for you. But how could he be in love with her after knowing her such a short time?"

"I have to admit they don't act very close. I keep thinking that if I tell him I'm still in love with him, I'd only be doing it in the hope he'd leave her for me."

"What's wrong with that?"

"Nothing, if he regrets having married her, especially now that he knows about Rose."

"Do you want him as a husband only because he wants to be a father to Rose?"

Not sure I meant it, I said, "No, of course not. But I really think he still cares about me. You tell me what you think later."

Mother walked out onto the porch and called to Father to come see what Santa had brought us all for Christmas. They were both very welcoming and received Irene's arrival with delight. The only free room was a very small one with a single bed and chest of drawers between my room and Sing's, but Irene insisted that with the window's view of the Sierra it was perfect.

That night, while my parents and most of Lone Pine's men and women danced at the town hall until the early hours of the morning, Irene and I sat on either side of the parlor fire in our night clothes with big mugs of hot chocolate. She brought me up-to-date with the happenings in Bridgeport, then we discussed how I could begin to accept the fact that Steven belonged to another woman. But we arrived at no conclusion.

A week of festivities followed where Irene and I had the opportunity to adjust to Steven and Lavinia as a couple. We all rode several times into the Alabama Hills through Lone Pine Canyon, took a buggy trip to Diaz Lake to see the swans that visit in the winter, and attended a card party one evening at the Edwards home. But at the end of that week, I still hadn't resolved myself to the rest of my life watching Steven and Lavinia grow old together with their children around them.

On a cold January afternoon, while Irene went into town with Mother and Charlotte for a visit to the shops with Rose in tow, I got on with my plans to dip candles. Father was as usual doing something outside, probably with Vince at least part of the time. And I had just heated the wax and laid out the string wicks next to the tin candle molds, when the back door opened and Steven walked in. I started to offer a cheery greeting, but the strained look on his face stopped me.

"Steven, what's wrong?"

"It's Lavinia. She had a lot of stomach pain late last night. The doctor said she might have had a bad reaction to something she'd eaten. We're out of coke syrup and I thought you might have some."

"Of course. It should help sooth her stomach." As I searched through a cupboard for the bottle, I said, "I can't imagine what she could have eaten to have such a reaction. We all had the same thing."

He was very quiet, not responding to my comment. When I turned back to him with the bottle in my hand, it was to find him watching me intently. "This isn't the first time this has happened in the last couple of weeks. The doctor thinks she could be developing a gastric condition brought on by the change in food, or nerves. Or something," he added lamely.

I picked up a glass on the table and walked to the sink to add it to the wash water. Behind me, he said, "She thought she might be expecting."

The crash of the glass as it hit the floor interrupted his musings. I stood stiffly amid the broken pieces while Steven fetched a broom and dust pan from the service porch off the kitchen, then offered them to me along with a wry smile. "But she's not."

As I swept the pieces of broken glass into a pile, I commented, "I suppose it's a possibility though."

After a slight hesitation, he stuffed his hands in his jacket pockets and said, "Well, yes, but pretty doubtful."

With my back to him, I murmured, "Oh?"

"Yeah, well," he mumbled, "she's been not feeling well or tired, or upset with me about something, or my parents were still up, or...anyway, you know what I mean."

"Yes, I do. Only too well." Then I added with a grimace, "At least I assume you two are sharing the same bedroom."

"You mean you and Alex had separate rooms?" He was as startled by the concept as I had been when I arrived at the Double R.

"Yes. Weeks would go by without my seeing him for more than a few minutes at meals, certainly not after retiring at night."

He looked at me with a tenderness and compassion that brought tears to my eyes. "You must have been very lonely."

"Yes," I admitted, "but for the last two years it was because I couldn't get home to you." Feeling heat spread over my face, I realized how vulnerable I'd left myself by such an admission.

"And when you finally do come home, I walk in with a wife." I shrugged as I realized he was choosing to ignore my hint that I was still in love with him. However, he did add, "Our timing seems to be lacking something."

"As long as you're happy," I intimated, "I guess that's what's important."

"Happy?" He mouthed the word as though it was a strange flavor on his tongue. "I was when I married her. I thought I'd found someone I could grow to love."

"*Grow* to love?"

"Well, yes. She was fun and beautiful and a little mysterious, and I thought she'd take away the hurt and disappointment I'd carried for so long." He looked into my eyes and held my gaze. "And she wanted me. I thought that would be enough."

I boldly asked, "It isn't?"

"I'm not sure now." He looked down at the bottle that he was gripping tightly with both hands. "So much has changed since we got here, including

Lavinia. In Los Angeles, she was fresh and lively, always laughing. Now she seems nervous all the time, and she keeps pressing me to move back to Los Angeles. I told her the other day that was out of the question and to stop asking me. She's withdrawn from me since then, barely responding to anything I say. So no, I'm not particularly happy, but neither is she."

Smiling ruefully, I told him, "I suppose I should be sorry to hear that, but I'm not."

"I know." He took a step toward me, then stopped. "If only...oh hell, it's so damn complicated." He then left without further words. I started after him, then thought better of it. When I turned back from the door, Irene was standing just inside the kitchen by the entry hall.

"Are you all back so soon?" I asked in surprise.

"I returned on my own. Emily and Charlotte ran into some women who wanted to see Rose, so I came home to help with the candles."

"That's sweet of you. I guess you heard my conversation with Steven just now."

"Some of it. What happened to Lavinia?"

"She was sick last night, and I guess a couple of times before that as well. The doctor thinks it's a form of gastric distress brought on by her nerves." With a strong hint of sarcasm, I added, "Evidently she's not all that fond of Lone Pine."

Irene shrugged. "Maybe she'll decide she's so unhappy that she'll leave him."

"I'm not counting on it," I told her. And indeed, no matter what Steven had just admitted to me, I was slowly realizing that I'd never have a future with him.

We spent the afternoon finishing the candles, carrying wood in to stack by the kitchen stove and the parlor fireplace, and grinding coffee for dinner and the next day's breakfast. Irene then went upstairs to rest and finish a book she'd been reading.

While cleaning the kitchen, I heard through the open window that Mother had returned home at the same time as Father. Sitting on the front porch swing chatting with him about her day, at one point Mother mentioned that she'd passed Lavinia starting out on a walk and not looking well at all.

"Lavinia told me that the fresh air seems to help when she feels this way, so I guess she's had periods of illness before this."

"Maybe she's not used to the purity of our water," Father chuckled. "Maybe once our water gets to the City, everyone there will have as hard a time digesting it when it starts clearing out the sludge they're used to having in their gut."

When they both laughed, it occurred to me that I'd heard other locals make slyly humorous gibes at the expense of Los Angeles citizens. But as I listened to my parents talking and laughing, the harmony of their tone brought to me a sense of welcome comfort--just as it had when I was a child falling asleep upstairs. The memory of some moments in life are so special that they last a lifetime.

On a cold day in mid-February of 1907, Father and Vince went to Independence, Father on Noble and Vince on a new horse he'd just trained for the trail. They were going first to the Court House on business and then a farm equipment auction. By noon, however, a snow storm hit the area without warning. This was not the most unusual of happenings along the Eastern Sierra, but rare as far south as Lone Pine. As the snow fell, it was blown sideways by a wind with gusts over forty miles per hour that quickly piled drifts against the side of the house.

But we weren't concerned, because we knew the men were still in Independence at the auction, and would stay there until the storm passed and visibility cleared. What we didn't know was that the auction had been cancelled before the storm hit, so they had already started for home.

When by late afternoon neither Mother nor Charlotte had received a telegram with the news that the men were staying in Independence, we all became a little anxious. Steven went to the telegraph office to see if a message had come in and had just not been delivered, but that wasn't the case.

Everyone gathered at our house just as the snow stopped and it began to rain. Irene and I made sandwiches and heated soup, then brought it all into the parlor where the street could be watched. Finally, shortly after it stopped raining but the clouds still made it too dark to see beyond the sycamores along the road, we heard a horse whinny loudly from that direction. Steven opened the front door first, a lantern in his hand as he hurried down the walk to the street. The rest of us crowded onto the front porch, trying to make out figures in the dark, but the lantern light illuminated only Steven.

The next sound was Steven's voice gasping out, "Oh, God!"

Mother and Charlotte gathered up their skirts and raced toward his voice, Charlotte quickly exclaiming, "Vince! Thank heaven you're back."

But then we heard Mother. "No! No! Frank, no!"

When clarity of awareness next came to me, I was standing beside Mother holding her rigid body in my arms while we both stared at Noble. Father's body was draped over his back. The exhausted horse was standing with a rear leg held off the ground and his head hanging almost to the ground.

Vince dismounted his horse and dropped the reins on the ground before he spoke, the words wrenched from him. "The storm caught us on the open flats by George's Creek. Lightening startled my horse and he reared. Noble spooked and went over backwards. Frank hit his head on a rock. He was dead when I got to him. Noble was hurt bad, but I needed him to carry Frank." He stopped talking, leaned against one of the sycamores, and covered his face with gloved hands stained with Father's blood. Charlotte stood helplessly next to him and patted his shoulder, her tears adding to the wet of his soaked jacket.

With great effort, Vince pulled himself together, and with Steven's help eased Father's body from the horse. They laid him gently on the ground, mercifully hiding the back of his head. Mother wrenched herself out of my arms and went to Father, kneeling next to him in the mud and stroking his forehead while murmuring words carried away on the wind.

Someone in town had informed the mortician that a body was being brought to the south end of town. When he arrived and saw the tableau before him, he stopped his open wagon and a gasp of shock escaped him. But he quickly assumed his public face and accepted Steven's assistance in lifting Father's body into his wagon, where he covered it with a tarp. When Mother began climbing into the back of the wagon, he helped her up.

Mother settled beside Father and pulled back the tarp until his head and shoulders were exposed. Her face was an unreadable mask, but tears slid down her cheeks as she laid a hand on his chest as though she might feel again his beating heart. The skirt of her wet dress had bunched above her knees, and I stepped forward to pull it down over her exposed legs. I then placed a lantern next to her and stepped back. Not one of us dared suggest she not go.

As the mortician urged his horses forward, the last of the rain clouds moved past the bright moon and its light illuminated the street. The wagon moved slowly north along Main where people vacated shops, houses, and saloons, to join other curious people gathered along the road. When the townspeople, every one a friend or neighbor, saw Emily in the back of the mortician's wagon, and on her lap Frank's dark head streaked with matted blood, some of the women began to openly weep. And more than a few of the men surreptitiously wiped at their eyes.

As soon as the wagon disappeared from our view, Vince and Charlotte walked up the path to the house. When Uncle Vince stumbled on the top step, Charlotte put her arm around him and helped him inside. I stood on the edge of the road like a lost orphan, not knowing what to do next. Turning for comfort to Steven, I found him checking Noble, running his hands down the injured leg. He then stood up and slowly lead the severely limping, thirteen year old animal around to the barn. Irene appeared at my side and blocked my view of Father's treasured horse in such obvious pain. With her arm around my shoulders, she forced me toward the house while I silently wondered why I felt so little emotion.

Almost as soon as we reached the kitchen, the loud report of a rifle sounded from out back, and I knew that Father's favorite horse was also now dead. I jerked out of Irene's grasp and threw open the back door. With my long skirts whipping about my legs in the rising wind, I ran toward the pasture behind the barn, slipping several times in the slush of rain and snow.

Opening the pasture gate, I ran to Royal and threw my arms around his neck, burying my face in the soft, thick fur of his winter coat. It had been a long time since I had paid attention to the old horse, but he welcomed me as always by nickering gently. With tears choking my throat, I told Royal that his beloved owner and his first son had just died. The absurdity that some might see in the situation escaped me completely. This calm and affectionate animal had always been for me a symbol of the happiness filling the early years of Frank and Emily's life together, and his energetic son Noble a symbol of its continuity. But now there was no future for Frank and Emily, or Noble. I didn't try to stifle my hard-wracking sobs as I hugged Royal's neck, the closest thing to Father's shoulder I could lean on.

Strong hands dragged me away from the horse, and I found myself wrapped in Steven's arms. He held me tightly until the energy of my initial grief was replaced by a numbness that was as much due to exhaustion as it was from the cold. Steven picked me up in his arms, the drape of my long skirts barely clear of the mud, and with the wind howling around us, he carried me back to the house and into the kitchen. I glimpsed Irene and Lavinia sitting by the fire in the parlor, and knew they must be wondering how to be helpful without being intrusive.

Expecting Steven to set me down in a chair near the fire, he instead passed through the entry hall and carried me directly upstairs to my room where I could recline against the pillows of my bed. After pouring a glass of water from the carafe on the nightstand, he made me drink it before leaving the room. However, he returned almost immediately, saying that he had spoken with Sing, who promised to keep Rose in his room for awhile.

"Mother." I grabbed Steven's arm. "We've got to go after Mother. We can't leave her alone at the mortuary."

"My parents have gone after her in their buggy. Don't worry about her."

"I can't not worry. He was her whole life." I lay back and stifled a sob. "For some reason, they always thought they'd go together. I think they couldn't imagine either one of them in the world without the other." When the tears started down my cheeks again, I didn't try to stop them. "Oh God, Steven, please wake me up!" He sat on the edge of the bed facing me and pulled me up into his arms. With my arms around him, I buried my face in his neck and slowly allowed myself to relax.

Lavinia entered the room and I heard the sharp intake of her breath. "Steven, really, I don't think this is appropriate at all! Why don't you let her rest and you return home with me?"

"I don't give a hot damn about what's appropriate," he snapped at her. "But I do think it's a good idea for you to return home. Maybe you can stoke the fire in the stove and make some coffee. And you can heat some soup for my parents when they get home."

"Me?"

"Yes, you. Even you can heat soup. Stop waiting for my mother to do everything."

"Steven!"

"Not now. Go home!"

The rustle of her skirts signaled her departure. Although I had stopped crying, I hadn't released Steven and now felt his arms tighten around me. He whispered softly, "I'm so sorry, Whitney. So sorry."

Not sure to what he was referring, I really didn't care. Only vaguely did I wonder what Irene was doing downstairs, but assumed that she would make sure there was lots of tea and coffee ready for anyone wanting it.

Food would not be a problem for days. Women from the town would be arriving first thing in the morning with covered dishes, condolences and offers of help. It was the way of our town, where everyone felt at least a little like family, celebrating the joyous times and lending support during the sorrowful ones.

CHAPTER 18

When beginning the process of convincing myself that Father was no longer to be in the rhythm of our days, I found myself occasionally pondering mundane if not odd thoughts. For instance, I spent fully five minutes wondering why sometimes my tears were cold upon my cheeks and at other times hot, and several more minutes on why I was surprised by the things that prompted them to begin. But after a week they ceased to flow as often, and when the first of the early wildflowers appeared in late March, I began to have an awareness of things outside myself, even hearing whole conversations.

Over the years I had seen many people grieve through tears, and even angry shouts at a God they thought had abandoned them, but I had never seen grief like I witnessed from Mother. There was little outward sign of it to most people other than a paleness of skin and a drawn look about the eyes and mouth. But those of us who knew her well missed her familiar spark of enthusiasm and the positive assertions she was always so quick to share. Now she moved apart from the rest of us, a body inhabiting the earth from habit rather than desire. Uncle Vince and Steven were busy at their ranch, as well as overseeing the care of our stock. Charlotte came to the house every day, but stayed only briefly. I could tell she was letting Mother adjust in her own way to what had so suddenly befallen her. But I think we were all surprised at how long it was taking--not for her to cease grieving, but to rise above the vacancy and withdrawal.

Eventually I began to wonder if she was trying to will herself to die, since she was eating barely enough to sustain life and staying to her room most of the time. At night I could hear her walking through the rest of the house until early morning. If she ventured outside at all, it was to sit on the front porch swing while wearing Father's old buckskin jacket.

Hope arose when one day she took a long walk and returned with some color in her cheeks. But the fact that she dressed too light for our chill March weather, and stared too long into the flames in the fireplace when she returned, suggested that little progress had been made in her adjustment. I was convinced of it when that night I again heard her downstairs at three in the morning.

One day I sat next to her on the porch swing and held her cool limp hand in mine. She ignored me, continuing to look up at the mountains while seeming to be even further away than the peaks. Her voice soft and full of regret, she murmured, "I never got the opportunity to tell Frank about the time Charlotte and I went down in a Bodie mine." She said nothing more.

Not understanding the importance of this lament and why it should cause her sadness, I related to Charlotte what Mother had said. After a moment of consideration, Charlotte told me, "If Emily had shared with Frank the story of that adventure, it would mean she'd have a strong memory of his reaction, and the opportunity to visit that moment again and again."

"After twenty-eight years of marriage, doesn't she have plenty of memories to recall?"

She smiled gently and put her arm around me. "When someone we love dies, we never have too many memories to recall. And we always regret that we didn't make more."

That was when I realized Mother was only inhabiting those places where she could produce strong recollections of Father. To break this pattern, I tried to talk her into coming with me to Bishop for a visit with Aunt Carrie, leaving Charlotte and Sing to care for Rose. But she put me off with reasonable sounding excuses.

Steven continued to help Vince with chores, not because Vince needed the help, but to keep him busy. They repaired fences, built a new storage shed and cleaned out an old one, worked with the stock and prepared for spring planting. Occasionally, Vince would stop and listen, as though hearing someone approaching, then shake his head and go back to work. Each time he observed this, Steven had to swallow the lump in his throat.

Of course, Steven also had to spend some of his time with Lavinia. Therefore, the only times I saw him were those few occasions when both families came together for a meal. Irene continued to live with us, having practically taken over the kitchen and garden. Only occasionally did I stop to wonder how she could stand to be away from her precious home. But I was deeply grateful that she did.

By the time Mother agreed to leave for Bishop, it was May, three months after Father's passing. Our train arrived at Bishop Station late in the afternoon and Aunt Carrie's warm embrace was there to greet us. The two friends since childhood talked late into the night, and I was sure then that bringing Mother to Bishop had been the right decision. However, the next day Mother insisted on returning home, and neither Aunt Carrie or myself could change her mind. Once home, pleading that she was tired from the journey, she went to bed early. But she didn't stay there, and I awoke several times during the night to hear her again walking through the house.

Sing meanwhile had met a Chinese widow lady who lived on the far side of town and with the remarkably American name of Ida Clair. During the day he cared for Rose and helped Irene in the garden, but each evening before leaving for Ida's home, he would prepare for us enticing meals that were so good I was amazed Mother could resist them.

Irene usually prepared the breakfast while I bathed and fed Rose, after which she assigned the daily girl her chores, shopped for what we needed, prepared a light mid-day meal, watered the garden, and made sure that the three young boys hired from town were properly caring for our animals. I couldn't have coped without her. Every evening she forced me to take a long walk before turning in, and I was therefore able to sleep at least for a few hours.

When Mother's behavior hadn't changed by the middle of April, I decided she couldn't be allowed to continue in her depressed pattern unchallenged. I entered her room one Sunday morning with a breakfast tray and a speech carefully prepared, only to find that Charlotte had preceded me by at least several hours. She reclined on the bed next to Mother with her back against the headboard and a shawl around her shoulders. But even more startling was the sight of Mother sound asleep with her head lying in Charlotte's lap. The fist of one hand was tucked beneath her chin like that of a sleeping child in its cradle. Charlotte held a finger to her lips, and I retreated quietly from the room.

It was after noon before they emerged, whereupon Mother ate a hearty meal, read the paper, and then went for a short walk. When she returned, she ate a piece of pie while standing at the kitchen sink and watching people passing by on Main. She then changed her clothes and spent two hours in the garden with the hoe, attacking any weed so foolish as to have put down roots within her line of sight.

After that I often found Mother rocking gently in the old rocking chair on the back porch where she could watch old Royal grazing in the pasture beyond the barn. Whenever I saw a certain wistful smile on her face, I knew she was spending a little time visiting with Father. If she got a bit too emotional or depressed, she would sit on the front porch swing looking up at her old friend, and her good spirits were soon restored. I longed to know how she did it. To me, Mt. Whitney was still just a mountain.

From that time on, life continued more normally. Mother often referred to Father, but it was either in a conversational context or recalling memories that made us all smile. Most importantly, she had returned to us for good.

Through all this, Steven had been readily available to listen to my concerns about Mother, lend advice, or help with repairs around the ranch. I soon realized that he had set himself up as our man of the house. But he continued to spend most of his time with his father, knowing that Vince felt keenly the absence of his old friend, even if he would never say so outright.

Because Steven spent so much time working outside, Lavinia was forced to become more domestic, and she resented it greatly. She and Charlotte had never developed a close rapport, and now with the added strain of grief shared by everyone but Lavinia, they were both finding their time together a trial. Lavinia's way of handling it was to withdraw and do as little as possible to help. One of the many arguments she and Steven had was when he found her buffing her nails while Charlotte prepared a large dinner. After Lavinia came in to help with the meal, the atmosphere in the kitchen was so tense that Charlotte told me she would have preferred Steven keep his mouth shut.

To give Lavinia credit, she did continue to have bouts of stomach cramping and nausea. I think it frightened her and made her wonder if it might indicate a serious problem. But such indisposition was not something women talked about unless with a close friend. And Lavinia didn't have one. I might have made more effort to befriend her, but she avoided being alone with me. I figured that she had heard one too many anecdotes about *Steven and Whitney growing up together*. Or maybe, as women are so good at doing, she sensed my true feelings for Steven.

The first time Steven and I were able to be alone in weeks, we headed to St. Mary's Café for breakfast. While waiting for our food, I told him how I'd found Charlotte in Mother's room.

"What did Mother say to Aunt Emily to snap her out of her funk?" he asked.

"I have no idea."

"You haven't asked one of them?" He was obviously incredulous that I would have so much restraint.

I shrugged in response. "I've spent my whole life realizing that I'll never understand the tie that binds them together. Besides, I'm simply relieved to have Mother functioning again. As to that, I'm relieved to feel myself as functioning again, too."

"I know this has been a very difficult time for you." He reached out and covered my hand with his. "I wish I could do more to help you."

"You've been wonderfully supportive, not to mention helpful around the ranch."

When he withdrew his hand, I almost grabbed it back, so hungry was I for his touch. Looking down into his coffee cup, he said, "Lavinia thinks I spend way too much time with you, and not nearly enough with her."

"It's not like we're unchaperoned. Rose or someone else is usually with us." I said it casually, but I felt it more as a complaint.

At the mention of Rose, he couldn't help but smile. "She's so beautiful. Her hair is turning dark auburn like yours."

"Yes, and her eyes are more and more like yours." I looked at him fondly. "She's taken to you so naturally."

"Lavinia thinks I'm too attentive to you and Rose. I've tried to explain to her that it's like spending time with family, but she doesn't see it that way."

I stared at him. "Is that what I am, then? Just family? Your sister?"

He looked at me with a start. "Of course not. I've never stopped loving you. You have to know that." My relief at finally hearing him say it out loud was obvious, and he smiled briefly before continuing. "But I'm a bit trapped, you know, and feeling guilty as hell. The poor girl said 'I do' expecting a real marriage. Not one based on her husband's anger and resentment toward the one he really loved, thinking she had rejected him."

Before I could respond, a shadow fell across the table and we looked up to find Lavinia standing beside us. From the look on her pale face it was easy to see she had heard much of our conversation.

"Poor girl?" she shrilled. "You're confused? You're trapped? Damn right I'm a poor girl!"

Steven stood up and grabbed her arm, pulling her from the restaurant and the curious, startled eyes of the other diners, most of whom we knew. The waitress waved me out after them, but when I got outside, Steven and Lavinia were already well down the street and just turning west onto South Street. Although I moved quickly, even several times hiking up my skirts and breaking into a subdued run, I only caught up with them as they reached the Perry barn. Steven led her into it before she jerked free of him.

She was posing questions one right after the other while choking on her fury. "Did I hear correctly? Rose is your child? When did that happen? When did you find out about her? Are you really in love with Whitney? How dare you ask me to marry you, and then bring me to this God-forsaken town where you could also be with her."

"Stop!" he shouted. "The whole town doesn't need to know our business."

"Oh, I think it does!" Her upper lip curled and she stood with clenched fists on her hips. "I think every bumpkin in this whole miserable town needs to know that you and Whitney have a bastard child. That way she can grow up knowing just what kind of parents she has!"

Standing in the doorway of the barn, I had watched the exchange between them, hesitant to interfere. But now I felt a rage so intense that it was a good thing Steven was present to keep me from jumping on her and ripping out every strand of her silky, yellow hair.

"How dare you threaten my family!" I yelled at her. Steven noted the look on my face and put a restraining hand on my arm.

Turning to Lavinia, he said, "I can't believe you're threatening me!"

"I hate this town. I hate you." She turned to me. "And I especially hate you."

"What did I ever do to you?"

"You've enjoyed every minute that you've tortured me with your knowing looks and insinuations of what you know. You're just playing innocent until you decide to make Steven yours."

"What are you talking about?" I asked her. Then, with a clarity that made me feel like a fool, I knew what she meant. "You're her!"

"Don't act so innocent," she snarled.

"I swear." Why am I trying to convince her, I wondered? But I continued, "Until just now I had no idea who you really are."

"Who she *really* is?" Steven repeated. "What does that mean?"

"No!" she shrieked. Then taking a deep breath, she stood up straighter and smoothed her dress with shaking hands. "I mean, you don't know anything about me."

"Oh, but I do." I turned to Steven. "Lavinia's last name is really Roberts. She's Alex's wife."

His mouth gaped open a moment before he closed it with a snap. Turning to her, he asked, "You were married to Alex? You never told me you were married before. And he never mentioned being divorced."

"He wasn't," I volunteered, enjoying the look of defeat on Lavinia's face. "In fact, she's actually his widow, not me."

"What?" He looked back and forth between us, not unexpectedly having a difficult time absorbing this confusing information.

"They never divorced," I explained, "because she ran away. She set it up in such a way that everyone believed she'd been killed and dragged off by a wild animal. So my marriage to him wasn't legal, and your marriage to her isn't legal because the ceremony took place while Alex was still alive."

He stared at Lavinia for a full minute before telling her, "I've never before in my life wanted to hit a woman. But if you don't pack your bags and get out of town immediately, I can't answer for my actions."

"You believe her?" Lavinia gasped.

"Of course, I believe her."

"But I'm your wife!"

"Evidently you're not!" Steven took a deep breath. "Now, get packed and get ready to leave town."

"Oh, I'll get out of town all right." The practiced repose was gone, replaced by an ugly sneer. "But before I leave, I'll make sure the right people hear a few home truths about you and Whitney." She turned and strode out of the barn with a look of furious determination on her face.

Steven turned to me. "She's going to tell my parents that Rose is ours, hoping to shock them. Isn't she?"

"Yes. But since they already know, she's likely to get quite an ear full. Especially from Charlotte." I couldn't help but laugh.

After a moment, he said, "How could I have been so wrong about her character?"

"You didn't know her all that long," I pointed out.

"No. I married her for all the wrong reasons, and I have no one to blame but myself."

He walked over to one of the horses and ran his hand down its neck. After a moment, he turned back to me. "So in other words, you and I are single people."

I couldn't suppress a smile. "That's right." When he walked up to me with a look that promised lingering moments in the hayloft, I held up my hand and said, "You'd better go to the house and make sure Lavinia doesn't pack the silver along with her undies."

"Good idea. I'll come by your place after I'm sure she's on the next stage, and hasn't had a chance to talk to anyone in town."

As I left the barn, I heard the murmur of voices coming from the side of the tool shed. Walking in that direction, I stopped in the shadows out of view when I heard Irene talking in a low voice.

"You don't remember me, Lavinia, because I was only a very young girl when you were married to Alex. But I remember you."

"You lived in Bridgeport, in town?"

"Yes. I had two very difficult parents, especially my father who ruled me with an iron fist that knew how to bruise without leaving a mark. And a mother who was too much of a coward to object. Or maybe she just didn't care."

"I'm sorry," Lavinia responded with impatience, "but what does this have to do with me?"

After a moment's hesitation, Irene asked, "Can't you call it even between you and Steven? Just keep your mouth shut and move on?"

"What do you mean 'even'?"

"You kept secret your relationship with Alex, and Steven and Whitney kept secret their relationship. Can't you just leave with some degree of grace?"

"What I did when I left Alex was survival," Lavinia returned, her voice hard with renewed anger. "What they did was betrayal."

"Oh, really!" Irene laughed with scorn. "You betrayed Alex, his father, and the whole town of Bridgeport. And especially Mrs. Lewis, who strangely enough thinks the world of you even after all this time. You had to know she'd be devastated by your so-called death. And she'd have gladly kept your secret. But besides that, from what I've observed, you don't even love Steven all that much."

"Maybe not," Lavinia responded, "but from the moment we arrived here, he's had second thoughts about having married me, so he doesn't love me either." Her voice rose again as she said, "He's made a fool of me. Before I leave here, people in this town are going to have second thoughts about Steven. And that whore Whitney, too!"

Irene's voice when next she spoke was calm and matter-of-fact. "You're a mean-spirited, empty-souled harpy that would be better off dead."

Lavinia gasped. "What a cruel thing to say. People aren't like a bug to be stepped on and casually removed from your path."

"No?" Irene was coolly dismissive. "Actually, I can arrange accidents quite easily and no one suspects a thing, especially of a fragile young woman like me. It's so easy to find toxic plants in the desert, or distill tobacco into a poison."

Lavinia must have looked stricken as she made the connection to her illnesses, because Irene added, "Don't worry. I only wanted you to get sick often enough that you'd decide you hated it here and leave Steven. It's not like you had a bad accident while out riding, or something." Startled, I risked a peak around the corner. Irene was looking beyond Lavinia toward the Alabama Hills, smiling slightly as she obviously recalled some memory of her own. Shaking her head slowly, she said, "So many people die in accidents."

Leaning against the old wood of the shed, I struggled not to be sick, knowing with blinding clarity that she was referring to the accident of the fiancé when she was seventeen. And no doubt the barn fire that killed her parents. For whom else might she have arranged an accident? The answer nearly brought me to my knees. Alex!

He would have allowed her to approach him because he'd become accustomed to her showing up unexpectedly. It would have been an easy matter for her to pick up the gun he was cleaning when he turned his attention to something else, slip in a bullet, raise the gun to his face as he turned back and pull the trigger before he could react. She must have dropped the gun near his hand and climbed back into her buggy. Remembering her arrival at the house that day, I marveled at how normal she had appeared. Not only had she not been rattled, she had been warm in her greeting and poised in the conversations that followed with those of us gathered there. I felt suffocated by the cold-blooded treachery of it all.

Turning my attention back to their conversation, I heard a shocked Lavinia ask, "Why are you telling me this? Do you plan on killing me, too?"

"Not if you leave immediately and say nothing about Whitney and Steven."

"You're insane," Lavinia snapped out. "I could tell Steven about you."

That was probably not the wisest thing to say to someone who was so obviously unstable, but Irene answered in a voice even and pitiless. "Do you really think anyone will believe the ravings of someone who has so outrageously lied about her past? Someone who faked their own death in such an ugly way? Someone who married a man when she knew it wasn't legal?"

"Yes, but he too..."

"You can leave here and still have a life in Los Angeles or San Francisco, where you can tell them anything you want. But if you say a word about Whitney and Steven to anyone, ever, the newspapers there will have the complete story of your duplicity and you'll be ruined. I'll see to that. And don't think I won't know."

Lavinia didn't argue further. "I'll be on the afternoon stage."

While Lavinia took the most direct route to the house, away from where I stood, I hurried home. By the time I'd reached my room, I was shaking and nauseated. Even the joy of knowing Steven and I could now be together could not relieve my distress.

Quickly rejecting from consideration one after another of those people I could tell, I couldn't help thinking, "If Father was alive, I could go to him." I certainly didn't want to burden Mother with such a problem. And I couldn't go to the sheriff without proof. Besides, going public about Irene might also reveal the truth about Steven and me, and Rose. Before I could figure out what to do, there was a soft knock on my door.

I ceased pacing and called out, "Yes?"

Irene stuck her head through the door. "I'm not bothering you, am I?"

"Come in. We need to talk."

Feeling my legs too weak to support me, I moved to one of the chairs by the west-facing window. Irene made herself comfortable in the chair across from me.

"You sound distressed, Whitney. Has something happened?"

She appeared so innocent that I wanted to slap her. But I only said, "Yes, something has happened. There was a confrontation between Lavinia, Steven and myself. We now know Lavinia is Alex's wife." I watched her react to my words as though she didn't already know.

"Well, that's a good thing, isn't it?" She settled back in her chair and smiled, the perfect picture of complacent success.

Looking out the window, and watching her only with my peripheral vision, I said, "Unfortunately, I now also know the truth about you and all you've done to sort through the difficult people in your life. And mine." I then looked directly at her, holding her gaze.

All color in her cheeks disappeared, and she asked quietly, "What do you mean?"

"Please, Irene." I had to stop and take a deep breath before I could continue. "We've been too important to one another for there to be dissembling between us now. I heard your conversation with Lavinia, and your threat to her."

In a soft voice, she asked, "And your reaction to this is, what?"

"I'm not sure I can put my feelings into words that describe them properly. At first there was disbelief, but then I thought of all the clues over the years, and I realized the extent of your handiwork."

"What do you plan to do about it?"

"Nothing." I got up and moved behind my chair, putting a physical if not symbolic barrier between us. My hands gripped the wood frame above the velvet fabric as I told her, "It's summer now, and you should be going home."

"Yes." She stood up slowly, looking out the window at the Sierra with its scattered patches of lingering snow along the ridge. "My garden will need tending now, and the house will need a good dusting." She looked back at me. "I'm no longer needed here."

"Irene, understand one thing." I took a step toward her. "If I hear that someone inconvenient to you has died in a suspicious accident, or an unexplained illness, I'll tell the authorities what I know and damn the consequences to either of us."

She looked at me with wet eyes shining. "I'm sorry it's come to this, Whitney. What I've done may have been drastic, but in all cases I just couldn't think of an alternative. I decided at a very early age that I'd survive my circumstances any way that was available to me, and I asked God to guide me. So whether or not you approve, I consider that God presented to me the means. And after all, everyone has to die sometime."

"You can't mean that! You have to know taking a life is wrong. Everyone has a conscience."

"I'm not sure I do." The small pucker of a frown appeared between her eyes. "At least not when it means my independence and safety." Looking me in the eyes, she added, "Or the well-being of someone I love."

I shook my head. "If you think I'm going to thank you for killing Alex, you're wrong. It might have been difficult to part from him, but as it turned out, we weren't actually married. So if you'd not interfered, the situation would have resolved itself. Wouldn't an all-knowing God know that? So where does the responsibility for murder truly lie?"

She looked at me strangely, as though she'd never considered the word *murder* as having anything to do with her actions.

"Alex was brooding and depressed when I found him in the tack room," she told me, all the while looking over my head as she pictured the moment. "He said his mother had abandoned him, his first wife had been killed trying to avoid him, you had betrayed him, and even his daughter didn't really belong to him. He said women were poison and he hated them all. But he said he couldn't do anything about any of them other than you." Looking at me once more, she announced, "He meant to make you suffer somehow."

"It was all talk, Irene. His pride would never have allowed the public to see the mess of his private life."

"I thought he meant it."

"So you killed him."

She shrugged. "God had given me the perfect opportunity. The gun was right there, and his back was turned."

"How self-serving you are in your justification." I was afraid I was going to gag.

"The other times that I arranged things may have served *my* needs, but with Alex I did what was needed for *you*."

"It was murder!" The effort I put forth not to shout made my head ache. "Don't you understand that?"

"It wasn't!" She took a step toward me, but when I backed up, she stopped and whispered, "It was putting order in the world. Order is everything."

I simply stared at her, not knowing how to respond to such a statement. But she offered no more words. After a moment observing my set expression, she left my room and went to hers where she immediately packed her bags. Sing drove her to the Robinsons Stables barely in time to catch the northbound stage.

Lavinia, meanwhile, had hurriedly sold her auto to someone in town who had previously shown an interest in it, and then had left on the stage going south that evening. By the end of one day both sources of deception were on their way to their origins.

Rose and I spent every minute of the next day together, and I allowed no one else to do anything for her. It was my attempt to feel again essential purity and innocence. If I couldn't change the fact of these qualities lacking in so much of my life, at least I could remind myself that they still existed in the world. Rose's laughter was the best demonstration of that.

A week later the town came together for a "Spring Cleaning" at the same time the quilting circle decided to host a quilt show. Both were a fundraiser for the schoolhouse that was in need of expensive repairs. Mother and I went through our closets, removing old clothes no longer worn or cared for very much, and piled them on the front porch. Together, we did the practical thing and put Father's clothes there too. However, Mother refused to give up his buckskin jacket or the hat she had bought him for Christmas one year when they had lived in Bodie. These she removed from the pile and stuffed under the buckboard seat.

We also tackled the kitchen and the dining room, deciding to donate items seldom used that were originally owned by Mrs. Kennedy or odd gifts received over the years. We then filled boxes with books, kitchen, and decorative items. Early Sunday afternoon, Vince and Charlotte brought their large wagon to our house and added our boxes to theirs.

Mother came out of the house last, carrying only her purse.

Standing on the porch with a last bag of clothes from my closet, I said, "I thought you were going to show Mrs. Kennedy's story quilt."

"Vince took it down from over my bed and it's wrapped and ready to go. But I've shown it so many times before that they're probably sick of seeing it."

"Nonsense. Everyone looks forward to it. And there may be a few new people who haven't seen it."

"Oh, okay." She went back in and emerged shortly with the story quilt wrapped in a sheet. It was composed of nine cloth squares, each representative of an important moment in the life of its maker, with the last appliquéd and embroidered squares illustrating my parents' importance in Mrs. Kennedy's life at its end. Mother had told me so many stories about the time she'd spent with Mrs. Kennedy there in the boardinghouse, as many still referred to our home, that I almost felt like this woman had been my grandmother.

After helping Mother onto the Perry's wagon, Steven and I followed in our buckboard with Rose, who we dropped off at a friend's house so she could play with their little girl. Sing was visiting his lady friend again, and we happily speculated if an announcement might not soon be forthcoming from him.

After an afternoon of successful sales, purchases, donations and visits with friends, we loaded the wagon preparatory to leaving for home. Mother wrapped the story quilt in its sheet and tucked it carefully at the back. We had only occasionally seen the wind as a problem during the day, with it several times carrying to us the rumble of thunder. But the gusts had increased and we were all glad to be heading home to a good meal after retrieving Rose.

Just as we started out, however, we were startled by the clanging of the fire bell. Approaching Main, we watched the fire wagons racing south down Main Street, the horses galloping as fast as they could. We pulled out onto Main, following behind the dozens of men running ahead of us who made up the volunteer fire department. Then we saw the smoke in the distance on the east side of the street, the steady wind blowing it away from the road toward the Inyos.

Someone shouted, "It's the boardinghouse!"

We looked at each other in disbelief, waiting for someone to holler back that it was a hay field or shed. But no one did. Vince urged his wagon forward while Steven and I passed it in the lighter buckboard. They were right. Our home was indeed on fire. Orange flames darted from the back of the house and smoke billowed from the windows of my room. My first thought was to remind myself of Rose's whereabouts, followed by concern for Sing. Was he still visiting in the Chinese section, or had he gotten home already?

For the third time in a year, I experienced the feeling that I was being held in the grip of a nightmare that should be ending but was not. Uncle Vince stopped his wagon behind ours, both of us far enough down the road from the house that we wouldn't be in the way. I helped Mother and Charlotte out of the wagon as Steven and Vince ran toward the house with the other men. The three of us started to follow, but when I realized the danger and futility of that, I hustled us across the street.

There we stood, Charlotte and I on either side of Mother as though we could protect her from this latest decimation of her world. Vince and Steven were helping wrestle the heavy hoses connected to the old pumper wagon. Men stood on either side with their hands on the long brass rails running the length of the water tank on wheels. At a command from the fire chief, the men began raising and lowering the rails, the alternating action of their efforts pumping the water down the hoses. Other men had broken down the picket fence in order to allow easier access to the house. Those with shovels were throwing smothering dirt onto the hot embers, while trampling the flowers Mother and I had so carefully planted only days before. I started to think that now we'd have to start over with new plants, then stopped myself as I realized that the men's efforts were going to be futile. The wall of flame was growing larger by the second and was quickly eating its way toward the front door. The only thing they could hope to accomplish was keeping the fire contained to our property.

From somewhere nearby a thoughtful man appeared with a chair for Mother, not bothering to waste useless words of comfort before disappearing into the crowd. I shuddered suddenly, and idly wondered why the temperature had dropped so fast.

Men ran from every direction with buckets, shovels, rakes and hoes as they shouted at one another things I couldn't make out. Thankfully, the wind was blowing away from us toward the Inyos or the billowing smoke would have made it impossible for us to have stayed where we were just across the road.

Steven suddenly dropped his section of the hose and ran into the house. If mother hadn't taken hold of my arm, I probably would have gone after him. He later told us that he'd seen a small window of opportunity right at the moment he realized all effort to save the house was useless. Almost immediately he reappeared with several items clutched in his arms and hurried across the street to us. He handed Mother the photo album, the stereoscopic cards from Bodie, Mrs. Kennedy's silver tea pot, and the Bodie photo of her and Father. It had all been on the tables near the parlor sofa.

"I'm afraid that's all I could grab before the back wall started to give way." He coughed hard several times.

When Steven bent over to place the items on the dirt at her feet, Mother reached out and grabbed the wedding photo from him. She hugged it and smiled up at Steven, "It's enough."

That's when I started to cry. I kept picturing the photos of Mrs. Kennedy and her husband, "dear Ben", melting amid the flames—and somehow knew Mother was picturing the same thing. Soft, despondent sobs caught in my throat as I remembered so many things that were being destroyed right before our eyes. They were only objects, but each one was attached to a memory that I feared we might not be able to recall without the gift, memento, or photo.

It was like watching a violent and horrible play on a stage filled with doom and destruction. But we weren't able to just walk out, and instead watched as walls gave way not with a crash, but with an exhausted sigh. When the ceiling collapsed right after, however, there was a lot of noise as wood splintered and the rocks from the fireplace tumbled away. The glass in the windows had already exploded from the intense heat.

Steven walked to my side and put an arm around my shoulders. I looked down at Mother sitting up straight and determined and outwardly composed, yet with two tears trickling down her cheek. From a distance, no one would have known she was crying at all.

"Where's Vince?" Charlotte suddenly asked.

Steven said, "I'll go get him. He went around back." He loped away, his long legs covering the distance quickly as he made his way around the flaming timbers and disappeared behind the crumbling house.

Suddenly thunder rumbled overhead. In all the excitement, none of us had noticed the dark clouds pushed along by the wind. Now, in the deepening dusk, we looked up and became aware of large gray thunderclouds packing the sky. It isn't often that the Eastern Sierra sees a summer storm so far south, and the moisture on the dry landscape is always welcome. But this time it was a cruel joke dropped into the middle of our horrid play, because no amount of water could have saved the house at that point. Nevertheless, without even a few introductory drops, the sky opened and poured down upon us. There wasn't much the volunteers could do other than put away the hoses and break apart the hot spots so the rain could reach them.

We were all quickly drenched, but also reluctant to move toward shelter. Several of the women nearby draped blankets around our shoulders and opened umbrellas that they shared with us. Steven said later that it was a very peculiar but touching tableau he and Vince approached. Poor Uncle Vince was not only soaked to the bone, but also limping severely.

Charlotte removed the blanket from around her shoulders and placed it around her husband, declaring, "We're going home."

Steven turned to me and shouted above the din of rain, thunder, shouting men, and barking dogs. "You and Emily need to go with them and get out of this. I'll be there as soon as I can." When both Mother and I started to object, he added with finality the saddest words possible. "There's nothing you can do."

I gave a last glance at the sodden, blackened ruin that had only that morning been a much loved home filled with the comfort of familiar possessions and the warmth of memories. Then, with my arm around Mother, I supported her all the way to Vince and Charlotte's small house on the edge of their ranch. There we silently removed our wet clothes and wrapped ourselves in robes and dry blankets. While I stoked the fire in the kitchen stove, Mother collapsed at the small kitchen table, shivering as much from shock as from cold. Meanwhile, Charlotte gave Vince a rubdown in their bedroom just off the back of the kitchen. Once he was in bed with a hot water bottle and extra blankets, and Charlotte had changed, she joined us in the kitchen.

Standing next to me by the fire, she said, "I'm concerned about him." Her expression matched her words.

"We're all dry now," I said.

"Yes, but Vince takes cold very easily." She shook her head slowly. "It's been that way since the accident in Bodie just before you were born, Whitney. His whole system has been weaker since then for some reason."

I put my arms around her. "Please don't worry, Aunt Charlotte. You nursed him through that, and you will this, too."

A little later Steven came in, walked up to Mother, and knelt before her while she held a mug of hot tea like it was a life line. "I'm sorry Aunt Emily, but it's all gone. There was nothing more we could do."

"How?" That was all she could get out.

"Someone said they saw a dry lightening strike near the house about half an hour before the fire was spotted. It looks like it caught the brush out by the garden, and then whipped by the wind, it spread quickly onto the house. That end of the house was the first to burn, so that makes sense."

Mother put a hand on Steven's cheek and sighed. "My dear, none of this makes sense."

He looked down and mumbled, "No. It's just not fair."

When he stood up and turned around, it was into my arms. I'm not sure who was supporting who, but we stood that way for a long time. Mother said later that watching us together like that was the best comfort she could have received right then.

CHAPTER 19

Early the next morning one of the women in charge of the previous day's rummage sale showed up with our donated clothes. There was also a bolt of soft cotton diapering fabric and baby clothes for Rose. The thoughtfulness of this almost broke my resolve to stay strong for Mother. Most welcome was Sing's arrival with Rose and his offer to keep her with him at Ida's house while we sorted out what to do next. I agreed, even while knowing that some of the townspeople would heartily disapprove of a white child being cared for "in the district". But Sing's thoughtfulness was only the first of many blessings we were to receive.

Women came by with food just like they did when a death had occurred, maybe realizing that for us it was much the same. One man told us that since the fire hadn't reached our barn, he would feed the animals for us until we could move them. He waved away our gratitude by mentioning some act of generosity Father had shown him some months before.

The women of the quilting circle brought us stacks of quilts, blankets, sheets and pillows. After they left, Mother and I reminisced with Charlotte and Steven about the women who had taught us how to quilt, women who had come west in wagons over the Oregon Trail. Passing on to us their skills with a needle and their stories of survival, they had also woven through our lives the influence of their courage and determination.

Mother said, "Even now those wonderful old friends are helping me find the will to persevere." And she smiled often during the next hour, I think remembering the times she had shared with old friends around the quilting frame. And maybe recalling the many times they had shared a meal in the boardinghouse around the old kitchen table made by Mrs. K's husband, forty years earlier.

More people arrived with food, clothes, and household items, all scoffing at the profuseness of our gratitude, saying that it was only payback for all that the Eastmans had done for them over the years. It all went into one of the Perry sheds until we once more had a house of our own. Several men even showed up with money they said was pay-back of a debt owed Father. To this day I'm not sure there was a debt involved at all. But they wanted to help us rebuild as quickly as possible, knowing it would keep us busy and help us focus on the future.

Two days later I changed into a gray dress I had donated with some reluctance to the rummage sale, and which had been returned to me the day before. Grateful that the day of the fire I had been wearing my most comfortable shoes instead of new fancy ones, I made my way to our ravaged home. Unsure if I could bear seeing the devastation, I steeled myself as I turned the corner onto Main.

The only thing left of the house where I'd spent a near idyllic youth, where my parents had shared a union so devoted and joyful that it had been the source of my adult expectations, was a pile of blackened rubble. The lower stones of the fireplace were still there, and they started the list of things in my mind that we could salvage. But the vegetable garden was gone, along with the bath house and clotheslines. The roses along the front walk were a barely recognizable tangle of broken twigs and mashed blooms. But I was glad to see that only some of the leaves on the sycamores along Main Street had been singed.

It was hard to believe that the house which Mother had felt to be a monument to her dear Mrs. Kennedy had disappeared in one night. As I looked at the pile of ashes and debris where our family had been sheltered for twenty-five years, reality faded away and was replaced by an emotional numbness. Blinking to clear my eyes, I noticed the stairwell. Badly charred it might have been, but it rose solidly above all the ugliness around it to a second floor that no longer existed. And I smiled, knowing that by some means yet to be revealed, our lives would repair and go forward. After all, if Mother and I could survive the loss of Father, we could certainly survive this.

A shadow moved into my line of sight and I turned around to find Steven standing a little apart. "Are you okay, Whitney?"

"Better than I expected the first time seeing all this."

We stood side by side for a few minutes, staring at the black pile of rubble. Steven finally said, "I wonder if there's anything we'll find in all this. Did you have your good jewelry in a place where it might have been protected?"

"It was in my dresser in a painted tin box Uncle Vince gave me last Christmas." I turned to him as I unbuttoned the high collar of my dress. "But I have the only thing that I count as truly valuable." Still on its original gold chain, I pulled out the cameo he had given me for my sixteenth birthday. "It's been around my neck since the first day I left here for Bridgeport."

It's the only time I've ever seen Steven so overwhelmed with emotion that he couldn't speak. We soon began a slow walk back to his house, our hands tightly clasped together.

After a few moments, he said, "Father's not doing well."

"Did he catch cold last night?"

"Yes. Mother sent for the doctor."

In fact, we arrived in the kitchen just as the doctor was leaving. He looked even more solemn than usual, and I hurried to Mother as she softly closed the door to the bedroom and walked into the kitchen. She sat down at the table and briefly put her head in her hands, then looked up at us with eyes almost as sad as when Father had died.

"Mother, what is it?"

"The doctor thinks he's developing pneumonia."

Steven immediately joined Charlotte in the bedroom, probably the first time he'd ever entered that room without knocking. As I pulled up a chair next to Mother, she gripped one of my hands and closed her eyes while struggling for control.

"Whitney, it doesn't look good. I've seen this kind of thing before. When it comes on this fast, it's difficult for even the strongest of people to fight. Vince looks big and strong, but he really isn't. Frank used to cover for him when they were working together, but in such a way that Vince wouldn't realize it."

"He's taken Father's death very hard too," I pointed out. "Best friends closer than some brothers, and Father died practically in his arms. He probably blames himself somehow."

"I wouldn't be surprised. If he does, such depression of mind isn't the best state for him to be in. He needs to fight." She looked out the window and struggled to smile. "But he has his love for Charlotte to support him, and of course Steven. Vince and Charlotte were never as publicly demonstrative as your father and I, but we always knew that the depth of their devotion was just as deep."

"Did the doctor leave any medicine for him?"

"Yes. But he keeps passing in and out of consciousness, so she has to wait until he's awake enough to swallow the liquid without choking."

The next several days were mostly spent helping Charlotte nurse Vince, who rallied well for most of one day before once again falling into a comatose state. Over the next few days our hopes rose and fell along with his progress until we settled for a permanent state of guarded optimism.

When not at home and by his father's bedside with Charlotte, Steven supervised the men helping with the clearing of our house. Meanwhile, Mother and I tried to figure out what to rebuild on the property.

On the fifth day of Vince's steadily improving recuperation, Steven took me for a buggy ride down to the river late one afternoon. While a mild breeze stirred the leaves of the cottonwood tree under which we sat, a wary young eagle watched us from the top of another, and small ground squirrels peaked out from the rocks along the water's edge. I thought it a most pleasant and calming place to be, but I was anxious being so far from the others.

After walking to the edge of the river, I grabbed a handful of long dry grass and began braiding the strands together. Steven watched me for several minutes in silence, then moved to my side. "Whitney, I brought you here for a reason. I wanted you alone, and in a place we've both shared so often in our lives."

"Why?"

"It's time we thought of how our plans for the future fit into those of your mother and my parents."

I tried not to sound coy. "Oh? And what is that?"

He threw a stick into the gently moving water of the river as it flowed toward Owens Lake. "I was thinking that if we get married, we could build our house on my parent's property. We could build it at the south end of the big pasture, so there'd be some grazing land between our houses. And I think your mother should stay with them."

"I don't think she'd like that."

"Well then, if she sells the boardinghouse property to Mr. Siliah, she'd have that money to build her own house north of my parent's place. I think the days are past when Aunt Emily should be keeping up a big house and garden, not to mention caring for livestock. Don't you?"

"Yes, I do. And I even think she'll agree." I turned to face him. "By the way, what do you mean *if* we get married?"

He smiled. "Well, it depends on whether or not you say yes."

Looking into his eyes and realizing how nervous he was, I told him gently, "You idiot, you haven't asked me yet."

He mumbled something under his breath before taking my hand in his. "Whitney, please marry me."

"Okay."

"Yes?"

"Yes." I laughed. "Oh, I suppose you thought I'd say no?"

"Some wise sage said never underestimate a woman's ability to shock the hell out of a man." With a wry smirk, he added, "I've learned to believe him."

We spent only a few moments in one another's arms, so eager were we to share the news of our engagement. I only hoped our plan for Mother would be received with relief instead of being considered a presumption.

We pulled up by the barn just as the doctor's rig rolled up to the front door. Tossing the reins to one of the ranch hands, we hurried into the house behind the doctor. However, Mother stopped me immediately inside the door and told Steven to go into the bedroom.

As Steven disappeared, I asked Mother, "What's happening?"

"He's failing quickly."

"No! He was getting better."

"Whitney, I don't think he's going to make it." A single tear rolled down her cheek and she reached for a handkerchief stuffed in a pocket of her apron. "Damn! You'd think I had no tears left, but it seems there's an endless supply."

"Oh, Mother." I took her in my arms and fought the aching strain of unshed tears choking in my throat.

Just as we settled on the sofa in the parlor, the doctor walked out of the bedroom and looked at us with a sadness that had only one interpretation. As the front door closed behind him, Steven came out of the bedroom and walked up to me with a look of grim determination. Grabbing my arm, he pulled me after him toward the bedroom. Charlotte was sitting on the far edge of the bed holding Vince's hand. The glassy brightness of her eyes as she looked up at us gave away her acceptance of what was shortly to follow.

Steven sat on the near edge of the bed and took hold of Vince's hand, encasing it in the warmth of his own. "Dad, I don't know if you can hear me or not, but I want you to know that I love you very much. And I also want you to know that Whitney and I are going to be married." In a voice barely above a whisper, he added, "All you've taught me both by word and example, about integrity and how to be a good man, it'll be the basis of what I'll teach your grandchildren. You'll live on in them."

Vince didn't open his eyes or speak, but for a moment there was a flush to his skin. A moment later Charlotte felt the barest of pressure from the hand she held, which she then leaned down and kissed. But the pressure ceased, the flush faded to a pale gray, and the exhaling of breath preceded an unequivocal stillness. Tears streamed down Charlotte's face as Steven went to her and knelt by her side, his arms holding her tight as she rocked back and forth while still clutching Vince's hand. I quickly left the room.

Finding Mother still in the small parlor, I sat down next to her and whispered the words, "He's gone."

Her only response was to take a deep breath, stand for a moment with her eyes closed, then walk to the bedroom, and to Charlotte.

Steven immediately left the house through the kitchen door. Against the side of the house he sunk to the ground, lay his forehead on arms folded across bent knees, and wept. Finding him there, I sat on the ground next to him and put my arm around his shoulders, comforting him as best I could.

That evening I took a long, solitary walk through the locust grove on the west side of town and eventually found myself alone by Tuttle Creek. Regardless of my deep sadness, I had myself in tight control. Feeling the radiating cool from the rushing water, I sat down on a large rock and started to relax. But when I took a deep breath, I found that a sob had found its way into it. I'm not sure if I then cried just for Vince's passing, or for all the tragedies that had recently been heaped upon us, but after several minutes I began to wonder if I'd ever stop.

Why was everything falling apart? Why was there so much sadness in our lives at a time when we should all be happily making plans for a wedding?

"It isn't fair!" I yelled at a squirrel watching from a tree branch. Several startled birds flushed from the streamside brush while chattering their indignation, and the squirrel scurried higher.

When I realized that I was sinking quickly into the ugliness of self-pity, I took a firm hold of myself. Then, like Mother earlier, my thoughts turned to old friends who had crossed the country in only a wagon, and who had lost so much along the way. Courage never failed them, nor their willingness to go forward with the faith that things would somehow get better even when surrounded by circumstances that suggested it would not. So just as those brave women had done half a century before, I rose up from the ground, brushed off my dress, squared my shoulders, and looked forward into an uncertain future.

CHAPTER 20

After Vince's funeral, so soon after the one for Father, the town proceeded through its days like a large family wrapped in a single despondency of grief. It didn't help that everyone had to pass the cleared land with the barn and corrals standing out as a reminder that there should have been a house there as well. Consequently, although we didn't feel alone in our slow adjustment to the losses in our world, it was difficult to find anyone to help boost our spirits.

True to their nature, Charlotte and Mother presented to everyone a brave and gracious face, no matter how they really felt. More than once, the person expressing their condolences was so overwhelmed with emotion while extolling the virtues of Frank Eastman or Vince Perry, that they ended up being the one in need of comfort.

Soon it became obvious that the town had assigned to us the status of *community project*. Women took turns bringing to us their favorite dishes for more days than usual, lingering long enough to be a diversion but not so long as to be intrusive. Mother swore that by the time we'd eaten the abundance of food brought to us, she and Charlotte would have forgotten how to cook. But we shared much of it with the ranch hands and their families, so it didn't go to waste.

When it was known that Mother had sold the property to Mr. Siliah, and that she would be rebuilding on the small lot just north of the Perry property, men came by in wagons filled with building materials. Soon we had a sizeable pile of lumber, nails, doors and window frames stacked on the side of the barn. Every man, after helping to unload the supplies, made Steven promise to call upon him for help when the construction began.

I never knew when Mother went to see the remnants of the boardinghouse. For her, saying good-bye to that house would have been an incredibly personal moment. Years later, however, she did admit that she had stopped by "to apologize to Mrs. Kennedy" for its loss.

We transferred the milk cow, chickens, hogs and Father's prize bull to the Perry property, while Royal nibbled grass in his new pasture unconcerned at the change of location. The same could not be said of Mother and myself. She and I shared what had before been Steven's room, thankfully containing a bunk bed and just enough space for Rose's crib in the corner. Steven slept on the sofa in the parlor or out in the bunk house with the ranch hands.

At the beginning of September, 1907, Steven convinced Mother, Charlotte, and myself to accept an invitation from Carrie to stay with her for awhile. Although Steven didn't tell our mothers, he confided to me that during our absence the house Mother and I had designed would be built. That way it would be ready for her to decorate when we returned; a new project to keep her busy for quite some while.

I thought it was the sweetest thing I'd ever known a man to do, and willingly kept the secret. So while I pictured men building for Mother a small, white house within easy walking distance of what was now Charlotte's house, we women slowly healed our hearts in Bishop. Almost immediately upon our arrival, Carrie's mare foaled a colt. Watching it stand and suckle, then wobble around on its thin legs, was the beginning of that healing.

We attended two quilting bees, so many card parties that I can't now count them, a barn-raising followed by a dance, bingo at one of the churches, and several supper parties. Of a more practical nature, we helped Carrie put up vegetables for the coming winter, while also drying fruit and making fruit leather. By the time we were through, her larder had an abundance to last for many months.

But as enjoyable and recuperative as our time with Carrie was, by the end of the month we were ready to return home and get on with the business of living. Interestingly, our absence from Lone Pine had given everyone there an opportunity to come to terms with the loss of two dear friends, and the fire's all too vivid reminder of the fragility of their own lives. By the time we got home, they had returned their focus to their own needs, which included the last harvests of the year.

When I stepped off the train practically into the arms of Steven, I clung to him much longer than many would have deemed proper for mere friends. He didn't seem to care. But I knew that until everyone understood that widowed Whitney and betrayed Steven were legally free to be together, we might shock local society if seen in such a compromising position. So I pushed him away.

Steven greeted his mother and his Aunt Emily with enthusiasm. But underlying the normal eagerness to have us home, I sensed a strange incidental excitement in his manner. He hurried us and our luggage to the buckboard, now rigged to carry four passengers.

Sitting next to Steven on the front seat, our shoulders touching, I felt inordinately pleased when passing along Main. People saw our little band returning and waved or called out, "Welcome home". Mrs. Edwards hollered, "Come by for coffee real soon." In whatever way the greeting was offered, by look or word or wave, we all felt embraced and happy to be home.

Pulling up in front of the Perry barn, I was puzzled in the extreme. There was no house built for Mother and, at least until I married Steven, for me. That property as we passed it was just as we had left it. When I looked at Steven for an explanation, he offered instead a big grin.

Once we'd stepped down from the wagon and turned toward the Perry home, Mother and I came to an abrupt halt and gaped while behind us Steven and Charlotte laughed at our reaction. Just before we had left, Charlotte had deduced what Steven had in mind for Mother, and instead told him to enlarge the existing house.

Now the kitchen was larger with more cupboards, and linoleum covered the old wood floor in a small white and black checked pattern. The walls were painted a soft creamy yellow and new white lace curtains hung at the windows over the sink in the corner. One of the best surprises sat in the middle of the kitchen. The old wooden table from the boardinghouse, built by Mrs. Kennedy's husband, had been salvaged. Although the drawers beneath the edge were slightly charred and there were several new gouges in the top, Mother and Charlotte lovingly ran their hands over its familiar surface. Both of them were no doubt recalling the many meals prepared and eaten at that table by the Eastmans and Perrys.

"How did this survive the fire?" Mother gasped, turning to Steven.

"Most of the kitchen was buried beneath the outside wall and the upper floor. The flames were extinguished by the rain just before the fire would have burned down to it."

"What else was salvaged then?" I asked, hoping there were at least a few more things.

Steven grinned and said, "The stones from the fireplace are out back. I thought I'd make a raised bed for you ladies. That way you won't have to bend over to play in the dirt."

Charlotte gently swatted his arm. "You won't call it play when you enjoy the fresh vegetables!"

"There were also a number of kitchen things from the cupboards that escaped the fire," he told us. "They're in boxes on the back porch." He walked over to the newly enlarged pantry and opened it. "And there was this." Having saved the silver tea pot the night of the fire, he now turned around with the rest of Mrs. Kennedy's tea service on its tray, all carefully polished. Mother covered her mouth with both hands, but she was smiling broadly.

Reaching back into the pantry, he said, "I managed to salvage something for you too, Whitney." He handed me the tin box in which I'd kept my jewelry. Although the box was black and pitted, with Steven's help the melted hinges gave way. Inside, each pin and bracelet given me by Father through the years was safe in its individual velvet pouch. In some inexplicable way, it was as though Father was reaching out to let me know that it was time to release my grief, and instead just hold dear the special times we had spent together. For several moments I was too overcome with emotion to even thank Steven, so I merely slipped my arms around his neck while he held me close.

Steven then gave us the rest of the tour. We soon discovered the addition of two large bedrooms across from each other on the north end of the house, at the end of a long hall that cut through the edge of what had once been Steven's room and was now part hallway and part open space. The addition of these bedrooms meant that the house had been extended north by twenty feet. The room off the kitchen that had in the past been Charlotte and Vince's bedroom would eventually be a guest room or a bedroom for live-in help if Mother and Charlotte ever needed it. But for now, it was Steven's room. All of this was the surprise Charlotte and Steven had planned the day before we left for Bishop.

But the surprise Steven had built for Charlotte extended south off the kitchen where before the small side door to the clotheslines had been. "Mom, would you mind going through that door now?"

"What did you do?" she grinned.

Mother and I were close on Charlotte's heals when she opened the door to an indoor bathroom. There was a large claw foot bath tub to the left and a pedestal sink on the back wall, both of which drained to the outside. The water still had to be heated on the nearby kitchen stove, but at least it could be drained to the exterior after use. In the far corner was a polished wooden box near the ceiling with a pipe leading down to a ceramic toilet. When the box was filled with water and the chain pulled, it would flush the toilet into a newly dug septic pit downhill from the house. We'd only ever seen something like it in a catalog or the big hotel in Bishop.

"Oh Steven, how wonderful!" Charlotte trilled. But it was her friend Emily whose hand she gripped. "Just think, Emily, now we can stretch out in a full plunge tub and soak in bubbles."

Mother was obviously confused. "I'm sorry, but I still don't understand all this."

"Emily," Charlotte said, "do you really think it makes sense for each of us to live alone? We'd just wear a rut in the ground between our houses going back and forth."

Mother slowly produced a smile above a chin that quivered, then whispered, "And the winter can be so cold when you're alone." She threw her arms around Charlotte's neck and they clung to each other, this time at least some of their tears those of joy.

Charlotte pulled back, wiped her hands across her cheeks and said, "Let's go see our bedrooms. Have you seen the new fabrics at the Meysan Store?" The two women bustled down the hall, from where we could hear their indistinct conversation frequently punctuated by laughter.

Throwing my arms around Steven and feeling the pressure of his body against mine, I seriously considered hustling him into his bedroom. But I thought better of it and merely said, "Thank you. It was just what they needed."

Taking my arm, he led me outside where we walked slowly along the edge of the south pasture. Royal immediately trotted across to us for the bite of carrot Steven held out to him.

"I noticed a small bed in the corner of Mother's room. Is that for me or Rose?"

He chuckled. "You. Sing is bringing Rose and her things by tomorrow. We'll set her up off the hall in the open space where my old room was. Of course, as soon as we're married, you'll be in my room off the kitchen until we get our house built. After Sing and his lady friend are married next week, he'll be living in Ida's house instead of with his friend's family."

"You've planned this all out, haven't you?"

"Yes." He had the grace to blush. "Have I assumed too much? Should I have consulted you more?"

I thought a moment. "No. Not considering everything that's happened." Slipping my arm through his, I told him, "But in the future, it'd be nice if you'd discuss with me things that affect us all."

"Okay." Steven then took my free hand and raised it to his lips. "I missed you so much."

"As busy as you've been?" I teased.

But he remained serious. "There was always the night."

I looked into his eyes and whispered, "I know."

No further words were required between us, and he wrapped me in his arms while we shared a long kiss.

"A question for you," I gasped.

"I must have lost my touch while you were gone. Let's practice now and talk later."

As he grabbed for me, I pushed him away and laughed. "No, seriously. How can we get married when everyone in town thinks you're already married?"

"Not by now they don't." His eyes twinkled as he explained. "I made sure that each man working with me on the house knew that Lavinia had tricked me into marrying her while already married to someone else. Of course, I didn't tell them who her husband had been."

"And they'll tell their wives," I laughed, "who will then tell several people."

"I figure by now everyone in town knows I'm a single man. And with you being the lovely widow, it leaves us free to marry whenever we want."

"Ah, the efficiency of gossip. It's one advantage of living in a small town." And we laughed together with a lightness not felt for a very long time.

Steven sobered suddenly and looked up to the mountains. Shaking his head, he said, "It's too bad Alex thought he had to take the coward's way out."

"What do you mean?"

"I know everyone said his death was an accident, but I just don't buy it. He couldn't have been that careless. It had to have been suicide, especially considering all that had happened in his life. But he was young enough to turn his life in a positive direction, and even find someone to love. Suicide is so...final." Again, he slowly shook his head.

Laying a hand on his arm, I told him, "Steven, I have something to tell you."

He looked at me and raised an eyebrow. "Go ahead."

"It wasn't suicide or an accident. He was murdered. By Irene."

"What? No! Really?" An appropriate reaction considering who I had accused.

The next half hour was spent detailing the story of Irene. I started with the odd conversation we'd had when I met her at age sixteen, and ended with our conversation in my bedroom that precipitated her abrupt departure.

"I've got to admit, Whitney, if it was anyone else other than you telling me this, I wouldn't believe it."

"I know. But imagine! Four people that we know of, and almost Lavinia. For all we know, there may have been others. I only hope my threat to her before she left keeps her from acting on that impulse in the future."

He looked at me curiously. "If you did have proof that she killed any of them, would you turn her in?"

I didn't hesitate long before telling him, "Yes, I would. Mostly because I'm not sure that she won't manage it again somehow. She has such a conviction that God is backing her up."

Several days later, a rancher from Bridgeport traveling south to Olancha stopped at the Richards Saloon while Steven was there with friends. The rancher gave them news of scandals and rumors from the north, and everyone listened intently. That night, Steven sat me down in the parlor and told me what he'd heard.

"This isn't going to be easy to hear, but it's only right that you know. Whitney, it's about Irene."

"What about her?"

"When she got home after leaving here, she found her house vandalized. It was almost destroyed. Outside, the vegetables had been ripped from the ground and thrown with force against the side of the house, leaving clods of mud sticking to the siding. All her plants and flowers had been stomped into the ground beneath a man's boot."

"Oh, how awful! That garden was everything to her."

"Inside was worse. The curtains and fabrics on the chairs were slashed to shreds, the pillows ripped open and the feathers tossed over the mess. Almost all of her books had been dumped on the floor after pages were torn from them, then her delicate dishes smashed and the pieces scattered over the books. Paintings were ripped out of their frames and ash from the stove had been dumped on the kitchen floor and smeared over the linoleum. Her bedroom had been trashed even more. All the bedding was torn and lamp oil poured on the mattress. Worse was the fact that the despoiler of her privacy had written with black tar on the wall over the bed the single word 'BITCH!'. The neighbors saw the ransacking the morning after it happened and reported it to the sheriff."

"Do they know who did it?"

He took a moment to answer, swallowing a mouthful of water before continuing. "Not for sure. But the reason she might have come here and stayed so long, could be due to a rumor that had been making the rounds. People were suggesting that her parents, and maybe even Alex, hadn't died the way everyone thought. That maybe she had something to do with their deaths."

I looked closely at him. "There's something else, isn't there?"

"Yes." He took another swallow of water. "A couple of days before the destruction, J.B. had been in town. But he wasn't seen after the morning she arrived home."

"But if he thought she had a hand in what happened to Alex, why wouldn't he have turned her over to the sheriff or even physically have harmed her?"

"What proof would he have had?" Again, he hesitated before continuing. "But even if he'd wanted to say or do something, he didn't get the chance."

"Why?" He reached for the glass of water, but I put my hand on his and said, "Just tell me."

"The neighbors said that when she got home, she stood silently in the garden for a long time, stiff as a board. Then she went inside and slowly walked through the house. When she got to the bedroom and saw the message left her on the wall above her bed, she opened her mouth and screamed. And she didn't stop. For all the time it took a neighbor to get into town and return with the sheriff, she screamed. And she continued until the doctor got there with a powerful shot of something. After that wore off, all she did was stare blankly, not responding to anyone or anything. She was taken to the state sanitarium."

Without saying anything, I got up and walked outside onto the front porch, suddenly in need of fresh air. Overcome by the urge to move, I began walking, and continued until I reached the cleared land of the boardinghouse. The old red barn stood with its doors wide open like arms ready to embrace me. Once inside and cloaked by its darkness and familiar smells, I knelt down in the middle of the floor on the remnants of straw, and wept. Not for Irene, who after all had reaped the consequence of her perverted actions, but for the loss of a friendship once so special. And maybe for the loss of what felt like the last of my youthful innocence.

Steven and I were married at the end of April, 1908, on a clear sunny day beneath the canopy of a bright blue Sierra sky. The ceremony took place on the edge of Lone Pine Creek where it cut through the Begole Grove at the north end of town, decorated by Nature with yellow, red and blue wildflowers along the water's edge. An open invitation had been issued to the whole town, and I think the whole town showed up.

Mother and Charlotte stood up with us as witnesses, their long blue dresses and large net-covered bonnets almost out-classing my arrival in pale pink satin and lace. The ceremony was punctuated by a few snuffles from the more sentimental ladies present, but Steven and I got through our exchange of vows without our emotions overcoming us.

Afterwards, there wasn't just one cake, but rather dozens of cakes made by many women. There were also piles of sandwiches, platters of fried chicken, bowls of potato salad, platters of cookies, and tubs of Lone Pine Beer on ice. Children slurped down glasses of sweet red punch with their cake, then ran along the creek while parents chastised them to take care of their good clothes. The celebrating continued until darkness descended and we were finally able to go home. When we got there, Mother had already moved my things to Steven's room off the kitchen.

Just as the holidays arrived, our house was finished, built with the help of dozens of men from the town. At last I lived in a house that I could decorate any way I wanted, and where I could plan menus that I would prepare. After a big party for everyone that had helped in the construction, we spent several weeks settling in and adjusting to being a family. But it wasn't long before we began entertaining friends, including Sing and his new wife. Sing continued to work for us part time, but it was mostly to care for Rose. He said it was so I could be free to do other things, but I knew he just missed spending time with her.

Soon there was a routine to our lives that was so comfortable that whenever old memories of the Double R returned to haunt me, it didn't take me long to shake them off and return to the present. After awhile, I simply never visited the unhappy events of those years.

In December of 1908, the construction of the aqueduct began in the San Fernando Valley, with the work crews slowly working their way toward us. But the preparation for it had begun a couple of years earlier. The City installed almost two hundred miles of telephone lines, carved over

500 miles of new roads into the Valley and up into the mountains, and set up over 2,000 buildings, tent houses and storage sheds along the proposed route. The City even built its own cement plant on the Tehachapi plateau, a little over 100 miles south of Lone Pine. Having discovered the presence of tufa in the sand there, they were able to create a stronger cement with which to line parts of the aqueduct, contributing to its lasting success. Because there was so little available water, however, they had to construct two hydroelectric plants on our creeks, with 169 miles of transmission lines. It was the first major engineering project in America that worked primarily off of electric power.

When the aqueduct was completed and the flood gates were opened in February of 1913, our water began its historic flow down the open ditch aqueduct along the Sierra foothills. We were there to see it, along with Rose's four year old brother, Adam.

Our water was collected in Haiwee Reservoir south of Owens Lake, then carried by closed conduit through a series of tunnels and steel siphons along the mountains forming the western rim of the Mojave Desert. A covered concrete flume carried it on to the Coast Range north of Los Angeles. After collecting in another reservoir, the water traveled five miles through the huge Elizabeth Tunnel that passed through the mountains, creating an electric power plant in San Francisquito Canyon. It then traveled through more tunnels, ending in another reservoir in the San Fernando Valley.

The Inyo County Board of Supervisors, citizen committees, the state's courts, California's congressional representatives, newspapers in sympathy with the Valley's 'victimization', private citizens, and even Mulholland's political foes--all had tried to stop the progress of the aqueduct, but no one had succeeded. To our great surprise, for a decade following its completion, there was only a subtle change to the Valley. But eventually many of the creeks dried up, causing the riparian wilderness along the river to slowly degrade and the Owens Lake to dry up even more rapidly than it already was doing. And, of course, deeply rooted trees that had for decades relied on a high water table slowly died.

There were also some conflicts between the ranchers and the City over the flow allowed into the irrigation ditches, especially as the 1920's approached and the City began to need more water for its growing population. But there were no changes to the land or the economy so monumental that it meant the immediate and total destruction of the ranches and towns. The slow decline of the Valley's prosperity had, however, begun.

Although the construction phase of the aqueduct had been a tense time for Valley citizens, and there were many who adamantly held a grudge against the City, most of us slowly adjusted to the presence of the big ditch cutting through our world. As a small mitigation, the construction created by-pass ponds that encouraged reeds and trees along their banks, the City planted trees they called wood lots, and allowed Diaz Lake to remain. And eventually the reservoirs took on the nature of lakes and were stocked with fish.

Some people were quick to point out that the City allowed some ranchers to stay on their land by leasing it to them, and even allowed the rancher sufficient water for stock or agriculture. For sometime this helped everyone regain a bit of hope that the Valley would continue to maintain and maybe even prosper. Only later did the reality set in that if the City decided it wanted any ranch's water, the tenants had no recourse but to leave.

How much water the City would eventually take, and how that would affect the long-term viability of the ranches and the health of the local environment, were questions no one could answer. Of course, as time passed, we received the answers when we had to deal with the consequences of living with less water than we, the land, and the animals required. But contend we all did, and some of us even thrived. Since most of us would never consider leaving the Valley, we had no other option.

Steven and Rose continued to develop a close relationship, but she also maintained her special bond with Sing and his wife Ida, and she spent as much time with them as she did at home. That was especially true after the blessing of Adam came into our lives.

Rose's friends included Paiute children from the local tribe, but also those of the Chinese, Basque and Mexican families. Rose thought nothing of this, but as she passed her twelfth birthday, several of the proper ladies in the town tried to council me out of letting her continue to "consort with such people". I thanked them for their advice, then ignored it. To Rose, all children were the same, and her chums.

Rose had already been introduced to bigotry. When only eight, she heard a man refer to Sing as "that yellow cookie that works for the Perrys". Her reaction was to kick him in the shin before running home to me in tears, for although she didn't exactly understand the reference, she did indeed understand the tone in which it had been said. It was then we discussed the concept of prejudice. Her intelligent comment was, "That's stupid!"

Mother and Charlotte found that living together suited them very well. Mother kept alive two of the sweetest memories of her past by hanging above her bed Mrs. Kennedy's story quilt and placing next to her bed the photograph of her and Father. And his buckskin coat and Bodie hat remained in her closet.

Both women enjoyed using Mrs. Kennedy's silver tea service while entertaining friends, which was a frequent event. The rest of their time was spent hosting fundraisers in support of the town's needs, or planting vegetable and flower gardens near the house.

Steven enlarged the back porch and hung there a swing big enough for two people. Mother spent a lot of time there, spring through fall. Watching her gently swinging back and forth, more than once I thought to myself that if she couldn't look up at Mt. Whitney and the Sierra crest, she'd cease to exist.

Several fires destroyed part of Bridgeport during the decade. Even though most of the relationships I developed there weren't happy ones, I still retained a great fondness for that region and was sorry to hear of the loss. Bridgeport continued to grow slowly, and in 1906 the town even paved its main street and gradually rerouted some of the roads. The area's beauty is unique, and the town retains the flavor of a small western village.

Bodie, however, has continued to slowly decline, and now in 1940 it is only a mere shadow of its former glory with only a few hundred living there. For a few years now two men have been working what they call the Roseklip Cyanide Plant where they process the Standard Mine's old dumps. So far, they have been successful enough that the mountains of waste rock are gradually being reduced to mere piles. The plant was recently enlarged so it can process 500 tons of rock per day, including the waste rock of the Bulwer Tunnel.

I doubt this will last for many years longer, but no matter what happens to Bodie in the future, it is still one of the largest and most complete of the old mining towns of the Old West. It's a special place where someone with just a little imagination can walk the streets beneath the looming Standard Mill and hear hurdy-gurdy music drift from crowded saloons. One might also hear desperados shooting it out in a nearby alley, and feel underfoot the thump of the stamps crushing ore in the mills scattered over Bodie Bluff.

I could tell you more about Rose, now a beautiful auburn-haired woman in her thirties, but she insists that she should write her own story. Since she was eighteen when the Valley began its next dramatic transformation at the beginning of the 1920's, I'm encouraging her to record the family's story as it parallels that of the Valley. Whether or not she will, remains to be seen.

But now I need to stop writing. Steven has come home and wants to share the events of his day with me. There really isn't any more to say about what happened so long ago anyway. This was written so future Eastman-Perry generations might know the truth of their heritage, and I can only hope that what I've revealed can be accepted, if not forgiven.

As for Steven and me, our marriage over the years hasn't been like that of my parents at all. When Steven disagrees with me, he doesn't hesitate to say so, although he usually listens to my ideas. Overall, I lead a traditional life as wife and mother, and I definitely care about my husband's opinions, even allowing them to influence mine. Well, some of the time. I am, after all, my mother's daughter.

Whitney Eastman Perry

DISCLAIMER

The story of how the Monte Diablo area became Convict Lake is true, as is the route traveled by the escaped prisoners, the events leading up to their capture, and much of their conversation. However, after 1872 the events and lives portrayed in this book related to the convicts is total speculation on my part, and was created only as a plot line for the novel. For all I know, the quality of their lives may have been completely opposite to what is portrayed here. Since I could find no record of what happened to these people, I have portrayed merely one "what if" possibility.

Many of the pioneers, freighters, stage drivers, Paiute peoples and locals are real people that existed in the Valley in the early 1900's. Although any interchange of action or conversation with the fictional characters is of my own creation, such contacts may be considered representational of the attitudes present at that time.

All of the locations are real. They are described as accurately as my research and visits to the described areas could reveal. If, therefore, I have portrayed any person, place or thing in any way not in accord with the recall of others, it must be attributed to individual perspective, and certainly no wish to deceive or misdirect the reader.

www.ingramcontent.com/pod-product-compliance
Lightning Source LLC
Chambersburg PA
CBHW031106030726
47496CB00002BA/408